THE FOLLOWER IN THE VOID

In the lightless Void ahead of Joanna, Suraklin's yellow shirt was a flitting blur. If she lost sight of that, she would be lost indeed.

Around her, the darkness was alive. She sensed the vast, amorphous things that floated in the frozen emptiness. She heard the dry whisper of something close behind, the panting, wheezing breath. Darkness was around her, and wind—or something else—was clawing the ends of her flying hair.

Joanna ran harder, sobbing, not daring to look behind her. Only the fact that she could not stop to catch her breath prevented her from screaming Suraklin's name, pleading for him to come back and fetch her. Surely, if he needed her services, as Antryg had said, he couldn't let her be lost in the Void.

Suddenly, he was gone!

By Barbara Hambly
Published by Ballantine Books:

DRAGONSBANE

THE LADIES OF MANDRIGYN
THE WITCHES OF WENSHAR

THE SILENT TOWER
THE SILICON MAGE

The Darwath Trilogy
THE TIME OF THE DARK
THE WALLS OF AIR
THE ARMIES OF DAYLIGHT

SEARCH THE SEVEN HILLS

The Silicon Mage

Barbara Hambly

A Del Rey Book

BALLANTINE BOOKS • NEW YORK

A Del Rey Book
Published by Ballantine Books
Copyright © 1988 by Barbara Hambly

Library of Congress Catalog Card Number: 87-91378

ISBN 0-345-33763-8

Manufactured in the United States of America

First Edition: April 1988

Cover art by Michael Whelan

Map by Shelly Shapiro

FOR BILL THE TIME LORD
AND THE BIONIC GIMP,
TWO TRUSTED FRIENDS.

My special thanks to Sam Pahalnuk, Diana Paxson, Carrie Dougherty, Adrian Butterfield, and Brynne Stevens for technical advice on a variety of subjects about which I knew nothing. This story could not have achieved its present shape without the wisdom and skill which they so generously shared.

A PORTION OF
THE EMPIRE
OF FERRYTH

CHAPTER I

THE WORST THING ABOUT KNOWING THAT GARY FAIRCHILD
had been dead for a month was seeing him every day at
work.

"So whatcha doing after we get outta here tonight,
babe?"

Joanna Sheraton tried not to stiffen, tried to recapture
the half-tolerant, half-evasive tone characteristic of her
conversations with him before . . . before. "I don't know,
Gary. Ruth and I had talked about going to the movies." It
sounded tinnily unconvincing even to her own ears.

Gary's face, as he leaned around the avocado burlap-
padded partition into her cluttered programming cubicle,
fell into its familiar pout. But there was a rehearsed quality
to it, as there was to the slouching stance of that compactly
muscled body in its assortment of Sears' best polyesters. It
was something he knew Gary used to do, but now and then
he forgot and stood straight and poised. There was an
amber glint far back in the brown eyes, worlds distant from
Gary's doglike eagerness.

Joanna felt her heart pounding fast and turned back to
comparing the green lines of information on her terminal
with the bug-riddled runout of the Tiger missile test analy-
sis program, so he wouldn't see the nervous tremor of her
mouth.

1

"Babe, what's the matter? You mad at me?" He had the whine down perfect that time.

She swung around a tad too quickly. "No. That is . . ." It was astonishingly difficult to remember patterns of voice and behavior several months old, particularly when she thought about them consciously—particularly with those brown eyes, watchful now, studying her face. She swallowed hard and pushed back the feathery tangle of untidy blond curls from her face.

"Babe, listen." He came around the partition, removed a stack of printouts from the cubicle's other chair, and sat down with that new, lithe grace, reaching out to take her hands. The nails were growing back—Gary had habitually bitten them to the quick. It was the closest that she'd let him get to her since she'd guessed what had happened to Gary—to the real Gary.

She made herself calm, made her eyes meet his.

He went on, "I don't know where you went when you disappeared at the end of August, or what happened to you . . ." That was a lie. He knew, all right; the only thing he didn't know was how much she had realized on the night of her return. "But I know something's been bothering you ever since you came back. You've been avoiding me."

"No!" Again it was too quick. The management of San Serano habitually turned off the air conditioning in Building Six around three in the afternoon; the close swelter of the October heat was, she hoped, enough to account for the crawl of sweat down her face and neck. Stammering, she tried to recoup. "I've been sort of avoiding everybody, Gary. Really, I just—I just don't want to see anyone now."

He smiled a little. "That's why you're going to the movies with Ruth?" His fingers tightened over hers. She hoped to hell they didn't feel as cold to him as they did to her. His eyes warmed with all Gary's old shallow charm. "You've got to deal with it sometime, babe. Get it out in the open." Past the cubicle door, voices sounded, and the scuff of feet echoed oddly in the high ceilings of the plant's testing bays just beyond the computer section where they sat. It was five o'clock. People were going home.

Hastily she pulled her hands away from him. Over her shoulder, as she began to stumble through backup procedures, he went on. "Why don't you come out to dinner with me, we go back to my place, and we talk. Okay?"

Two and a half months ago the invitation would have meant merely that he was going to try and talk her into bed with him. Now she knew, with a cold that seemed to spread from her hands and feet to the very pit of her stomach, that what he wanted was to get her alone.

"Another time, Gary." Her hands fumbled the typed commands; she hit the ESCAPE button and tried again, hoping he wouldn't read her fear and begin to ask himself why.

"Babe ..." He came around behind her and put his hands on her shoulders, bare in the sleeveless top that was the only answer to the heat of an unspeakable California autumn. She had to clench her teeth and fight not to strike his hands away with loathing and terror. "Next week?"

"Maybe ..." For a horrifying instant she blocked on the proper command to get out of the mainframe, her distracted mind praying he wouldn't notice.

"Tuesday?"

She was about to say "Maybe" again, then realized that every moment the discussion lasted, people were leaving the plant. In a very few minutes Building Six would be virtually empty, and he wouldn't have to maneuver to get her alone ...

She turned in her swivel chair, looked up into his eyes, and conjured up a sigh. "All right."

He smiled, but there was a gleam of a different triumph in his eyes.

She was shaking all over as she walked out to the parking lot.

He had been trying for weeks to get her alone, sometimes subtly, sometimes blatantly; like her, he was working delicately around things that he wasn't supposed to know, pretending he didn't know exactly what had happened to her in those weeks at the end of summer when she'd been gone, pretending he hadn't met her on the other side of the dark Void that separated universe from universe.

He hadn't been Gary then, of course.

Joanna shivered as she started up the car, a decrepit blue bomber of a '75 Mustang, remembering the frail, delicate old Archmage, the head of the Council of Wizards, Salteris Solaris. He'd fooled them all: his grandson the young warrior Stonne Caris; Gary—the real Gary, in those days—whom he'd duped into acting for him on this side of the Void; and all the Wizards of the Council... herself... He'd fooled them, and had left poor Salteris' stripped-out husk of body and mind to migrate on and devour Gary's self in his turn, as he'd left others.

He was Suraklin the Dark Mage, now after her.

The damnable thing was that there was no proof.

It was no wonder, she thought, that Antryg Windrose went insane.

She guided the car down the long stretch of Lost Canyon Road to where the Ventura Freeway lay, a glittering snake of constipated steel wavering with heat-dance, and wondered bleakly if Antryg were still alive.

He has to be, she thought, a threadbare litany with which she had tried to sustain herself for the last four weeks. *Please, God, don't let him be dead.*

She had no proof of that, either.

Tears of remorse, anger, and shame burned her eyes.

Likewise, she had no proof that those blank periods of gray and causeless depression that had more and more often troubled her and everyone she knew were anything other than her own unsettled mind. Yes, at such times no one at San Serano seemed to be able to do any work or to perform such tasks as they attempted correctly; yes, such spells coincided with an increase in newspaper accounts of both suicides and senseless gang violence, not only in Los

Angeles, but in San Francisco, New York, Tokyo, London, or anywhere else she could read about. One or two newspapers had come up with facile sociological theories about economic anxiety and shifts in demographics. They might even have been right. But going downstairs to visit her friend Ruth after one such spell, Joanna had seen the painting on which Ruth had spent weeks, gessoed over with great, impatient smears of hardening white.

That was still not proof that the life-energy of the world was being intermittently drained and bled—not fatally, or at least not intrinsically fatally—across the Void, to create electricity to power a computer in a world which had neither.

In the last four weeks, Joanna had read a great deal about that computer in Suraklin's files.

She nosed the Mustang up the freeway on ramp, one tedious car length at a time, and into the sluggish flow of traffic. Whatever air-conditioning system the car had once possessed had bitten the big one years ago; she relied on what Ruth called four-eighty air conditioning; one opened all four windows and drove at eighty. It worked when one wasn't trying to get down the 101 at five-fifteen on a Friday afternoon with everybody else in the southern half of the state of California. At least she was inbound, toward L.A. instead of away from it; the traffic *was* moving—at about two yards per hour, but moving. The outbound lanes were stopped in both directions as far as the eye could see.

The slowness gave her time to think about tonight, and with thought came fear.

She'd been living with fear for over a month now and she hadn't gotten used to it yet. The abnormally heavy traffic reminded her again that it was Friday, making her heart triphammer with dread. There was a good chance that it would be tonight. . . .

She and Antryg Windrose had guessed that Suraklin had a computer whose electrical/magical power relays fed on life, hidden in some fortress, some cavern, or some other hideaway in the Empire of Ferryth, the world on the other side of the Void, before she'd ever tapped into Suraklin's files. For months Gary had been programming them into the big Cray mainframe at San Serano, while he'd worked at stealing by modem-powered computer-scam an experimental mainframe of artificial-intelligence proportions to set up on the other side of the Void. It was ultimately ironic, she thought wryly, that, having stolen via computer, Gary's personality, his self, should now be nothing more than a series of programs logged in a computer's electronic guts.

She'd seen that program. Everything about Gary—his likes and dislikes, his intricate network of computer-tapped bank accounts, the affairs he'd carried on with other women while he'd sworn his undying love to her, and the details of the particularly nasty variety of pornography he'd favored—had all been neatly digitalized. In other files, she'd found the details of the old Archmage Salteris' personality and what had been that of the poor imbecilic Emperor of Ferryth, whose shell still stumbled drooling through the palace at Angelshand while his mad son ruled the Empire.

And with them was the personality, the memories, and the knowledge of the man who had stolen and inhabited the bodies and minds of the Emperor, of Salteris, and of Gary in turn—the evil old man whose speech patterns and gestures Gary occasionally used and whose amber cat-glint eyes had watched her so intently today, the wizard Suraklin, whom all had once called the Dark Mage.

The computer was his ticket to eternity. Joanna knew it existed and knew he was programming his personality, petrifying it in everlasting silicon, so that he would at last live forever. The drain on the life-energies of her own world and of the world in which the computer itself was situated —the world across the Void—wasn't strong enough to kill. It would only maim, in a way for which there was no word, forever.

She knew it existed, but she had no proof.

She was fighting him absolutely alone.

She edged the car out of traffic, off the freeway and into a supermarket parking lot in Encino, still halfway across the San Fernando Valley from her home. From the front seat, she fished her purse, a monstrous affair of macramé and bunny skins the size and weight of a dead Labrador dog; from the trash pit of the trunk she dug a blue nylon backpack of the kind schoolkids carry books in, crammed to bursting and heavy as if it contained lead. Slinging these over her shoulder, she locked up the car and crossed the parking lot on foot, a small, sturdy girl, her untidy blond curls now damp and matted with sweat, like a schoolkid herself in her worn blue jeans and sleeveless top. Within fifteen minutes she was on a bus headed back toward San Serano.

Definitely, she thought, *a candidate for the Academy for the Bewildered.* Her behavior in the last month—breaking into computer files, hiding her car and sneaking back to the darkened plant after everyone was gone, avoiding the man she'd been sleeping with for the last two years—was bizarre enough to qualify her as a paranoid in anybody's book. Her dreams were something she wouldn't wish on her worst enemy.

"I've spent most of my life terrified of a man who's been dead for years," Antryg Windrose had told her once. And she understood now how the Prince Regent had become a hopeless paranoid at the age of ten, positive that his father the Emperor had ceased to be his father and unable to prove it to a soul.

She leaned her head against the vibrating metal of the window frame of the bus, closed her eyes, and tried not to smell the fattish man in a brown leisure suit who'd come to sit next to her on the crowded conveyance.

The whole situation—the events of her disappearance, the terrible thing she had learned, the tall, gentle madman who had kept her safe both from the Inquisition and from the random abominations traveling now through the Void between universes—had the aspect of some hideous quadratic equation, with two solutions and no means of determining which was correct.

The daylight side of the equation was simply that she had been temporarily insane. That was easy. At Gary's house party last August, she'd imbibed some chemically enhanced punch, of which there'd been a fair amount, and had undergone a long period of illness and violent hallucinations, peopled by wizards, warriors, evil princes, and the kind of man whose love she had always craved. And, like Judy Garland in *The Wizard of Oz*, she had waked again to a black-and-white world of people she had known all her life saying soothingly to her, "It was only a dream, dear; only a dream."

The night side of the equation was also a dream.

That dream had come to her a few nights after her return to this world from wherever she had been. It had recurred —cloudy, haunting, terrible—five or six times since.

In the dream she was in a stone-walled room, like the dungeon of the Inquisition from which Antryg had rescued her; by its heavy proportions, it was somewhere underground. Clammy cold radiated from the damp wall behind her, but she was sweating from the heat that blazed from the condensed cherry flames on the room's small hearth. A man was working at the fire, bent over it with his troll shadow flung vast and fidgeting on the curved stone of wall and roof groin, stripped to loincloth and shoes in the heat, with his skull shaved bald. In the corner where she stood, Joanna could smell the acrid reek of his sweat. The faint, brisk tapping of his little hammer on iron sounded loud in the silence, punctuating the crackle of the coals and the asthmatic hiss of the bellows being worked for him by a girl apprentice whose sleeveless shift showed biceps like a man's. She, too, was shaved bald, as was the big, clumsy-looking woman in gray velvet robes who stood before the hearth, perspiration trickling down the fatty rolls of her neck. The smell of unwashed wool, wet earth, and smoke lay heavy on the air.

That fat woman was looking, not at what the smith was doing by the fire, but at the doorway opposite, a low black arch of shadows, sinister as the maw of some Boschian beast.

In time, there was movement in that dark, and the fat woman in gray folded her hands over her stomach and smiled.

The man they brought in was taller than all but two of the guards who held him. When Joanna had stood in the circle of his arms, her head had not come as high as those broad, bony shoulders. Framed in a tangled explosion of graying brown hair, his face was chalky with exhaustion, the wide gray eyes in their bistered hollows dilated with drugs.

The big woman stepped forward, her eyes like pieces of chipped blue glass in the pouchy flesh. "Antryg Windrose," she said, and the prisoner raised his head.

Without his spectacles, Joanna knew he was half-blind. She saw the swooping network of lines—raying back from eyelids to temples and down over his cheeks—tighten as he tried to get her into focus.

"Antryg Windrose, do you confess to the crimes of which you have been accused?"

He drew in breath to speak, then paused. Sweat shone in the torchlight on his upper lip, the preposterous arch of his nose, and the pit of his throat, visible through the tattered collar of the coarse robe he wore. Asleep, dead—fifty years from now, Joanna knew she would recognize his voice in her dreams.

"Herthe, I don't care what you do to me, but please believe that killing me will not remove the danger you're all in. Suraklin . . ."

A guard behind him did something to one of his pinioned arms; he cried out and the other guard caught him as his knees buckled. In the crazily leaping shadows, Joanna could see that the first guard was Stonne Caris, the Archmage's grandson.

The woman Herthe stepped forward as the guards dragged Antryg upright again. "Do not name your master to us," she said softly. "And do not think to frighten us into letting you live. You have already signed the confession of your crimes." Her voice sank lower, cold as poisoned ice. "Is it necessary that, as Bishop in charge of this Inquisition, I require you to do so again?"

He looked away from that flat stare, and a shudder went through his body. His voice was almost inaudible. "No."

"Do you confess to violating the first law of the Council of Wizards, to breaking your vows to the Council never to use your powers, either for ill or for what seems good, in the affairs of humankind?"

He nodded, still not meeting her eyes. "Yes."

"Do you confess to attempting to murder the Prince Regent Pharos by means of magic?"

"Yes."

"Do you confess to the murder of Salteris Solaris, Archmage of the Council?"

He closed his eyes, fighting within himself against grief, guilt, and despair. It was a long time before he could speak; and then, it was only the soundless movement of his lips. "Yes."

The Bishop signed to the blacksmith beside the hearth. He straightened up, holding in his hands the thing he had been forging. Those of Antryg's guards whom Joanna recognized by their black robes as wizards fell hastily back. Caris, too, a wizard born, flinched and averted his face from it, though he did not release his grip on Antryg's arm.

Panic and despair flooded the mad wizard's gray eyes. "No," he whispered desperately, and tried to back away; Caris twisted his arm again, brutally forcing him forward. "Herthe, that isn't necessary. The Sigil of Darkness is on the Tower door; that is enough. I can't touch it, can't pass it, no wizard can . . ."

"Yet you escaped from this Silent Tower before," the Bishop said impassively. A spurt of yellow firelight winked balefully on the iron collar in the smith's hands, flaring across the crooked symbol of lead and jewels worked into its center. "The Sigil of Darkness is the Seal of the Dead God, the death of power. It should keep you from escaping again until the time of your execution."

"I won't," Antryg said, his voice low and desperate, staring at the thing in the smith's hands as if hypnotized. "I swear to you I won't try to escape, only don't . . . You don't understand, you're not a wizard, please . . ."

The smith stepped forward, the iron collar in his hands. It took four guards to force Antryg to his knees, to strip back his faded robes, and to hold him immobile by the hair, the arms, the shoulders, while the smith fixed the collar around his neck and soldered shut its lock. Caris was one of them; but, mageborn as he was, even the proximity of the Sigil left him sweating and gray-lipped. Though his grip never slacked, not once throughout did he look at the thing they were fastening against Antryg's flesh. Only when they were done and the other guards released him did Caris thrust the renegade wizard from him, sending him sprawling to the filth of the stone floor.

Every time she had dreamed this, Joanna fought to leave the shadowy corner where she stood to go to his side. It was like trying to move, not under water, but smothered like a fly in the treacly amber of the firelight. Even her cries were stillborn in her aching throat. For a long minute, there was no sound in that dreadful room, save the cracking of the fire, and Antryg's hoarse, sobbing breath.

Then Caris asked quietly, "Why this?"

The Bishop fixed upon him her clammy blue gaze.

In a face still white from the mere closeness to the Sigil of Darkness, the young man's brown eyes smoldered with hate. "He has confessed and been condemned by the Emperor, by the Witchfinders, and by the Council of Wizards. Why take the trouble of binding his powers, instead of killing him now? Has someone on the Council gotten jealous of the Council's rights to judge its own?"

"You are a sasennan of the Council, Caris, their living weapon." The words came out as flat and cold as her fish-belly eyes. "It is not for the sword to question the hand that wields it."

Passion shook his low voice. "Salteris was my grandfather, damn you!"

"Caris." Ghostlike, the form of the wizard Lady Rosamund materialized in the darkness of the low doorway, the mage who had led in Antryg's arrest. Behind the glitter of her bullion-stitched stole of office, she seemed little more than shadow within shadow, and those gathered behind her even less than that. "You put that away," she reminded him, "when you took your vows as sasennan. From that moment, you had no grandfather. It is nothing to you which member of the Council has spoken for this man's life, or why. Until that vote changes, he remains as he is."

Huddled in the shadows, Antryg had turned his face from the other wizards and covered it with his hands, as if by so doing he could hide from them. Twice Joanna had seen his fingers move toward the iron collar, but he could not bring himself to touch it. His whole body shivered. She thought he wept.

The hearth fire had sunk to a bed of rubies on powdery ash. The smith and his apprentice had already departed. In the blood-colored glare, the Bishop gave that crumpled form one last scornful glance and followed, with her black-clothed guards about her; the wizards faded back into the shadows from whence they had come. For a time Caris alone remained, looking after them, his face like carved bone dyed by the sinking embers, motionless but for the somber glint of his eyes.

Then he turned and walked to where Antryg lay.

The wizard was silent. Only by the shaky draw and release of his breath could Joanna tell that he was alive at all or conscious. The rags of his robe had been pulled down off his shoulders; in the dull carmine light, she could make out the angles of scapula and vertebrae under taut, fine-textured white skin.

Caris knelt beside him and drew his dagger. At the noise, Antryg raised his head, struggling up against some great weight of despair. Seizing him by the shoulder, the young man thrust him back against the stones of the wall. Coppery reflections of the fire glinted on the long blade, on the sweat that ran down Antryg's face and chest, and on the evil jewels in the iron and lead of the collar.

For a time Antryg looked, not at the blade that hung inches from his naked throat, but at the sasennan's eyes. Then very slowly he brought up his hands, and Joanna saw that his fingers were all splinted and bandaged, swollen as if every joint had been dislocated. Gritting his teeth slightly against the pain, with the edge of one wrist he pushed back the sleeve of his robe to expose ropy muscle and veins tracked to the elbows with whitened scars.

"Please," he said softly. "I'd take it as a great favor."

In one savage move Caris hurled him aside and jerked upright to stand over him. For that instant, no matter how many times Joanna had dreamed this scene, she thought that he would kick Antryg with fury and frustration and hate. But he turned on one booted heel and snapped the dagger back into its sheathe. The firelight blinked on its hilt as he strode into the darkness of the doorway, leaving Antryg lying alone, like a broken scarecrow in the gathering dark.

After a long time, the wizard crawled to his feet. Holding himself upright against the walls with his bandaged hands, he stumbled toward the door and beyond its darkness to the stair that led to his prison in the Silent Tower above.

The bus lurched to a stop at the gates of San Serano, and Joanna got out. The shuddering heat of the day radiated through the soles of her battered hightop sneakers from the asphalt as she crossed the parking lot to Building Six; the empty hills that surrounded the plant loomed like brownish cardboard cutouts in the smog.

You mustn't think about Antryg, she told herself wearily. Not of the lightness of those big hands as he'd taught her to drive Prince Cerdic's carriage nor those evenings they'd spent at the posthouses along the road from Kymil to Angelshand, drinking ale and talking. Not the tones of that remarkable voice, deep and beautiful like some lunatic Shakespearean actor's nor the desperate heat of his lips against hers. That was one thing nobody ever mentioned, she thought wryly—that the obverse side of learning to care for someone was that you couldn't stop caring when it hurt.

The straps of the heavy backpack cut into her shoulder. It contained a variety of things, mostly bought out of money pilfered by computer from Gary's various illegal bank accounts—bank accounts he had filled by computer theft from financial institutions across the United States. She'd found everything about them—account numbers, amounts, even the break-in program he'd modemed into all those banking computers after hours—in the programs of his personality in the DARKMAGE files. It hadn't taken much tinkering to help herself. Gary and Suraklin between them—*between him*? she couldn't help wondering—had done a good deal of evil. She considered it only right that they should finance her expedition to free Antryg—And he *is* alive! she insisted desperately to herself. He *is*!—and defeat Suraklin's plan.

She couldn't go on fighting him alone.

So she'd bought cultured pearls and synthetic sapphires and rubies, beef jerky and Granola bars, a lightweight water bottle and a six-inch sheathe knife to go with the Swiss Army knife she already had, duct tape, nylon cord, a bundle of plastic-coated copper wire, carbide hacksaw blades, and various other supplies. From a pair of costumers she knew who catered to the Renaissance Faire crowd, she'd ordered a gown made to the best of her recollections that would pack small, but, once unpacked, would allow her to pass inconspicuously in a society that frowned upon women wearing trousers. The thought of passing herself off as a boy, as so many romantic heroines seemed able to do, had crossed her mind, but one glance in the mirror put the kibosh on that one.

She'd bought a .38 Colt Diamondback and a cleaning kit and had practiced until the blasting roar and the kick no longer twitched at her aim. She had toyed with the notion of going to one of the jock hackers she knew for some kind of portable induction coil simply to degauss the stolen computer's circuits; but from what she had read of its specs, she knew its shielding was up to anything a battery was likely to generate, and there was no guarantee she'd be able to tap into the computer's magical electrical source herself. The idea of high explosive she'd simply discarded; aside from the legal restrictions entailed in acquiring it, she knew herself to be far too inexperienced to use or transport it with anything resembling safety.

But input is input. If Gary—Suraklin—could transfer programs from the San Serano mainframe to his new computer, so could she. So in a special pocket of her backpack, reinforced with metal and wrapped in layer after layer of plastic, was her best and most illegal wipe-the-disk worm program.

For the rest, her backpack was jammed with hardcopy. Some of it photoreduced and Xeroxed almost to illegibility, some merely shoved in at random as it came off the modem-lines that she hadn't even had time to look at. She'd been hacking into the DARKMAGE files for a month; but owing to the sheer volume of them, there had been so little time. So little time, she thought—but more than enough for Antryg to be . . .

Stop that! she ordered herself. *Antryg is alive. He has to be. He has to . . .*

And if he wasn't, she knew, with cold and sinking dread, she'd have to stop Suraklin herself.

They'd already shut down most of the lights in Building Six. Very quietly, Joanna moved down the blue-carpeted corridors of the empty typing pools, between programmers' deserted cubicles. She had stolen back into San Serano this way at least twice a week for the last month, and it always brought up in her a variety of emotions; but paramount, horrifying, in her mind was the knowledge that Suraklin still needed her. He had kidnapped her once before when he was planning to take over Gary's body, and knew he'd need a programmer in his universe under his influence to take Gary's place. Rather, he had gotten Gary to kidnap her and had himself taken her across the Void. Had Antryg not been following him, she would even now be the Dark Mage's helpless puppet and slave.

Almost the last thing Antryg had said to her when they'd finally taken him was to warn her. And of course she hadn't listened.

Nearly ill with the violence of her hammering heart, she walked swiftly along those darkened halls. If he met her now, he'd have her, and every step she took closer to the Main Computer Room made her danger worse.

Relax, she commanded shakily. *You've done this a dozen times.*

She was still shaking all over by the time she slipped into one of the programming cubicles across the hall from the mainframe.

You've done this a dozen times . . .

Left work with everyone else, to stash your car in a parking lot en route, but never the same parking lot, and sneaked back here by bus to take a roundabout way back into the plant to wait . . . Spent your time raiding computer files and toting around twenty pounds of backpack . . .

Altogether, she thought wryly, to quiet the shakiness in her chest, *this had damn well better not be a hallucination after all.*

She felt a little like a white-robed cultist who, having sold everything he owns, stands expectantly on his mountaintop, awaiting the end of the world. *And I'm going to feel just as silly,* she added, *trudging down home again . . .*

Feet swished softly on the carpet outside. Joanna flattened her body against the wall behind the cubicle's half-open door and angled her head sideways to look through its crack. For one flashing instant she identified Gary as he passed.

The Gary who was no longer Gary now, in the absence of anyone who had known Gary, didn't bother to keep up the pretense. In spite of years of conscientious weight-lifting, Gary—of medium height and slender build, despite a recent tendency toward paunchiness— had never looked particularly comfortable with his body. He walked now with an animal grace subtly at odds with the sensible gray polyester trousers and the pale quiana shirt.

Joanna saw he was carrying a briefcase, and her heart turned perfectly cold within her.

It was, after all, going to be tonight.

She'd guessed it when she'd tapped into the DARK-MAGE files early this morning and found large sections of them gone. No modem-lines stretched across the Void. He was doing his programming on the San Serano mainframe, but he had to transfer his files across the Void by hand.

She felt the terrified urge to cry. *Don't think about it,* she told herself severely and tiptoed soundlessly across the darkened cubicle to the phone. To her infinite relief, she got Ruth's answering machine. It had been a good bet she would—Ruth was rarely home—but the last thing she wanted right now was questions.

She said, simply, "Ruth, this is Joanna. Use your key to my place. There's a manila envelope on the table, with some instructions. *Please* carry them out. I'll explain when I see you, but that might not be for a few weeks. I'm not in any trouble. 'Bye."

Paranoid, schizo, obsessive, insane.

Why does it have to be me?

Antryg, she thought, must have felt the same.

Then something changed in the air. It was a sensation she would have been totally unable to describe——an unreasoning terror, a strange tingling of the nerves, a sense of standing on a beach whose shoreline is not water but the black drop-off into eternity. But once felt, it could not be mistaken for anything else. Dark winds seemed to whisper across her bones; she felt she could hear the murmuring echoes of unknown forces, moving in blackness.

The Void between the universes was being bridged. Suraklin was going across.

She was keyed to the shaking point as she slid out the cubicle door. *I can't let Suraklin see me*, she thought desperately. *As of now I've disappeared and left a plausible story for why I won't be seen for a couple of weeks. No one will look for me.*

But of course, if Suraklin took her now, it wouldn't matter if the search started tomorrow. No one would find her until she returned, her mind not her own.

Cold white light poured through the computer room door into the darkened corridor. The backpack with the purse strapped to it now dragged her shoulders, but she scarcely noticed. She thought, quite reasonably, *There's a nine o'clock bus back to Encino* . . . and put her head around the door.

And the good news is, she thought half-hysterically, *it wasn't all a hallucination.*

That is, unless I'm having a hallucination now.

There was darkness in the computer room.

Darkness, hideously, surrounded by the fluorescent blaze of the lights; like a cloud of gas, but definitely not a vapor, not a substance at all. A darkness that seemed to stretch away, never reaching the rear wall with its banks of green-eyed monitor lights, but seeming to extend far past it, a ghostly corridor that stretched to the abysses of infinity. Far off, along that great gulf of nothing, she sensed movement.

There was no one now in the computer room. At its edges, the darkness was already beginning to disperse.

And the bad news is . . .

. . . It wasn't all a hallucination.

And you're going to have to walk into it.

A small voice within her suggested timidly, *Can't I just go home and forget the whole thing?*

Not allowing herself to think any further about that very real option, Joanna strode forward into that darkness.

CHAPTER II

IT WAS BEYOND A DOUBT THE MOST FRIGHTENING THING she had ever done. She hadn't gone two steps when she wanted to turn around and go back, but she knew already she dare not even look over her shoulder to see if it were possible. Far in the lightless Void ahead of her Gary's—Suraklin's—yellow polyester shirt was a flitting blur. If she lost sight of that, she would be lost indeed.

Vertigo swamped her, the sensation of falling, the terror of feeling nothing beneath her feet. She struggled forward, half-running, half-swimming, tractionless and desperate to keep that pale will-o'-the-wisp in sight, smothering in darkness such as she had never known. Tears burned her eyes, tears of terror and resentment. When she had gone through to that other world the first time she had been unconscious; coming back, Salteris'—Suraklin's—thin, strong hand had been her guide.

Don't think, she told herself. *Caris could follow a man through the Void unguided; you can, too.* Cold that was not really cold was leeching the strength from her veins. She ran/swam/flew through the darkness, fighting frantically not to lose sight of the man who would destroy her if he found her now.

The darkness was alive. She knew it, felt it, sensed the vast amorphous things that floated in that frozen emptiness;

she heard the dry, glittery whisper of something close behind. Panting, wheezing breath, she wondered, or her own desperate gasping as she struggled to keep Suraklin in sight? Her sweat, dripping from her hair in icy droplets, cold on the bare flesh of her arms, or . . . ?

She ran harder, sobbing, not daring to look behind her. Only the fact that she could not stop to get her breath prevented her from screaming Suraklin's name, pleading with him to come back and fetch her. If he needed her services as Antryg had said, he couldn't let her be lost in the Void.

He was gone.

Darkness was around her, wind—or something else—clawing the ends of her flying hair. There was no blur ahead of her, only plunging darkness, livid with the sense of writhing things. Far off to her right, something bright caught her eye, fragile, milky light, and she sensed the smell of rain. Though it was nowhere near the direction she had last seen Suraklin, she veered toward it, running as she had never run before, running in heartbursting panic, with the pack dragging her shoulders, like the weighted flight of nightmare. Something swooped at her, some winged and flabby thing whirling out of the aphotic pits of this nonbeing; she felt it cut her arm, felt blood hot on the cold flesh. She didn't look, only ran harder. Time had stopped; she felt as if she had been running for hours, aimless and in terror. What if she had been? she wondered frantically. What if the light before her vanished as Suraklin had? What if it was only a lure? What if she never got out, if this would go on until she died? What if she didn't die? Her hair tangled in her eyes, the pack was dragging on her, pulling her back, and the light was drifting away, fainter and fainter . . .

Then it was clear before her, a white moon burning full and clear in a wide-flung double ring of ice mists above a broken line of standing-stones. Sodden grasses whipped Joanna's calves as she ran; cold sliced her arms, damp and raw. Behind her she heard the chitter and hiss that had filled her ears in the Void. Risking a glance over her shoulder, she saw it, as much of it as there was to see— something dark and floating, a chitinous tangle of long, knobby legs, with moonlight edging an aureole of floating tendrils like a woman's long hair in water. The tendrils reached out toward her, and, in the knot of darkness at the creature's center, things like specks of faceted glass caught the moonlight.

Her mind blurred with terror she ran, stumbling on the rough rise of the ground, racing until she felt her heart must burst toward the staring silver eye of the moon. She had the confused impression that, if she could get her back to one of the bigger standing-stones, she might at least have some chance. Where she had come through the Void, they were only low stumps, like broken fenceposts along the ancient path, if anything remained of them at all. Even as she ran, she cursed herself. Her knife was in her pack; she'd never get it out in time. *Caris would never let himself get caught like this . . .*

She flung herself against the nearest of the large stones, the pitted surface tearing at her hands. Blind with horror, she scrabbled at her pack and ripped free the velcro pocket. The blood was hot on her arm where the creature had cut her. In another second all those dangling claws would be on her. She dropped the pack and jerked the knife free of its sheathe, the blade jamming in its newness. Any second . . . Any second . . .

Barely able to breathe, she flattened back against the stone and faced her adversary.

It was gone.

It was out there in the darkness; she knew it, felt it, and could almost hear its faint, crackling whisper. But there was another sound, a muffled, rumbling thud in the earth, a groan.

She spun around, looking down the track into the moonwashed slot between the stones.

A rustling, moving shadow spread over the ground like

water. Even with the thin lucency of the moon, it was hard
to distinguish shapes, but after a moment she heard the
groan again, deep and plaintive, and realized it was the
lowing of a cow. Sheep bleated. Straining her eyes, Joanna
could make them out now in the shadow: cloudy blobs of
whitish wool; the blunted spark of brass horn-tips; and a
vertical shape that could only be a walking man. Sweet,
cold, and unbearably lonely, music curled like a black ribbon into the night, a haunted piping that threaded its way
like wind between the stones. Like a counterpoint against
the thudding of her heart, she heard the hollow pat of a
drum.

Somewhere beyond the line of stones, out in the huge
gulf of blackness that lay like a single velvet entity up to
the glowing violet hem of the hill-crowded sky, the abomination waited.

Joanna remembered Antryg saying that whenever the
Void was breached the whole fabric of the universe weakened; holes appeared not only in the vicinity of the Gate,
but elsewhere in other universes, and through these holes
abominations would drift. In veering from Suraklin's route,
she might have stumbled through a hole opened along one
of the energy-tracks that crossed the Empire of Ferryth. Or,
she thought with a shiver, she might have fallen through to
some other universe altogether, neither her own nor the one
she sought.

Fine, she thought, with half-hysterical irony. *I've managed to screw up before I even got through the Void.*

She stepped cautiously back out of the main track between the stones, keeping her body still pressed to the icy,
uneven surface of the menhir, the cold making her hands
ache around the unaccustomed handle of the knife. The
bobbing darkness down the track was coming nearer, re-
solving itself into a blur of dark shapes and green eyes
flashing queerly in the moonlight. She smelled dung and
dust in the sweetness of the trampled grass; fragile and

terrible, the aching, single voice of the pipe tugged at her heart.

A sheep passed her, then a cow with a yearling calf. More cows followed, jostling one another, one of them so close she could feel the warmth of its body, then sheep in a dusty choke of wool-smell and hay. Dogs trotted between them, silent; then goats, a couple of pigs, a plowhorse the size of a Panzer tank, with a small boy walking nearly hidden in its shadow along that dark and silent track toward the moon. Other men and women walked among the animals, silent as they in the false, quicksilver light; dogs trotted at their master's heels, and half-grown girls carried cats in their arms.

In the trampled wake of the beasts walked a line of men, heads dark and disfigured by the horned beast masks they wore. There was something indescribably lonely and terrible about the dirge they played, like no music Joanna had ever heard, mourning for something no one understood anymore. The black horns bobbed and swayed in the ashy moonlight. Under the jutting muzzles gleamed the silvery reflection of masked eyes. If they saw her as they passed her, standing shivering in the black pool of moonshadow, they gave no sign.

Last of all she saw what she thought was a catafalque made up from a farm wagon, drawn by cows and sheep, though it was almost impossible to tell in the darkness. She thought that on it lay the body of a man, eyes shut, face and hands blackened, clothed in rags, with a deer's antlers fixed to his dark forehead. She seemed to hear Antryg's deep voice: "All things travel along the lines, resonating forward and back . . . On certain nights of the year the peasants still drive their herds along them, in commemoration of the Dead God, though they've forgotten why he died . . ."

Well, at least, Joanna thought wryly, *I've come to the right world.*

Fine. Now you have to worry about Suraklin.

Her first impulse was to follow them, knowing they would lead her eventually back to their village, to shelter and warmth for the night. It was bitterly cold—belatedly, Joanna remembered that, for all its damp and smothering heat in midsummer, the Empire of Ferryth lay well to the north of the latitudes of California. The thin windbreaker wadded in her backpack would be about as much use to her as a pair of lace ankle sox. *Swell. You not only screwed up while you got through the Void, but you didn't do so good before you entered it, either.*

But even as she moved to pick up her backpack and follow, Joanna glanced out into the darkness, and saw something moving, like a floating spider, far out in the darkness, paralleling the course of the stones. Moonlight tipped the end of a floating spun-glass tendril. The abomination, too, was following the funeral of the Dead God.

Was it the music that drew it? she wondered. Or the smell and the heat of blood? She huddled down again, her back to the blue-black shadow of the eroded stone, trembling as she pulled the useless windbreaker from her pack and prepared to wait out the night. Far off, like the voices of the dead, the pipes cried alone in the darkness.

Had it not been for the abomination, Joanna might have backtrailed the swathe of trampled grass and animal dung back to the village from which the macabre procession had set out. She felt cold and hungry and, once the first rush of adrenaline seeped from her veins, exhausted; even if the villagers had left watchdogs prowling around their homes, even if they weren't likely to welcome a stranger snooping about the place in their absence, surely she could take refuge in some friendly haybarn until dawn. But the thought of being in any enclosed place in this black gloom—the thought of being without a clear line of sight in all directions and something absolutely solid at her back—gave her a shrinking feeling in the pit of her stomach; she huddled all the tighter into her thin jacket and stayed where she was. The long trough of the energy-track, marked only here and there with an occasional small menhir in the direction of the village, but as visible in the wan moonlight as a paved highway, stretched away into the shadowy hills. It was a long walk, not knowing what might drift above or behind her in the dark.

The depression, when it came, turning the fragile beauty of the moonlight to flint, even as it sucked the hope from Joanna's soul, made everything a thousand times worse.

Joanna knew what it was and had been expecting it. After all, Suraklin had crossed the Void to use his computer on this side of it, and the computer fed on electricity converted by relays of teles-balls from the energy, the hope, and the life-force of every human being in her own world, this one, and who knew how many besides.

She, at least, was aware now that the numbness in her soul was externally caused, not the result of some fading within herself, and that put her ahead of literally every other victim of the computer's far-reaching field. It didn't help, of course. She was still tormented by the knowledge that she would fail and that what she did was pointless and would result, at best, in her permanent exile to this inconvenient, smelly world and, at worst, in her death or enslavement. She felt a growing conviction that Antryg was, in fact, long dead. It had been a month and more since the wizards had taken him. Even worse was the part of her that shrugged and said, "So what?" That part of her was seized with an impatience to get up and set out through the darkness for the village, half forgetting, as an alcoholic forgets his last bender when the liquor-fumes rise to his nose, that the abomination was somewhere out there. *It's following them—it won't get me,* she thought, resentment at her chapped hands and cramped knees flooding her, and only a mechanical resolution to do everything completely by the numbers made her stay where she was.

When a steel-colored dawn finally gave her a clear enough view of the surrounding countryside to make sure she was absolutely unthreatened and unobserved from any direction in the crowding shoulders of the hills, she got stiffly to her feet and changed into her dress—not particularly easy to do while keeping an eye on the landscape. The depression that choked her soul like sifted ash had not abated. Since this was Saturday, she didn't particularly expect it to. Gary—Suraklin—would undoubtedly continue his programming all morning and into the afternoon, and there would most likely be another such spell tomorrow.

At least, she thought, viewing the bony landscape of granite hills beneath its thin garment of rusty autumn grass, *I seem to have come to the right place*. But Antryg had said that the Sykerst, the rolling, barren lands of steppe and moor and waving lakes of grass through which they had walked from Kymil to Angelshand that summer, stretched two thousand miles to the east of the more populous areas of the Empire. If she were somewhere in the Sykerst—and these hills looked exactly similar to those she remembered —she could easily be anywhere in them.

Please don't let me be fifteen hundred miles from the nearest civilization, she prayed drearily, hoisting her backpack to her shoulder and cursing herself for filling it with paper. *Gimme a break, for Chrissake. This is going to be tough enough.*

As she trudged down the trampled path of the Dead God and his followers, the hem of her petticoat swirling around the hightop sneakers she had decided would be better for walking in, the other half of her mind retorted, *Don't bitch, baby, you made it to the right universe, didn't you?*

Did I?

I should have taken that nine o'clock bus back to En-cino. Oddly enough, a glance at her watch sometime in the course of the night had showed her that, though it had felt as if she had run through the Void for at least half an hour, the time had not registered on her watch at all. As near as she could calculate, she had emerged a few minutes before nine o'clock—precisely the same time that she had stepped in.

It was now full daylight, the morning hard and clear and hot in the sky, when she saw the village, tucked into a little pocket of semifertile land among the looming gray hills. A few workers toiled desultorily among the tawny grain in the fields; harvesting, guessed Joanna, by the half-shaved stubble, but not going about it with any great enthusiasm. The sun seemed stiflingly hot on her unprotected head. *I should have remembered to bring a hat,* she told herself irritably, *and a groundcloth to sit on last night would have helped, too.* But here on the tall slope of a granite hill, she could feel the bite in the wind. She remembered how, all through the tail end of summer, the bleak weariness of these times had kept the haymakers from the fields—a physical exhaustion as much as an emotional one, for the drawing of energy down the paths to Suraklin's computer affected the body as well as the soul. Part of her recognized that the ruin of the harvest would mean hunger throughout the land. Another part simply did not care.

All she wanted now was a meal and a bed to sleep in. If possible, she wanted to sleep through tomorrow—to deal with all this later.

The wind turned; the smell of blood hit her nostrils as if she'd inhaled a dose of ammonia.

She knew the smell of blood. At the summer's end, on an island in the sluggish green Shan, she'd shot a Witch-finder at a range of under two feet. The blood had sprayed her as if from a hose. Antryg had dragged her into the water, washed the sticky horror from her clothes and hair almost before what she had done sank into her. But she'd never forget that cloying, sweetish reek.

Turning her head, she saw the distant clump of gorse on the hillside and how the iridescent cloud of flies glittered around it in the early sun. Not wanting to, but knowing that she'd have to know, Joanna gathered up handfuls of petticoat and skirts in a gesture that was to become second nature to her, and picked her way over the sloping ground.

It had been a pig. It lay in a little hollow, behind the stiff, gray-green clump of the gorse. Flies swarmed over it, industrial-strength rural flies, some of them two inches long, buzzing like B-52s in the stillness of the sheltered hillslope. The pig's flesh had fallen in over its bones, like a punctured balloon, as if all the fluids of its body had been sucked forth at once, though Joanna could tell that the kill was fresh, last night. It had not yet begun to stink. Its hide, what she could see of it, was beaded all over with dots of blood, as if it had been pricked with a thousand needles simultaneously. She remembered the floating, angel-hair tendrils of the abomination, reaching out in the shimmer of the moon.

Stumbling jerkily on the uneven ground, Joanna turned and walked swiftly away from it. She made her way downhill, not toward the village, where people might delay her with questions, but toward the narrow wagon track of ash-colored dust that wound away from it to the south. In spite of the exhaustion that dragged upon her and the dreadful sick weariness that filled her body like a bloating disease, she wanted to get away from this accursed country as far and as fast as she could.

A wagon was coming from the village, driven brutally fast, with an angry disregard of the horse or the road. Joanna thought, *To hell with him, I don't need that kind of driving, I'll wait for the next one*, and then realized that, as small as this village was, in the midst of the harvest season, this was probably the only outgoing vehicle she was going to catch all week. The fear of the abomination alive in her mind, if not in her numb heart, she ran to reach the edge of the road before the wagon passed.

"Stop!" she pleaded in English, hoping to goodness the spell of tongues Antryg had once laid on her would hold. "Help me!"

The driver stopped the horse with a savage yank of the reins; she saw the flecks of foam spray from the beast's wrenched mouth. The driver was a youngish man who had once been stout, but now had the slightly wrinkled, fallen-in appearance of a fast and unhealthy weight loss; his face was gray and pinched with anger. "What the hell do you be wanting, girl?" he yelled at her.

Thank God the spell works. "I'm trying to get to Angels-hand. We were set on by highwaymen—they killed my brother." She wished as she said it that she could work up a more convincing delivery, but with the hot buzzing weariness in her head it was the best she could do. "Can you take me to the nearest town where I can get a stage? I have money..."

"What, that the highwaymen left you?" the driver jeered. "Money you stole from those you worked for, more like, when they turned you off!" He lashed his horse. The wheels flung dust on her as the wagon pulled away.

Joanna stood for a moment, her throat hurting with tears of resentment and rage. Blindingly, crazily, she wanted to fling rocks after the departing wagon and scream curses at its driver, the horse, and their whole smelly little village. Suddenly, overwhelmingly, she wanted to pull the gun from her pack and...

LIQUOR-STORE ROBBERS SHOOT THREE, the headlines had said last week. GANG SHOOTING SPREE KILLS FIVE. WOMAN SHOOTS TEENAGE DAUGHTER...

Among other things, that deadness, that uncaring in the soul, made it very easy to pull a trigger if you happened to have one in your hand.

Joanna sighed. Beyond a doubt the yokel in the wagon had spoken out of the same bled, gray ache that filled her own heart. After this spell of draining ended, she supposed she'd feel sympathy for him. Right now the rage in her, like the pus of an unburst boil, began its nauseating reabsorption into her body. She scrambled over the weed-grown ditch and bank, brambles snagging her petticoat and the backpack straps cutting into her shoulders, and began walking away from the village, but not really caring where she went or why.

She was almost on top of the wagon before she realized it had stopped and was waiting for her.

"I'm sorry, lass," the driver said in a weary, beaten voice. He pushed back his sweat-stained felt hat and wiped his brow with an arm that Joanna could have done chin-ups on, had not such exercises always been beyond her. "I didn't mean to shout at you as I did." He extended a hand the size of a small typewriter to help her over the high front wheels to the straw-strewn board of the seat. Puzzlement and exhaustion struggled for a moment behind his clear green eyes, and with them a hidden fear. "It's just . . . I don't know what it is that's come over me of late."

Joanna could have told him, but it was no more believable in this world than it was in her own.

It took her nine days to reach Angelshand; nine exhausting days of being jolted, first in wagons, then in the public stagecoach, elbow-to-elbow with coarse country squires, broadcloth-suited businessmen, talkative matrons, and bald-shaved prelates, over roads deep in autumnal mud. The gap in the Void through which she had come had opened deep in the Sykerst, hundreds of miles from either Kymil, where she was almost certain Antryg was being held, or Angelshand, where she hoped to find help in rescuing him. Once the weary spell of deadness lifted, as it did late that first afternoon, she realized she was extremely lucky she hadn't come through on the other side of the world.

Still, it meant eight nights in some of the worst accommodations she had ever encountered, sharing straw mattresses crawling with bedbugs with whatever other female passengers happened to be on the stage that day—and their babies, if they had them—lying awake, half-choked with the foetor of unwashed clothes and bodies, scratching furiously at flea bites, staring at the dark rafters overhead, and listening to the steady beat of the rain on the shingles. *This doesn't even qualify as one-star,* she thought tiredly. *I'll give this two black holes. Why couldn't I be like those heroines who come through the time-warp or the dimensional vortex at most a day's walk from where they're trying to get to?*

The farmer who had given her a ride had introduced her to a friend of his in the next village, with instructions to take her on to a mutual acquaintance, a trusted Old Believer merchant in Sug's Beck, the nearest large town. Neither would even listen to her offers of payment, but she had left a sapphire with the merchant, who, like most of his faith, turned a few crowns in whatever he could, telling him to give them both whatever credit the jewel would buy. The merchant, an elderly man in the long black robes and elaborately braided hair of his people, had bought other jewels from her to give her money for the journey and had thrown in gratis a hot meal—care of his wife—a cloak, since by then the rains had begun, and a new dress, "Because a nice girl like you needs more than one dress."

The journey itself was exhausting and uncomfortable beyond belief. Joanna spent the first three days in a stupor of exhaustion and afterward alternated between almost unbearable anxiety over how long it was taking, the gnawing awareness that if Antryg were dead or if she couldn't manage his escape there was no way out of this world for her, and the unspeakable tedium of her fellow-passengers' conversation. The Council could change their vote and execute Antryg at any time, if they hadn't done so weeks ago while she was still raiding the DARKMAGE files from the San Serano computer.

Altogether, Joanna was heartily glad when the huge, unwieldy coach pulled into the yard of the Horn of the Hunter on the southern outskirts of Angelshand, and she stumbled—cramped, weary, and, she suspected, lousy—out of it for the last time into the raw, misty gloom of the early afternoon.

"Call you a hack, ma'am?" one of the porters inquired, and Joanna nodded, though the thought of getting into another horse-drawn conveyance affected her with an almost physical nausea. As the cab rattled north through first the suburbs, then the outlying slums and factory districts of the capital of the Empire of Ferryth, Joanna felt again the quickening of her heart and the hard twist of anxiety in her belly as she recognized landmark after landmark in that dark granite city. Buildings the color of iron loomed above the sheet-steel of the river against a sky dark with autumn and factory soot. Above the jammed higgledy-piggledy of rotting half-timbered gambrels on Angel's Island she caught a glimpse of the towers of the St. Cyr fortress, where the Bishop of Angelshand presided over the Inquisition and its Witchfinders. Even in this raw weather the streets teemed with beggars in rags, servants in a rainbow of livery, and swaggering sasenna in their black uniforms and razor-bright swords. Scarf-sellers, whores, and match and noodle vendors rubbed elbows with bourgeois ladies out for walks with their companions, clerks hurrying to their countinghouses, crossing-sweepers busily clearing horse dung out of the way for a copper, chimney sweeps, pickpockets, constables in red and blue uniforms, and butchers' boys driving their quick-footed ponies and trailed by gangs of yapping pariah dogs. From the packed bridge that joined Angel's Island with the wealthier precincts north of the river, Joanna glanced downstream to the harbor, where masts rose like a fire-stripped forest and the faint cries of the stevedores unloading all the wealth of the Empire mingled with the melancholy mewing of the gulls. Swirling below against the arches of the bridge, the river stank like the sewer it was.

The cabman had known the house she'd asked for—a fortunate circumstance, since Joanna couldn't remember the name of the square. By the time she climbed down and paid off the jarvey, the tightness in her chest had become almost unbearable; the fear that had slept in her all these last nine dreary days swelled again to smother her, the fear of being done with one stage and having to start on the next.

It was Joanna's nature to think in subroutines. It was, she supposed, the only thing which had permitted her to undertake her current impossible task. She had obtained as much of Suraklin's files, Suraklin's knowledge and personality, as she would be able to; she had prepared herself for the expedition—with the omission of a warm jacket, a hat, and a groundcloth, she reminded herself; she had made it this far. Over the course of the last nine interminable days she had tortured herself, like the victim of a Sunday-afternoon toothache, prodding at the pain and waiting for the dentist's office to open on Monday, by wondering, *What if he's gone? What if he was arrested? What if he won't help me . . . ?* until she was almost ill with apprehension.

But the narrow, disdainful townhouse in its fashionable setting was unchanged as she crossed the broad rectangle of autumn-brown grass in the center of Governor's Square. Five or six carriages, their teams thickly blanketed and puffing steam from their nostrils like dragons in idle, stood near the curb. The coachmen, both male and female, had gotten up a coal fire in a brazier on one corner and were huddled around it, warming their hands and talking shop. Her heart pounding, Joanna hitched her overstuffed backpack up over one shoulder and climbed the marble steps of the one house in this world in which she hoped for refuge while she made her plans.

An extremely gorgeous young footman in fuchsia livery answered her knock, and looked down his beautiful nose at her when she admitted, blushing, that she didn't have a card to lay upon his little silver tray. *Add calling cards*, she thought irrelevantly, *to the list for next time*. "I'm afraid I haven't any with me," she said meekly, wishing she had had access to a hot bath and a dress that hadn't been worn for six or seven consecutive days in a crowded coach. The young footman's expression of disbelief deepened; Joanna found herself picturing what the Prince Regent would say about him, and immediately felt better. "If you'll tell Magister Magus that Joanna Sheraton is here, I think he'll want to see me."

The young man looked as if he did not see how this could be possible, but only said, "Very well, Miss. Walk this way," an unconscious Marx Brothers straight line which made Joanna want to giggle. It was odd, she thought, following him up the oval curve of the open stairway, how fleeing for her life from the abomination in the darkness had seemed less anxiety-producing than facing another person and asking for help.

And he has to help me, she thought blindly. *I have to start somewhere . . .*

Magister Magus' drawing room was, as usual, crowded with overdressed ladies with high-piled hair, an ocean of jacquard petticoats, lace sleeve flounces, and jewelry that reduced Joanna's paltry hoard to bargain-basement gleanings. Most of their maids were better dressed than Joanna, and all of them looked down their rice-powdered noses at her travel-stained blue dress and the limp cloak that the footman took away. One elegant young matron who couldn't have been more than eighteen nudged her neighbor and nodded toward Joanna with a remark concealed behind a painted chicken-skin fan. The others, after a cursory glance, simply ignored her.

After nine days of stagecoach gossip and the endless accounts of her fellow passengers' illnesses and childbirths, Joanna was just as glad.

She was human enough to be thoroughly gratified, however, when a second footman opened the inner ebony doors of the drawing room, to usher out a solemn-looking lady in her sixties, and said, "Miss Sheraton?"

Demurely, Joanna got to her feet. As the doors shut behind her she heard a muffled, "Well, *really!*" The footman lifted a curtain from an arch, and Joanna found herself in a small consulting chamber even more opulently fur-

nished than the lush pink-and-black room outside. Incense
burned before a hematite statue of Kahieret, God of the
Mages, withdrawn and dark as the velvet that draped its
niche, and Magister Magus himself was just rising from his
chair of inlaid ebony.

"My dear child!" He strode to her across the tufted silk
of the carpet and caught her hands. "Antryg's friend the
systems designer—your hands are freezing! I can spare but
a moment now, my dear, but I've ordered tea for you in the
dining room . . ."

She grinned shakily, relief at being recognized, let alone
welcomed, making her throat feel suddenly hot and close.
"It's all right. I can't have your customers getting in a
snit."

"Are you hungry?" His eyes were anxious—light, almost white-green, within startling dark rings around the
irises; he must have been months tracking down the peri-
dots of just that color set among the diamonds of his pectoral cross. In spite of the black velvet robe and all the
trappings of a fashionable society charlatan, there was a
genuine warmth to him, a caring wholly apart from his
professional charm. "My dear child, I'd heard . . ." He hesitated, seeing the sudden tightness of her expression, and
veered from mentioning what she already must know.
"Well, I was afraid you'd been hurt as well."

She shook her head, furiously fighting the urge to lean
on that slender velvet shoulder and cry. It was unexpectedly, achingly good to be with someone who believed her
and who would understand.

She was looking away from the Magus, and in any case
her sight was suddenly blurred, but she felt the gentle
touch of his hand on her shoulder. "Now, my dear," that
fluent, beautiful voice said. "We'll talk about it after you've
rested a little and eaten. Are you . . . ?" He hesitated again.
Looking up, Joanna saw tact and concern for her struggling
in his face with worry for himself and almost laughed in
spite of her tears.

"No, I'm not on the run. Nobody's after me." *At least*, she amended, *not the authorities*. She decided not to mention Suraklin until Magus was sitting down.

He made a deprecating noise, as if such considerations were the furthest thing from his mind, but looked relieved.

Then silence hung between them, silence balanced on the edge of an indrawn breath, like the silence in a lovers' quarrel in which neither dares speak for fear of the chain of events the next, inevitable utterance must unleash. The swollen hurt of the dread she had carried in her for nearly six weeks was nearly unbearable, but now that she faced the first person whom she could ask, the first person who could tell her, she found the words stuck in her throat.

And the Magus, looking down into her eyes, wore an expression of such pity and such unhappiness that he must be the one to answer the question which he knew she would ask that she felt her heart and bowels turn to sodden and ruinous ash. He knew what she was going to ask him, she thought, and he knew he'd have to be the one to tell her she had failed before she had begun.

Her voice was very small. "He's dead, isn't he?"

Magus sighed, not pretending he did not understand of whom they spoke. "I wish it wasn't me who has to tell you this," he said gently and took her hand in his, as if the touch of his fingers could somehow lessen what was to come. "No, he isn't dead, but—his mind is gone. The Inquisition tortured him, you know. I'm not sure what all they did, but when they were done, there wasn't much left. My child, I'm sorry."

CHAPTER III

I'M GOING TO HAVE TO DO THIS ALL BY MYSELF. JOANNA stared blankly out into the misty charcoal gloom visible beyond the dining room windows, feeling the weight of terror constricting her chest like an iron band.

And then, *Oh, Antryg, I'm sorry.*

Joanna had never been a believer in *sorry*. Up until the last moment, when the wizards walked through the patio doors of Gary's house in Agoura, she could have cut Antryg's bonds and let him flee into the night.

She wondered why she had believed that a love as intense as the one she felt for him had to be suspect, that anything she wanted that badly couldn't be right.

Weak tears gathered in the inner corners of her eyes and she gritted her teeth against them, thankful for the warmth of the cup of steaming tea cradled in her cold hands.

"I doubt that either of us would even recognize him anymore," Magister Magus was saying gently. "They say for days all he did was huddle in a corner and weep, or scream and pound on the walls with his hands." Joanna shut her eyes, remembering the splints on those twisted fingers. "I've heard that these days he has visions and holds long conversations with obscure saints."

I betrayed him to that, Joanna thought, her mind numb with fear and grief. *I betrayed him and now I have to face*

38

Suraklin alone. She didn't know which was worse.

It was six in the evening and already quite dark. The Magus' ladies had all departed to have their hair done up for the evening's balls and opera visits, and the narrow townhouse was quiet, save for the distant clink of metal and porcelain in the kitchen where dinner was being prepared. A steady drizzle pattered against the window beyond its claret-red velvet drapes, and Joanna felt cold to the bottommost reaches of her soul.

She realized she had let her silence last too long. Looking around, she saw the Magus regarding her anxiously, kindly concern in his fashionably painted eyes. She swallowed and set her teacup down unsipped, forcing her voice steady. "Who told you that?"

He shook his head, as if to dispel her forlorn hope it was all rumor. "It's common knowledge, child. I've spoken to Church sasenna and hasu who've guarded him. The guard on the Tower has been trebled; since he's taken to having visions, the Bishop changes them nearly every week. Most of the Church sasenna have taken monks' vows as well; the visions inspired a certain amount of sympathy and awe, since he describes quite accurately saints of whom he's obviously never heard."

He folded his slender hands, clearly concerned both for his friend and for her. Out of his impressive black velvet robes, he looked like any well-to-do professional of the city in his white shirtsleeves, stockings, dark breeches, and vest. The Prince Regent, Joanna reflected with tired irony, in his sable linen and black-jeweled rings, looked far more like a necromancer than this dapper little faker.

"Would the Sigil of Darkness do that to him?"

The Magus thought about it a moment, frowning. "I don't see how it would," he said finally. "After all, he was imprisoned under its influence for seven years and it did him no harm."

"But then it was just on the doors of the Tower, wasn't it, and not around his neck?"

"Around his neck?" The revulsion on his face was almost nausea.

"On an iron collar," Joanna said. "They soldered it there, after he had signed his confession, I think because someone on the Council was holding out against voting for his execution."

The dog wizard looked away, utterly sickened.

Hesitantly, she added, "I saw it in a dream . . ."

"I don't wonder that you did. The screaming of his soul at the touch of that thing . . ." He swung back to look at her. "Do you know what the Sigil of Darkness is, child? What it does?" And, when she only looked blankly at him, he went on, "It is an utterly abominable thing to wizards, utterly abominable. It does more than cripple our power. It is the antithesis of power; it is anti-power, and the greater one's strength, the greater the—I suppose pain is the closest word, but it isn't that. It eats power, eats at us through our power. Torturing him these last six weeks would have been more merciful. God help him, no wonder he went mad." He flinched, pressing his long fingers against his mouth in the frame of its silky little Van Dyke beard, as if he could feel the cold stain of that poison through the secret magic that underlay his flamboyant charlatanry.

Frostbitten fingers hurt when they were warmed—Joanna recognized the stabbing ache somewhere in her chest as being of the same order, the pain of hope flaring in the ash. "Then if the Sigil were removed . . ."

Pity in his thin face, the Magus took her hands. "Child, it's hopeless. You would only destroy yourself. Antryg is my friend. Since I wasn't blind when you were here with him, I know you love him . . ."

"It isn't that," Joanna said stubbornly. "My—love for him—has nothing to do with this, nor the fact that I put him where he is now, that I was the one who drugged him and gave him to the Council . . ."

Magus made a shocked noise.

"It's that I have a job to do and I can't do it without a

wizard's help. I can't do it without Antryg's help. He's the only one besides myself who even believes there *is* a threat, a worldwide threat, in these—these periods of deadness, of draining, of the death of magic and hope. And from everything I've heard, he's for damn sure the only mage who's capable of taking on Suraklin."

She hadn't meant to speak that name to him so soon. The silence that followed it was curiously like that which follows thunder in the night, a hush through which the tiny sounds of the servants in the kitchen, the faint patter of the rain, and the tinkly rattle of a carriage over the wet cobblestones outside seemed clear as music. Magus' black eyebrows seemed to stand out like smudges of ink against a face gone suddenly very white.

He said softly, "That's impossible. Suraklin is dead."

"Suraklin's original body is dead." Joanna's grip tightened slightly over the Magus' fingers as they flinched, as if to keep him from flight at the mere mention of the Dark Mage. "Suraklin's mind, his knowledge, and his personality have been living in the minds of others, like a self-perpetuating worm-program on a computer disk that lies about its own existence and eventually eats up all the other programs. And now he's getting ready to download into a computer for real, a computer powered by electricity that will be generated by the life-energies of everyone in the world. The deadness is going to become permanent, Magus. Everyone's magic will fade, as yours has faded. Suraklin will have it all."

She looked across the table at the Magus and saw in his horror-stricken green eyes that, deny it though he might to her, to others, or to himself, he knew she spoke the truth. He whispered, "Then when Antryg was here with you in the fall . . ."

"He was looking for Suraklin."

The Magus pulled his hands away from her and stared out into the rainy darkness. "Dear God."

"And he couldn't confide in you or me or anyone, because he knew that anyone at all might be under Suraklin's influence." *As Magus might be*, Joanna thought, with sudden disgust at herself. *Oh, well, too late now. No wonder Antryg came across as a hopeless paranoid.* "Magus, I need help."

"Not against Suraklin."

"He doesn't know I'm here."

"He will. By the saints, girl, don't you listen to anything?" He swung back to face her, anger struggling with fear in his absinthe-colored eyes. "I never lived in Kymil—the Church has always been too strong in that town for a dog wizard to be comfortable—but I passed through it when Suraklin was alive. I tell you there was nothing that went on there that he didn't know, no one whose life he could not tamper with if they did not obey his . . . He called them 'requests.'

"The first time I saw him was in the marketplace, a thin, biscuit-colored man with his long hair tied in a tail down his back and his yellow eyes like a cat's, watching the stall holders' children playing in the gutters. He walked over to a little girl of about four and took her—just took her by the hand and led her away through the market, in front of the whole population of Kymil, *and nobody did a thing!* I was so shocked I wondered for a moment whether he mightn't have been using some kind of cloaking-spell—which, as mageborn myself, I could see through when others couldn't. But one of the little boys ran to the girl's mother, pointing after them and telling her. And she shushed him. I'll never forget the tears running down her face as she watched them leave the market nor that damned, smug look of satisfaction on Suraklin's. My child, I'll have nothing to do with Suraklin."

Had Suraklin done that with Antryg? Joanna wondered —just walked up to that overgrown, skinny boy of nine in some outback Sykerst town and taken him by the hand, smelling out the powers in his mind and wanting them for his own? Or because of the boy's powers, had he seduced

Antryg through dreams, as he had seduced Gary, long before they met, to win *his* trust?

"Then help me save Antryg," she said quietly. When he averted his gaze from her again, she reached across the table and caught at the pleated ruffle of his wrist. "Magus, please! I have to start somewhere . . ."

"Even if you could somehow get into the Tower itself, getting the Sigil off him might not help, after this long."

Her voice breaking with despair, she cried, "I have to try! Magus, I can't do this all by myself! Suraklin has to be defeated . . ."

With the gentle swiftness of one long used to dealing with female hysterics, Magister Magus was on his feet, around the table, and holding her comfortingly in his arms. And, in spite of her fury at him and her frustrated rage at his cowardice, Joanna found a great deal of comfort in the firm strength of his hold, the warmth of his hands on hers, and the mingled smell of perfume, candlewax, and incense that clung to his clothes. "My child, I'm telling you he can't be," the Magus said softly. "I know you consider me a coward and a villain . . ."

She raised her head from that strong, slender shoulder and looked into the green eyes beneath the silver-shot black brows, seeing in them the man's genuine quixotic chivalry struggling with his fear of pain and death.

He went on, with a kind of apologetic dignity, "My position was bad enough before, with the Witchfinders always sniffing at my heels and the Regent staring daggers at me every time our paths crossed at the Palace, in spite of my being under the protection of his cousin and heir. Now with the abominations multiplying in the countryside, with the harvest on the verge of failing, the Saarieque trade-fleet not yet in and every fortune in the Empire in a tizzy, with rumors of plots by wizards flying thick as grasshoppers in a dry summer . . . My child, it would take so little for me to end up before the Inquisition myself. It would be safer for me not to let you stay here at all . . ."

Panic clutched her; he touched her hair reassuringly, the dozen candles in their holder on the table throwing faint, multiple shadows across the tired lines of hopelessness on his face. "I can only beg you to remember my position here and not bring down the Witchfinders, the Council of Wizards, or the abominable Prince Regent's notice on me while you're under my roof. Further than that I cannot go. I have met Suraklin, my child; I've seen his power. Believe me, the consequences of going against him are one of the few things I can think of worse than death."

Joanna sighed, feeling very weak and wishing there were someone else to do all this for her. "Unfortunately," she said, "so are the consequences of not going against him. So I really have no choice."

The noodle vendor whose little cart leaked steam into the damp air looked askance at Joanna, but pointed out to her the direction she had asked. This part of Angelshand was a far cry from Governor's Square. Crumbling brick tenements and soot-rotted half-timbered edifices leaned against one another in the fog like homeward-bound drunks. Down alleyways which Joanna could have spanned with her arms, mazes of laundry fluttered above reeking streams of half-frozen sewage through which beggar-children splashed, shrieking, their feet wrapped in rags. The shops that gazed like the gloomy eyesockets of skulls into the narrow lanes seemed to be of only three types—secondhand clothes, pawnshops, or gin palaces from whose doors, even at this hour of the afternoon, trickled snatches of drunken singing. The men and women whose feet churned at the icy slime that smeared the flagways increasingly wore the dark gabardine and looped-up braids of the Old Believers, and once Joanna glimpsed across the street a red-haired girl in the billowing black robes of a mage.

Nervously, Joanna patted under her cloak the awkward bulge of the .38 that distended the pocket of her dress. She wasn't sure what Caris' reaction to her return would be, but she didn't believe in taking chances. Knowing what he knew, Caris would guess at once that there could be only one reason for her to come back.

The Mages' Yard was a narrow court of eight or nine shabby houses, brooding in the raw brown mists over scummed and uneven cobblestones. As she passed it, Joanna saw few people about, save for an Old Believer woman sweeping her doorstep and a boy in rags peddling kindling from house to house. Autumn in Angelshand was a dreary time. The long winds from the southwest, the ship-winds, slacked as the trade season drew to its close, and the fogs and rains settled in. Iron cold was locking down on the land. The Sykerst would already be under snow.

The harvest had failed; from the number of beggars Joanna had seen she guessed the cost of bread was up. According to Magister Magus, poverty was always worst in the city in early autumn, just before the great silk and tea fleets came in from Saarieque to provide their annual stimulus to the economy. He had spoken of this philosophically. Joanna, raised with the comfort of a public welfare system that never *really* let anybody starve, found those hollowed eyes and emaciated faces horribly disquieting.

As she lingered at the head of the Mages' Yard, one of the house doors opened, and a small group of wizards and sasenna emerged. In their center she recognized the Lady Rosamund, coldly beautiful and seemingly oblivious to the bitter chill of the afternoon, laying down the law about something to a silver-haired androgyne who flitted along at her side like a dandelion seed. Her breath steamed cloudy in the grimy air, and her voice struck fragments of words, like glass chimes, from the hard walls of the court. Mindful not to call attention to herself by hurrying, Joanna idled away down the street, glad for the concealing hood of her cloak.

Of all the mages, she feared most to meet the Lady Rosamund.

In a tavern down the block, she gave the innkeeper's boy a copper bit to take a message to Stonne Caris in the Mages' Yard. Sitting in the half-empty ordinary room, she wondered what she would say to the Archmage's grandson, the young man who had risked his life to pursue and capture Antryg and bring him to the Council's justice. The last time she had seen him came back to her, when he and the Church wizards had beaten Antryg to his knees at his last, desperate attempt at flight, and had dragged him back through the dark Gate in the Void. Caris had worn a look of calm, the serenity of a man once more back in the world he knew. She recalled, too, the dark scenes of her dream.

But Caris had traveled with Antryg and her from Kymil to Angelshand. With his rudimentary powers, he had felt the draining-off of the world's life to fuel Suraklin's computer; he had dealt with the abominations which came through the Void at its opening; and he had heard Antryg speak of the danger that lay in those gray times of grief. He was, Joanna realized, one of the very few people who might conceivably believe what was going on. And, though she wasn't sure how much bearing it would have on Caris' attitude, Antryg had saved his life.

The door opened. Murky whitish light filtered dimly into the brown gloom. Looking up, Joanna saw Caris silhouetted against the gray cold of the street—a young Greek god, foster-raised in Valhalla, with the loose black clothing of a sasennan and a thickly quilted jacket not quite blurring the gymnast poise of the body and his short quiff of cornsilk-yellow hair falling over his forehead. The sword and daggers of the ancient order of sworn warriors glinted among a brass-buckled strapwork of weapons belts and a dark silk sword sash. Coffee-brown, tip-tilted eyes touched her, went on to scan the room for potential dangers, and returned to her.

His face expressionless, he turned on his heel and strode out again.

Startled and hurt, Joanna lunged to her feet, tripped on

her petticoats, and cursed. The cold outside was like a slap in the face; in the bleak, narrow street, Caris was nowhere to be seen. A glance at the black mud underfoot showed her the marks of his soft-soled boots; holding up her skirts, she followed around the corner into an alley...

Hard hands grabbed her elbows from behind. Joanna cried out with shock as she was shoved face-forward against the sooty brick of a wall; a hand blocked her jabbing elbow as another clawed through the layers of her cloak at the pocket of her skirt.

It was all over in less than a second, and Caris turned her around, holding her hard against the wall with one hand while he shoved the .38 into his sword sash with the other. His brown eyes were flat and cold, as if they had never met.

"Come with me," he said.

She braced her feet against the jerk of his hand. His beauty had always intimidated her, but she had never had cause to feel his strength before. It was terrifying. Of course, she thought, he's been working out eight hours a day since he was fourteen. "Caris, no..."

He paused. His face was as she had seen it in her dream, expressionless, but with emotion raging far back in the depths of his eyes. "You shouldn't have come back, Joanna. You understand that now the Archmage won't be able to let you go." Like his face, there was nothing in his voice.

It was something Joanna hadn't counted on and it hit her like a blow to the stomach. She had known that if she met Lady Rosamund she would be recognized and identified as what she was now, Antryg's willing accomplice instead of his victim. The thought that she, too, might be imprisoned by the wizards hadn't even occurred to her. With it came the sinking realization that, while she had given plausible reasons for her disappearance in her own world which would prevent people from looking for her, in this world, legally, she did not exist at all. If she vanished, no one would know, except Magister Magus, who would undoubtedly be too terrified to inquire.

Her first impulse was to plead. But something in Caris' inhuman blankness sparked anger in her instead, and she set her feet and twisted her arm defiantly against the steel grip. "Look, would you pretend you have a will of your own for about five minutes?"

She saw the flare of his nostrils with his responding anger; but, as is the Way of the Sasenna, he mastered it and only said levelly, "Having a will of my own kept me from killing Antryg Windrose the moment I caught him. Had I been obedient to the dictates of the council, my grandfather would be alive today."

Joanna used a phrase she'd picked up from the stagecoach drivers on the way to Angelshand and added, "You were obedient to the dictates of the Council when you let your grandfather go to meet him alone, both times, first at the Silent Tower, then at Gary's. Even if he wasn't duping you, do you think your unthinking obedience helped him any?"

The breath steamed from his lips—one, two breaths. His grip didn't change. "When I took my vows as sasennan, I turned my will over to the Council of Wizards," he said. "Whether your arguments are right or wrong doesn't concern me."

"Does it concern you that even having Antryg under lock and key, sealed in the Silent Tower under the Sigil of Darkness and driven out of his mind by what they've done to him, the fading of magic, the draining of life, *is still going on*? If the abominations were Antryg's doing, why are they still appearing?"

"Because he still lives." He thrust her toward the mouth of the alley; Joanna pulled vainly against that frightening strength. Terrified at the thought of facing the Council, she forced her mind to focus, not on her fear, but on her rage.

"Dammit, would you act like a man instead of a goddam computer!"

That offended him out of his stony calm. "It is a man who is loyal . . ."

She finally succeeded in wrenching her arm free of his grip and stood, angrily rubbing it through her cloak. "I've talked to a lot of computers in my time and, believe me, I've gotten more discrimination and judgment out of a six-K ops program than I'm getting out of you!"

They stood close together in the murky shades of the alley, like a fair-haired brother and sister at the tail end of a shouting match. Caris was breathing hard now with fury, his hand half drawn back, as if he would strike her. *If he does*, she thought, too angry now to let herself fear, *so help me I'll rip his ears off*.

But slowly, the iron expression on Caris' face faded. Fleetingly, it looked young and troubled—she remembered he was only nineteen—as it had before his grandfather's murder had hardened his soul into the perfection of his vows. Quietly, he said, "It isn't up to me to discriminate or to judge—or even to listen. I know you to be an enemy of the will of the Council. You're here to rescue Antryg, aren't you?"

"You flatter him," Joanna said slowly. "And you insult me, by the way. I'm here because I know, and you know, that Antryg's old master Suraklin didn't die twenty-five years ago when he was supposed to have been killed. Only two people knew that—Antryg and Suraklin himself. Caris, for the last four years Suraklin was occupying the brain and body of your grandfather Salteris."

"No." The flat harshness returned to his voice, the rage to his eyes. "He told you that, didn't he? To save his own skin. Had I known he had calumnated Salteris so, I would have . . ."

"Slit his wrists back at the Tower when he begged you to?" That threw him off balance. She pressed on. "There was a man I knew back in my own world, the owner of the house where we were, the house where all Suraklin's marks were found. After your grandfather died—after

Suraklin left his body, imbecile as he left the Emperor's—
this man had all the mannerisms and the patterns of speech
that I knew in your grandfather. According to your grandfather himself, who else could download his personality
from body to body, from brain to brain, except Suraklin?
Caris, we got the wrong man. We were both duped. And
now we have to stop Suraklin, and Antryg—*if* we can get
him out of the Silent Tower, *if* we can get the Sigil of
Darkness off him—is the only one who might be able to
help us."

"That's a lie," the sasennan said, his voice like the iron
earth of winter. "Antryg murdered my grandfather. He betrayed his trust—*he* was Suraklin . . ."

"Caris," Joanna said quietly, "wasn't there ever a time
when your grandfather—changed?"

He looked away. "No. . . . It was because of my grandmother's death. He loved her." His jaw tightened. For a
moment, the grief and anger in him seemed to seethe up
beneath the stiff rock barriers erected by the Way of the
Sasenna. When he looked back at her, there was something
close to hatred in his brown eyes.

"Don't you understand that what I think about it doesn't
matter?" The words came jerkily, as if the very framing of
them were difficult. "Your telling me this . . . I am sworn to
be the weapon of the Council and only that. I'm not—
qualified—to judge these matters. It is not the Way of the
Sasenna to be."

Looking up into his face, Joanna suddenly felt very
sorry for this gorgeous, muscular young man, this honed
and glistening blade. After all, she thought, he had traded
in the pain of making decisions for the steady comfort of
knowing that in following orders, no matter what they
were, he would always be in the right. Pain like that could
be turned away from, but it was always there waiting, and
now he had no experience in dealing with it.

Her anger at him faded. "I'm sorry," she said. Turning,
she walked away down the alley toward the muddy pave-

ment of the street. Grief and defeat filled her, as exhausting as if she had indeed fought him hand to hand. Caris remained standing where he was, looking after that small, cloaked figure, like a statue, save for the mist of his breath. Only when she was halfway back to Magister Magus' did Joanna realize that he hadn't, after all, followed his duty and caught her again and only much later that evening did she remember that he had kept her gun.

CHAPTER IV

THIS IS MY LAST CHANCE. A FOOTMAN IN THE EMERALD green velvet livery of the Prince Cerdic's household opened the door of Magister Magus' anonymous dark carriage, and helped Joanna down—a gesture she had always considered a quaint formality until she'd actually tried getting out of a high-slung vehicle in half a dozen layers of petticoats and skirts. *This had better work.*

If it didn't, she had no idea where to go next.

She tipped the man the amount prescribed by Magister Magus, that expert in the nuances of Court conduct, and walked up the pink marble steps of the Dower House, one of the smallest of the several palaces which dotted the vast, fairy-tale parklands comprising the Imperial Seat. She found that, on the whole, she felt worse than she had when she'd knocked on Magister Magus' door for the first time. On that occasion at least, she reflected, she'd had the comfort of several courses of action open to her—if not Magister Magus, then Caris; if not Caris, then Cerdic the Prince, first cousin of the Regent and Heir, after him, to the Empire.

She was now down to one, with nothing open to her beyond that, and no way of getting home.

Literally no way of getting home, she added to herself with a rueful grin, watching the coachman turn the small,

single-horse brougham in the drive and move briskly away
down the rain-puddled road up which they had come, until
it vanished beyond a copse of wet trees. Magister Magus
had been horrified by her request to be taken to Court.
"Are you mad, girl? With things as they are? The abomination that killed those children in the factory district last
night; the rumors in the Sykerst that the religion of the old
gods is coming back; the Witchfinders up in arms; pogroms
in Mellidane; the Stock Exchange shaky—it always is, in
autumn—mutinies on the trade-ships coming back from
Saarieque and the Spice Lands; the worst harvest in thirty
years . . . My life wouldn't be worth two coppers if I went
anywhere *near* the Imperial Palaces!"

"But I have to see Prince Cerdic," Joanna had insisted
quietly from the depths of one of the dog wizard's gilded
ebony armchairs. "I may not know a lot about Courts and
Princes and things, but I do know you can't just walk in off
the street and ask to see the dude who's second-in-line for
the throne. But he's a friend of yours and he favors the
wizards. If anyone could help me get Antryg out, he
could."

"*If* anyone," the dog wizard repeated softly. That had
been last night, after Joanna had returned from her abortive
interview with Caris; they had shared a glass of port in the
library while the Magus had read over the various newspapers, broadsides, and scandal sheets from which he
gleaned the raw material for his seemingly magical deduc-
tions about his clients' lives. "The problem is, child, I'm
not sure anyone can help Antryg now. And in any case, I'd
hesitate to ask. Part of the secret of dealing with Courts is
knowing when to disappear. Now that the Prince Regent is
married, he keeps an even closer eye on Cerdic . . ."

"Married?"

"Last month—my dear child, the town rang with it."

The Regent's high, harsh voice came back to her . . .
that brainless bitch I'm to marry . . . and Antryg's, in the

firelight of the posthouse, *Come, Pharos, you know you haven't any use for a woman . . .*

"Pellicida, niece of the King of Senterwing," the Magus went on. "They say at court his Grace calls her the Black Mare. But until he gets her with child—if he ever manages to—Cerdic is still his heir; and at the moment, both Cerdic and I know it is not the time for Cerdic to be seen associating with the mageborn."

By dint of coaxing, Joanna had managed to secure the loan of his carriage and a letter of introduction. "Anything else?" the Magus had inquired, with some acerbity. "A team of running-footmen to announce you? A brass band? Fireworks, maybe?" But he had flung himself gracefully into a chair before his desk, waved absentmindedly in the direction of the two branches of candles flanking its inlaid writing surface and caused all twelve wicks to burst into a simultaneous flutter of light, then began to write.

His sole condition had been that his coachman wait for her at the gates of the Imperial Park, not at the Dower House where Cerdic stayed when he was in Angelshand. Knowing that the Regent would probably have spies in the stables, Joanna had agreed. Last night, with the rain drumming softly on the roof, this had not seemed like such a good idea, but this morning the soft autumn ship winds had blown again from the southwest, dispersing the clinging mists. The first of the Saarieque trade fleet had finally been sighted, a day or two off the out-islands. Magister Magus, like everybody else in the city, had money invested in their cargoes and had cheered up considerably and given Joanna innumerable small pointers about the proper conduct at Court.

It appeared that Magister Magus wasn't the only person in Angelshand familiar with the secret of knowing when to disappear. Pharos' paranoia about Cerdic was evidently only too well-known. After a condescending scrutiny which made Joanna glad she'd invested the remainder of her dwindling funds in a new gown, an elderly majordomo conducted her to what was apparently the reception room for the better class of petitioners, a sort of long drawing room in oak and red velvet, whose French windows looked out on a vista of wet, brown garden, shivering in the wind-blown restlessness of the sunlight. The room boasted several life-sized bronze statues in velvet-draped wall niches, a marble fireplace in which a fire had been newly made up, and not another living soul.

"His Grace is rather occupied this morning," the major-domo said, with a chilly bow, a statement which Joanna interpreted as a warning that she was in for a long wait. "I will inform him of your presence." And he departed, bearing her letter of introduction and the sizable tip the Magus had advised would insure its prompt delivery.

At least, Joanna thought, there was a fire in the fireplace, not at all a usual consideration, according to Magister Magus, in the rooms where the humble waited to present their petitions to the great. Thinking back on it later, she knew that it should have alerted her that someone else was expected and, in fact, someone fairly important—but it didn't.

Thus the first warning she had was the sound of voices approaching in the garden beyond the French doors. She looked up, startled, in time to see through the glass Prince Cerdic himself coming up the steps of the small terrace just outside, looking back over his shoulder to talk to a man behind him.

The second man was Gary.

Joanna was so shocked, so disoriented at seeing Gary—possessed by Suraklin or not, her first impression was that it was Gary—in the context of this world that Prince Cerdic was actually starting to open the door before she moved. Her mind was staggering under the realization of what Suraklin's presence here implied, the collapsing hurt of her last hope vanishing; only a half-second later did she realize her own appalling peril, and then it was far too late to make it across the room to the inner door. Her only refuge was in the velvet-draped niche beside the fireplace which housed a heroic bronze of some ancient warrior who bore a startling resemblance to Tom Selleck, close enough to have reached out and touched either of the two men as they came to warm their hands at the fire.

"My dear Gaire, of course he's mad, but why should the nobles care about that?" Cerdic was asking. "As long as he doesn't offend the Church, retains a favorable trade balance with Saarieque, and keeps the peasants in line, they wouldn't care if he slept with sheep and pigs, never mind boys." The young Prince had put on a little weight since Joanna had last seen him, his round cheeks somewhat rounder against the artful clusters of dark brown curls. But he still had the same pleasant expression in his painted hazel eyes and the same open brow and air of clean, healthy good looks. Against Cerdic's resplendent mauve satin and clouds of rose-point lace, Suraklin's dust-colored velvet seemed almost severe.

"So far." The Dark Mage had discarded all of Gary's old mannerisms. Even the voice sounded different, though its pitch and timbre were the same. "Nobles favor any man under whose rule they prosper. When they feel the pinch of lost revenues and when they come to you for money, you'll find yourself a good deal more popular."

Cerdic nodded in eager agreement. "Of course your investment advice is superb, as all advice from one in touch with the Ancient Powers of Magic must be." Suraklin nodded in deprecating agreement. Joanna, in her hiding place and half-suffocated by the heat trapped between the fireplace wall and the crimson velvet draperies, remembered the young Prince's slavish adherence to anything Antryg had said, too, and wondered how she could possibly have considered that kind of unthinking championship anything but moronic.

"But all support doesn't come from money alone. Popular feeling plays a great part in it, especially now..."

"And so it shall," the wizard responded kindly. "It's

why I asked you to extend your invitation to both your cousin and his bride today. The Lady Pellicida is surprisingly popular..."

Cerdic's plucked eyebrows lifted. "Pella? That overdressed, homely gawk of a girl?"

"They see in her one more victim of your cousin's evil." He shrugged. "As indeed she is. When you have your conference with the Regent, then I shall speak to Pella, to offer her your support and help."

"But..." The Prince frowned, genuinely concerned. "I can't allow you to endanger yourself by remaining. Indeed, the Regent might have with him one of those disgraceful catamites he keeps about him. He often brings them with him. That poor girl! If you're seen here—if word gets to my cousin that you're one of the mageborn... Your person is too precious to go into such peril alone!"

Suraklin smiled, like a saint making light of an impending martyrdom, but there was an amused glint in his eye, as if he snickered up his sleeve ruffles at his patron. Had he done so, she wondered, suddenly angry, at her belief in him and at Caris' love? "Do you think I cannot deal with such matters?" he asked mildly. "You'll see; there will be no danger or certainly not much. And in any case, it's your cause I'm thinking about, my Prince, not mine."

And if you were Pinocchio, Joanna thought sourly, *the Prince would have just gotten impaled on about seven feet of nose.*

The two men strolled back to the French window together, talking quietly of a masked ball to be given by the merchant noble Calve Dirham the following night; against the misty brightness of the glass, Joanna saw with some surprise that Suraklin and Cerdic were the same height. She had gained the impression that Gary's very body had altered and that he was taller, thinner, older—so much older. She knew Gary was thirty-four, ten or twelve years older than Cerdic at the most. But those brown eyes, with their disquieting yellow glint, were the eyes of fathomless age.

The hold of Suraklin over the minds of those he sought to control was almost unbreakable. She had been warned of it, over and over again; she had seen it only yesterday, in Caris' stubborn adherence to his love for the old man. She was far too familiar with it to believe that the credulous Cerdic could be convinced to help her, or indeed to do anything but turn her over to Suraklin.

The thought made the sweat trickle down her sides under the forest-green satin of her gown. *Jesus Christ*, she thought suddenly, *if he's here at Court, he'll be maneuvering to get Antryg's death expedited*. The fact that to do so he would probably have to go through the Regent, suspicious of all mages, didn't matter. She'd had devastating experience with the Dark Mage's abilities as a manipulator. *I have to get Antryg out of there!*

But without support of any kind, she could see no way that she could.

There's nothing further I can do in Angelshand, she began, falling subconsciously back into programmer mode and groping for a next step to get her beyond the panic that began to hammer in her chest. *First, I have to touch Magister Magus for a monster loan. Second, I have to get to Kymil . . .*

"My lord," the majordomo's voice said from the inner door. "His Grace the Prince Regent is here."

Cerdic laid a hand on Suraklin's sleeve and said softly, "Do be careful, lord wizard." Turning, he hastened across the room and out into the main hall beyond. With an ironic smile, Suraklin slipped through the French doors onto the terrace.

Oh, swell, Joanna thought, weak with fear. *So now I have a choice of splitting and walking smack into him outside or staying where I am and getting rousted out by Pharos' sasenna, if they decide to search the room . . . Holy Christ, Pharos will recognize me, too!* She leaned her head back against the paneling behind the drapes, caught between panic and an ironic understanding of the impulse to pound one's head against a wall.

But stronger than either of those was a violent and personal loathing for the wizard Suraklin. Seeing him at San Serano, in Gary's body, was one thing; while he was imitating Gary's mannerisms it had seemed, at times, that it was in fact only a segment of Gary. She had known that Gary was dead. But not until now, not until she had seen Suraklin *as Suraklin*, gesturing casually with Gary's hands and smiling his lies through Gary's mouth, did it come home to her that Suraklin had killed Gary for his body and the contents of his brain as surely and as offhandedly as he'd have killed a rabbit to make slippers out of its skin. In the last year she hadn't liked Gary much and, reading his programs and the motivations and thoughts that had watchspringed his actions, she liked him less. But her dislike of him in no way altered the callous brutality of his murder.

The door opened. The elderly majordomo ushered in the Prince Regent Pharos Destramor, Heir to the Empire and its de facto ruler, small and dainty as ever in his gold-laced black velvet and leaning on the arm of the prettiest teen-aged boy Joanna had ever seen. Only a year or so younger than Caris, the boy was darkly handsome in blueberry silk; but unlike Caris, he appeared highly conscious of his own good looks and preened himself at the Prince's every admiring glance. Behind them walked a girl of about the same age, fully as tall as the Prince's companion and nearly a head taller than the Prince himself, her coarse black hair curled unbecomingly around a dark, strong-featured face, wearing far too much makeup and an overdecorated pink satin gown. A pampered-looking lapdog trotted at her heels, like a miniaturized Borzoi with a diamond collar on its neck.

The Black Mare, Joanna thought, looking at that broad-shouldered, big-boned figure. It was a cruel nickname and

regrettably apt. Only at second glance did Joanna see how
young she was.

The Regent and his eromenos had come to stand near
the fire. The perfume they wore was rank and sweet in
Joanna's nostrils. The girl Pellicida lingered awkwardly in
the background, and Joanna saw a private smirk of triumph
at having shut her out slip between the Prince's pale-blue,
paint-crusted eyes and his boyfriend's violet ones. The boy
whispered something and glanced; the man giggled.

At that point the lapdog, sniffing exploringly around the
room, reached the wall niche in which Joanna had taken
refuge. It cocked its feathered ears toward her. Joanna had
one instant's total fright; then the Prince said, loudly
enough for his miserable bride to hear, "Useless bitches, all
of them." He knelt and snapped his fingers peremptorily.
"Kysshenka—Kyssha . . ."

The little dog, her attention diverted from Joanna, trotted obediently over; the Prince's soft hand stroked the tiny
head. "Mangey little ragmops—this one and those two fat
pugs. I've always wanted to shave the lot of them . . ."

"Stop it," Pellicida said from the other end of the room.
Hearing her voice, the little dog made an effort to get
away, but the Prince, with that surprising quickness of
hand Joanna had noticed in him before, caught the scruff of
the slender neck.

"'Stop it,'" Pharos mimicked in a nasal whine and
added to the dog, "Bite me, would you?" as the little creature, panicking, made a hesitant nip or two at his sleeve
ruffles, though it was obvious she knew full well she was
forbidden to bite humans. There was a look of terror and
horrible dilemma in her enormous brown eyes.

Pellicida strode down the length of the salon, her vast
carnation petticoats bringing down a small table unnoticed
in her wake. "Let her go."

"Why should I, my little Princess? She's my dog, after
all—as all your property is mine to do with as I choose. If
I decided to set that fluffy little tail on fire . . ." He caught

the dog Kyssha's feathery tail in his other hand and pulled her by it toward the blazing hearth.

Whether he would actually have thrust the terrified lap-dog's tail into the fire or not Joanna never found out, though she had her suspicions. This was because Pellicida, reaching him, grabbed him by the shoulder of his coat and hauled him to his feet, making him release the dog in sheer surprise. With the other hand she delivered an open-hand slap across his face that staggered him back against the marble mantel.

For an instant Joanna thought he would strike at her; from where she hid in the thick folds of the niche curtains, she could see him, pressed against the pink and white carvings like a snake coiling, an ugly red bruise mottling his pasty skin. Pellicida faced him, tears of anger blazing in her hazel eyes. Kyssha, flattened against her mistress' skirts, seemed to sense the violence of his rage and bared her tiny fangs in a soprano growl.

Quietly, Pharos said, "You'll regret that." He walked unhurriedly past her and out the hall door, his boyfriend hurrying solicitously in his wake. The Princess looked after him until the door shut. Then she crumpled down onto one of the settees near the fire, gathered up the dog who had jumped immediately into her arms, and began to cry.

As in her dream of the Silent Tower, for an instant Joanna felt trapped where she was, held from comforting this big, dark, homely child by her fear of discovery should Pharos come suddenly back. *To hell with that*, she thought, stepping out of the dusty tangle of crimson curtains. *Anybody who has to put up with that kind of public humiliation every day needs all the help she can get.* She was halfway to the settee when a shadow crossed the garden windows and the dog Kyssha raised her head with a quick, high-pitched growl. Looking across at the tall, narrow bands of window light, Joanna recognized Suraklin's returning shape.

The Princess had seen him, too. Still holding Kyssha in

her arms she got quickly to her feet, stumbling when she trod on the hem of one of her flowerlike layers of skirts, and headed for the curtained niche by the fireplace, blundering straight into Joanna.

For an instant the two women stared at each other, startled and disoriented; then Joanna turned back and made a dash for the niche, the tall Princess at her heels.

"I can't let him see me!" Joanna gasped, and Pellicida shook her head in agreement and felt quickly behind the deeply carved molding of the wall panels at the back of the niche. A narrow door opened.

"Through here," whispered the Princess. "I can't let him see me, either."

The panel slid back into place behind them, the sigh of air settling from beneath the heavy drape as Suraklin the Dark Mage was left to enter an empty hall.

"Why not?" asked Joanna quietly. "Gaire, I mean." She used the name Cerdic had called him.

Pellicida glanced quickly down at her, then away. After a moment she let out her breath in a sigh. "It isn't important." Her mouth trembled on the words, but she pursed it closed.

The sliding panel had admitted them into another room along the garden side of the house, this one a sort of private bookroom-cum-study filled with Cerdic's usual collection of statues of the Old Gods, tomes of cantrip and quackery, star-mandallas, and armillary spheres. From it the two girls had stepped through another French window into the gardens, crossing to the nearest copse of trees and taking one of the winding paths that would lead, eventually, to the other palaces of the grounds and to the outer gates where Magister Magus' coach awaited Joanna. In spite of the sharp-edged sunlight, the afternoon was quite cold, but by tacit consent neither suggested returning to search for their cloaks.

The Princess sniffled, and Joanna dug into the deep

pocket of her dress for a clean handkerchief to offer her. Pella was not the delicate type of girl who could cry without rendering herself hideous; her nose was swollen, and her face, under a layer of half-wiped-off cosmetics, reddened in fading blotches. Kyssha, trotting at the hem of her swagged petticoats, looked up at her and whined in concern, and Pella reached down and took the little dog into the crook of her arm.

Joanna sighed. "I realize this is a stupid question under the circumstances, but can I do anything? Short of murdering Pharos, that is—though honestly I don't think Cerdic would be an improvement as a ruler."

Pella glanced quickly at her again, as if to reassure herself of the jesting tone in her voice. In spite of the japes about it, her height wasn't excessive, though at five-nine or so she was a head taller than Joanna and the diminutive Prince. It was her air of hesitancy which made her seem clumsy and outsize, something not helped by the bouffant extravagance of her gown. "It's all right," she said wearily. "I suppose I'd agree with Gaire about—it—if I didn't know what kind of ruler Cerdic would make." She gave her eyes a final wipe, completing the ruin of her makeup, and stroked Kyssha's head protectively. The little dog licked at her hands and whined again, shivering in the sharpness of the wind. Pella's mouth twitched in a bitter expression far older than her years. "Do you know Gaire well?"

"I did," said Joanna softly. "Once."

"I didn't know he'd come back." They emerged from the trees into a long, formal parterre which must have been like close-napped green velvet in the summer, brown now and edged with naked trees gray as pewter in the changeable brightness of the day. "Tell me about him."

Joanna shook her head. "I don't know if I can. It's—it's hard to explain."

"I have to know."

The urgency in her voice and the intentness of those

hazel-green eyes stopped Joanna. She stood looking up at the girl, sensing the echo of that hateful sensation of knowing but of having no proof. Suraklin must have tried to put the influence of his mind over hers; she had fled him, not knowing why.

Then, rather quickly, Pella looked away. "He comes and goes. Nobody knows anything about him. Except what signifies—that he's Cerdic's latest fad, his 'Spiritual Advisor,' which is what he calls himself so no one can point to him and say 'wizard.' But he is a wizard, isn't he?"

"Yes," Joanna said softly.

Pellicida let out her breath in another short little sigh and stood for a time, cradling her little dog in her arms, staring out across the two acres of flawlessly smooth brown lawn toward the gilded roof trees of the Imperial Palace, visible beyond the cindery lace of the trees. "He made me . . ." she began, and broke off. Then she said, "I didn't even *like* him—I didn't understand what happened. I haven't—haven't ever been in love, but I didn't think it could be like that. It was a spell, wasn't it?"

"Yes," Joanna said, guessing what had happened and why Pellicida had run from him rather than face him again. After a moment she added, "I think legally that counts as rape—or it should, anyway."

Pellicida's glance was wry, to hide a hurt that had clearly been one of many in the last wretched month. She started walking again, a solitary figure, like a huge pink peony dropped on the sepia ground. The wind pulled loose strands of her black hair from their ridiculous masses of curls and tangled them with the dog's silky fur. "Did he do that to you?"

"He tried."

"Because you could be useful to him?"

Joanna nodded. She wondered morbidly whether, if she had agreed, he would have imitated Gary's rather unsatisfying sexual technique.

"Why did he do it?" Pella asked, as if asking about

something that had been done to someone other than herself. "To get me to—to connive at his killing Pharos?"

She was a stranger in a strange land, a world alien to her own customs and wants, eighteen years old and married to a man who scorned and humiliated her. She held herself straight as any of the marble statues of heroes that lined the parterre, her profile cut like stone against the dark chaos of her hair.

Joanna said, "Probably."

"Tell me about him," Pella said again. "There's something about him, something evil . . . I don't know. Tell me who he is, and what he wants; tell me what's going on."

During winters in Angelshand, dawn came late; in the pre-solstice depths, a heatless daylight lasted five or six hours. Now, with autumn fully come, workers sought the grim riverside factories in darkness. The bells of the city's many churches were tolling matins. In summer the sky would have already been pale. Unnaturally clear and cold for this season of the year, the stars blazed queerly above the black angles of jutting roofs.

Stonne Caris, grandson of the dead Archmage Salteris Solaris, thrust his hands into the sleeves of his padded jacket and shivered as he strode the silent alleyways. In spite of the unseasonal clearness of the predawn darkness, it was bitterly cold. Usually at this hour of the morning from where he stood at the top of Threadneedle Street, where its cobbled slope turned down toward the river, nothing could be seen but a sea of white mist rising from that oily brown expanse, but now even the winking nets of riding lights on the ships in the harbor seemed to dance in the dark. It made him uneasy, with a strange sense of things not being as they should be. But his mageborn eyes showed him nothing to fear in the darkness of the alleys around him, and his hearing, trained through grueling blindfold obstacle courses, spoke of no danger. Still, he hesitated for a moment at the top of the street, as if his nose could tell him what was wrong.

But all he smelled was the usual fishy reek of the bare mudflats below the granite embankments and, more strongly than usual, the nauseating whiff of spoiling meat and cheese from the garbage dump near the Grand Market.

Cautiously, he felt the pistol he had taken from Joanna, thrust through his sword sash, hard against his stomach through the padding of coat, jacket, and shirt. He slid his sword, still in its sheathe, from his sash; carrying the sheathe loosely in his left hand, he descended to the flats, his footfalls a moist whisper in the iron dawn.

He was pleased to find the mudflats empty. At this hour, they often weren't—during the summer they were a favorite dueling ground for young blades with scores to settle. Generally the coming of the autumn mists put a stop to such proceedings. This morning, however, was exceptionally clear. His breath escaped him in a cold thread of white; somewhere a dog barked, but he missed the crying of the gulls usually to be found arguing over the river garbage left by the turn of the tide.

He stopped, puzzling for a moment over that.

Upriver and down, dull orange lights glowed in kitchen windows of the dark houses that overhung the embankments. Across the rippling sheet of the water, the lights of the massive St. Cyr fortress gleamed unnaturally bright. An icy skiff of wind tugged at his cropped blond hair. He slipped the sword sheathe back into his sash and took out the gun.

When he had taken it from Joanna, he had assumed it was a gun like any other; only when he had examined it later, after he had come off-shift in his duties as guard at the Mages' Yard, did he realize that, in their weaponry as well as their strange machines, Joanna's people were vastly different from his own. The weapon itself was alien to those with which he was familiar, but the principles were the same. Instead of a ball, it fired pointed projectiles, encapsuled in what he guessed were cartridges already filled with premeasured loads, apparently loaded from the breech instead of the muzzle. In addition, this weapon had a revolving chamber, holding six bullets.

Lost in admiration of the efficiency of it, he had at first not realized what it could mean—that a weapon existed which fired several times in rapid succession.

When he realized it, it had shaken him to the roots.

The air down here was still, though he could now hear the rising whine of wind across the roofs of the houses above him. The cold damped much of the smell of the mudflats. It was not an ideal place for his experiment—it was more open here than it had been in the Mages' Yard on the night of Thirle's murder, and there was some movement of air—but it would do.

He pointed the gun downriver, aiming high in the air, braced both his hands on the butt in case it kicked more strongly than an ordinary pistol, and squeezed the trigger. Instantly the flat crack of it echoed out across the water; there was no delay between the fall of the hammer and the ignition of the powder, and it hardly kicked at all. He fired a second shot immediately, the cylinder revolving with deadly, beautiful smoothness into place. There was a little flash. That was all.

There was very little smell of powder and no smoke whatsoever.

Caris felt his stomach sink.

This is none of my business, he thought despairingly. *I shouldn't even be here. I am sasennan of the Council—it isn't up to me to decide right and wrong. Antryg confessed to the murder of Thirle and other things besides . . .*

But the murder was done with a gun like this one.

Where had he gotten it?

The thought intruded itself into his mind that Joanna could have been right.

And if that is the case . . .

The wind was rising as Caris strode up the steep angle of Threadneedle Street again. Black clouds had moved in to blot the stars. The ships at rest in the harbor began to rock uneasily, like horses tied in a barn, nervous at a sudden whiff of smoke.

As he made his way back through the alleys to the Ghetto, Caris remembered the scene. It was his dreams that had wakened him then, troubled, inchoate dreams of loss —his dreams and the fading of his magic. His powers had never been much, but once before he had sensed their waning; that second time, waking in the muggy, stinking heat of the summer night, it had been like death. He had, he remembered, some notion of crossing the Yard from the house where the sasenna slept to see if his grandfather was back; but with the desolation that had come over him, it had suddenly seemed pointless. It was as if, with his magic, all hope had been bled from the world.

Then he had heard Thirle scream.

Thirle had been standing in the mouth of the alley known as Stinking Lane, the alley where that dreadful Gate of darkness had opened through the Void. He had been shot from the shadows of the houses on the opposite side of the square, and from those shadows a man had come running. A second shot had been fired at Caris, but he did not know, now that he thought of it, whether the fleeing man had fired it, or it had come from the shadows of the houses, like the first.

The killer had not been the man he had seen—the man who had run back through the Void—at all, but rather someone who had remained in the Court, who had fired the shots to cover the fugitive's tracks and to get Thirle out of the way.

Although Caris' memories of that time were surprisingly blurred—due, he supposed, to the draining hopelessness which had been on him then—it came to him now that the aim had been startlingly good for a running man's.

The first spits of rain were beginning to fall by the time he reached the Mages' Yard.

It made it easier for him. Though no sasennan would

take shelter to the neglect of his duties, the noise of the wind howling through the narrow alleyways around the Yard would cover any sounds he might make better than the foggy stillness typical of autumn. After his grandfather's death, there had been talk of the narrow little house being taken over by the Lady Rosamund, but nothing had been done about it yet. The place had been locked and fear-spells put on the doors and windows; Caris could see them, glowing faintly through the slashing rain. He had not the power to override them, but simply his awareness of them—his knowledge that they were merely spells—let him force the catches on the rear window and scramble through with hammering heart, where an ordinary house-breaker would have thought better of the entire project.

The whole house spoke to him of his grandfather, with a terrible immediacy which brought back all his grief and rage at the old man's death.

If Joanna had been right . . .

Had there been a time when he had changed?

Standing in the close, crowded darkness of the narrow room that had been Salteris' study, while the rain slammed dementedly against the window glass as if hurled from buckets, Caris let his mind rove back.

He had not seen his grandfather from the time he was thirteen until he was eighteen, nearly two years ago now; he was aware that there was no greater gap in perceptions than that which existed between those two ages. His memories of his grandfather before that were a child's memories—running behind the old man through the sweet-marshes of the river Strebwell, hunting polliwogs while the Archmage gathered mallows or observed the comings and goings of birds. One summer there had been an epidemic of little pox in the village, and Caris had been drafted as assistant, to brew tisanes and hunt herbs; later his grandfather, still young, with the wiry strength of wizards, had stripped to a breechclout, braided back his long dark hair, and had helped Caris and the few villagers who

were still on their feet get the hay in. Caris remembered as
if it were yesterday the shine of drying sweat on the muscles of Salteris' arms and back as he'd sat with the other
villagers under shelter, drinking beer as the rains swept in
over the stubble fields; he remembered the thick, green
smell of the air, heady as brandy, and Salteris' joyful
laughter.

Since Caris had come to serve the Council of Mages as
sasennan, since he had sworn his unthinking allegiance to
his grandfather as head of that Council, he had not heard
his grandfather laugh. He thought the glint of ironic mockery in the old man's eyes was new, but couldn't be sure; he
did not remember in any of his childhood the haughty
touchiness of temper which had characterized the wizard
lately, nor that suave note in the voice which seemed to
speak of some private joke with himself at his listener's
expense. It might, Caris had thought, have had something
to do with his grandmother's death, which had happened
after he had gone to Innkitar to begin his training as sasennan; it might simply have been that, as a child, he had not
seen that side of his grandfather.

Or it might be as Joanna had said.

If it was, he thought, sudden heat firing through his
veins, it was Suraklin who killed him—Suraklin who
ended that laughter, who stripped away that joyful life.
Suraklin the Dark Mage . . .

I will kill him, he thought. *Dear God, I will kill him . . .*

Antryg, too, he realized, had loved Salteris. If what
Joanna said was true—if Suraklin had left his grandfather
alive and imbecile, to go on to this other man, this man of
her world who understood computers—what must it have
cost Antryg to kill in mercy the part that was left?

Stop it, he told himself. *Stop it until you have proof.*

He knew in his heart that the Way of the Sasenna is not
to ask for proof. The Council had decided; it was no longer
his affair. Nevertheless, he began to search the darkened
study.

As it had been in Salteris' lifetime, the room was crowded with books, tablets, charts, astrolabes, and armillaries, but scrupulously neat. The old man's desk towered above it all in its little niche near the fire, like some massive black castle, turreted and crenellated with scroll-edged pigeonholes and a treasure house of secret compartments. A couple of candleholders arched out over the slanted writing surface, but the waxen shafts they bore were unburned and covered with dust. Salteris had seldom bothered to light them when he worked, seeing, as all mageborn could, in the dark.

Caris' own sight in darkness was not as good as most mages', but it would have to suffice. The wind, which had risen to a screaming frenzy over the rooftops, would cover any noises he might make, but he could not hide light.

Methodically, he searched.

His grandmother, Salteris' wife in all but name for forty years, had told him of this desk, fascinating him with its marvels while he, a fair-haired child with dirt on his hands, sat on her knee. His fingers, light and sure as a craftsman's, probed delicately for hidden springs and secret doors, compartments tucked into what appeared to be mere partitions. Outside, the wind howled down from the north, driving sleet and rain before it; in the darkness around him, the old house rocked uneasily on its timbers. In one compartment he found his grandfather's porcelain flute—a flute that he remembered the old man playing for his grandmother, but had not heard Salteris play since.

In another, he found a handful of bullets. There was no mistaking them—point-nosed, gleaming, wrapped in their brass cartridges. He drew the gun from his sash, and broke open the cylinder; they were too large to fit, but clearly of the same manufacture. A little more search of the desk yielded the gun itself. Two of its chambers were empty.

Caris set the gun down on the desk. He was so angry his hands shook, cold, furious rage that felt queerly impersonal in its intensity. Suraklin had murdered his grandfa-

ther, years ago, calmly, greedily, tricking him with a play
of friendship and understanding in his former guise as the
Emperor Hieraldus until he was ready to strike. He had
murdered poor Thirle, stout and affable and trusting, simply because he was in the way. Who knew how many
others besides? He had used Caris' love, twisted and
tricked him and tried to manipulate him into killing the one
man who might have been able to offer effective opposi-
tion.

Caris' fisted hands tightened until the bones hurt.

And Suraklin had gotten away with it. He was still at
large. Bound by his vows to the Council, there was nothing
Caris could do.

Though the storm-darkness still blotted the windows,
Caris knew it would soon be time for morning training with
the other sasenna. Quietly, he wrapped both guns in the
oiled cloth, along with the bullets. Then he rose and
slipped the catch from a window nearby, to account for the
rainwater that had dripped from his clothes. Retracing his
steps to the window at the back of the house, he scrambled
out again into the storm, taking guns and bullets with him.

CHAPTER V

THE STORM, THE WORST IN HUMAN MEMORY, LASTED UNTIL early the following afternoon. Joanna watched its fury from the secrecy of a small boudoir attached to Princess Pellicida's rooms in the north wing of the Imperial Palace, a hidden love nest furnished for some forgotten princely mistress of the last generation and enterable only through a hinged wall panel near the head of Pella's bed. The previous night she and the Regent's wife had arranged to meet at a masked ball at the merchant prince Calve Dirham's extensive townhouse near the palace park. They had talked until nearly four in the morning, watching Prince Cerdic, who probably believed himself incognito behind a mask of seashells and pearls, winning thousands of Imperial Eagle coins in the gambling rooms while Suraklin had looked on, his suit of old-fashioned blue velvet and lace transformed into a macabre incongruity by the grinning mask of a skull.

The Prince's streak of uncanny luck at cards, at dice, and at roulette—Dirham's gaming room had boasted a roulette wheel, which for some reason reminded Joanna of the arcade-size videogame which Gary Fairchild had made available to his guests—had lasted for four hours, causing Joanna to remark, "I bet that's the *real* reason they outlawed wizards meddling in human affairs." She'd seen Cerdic's old suit of magic-proof armor, and wondered facetiously if there existed, in the attics of the nobility, na-aar roulette wheels, dice, and card decks.

It was not until this morning that she understood the true reason.

By the time she and Pella had discussed plans for freeing Antryg, the wind had begun—violent, unseasonable, arctic. Rather than have Joanna go seeking a cab in the pouring rain or scandalize the entire servant population into an orgy of gossip by instructing Pellicida's coachman to drive to Magister Magus' house, Pella had offered her the hospitality of the little hideaway in her suite. "You don't have to worry about Pharos," the Princess said, as the carriage had pulled away from Dirham's in the pitch-black, screaming darkness. "He stays in his own palace. I'm told he's even given his paramour Leynart rooms there."

Joanna had laughed. "I don't imagine Pharos even knows where your rooms are."

Beneath the trailing black-and-white feathers of the mask she still wore, Pella's mouth had tightened. She looked away. Her voice sounded very small. "He does."

Joanna blushed hotly in the darkness of the coach. Whatever brief honeymoon this girl had known with the Regent, Joanna thought, as a first experience Pharos would undoubtedly tie for last with Jack the Ripper. No wonder Suraklin had found her easy prey. As they drove slowly through the palace park, blind with the rain and stopping continually as huge branches and even young trees were literally ripped from their roots to come careening like drunken witches through the howling air, Joanna could see the dim lights of the Regent's palace, glimmering through the thick trees that hemmed it in. She wondered if he were in his study reading a good book—the Marquis de Sade, for preference—or merely spending a quiet evening in the basement, whipping his servants.

"I wish it didn't matter to me," that sweet, curiously husky voice went on after a long time of silence. "I wish I could just—I don't know. Shut my eyes and not care whether someone murdered him or not. Then I could be rid of him, and not—not have to put up with . . . with all this." She sighed, and looked back at Joanna, her white wig, mingled with the long black feathers of the concealing mask she wore, starkly pale against the dusky oval of her face in the reflected glow of the carriage lamps. "The thing is, I know he's a good ruler. I've seen good rule at home. Senterwing isn't a very large country, but Uncle Tye makes the most of what he has. He's always spoken well of Pharos' policies. Pharos understands trade and industry and all the things landholders aren't supposed to concern themselves with. That's why he married me, because Senterwing is a country of factories and banks. It's just that—I suppose being a good ruler is different from being a good man."

"I know," Joanna said. "And as a matter of fact, it's because he's a good ruler—or a strong ruler, anyway— that Suraklin wants to get rid of him and put Cerdic on the throne. Cerdic would sure as hell let him run the country."

Pellicida sighed. "It sounds—I don't know, pompous I suppose—to say so, but it's one reason I want to help you. It isn't fashionable here to be concerned about it, but I was brought up to believe in good rulership. So much depends on it." She toyed with her fan, her big, awkward hands dwarfing the delicate confection of ivory and silk, keeping her eyes on it rather than meeting Joanna's. Silhouetted against the sodden gloom, her strong-featured face seemed older than its eighteen years, momentarily the face of a woman and a queen. Then she ducked her head—Joanna sensed rather than saw her blotchy, unbecoming blush. "And then these times of deadness, these drained patches, that you say are caused by this machine of Suraklin's . . . One of them took place not too long after I let him seduce me. I came very close to killing myself then. Not out of guilt—not really. Just a kind of hopelessness. It seemed to me that from then on there would be nothing else for me but that, going from lover to lover because there was nothing else to do here. It all seemed so stale and dirty. And I wonder how many other people have felt like that during those times, and how many went through with it?"

The Princess was out when Joanna woke. It was eleven o'clock by the digital watch stashed in the pockets of her petticoats and by the delicate ormolu clock on the mantelpiece, but there was a covered breakfast tray in the empty sitting room. A fire burned in the small marble grate, warming the little suite; indoor plants clustered near it like fragile children shunning the rough world outside. The place was cluttered and cozy, filled with knickknacks and pets: a cageful of ornamental finches whose aimless twittering gave Joanna a whole new insight into the term "bird-brained"; Pella's two fat pugs about whom Joanna, a cat person, privately agreed with the Regent; and, to Joanna's great delight, a five-foot boa constrictor dozing in wintry torpor in a big glass cabinet built into the side of the chimney. "Mellachior spends most of his winters asleep," Pella had remarked, tapping the glass gently; the shining earth-colored coils within did not shift. "They laugh at me around here, but I was brought up with animals. As things worked out, I'm glad I brought them along."

Wind still ravenned at the windows, though, by the sound of it, the storm was lessening. Pella's two fat pugs, clearly unhappy at the tumult, crouched beside Joanna on the windowseat as she looked out across the devastated park. The naked shrubs had been stripped of most of their branches and whole trees snapped off short, to lie tangled and dead in the slate-colored lakes of the flooded paths.

Joanna pulled more closely about her the overlong plush robe she'd borrowed from her hostess and shivered. Through what little had remained of the dark hours, she'd listened to the rain slashing against the secret room's small, round window. It had come to her then why the interference of wizards in human affairs was—and should be—punishable by death.

The door opened. She glanced up as Pella entered, Kyssha pattering restlessly at her heels. The little dog dashed over to greet Joanna, then to engage in an orgy of sniffing and licking with the two lapdogs. Pella only stood like an outsize bird of paradise in her primrose and green riding dress, her face somber and her eyes filled with sorrow and concern.

Pella was the daughter of merchant kings. Joanna guessed that she, too, had understood what the storm had done.

"It destroyed the trade-fleet," she asked quietly, "didn't it?"

Pella nodded. She seemed stunned, shedding her enormous greatcoat and shaking the last flecks of the fitful, windblown drizzle from her coarse black hair. "All the first-comers, the ones that would have put in today to get the cream of the market. God knows how many others out among the islands." She dropped her gloves and her coat, moving as if the loss, the tragedy, were hers and not others'. "Autumn's a quiet season," she went on. "Fogs and rain, yes, but never winds like that. The whole harbor is one lake of fouled masts; they've pulled hundreds of bodies out so far. They say Calve Dirham hanged himself this morning, rather than face his investors."

Joanna remembered him vaguely from last night, a jovial little man, vulgar but anxious for everyone to have a good time. Wrath stirred in her, the hot wrath she had felt yesterday while watching Suraklin smiling through poor Gary's mouth. She felt the cold of the window glass breathe against her back as she leaned against it. Her voice came out surprisingly level. "Were any of the ships Cerdic invested in wrecked?"

The Princess shook her head wearily. "I don't know, Joanna. There were so many..." Then she stopped, realizing what Joanna had asked. She stared at her in silence, her hazel eyes wide with first shock, then dawning horror. "That's impossible."

"Think about it." In her mind Joanna saw Suraklin again as she had seen him last night—the skull smiling above blue velvet and lace.

"He *couldn't*," Pella whispered. "I know Cerdic's ships were supposed to be far in the rear, but... Most of the fleet was wrecked, Joanna! Hundreds were killed..."

"It wiped out fortunes, didn't it?" Joanna folded her arms across her drawn-up knees, regarding the gawky young Princess in her coat of daffodil velvet, still standing beside the hearth and the gilded snake cage. "And people who lost their year's income will be turning to a man who has money. You saw how much he won last night, and I'd be willing to bet none of the ships he invested in were in the harbor last night. I don't think Cerdic's going to let himself believe Suraklin did this to buy him power, and Suraklin's probably going to come up with some plausible explanation so Cerdic doesn't have to believe it. But I think that's what happened.

"I didn't really understand before," she went on, standing up, the folds of the robe falling thickly around her feet, "why the Council would make it punishable by death for the mageborn to interfere in human affairs." She kicked the dragging weight of the lavender velvet out of the way and crossed to where Pella stood. "Even watching Suraklin making the cards fall right for Cerdic, or spinning the roulette wheel his way... Maybe there are people who'd even forgive a love-spell or two, like the one he put on you. So what? they'd say. But I know now the kind of thing that they meant, five hundred years ago, when they fought the Battle of Stellith over it; I know the potential for destruction of someone really powerful who doesn't give a damn, so long as he gets what he wants. And do you know what else I know?"

The Princess looked at her apprehensively, this small, outlander woman with her tangled blond curls hanging over the robe's gray fur collar, her arms folded over her breasts.

"They're going to find some way to blame it on Antryg."

"The Prince won't ask questions if I say I'm going to one of the royal residences near Kymil." Pella deftly steered her chestnut team around the ruins of a chimney which had literally been blown into the street, the long wreckage of brick stretching like a snake across the flooded cobblestones and on into the tangle of glass, broken shutters, and ruined goods in a shop window. "Everyone makes jokes about Senterwing being a swamp, but it's warmer than Angelshand. I can probably get away with saying I can't stand the cold."

With her black hair braided up under a close-fitting cap and her tall form muffled in a many-caped cloak such as coachmen wore, the Princess was sufficiently anonymous at the reins of her unmarked phaeton. The masculine style suited her far better than her frilled court dresses did; by no longer trying to apologize for her square jaw and wide mouth, she gave them dignity and a kind of severe beauty. Joanna, huddled beside her on the high seat with a cloak covering the elaborately silly gown she'd worn to the ball last night, had leisure to look around at the swamped streets of the town.

Most of them were flooded right across, and the phaeton's wheels threw up little wings of water as it passed servants and laborers working ankle-deep at clearing away the wreckage of broken trees, fallen chimneys, and scattered roof tiles. In the poorer districts of the town south of the river, Joanna thought, the damage would be worse. She remembered the rickety tenements that leaned so perilously against one another and the vendors' stands in the streets. Even in the relatively affluent neighborhoods near Governor's Square, there was a silence, an air of calamity, and a ghastly realization that money borrowed or spent against the expectation of those investments was truly gone.

But in the poor quarters it would not be a question of

money, but of husbands, brothers, fathers, and sons, dragged dead out of the broken tangle of fouled spars and lines that stretched for miles along the smoke-colored waters of the harbor. It was a question of marginal poverty turning into starving destitution and of cold beds and children who would never see their fathers—or days without hunger—again.

Joanna shivered, oppressed as she had been her first morning in Kymil, by the sense of being brought face-to-face with intolerable situations which she had no power to rectify—except, she thought, by doing what she was doing, by attending to the matter at hand. "Can you get a copy of Pharos' seal?" she asked and Pellicida nodded. For all her youth she had a bluntly matter-of-fact grasp of the essentials.

"He keeps the seal itself guarded, I don't know where. But I have two or three letters from him with it on the bottom."

"Magister Magus will know how to remove them," Joanna said. *And he'll do it*, she added grimly to herself, *or I'll know the reason why.* He'd be horrified, of course, as he'd been horrified yesterday when Joanna had told him she'd found an ally in the Regent's wife, but it couldn't be helped. If they were to free Antryg, they'd need forged signatures and faked seals to get into the Tower, and she had a shrewd idea the Magus knew who in Angelshand could provide such things at short notice.

And the notice, she thought, looking around her at the sheets of leaden water and at the desperate, angry faces, would be very short indeed. They were people mortally injured, seeking someone to blame. It wouldn't take much of a manipulator to turn that anger against anyone who might stand in his way.

She stroked Kyssha's fluffy head; the dog lay like a little muff across her lap, Pella needing all her freedom of action to control the team in the flooded debris through which they passed. Clumsy and gawky as the tall Princess seemed on foot in her tasseled and overjeweled gowns, she was a steady and light-handed driver. She was careful of her team, too, getting out and testing the deeply flooded patches of street for submerged wreckage; and restive as they were, the horses stood obediently with Joanna's hand on the rein until Pella had scrambled up to the high seat again.

"I helped train them," she said, when Joanna spoke of it. "We had a marvel of a trainer at home. He taught me everything he could when Mother wasn't looking. I was always more at home in the stables than I was at dancing lessons. At least no one laughed when I tripped over my own feet." She sighed, looking out across the team's sharp-pricked ears as she guided them around the broken corpse of a tree that blocked half the lane. "I never really cared for being a Princess."

Down at the far end of the street, voices shouted, a rumble of angry sound punctuated suddenly by a yell. "Lynch him! String him up! Storm caller—he did this!" Other voices joined in like a hellish chorus baying, "Hang him! Hang the wizard!"

"Oh God," Joanna whispered, knowing what it had to be. Pella exchanged a quick, scared glance with her, then clucked encouragement to her team, who trotted nervously forward with a hissing swish of muddy water.

There must have been thirty or forty people in Governor's Square, men and women both, mostly laborers and servants. They were rudely armed with makeshift clubs, bread knives, and bits of timber from broken shutters. A knot of black-clothed sasenna clustered around the steps of Magister Magus' house, keeping them back.

". . . behind it all summer!" a man in the long caped cloak and muffler of a cab driver was yelling. "It's him that called up them abominations, those things setting fire to the houses in the Haymarket! Ruined the harvest, belike, too! And now this . . . !"

The doors opened. Four sasenna and two men in the

narrow gray garments of Witchfinders emerged, leading
Magister Magus between them. Around the steps, the
crowd set up a yammering like the hounds of hell. Clods of
dirt and horse dung splattered against the wall on all sides
of the door, and Magus flinched, trying to hide his face
against his shoulder as best he could in wretchedness and
shame. His hands were bound behind him; even at this
distance, Joanna saw the blood-bright ribbon of spell-cord
twisted through the bonds. She only realized she had half
risen in the phaeton seat when Pella pulled her back down.

"There's nothing we can do."

The mob was pushing in. The sasenna descended the
steps, thrusting them back. Two remained by the door with
their prisoner, their crossbows leveled on him, as if they
expected him to attempt to fell them with a Bruce Lee
wheel kick, leap over the heads of the crowd, and make
good his escape. The dog wizard's thin face was white
against his disheveled black hair; a bruise was already
blackening on his temple.

Joanna looked across at Pella, fear kicking hard at her
chest. "It isn't that. My backpack's in the house. It's got
the program disk in it, the only thing that can take out the
programming in Suraklin's computer."

Pella's full, square lips pressed taut; her eyes narrowed
as she scanned the square and the little group before the
house. "They'll need their whole force to keep the crowd
off him. One of us could get in the back now before they
search the house."

Joanna's stomach curled up in terror at the possibility of
capture by the Witchfinders and the thought of facing the
Witchfinder Peelbone again. But she knew the Princess
was right. She took a deep breath, "Okay. If I'm not back
in . . ."

Pella handed her the reins. "I'll go. Can you hold
them?" And when Joanna moved to make a totally half-
hearted protest, she asked, "What can they do to me if they

catch me? I'm the wife of the Heir. What does this back-pack thing look like?"

Joanna told her and held Kyssha back from joining her as the tall girl sprang down from the seat and pushed her way off through the crowd.

A small black carriage had been brought up to the house doors, enclosed and heavily curtained. Joanna remembered it well. She had ridden in a similar one from the house of the murdered Dr. Skipfrag to the St. Cyr fortress after her own arrest.

The guards formed a flying wedge around Magus, breasting like swimmers through the crowd to get him there; angry fists were shaken at them, and now and then a stick flailed out of the mob to strike one or another on their shoulders. The Magus cowered in the midst of his guards, with the look on his face of a rabbit in a trap. Remember-ing his kindness to her and the fact that it was he who had helped Antryg rescue her from Peelbone and his Witch-finders, Joanna felt like a traitor.

A voice said close to her knee, "You know he'll be safer with them than he would if he stayed in his house."

Startled, she looked down. Caris stood beside the pha-eton.

"What will be done to him?" she asked quietly.

"Magus?" Caris shrugged, watching the progress of the mêlée by the steps with a professional eye. "If Cerdic speaks up for him, probably only a public flogging and banishment. But rumor has it that Cerdic's found himself a new Spiritual Advisor these days."

Voices rose, and dung and pieces of broken brick rained down on the closed black carriage as it began to move away. A stray chunk of dirt struck one of Pella's phaeton team and the horse flung up its head nervously. Caris caught the rein and drew the beast back down, talking gently and stroking the soft nose. A moment later Pella reappeared, the bulk of her tweed cloak appearing even bulkier with the backpack hidden beneath it. She saw Caris

and stopped, her brisk competence fading to awkwardness
at once.

"It's all right," Joanna said. "At least—I think it's all
right. But we'd probably better get out of here." The crowd
around the Magus' house was dispersing as three sasenna
went back up the steps. One of them removed from the
pouch at his belt a bar of red wax and a seal; Joanna suspected reinforcements would be on the way.

"It's all right," Caris assured her. His voice even and
impersonal, he went on, "I've just heard that Cerdic's two
ships have been sighted coming in past the Chittern Islands. It seems one of them sprang a plank or something
and had to put in at Felwip a few days ago. I don't know
what happened with the other, but something similar, some
accident that kept them in port in the islands."

"Dear God," Pella said softly. Her green-gold eyes filled
with pain, either at the destruction itself or at this final
proof of cold-blooded perfidy; half-subconsciously she put
out her hand to touch the flank of her near horse, as if
seeking in the animal contact some grounding to the gentler
life she had left behind. After a silent moment, she handed
the backpack up to Joanna, swung herself up onto the high
driver's seat again, and collected the reins.

Without a word, Caris sprang up to the groom's perch
behind them. Still in that same automatic fashion, as if she
were handling a car instead of two nervous animals, Pella
backed her team neatly, turned them, and guided them
across the flooded cobbles of the square. She looked
stunned; Joanna found herself remembering that most people in this world only half believed in magic, if they believed in it at all. It was one thing, she supposed, to have a
love-spell put on you. It was another to see spells used on
that scale with that kind of cold-blooded selfishness.

To Caris, Joanna only said, "Suraklin's staying with
Cerdic. He's been helping him win money in the gambling
halls; Cerdic will have a fortune now to buy friends with.

We don't know, but we think Suraklin means to murder Pharos and get control of the Empire."

"That would make sense," Caris said quietly. "He will be trying to protect himself, if it is in fact his aim to become one of these computer machines." Then for a long time he said nothing, only held onto the brass railing of the groom's perch, staring out in front of him as Pella drove through the flooded, half-empty streets of the town. Kyssha put her paws on the seatback and nosed at his hand; Caris stroked her head absently, as if not truly aware of her presence. Then he sighed. "I found this in Grandfather's house." He took a revolver from his belt. Glimpsing it there earlier, Joanna had assumed that it was the one he'd taken from her, but she saw now it was a .45, not a .38. She glanced quickly up at his face, and saw it strained and bitter, as if he had taken some scouring drug.

He had wept, she remembered, over the dead Archmage's body, sobs that had seemed to tear him apart. "I'm sorry."

He shook his head, as if he would say something; but after a false start, he was silent.

Hesitantly, Joanna said, "Maybe if you showed it to the new Archmage . . ."

"It wouldn't do me any good," Caris said, his voice quiet but hard as stone. "For one thing, it is not for me, as sasennan, even to have investigated; the Lady Rosamund has already told me that the matter is closed. Then, too, most of the mages have left the Yard. They know the storm was caused by magic. They tried to trace it, but weather tampering is very hard to track. They knew they'd be blamed. After their arrest last summer, even the few who stayed in town have kept getaway bags packed. The last of them left before noon." He sounded remote, as if it barely concerned him; had she trained with him as sasennan, Joanna would have recognized the tone he used when he was injured and trying to speak around gut-tearing pain. Pella glanced back at him, comprehension and worry in her eyes. "Some of them took sasenna with them, but I was one of the ones ordered to stay as a guard against looters."

There was a moment's silence, broken by the milky swish of the wheels in the flooded street and the splashing of the horses' hooves. Joanna knew it was an unfair question, but asked it anyway. "And will you?"

He didn't look at her. "Joanna, you don't understand."

She half turned in her seat, looking up at that tense, beautiful face in the sunless light. "I do understand, a little —at least as much as anyone can understand who hasn't been brought up with that strong a concept of honor. And after seeing the destruction Suraklin has wrought, I think I understand the vows of the sasenna as analogous to those of the mages; that one who is trained to kill *can not* be permitted to choose his own places and times for it, any more than one who has been trained to alter the physical world by an act of his own will. But that doesn't change what Suraklin is doing. It doesn't change the fact that he's got to be stopped at whatever the cost."

Keeping clear of the poorer districts near the river, Pella guided her horses through a broad square past a neoclassical domed building that was obviously a bank. Its granite steps churned with businessmen in dark broadcloth like a hosed-out anthill. One young man came quickly down the steps and climbed into a closed carriage as Pella drove past. Through the windows, Joanna could see him, once he thought himself out of sight of his colleagues, bury his face in his hands like a man who has heard the sentence of his own death.

Behind her, Caris' voice was desperate. "Don't do this to me, Joanna."

Antryg had said that, she remembered, lying with bound hands, waiting for the wizards to come for him.

She did not look back at him, only pleated at the knots of green silk ribbon that bordered the sleeves of last night's ballgown. "Why did you come looking for me, then?"

Caris sighed, bitter and weary, as if he had not even

been sure he meant to speak to her until now. "To tell you that the rumor in the Mages' Yard is that Peelbone the Witchfinder left Angelshand this morning, as soon as the wind eased enough to let him travel. He's heading south, for Kymil."

"Are you angry with Caris?" Pella asked later, pausing in her search for a spill of kindling to light the candles in the rapidly encroaching gloom of her apartments. "Because you shouldn't be."

"Not really." Joanna's small hands continued to move as she talked, folding the mountains of petticoats, night-dresses, and chemises whose packing she had taken over after Pella had, for the fifth time, gone wandering around the chaos of the room looking for a mislaid glove. "I know he takes his vows as a sasennan very seriously; I suppose it's like a devoutly religious person being asked to deny God in order to save the life of someone he loves."

Pella nodded. "Only of course all sasenna are automatically excommunicate—except the Church's, that is. They don't deny God, but they certainly must choose their master's wishes over the Church's without an instant's thought. It's the same reason they don't make legal marriages." Around her feet, Kyssha and the two lapdogs played hide-and-seek among the lace ruffles of half a dozen petticoats tossed carelessly on the floor. "You know it is in the Council's power to have him killed for disobedience?"

"I know if a sasennan becomes—flawed, or crippled, he's supposed to kill himself," Joanna said slowly, thinking of the Regent's deaf servant Kanner. "But I don't think that fear was a factor in Caris' decision to stay here."

"No," Pella agreed quietly. Forgetting her quest for illumination, she returned to the dense shadows of the bed and helped Joanna dump the latest heap of lace-edged lawn into the trunk at her side. "Do we *have* to pack all this?"

"We do if it's going to look as if you're heading south for a leisurely change of climate," Joanna declared. In straightforward matters of animals or physical courage or, Joanna suspected, policy, the Princess had a powerful and instinctive grace, like an animal herself; but faced with the nuanced complexities of clothing or behavior, she lapsed into gauchery. Joanna, morbidly sensitive to all the things she herself had been urged to do, felt an overwhelming sympathy. She fished her backpack from the floor and dug from it a notebook, from which she ripped half a page. She twisted the paper into a makeshift spill and handed it to Pella, who remembered what she was about and hurried to the fireplace to touch one end to the small blaze there. "The minute it's light enough and we're away from Angelshand, we're going to leave it behind with the baggage wagons and go on in your phaeton, remember."

The Princess froze in the act of touching the lighted end to a candle wick. "The letters of credit for changing horses . . ."

"I have them here." Joanna nudged her backpack with one toe. After watching Pellicida's absentminded packing all afternoon, she had taken the precaution of stowing everything they would truly need in various pockets of the bulging sack—the aforesaid provision for changing horses en route, a great deal of money, and a sheaf of letters and orders from Pharos, several of which bore his seal which Joanna hoped she'd be able to remove with a hot knife, once she'd forged permits to get in to the Tower itself.

Returning to the former topic, she went on, "I think it would be easier for one of us to get in to see Antryg if we had a sasennan along to make it look more official . . ."

"At a pinch, I could pass myself off as a sasennan," Pella said thoughtfully. "That is, I've had some training. We all did—my cousins and I, back home, though of course, since we would never be allowed to take vows, we were never trained at the higher levels. But I've got a uniform and a sword, as well as a clerk's robe for you."

"*Are* there female clerks?"

Pella looked startled that Joanna would ask. "Of course.

A man doesn't write with his—er—whiskers." The spill burned down to her fingers; looking startled, she hastily lit the candle with it and tossed the flaming paper into the hearth. Then she proceeded to rove restlessly around the little bedchamber, lighting the candles that stood in holders of crystal, gilt bronze, and creamy porcelain. "Speaking of writing, I can fill out the text of the passes to get us into the Tower—any clerk would do that—but Pharos' signature is another matter. I was never any good at drawing. Besides, he's left-handed."

"I think I can manage that," Joanna said. "At least, I could always forge my mother's, and *she's* left-handed, not to mention signing her name like a Rorschach test. You know, in a way I feel rather sorry for Caris."

"Sorry?" Pella bristled.

"He's in an almost impossible situation," she explained quietly. Elsewhere in the palace, on the floor below, voices were momentarily raised and a hurrying of feet was heard; Pella swung around, her greenish eyes darkening, and she stood frozen like a deer in stillness until the sounds passed away. "What is it?"

"Nothing," the girl said and blushed again. "That is— whenever my mother went traveling, which wasn't often, my father used to come up to her rooms and bid her good- bye. It isn't that I expect Pharos to, but..." She stam- mered to a conclusion, as if realizing how ludicrous the comparison was.

Her parents must have loved one another a great deal, Joanna thought, torn between cynicism and envy, to have given her such ineradicable hopes about marriage.

She, too, had been listening for Pharos' chance coming, though for different reasons. When she went back to her packing, the leftover adrenaline flash made her fingers shake.

All it would need, she thought, was the smallest suspi- cion on his part. All it would need was one servant's rumor, one bit of gossip about his wife's new friend. For he would recognize her, of course. He might or might not take out his vicious sense of betrayal by Antryg on her, but whatever happened, at a screamingly optimistic least it would mean delay.

There could be no delay. Not now.

On their return to the north wing of the Imperial Palace Pellicida had been all for ordering a fresh change of horses for her phaeton and setting forth then and there, in the hopes of overtaking the Witchfinder's equipage and holding the lead all the way to Kymil. It had taken considerable persuasion on Joanna's part to convince her to wait for tomorrow morning, as even the most precipitate journey would under normal circumstances. Hence the long and tedious business of packing, of ordering the great traveling coach and a smaller vehicle for the servants and extra luggage, and of sending postriders ahead with orders to prepare Larkmoor, the small royal manor near Kymil.

Much as it drove Joanna insane to watch the failing of the afternoon light—it was only three-thirty—and to know that they couldn't leave for another fifteen hours or so, she knew that it was necessary to avert suspicion. She had no idea whether Suraklin was still with Cerdic at the Dower House and no idea if or how intently he kept track of Pella's movements. Throughout Pella's packing—or rather Joanna's packing of Pella's things while the Princess roved abstractedly around the apartment, looking for items Joanna had already packed—Joanna had been burningly conscious of the slow-moving gilt hands of the mantelpiece clock, half-buried under an orgy of enamel-and-gold nymphs, and of the gathering darkness outside. Peelbone the Witchfinder was on his way south, undoubtedly with the final warrant for Antryg's death in his pocket. At this point, the Council of Wizards was in no shape to prevent it, as Suraklin had clearly intended. And she knew she was doomed to sit in these rooms until enough time had passed for someone to sleep and wake up before she could do anything about it.

Screaming with frustration will not help, she told herself firmly, with wry and involuntary humor, *and will only cause talk among the servants*. With the hideous sensation of having her plans ravel once again from her hands, she went back to her packing, wondering how she would pass the night until morning.

It was seven A.M., black as the pits of hell and bitterly cold, when the Princess' huge traveling carriage finally lumbered away. To the last, Pellicida had been listening, waiting for some sign of her husband's coming, some acknowledgment from him that her movements mattered to him, and Joanna had fretted herself nearly ill with apprehension. He had not come, of course. Perhaps the girl did not consciously expect that he would, but Joanna could sense her disappointment and her hurt, ridiculous though it was, and was fond enough of the big, gawky girl to feel sorry for her. She herself had been more fearful that Suraklin would choose that inopportune moment to renew his attempt to seduce the Prince's wife. Then the game would have been up indeed.

River fog had risen to blanket the palace grounds and the city that lay beyond the walls; through it Joanna could see nothing, but now and then she heard the slop and drip of the horses' hooves in puddles and knew that the landscape would be one of absolute desolation. It was wretchedly cold in the coach, in spite of heated bricks wrapped up in the fur robes at their feet, and Joanna watched the soft steam of her breath float in the reflected glow of the carriage lamps. The coach was badly sprung; though the Princess' phaeton, which followed behind, ostensibly for Pella's use once they reached Larkmoor, was slightly better, she was miserably anticipating several days of jolting discomfort. She tried to keep herself from thinking about Antryg, about what would happen to her if she failed to rescue him, or if, having gotten the accursed Sigil off his throat, she found him permanently mind-broken as Magister Magus had feared. She tried not to think of the Magus, either.

He would be in the St. Cyr fortress now, in one of the vermin-ridden cells whose walls, like those of the Silent Tower, were spelled against the working of magic, perhaps the same cell in which she and the tiny, decrepit old crone Minhyrdin the Fair had been locked. It had been his spell, she remembered unhappily, that had allowed Antryg to break her out.

She leaned her head back against the soft plush of the seat squabs and shut her eyes, her head aching. She could think of no way in which she had betrayed him; it was sheer luck that she herself had spent last night at the palace instead of going home to be arrested with him. She could not help him. In fact, tarrying here would put her in danger of arrest herself when the Witchfinders began questioning him, even had Antryg not been facing immediate death. But she still felt guilty at abandoning the poor little quack to his fate.

The jolt of the carriage as it lurched to a stop made her open her eyes. At the same time she heard Pella gasp, and the Princess' big, clumsy hand sought hers under the velvet softness of the furs. Her heart seeming to shrink in her breast to something the size of a filbert, Joanna sat up and followed the younger girl's gaze through the carriage window, out into the blackness of the iron dawn.

Dark against the fog, a black shape stood on the verge of the road; a black cloak fell back from a raised arm. The horses drew up, their breath smoking like dragons' in the cold. Wet gravel crunched under soft boots. The lamps caught the glint of blond hair.

After an instant's frozen shock, Pella opened the carriage door. Caris climbed in without a word, the soft leather of his dagger belts creaking as he slumped back into the seat opposite the two girls. He did not look at them, nor did he speak; he just stared furiously out into the charcoal blackness of the mist as the coachman whipped up the horses, and, with a rattle of brasses and leather, they started forward again.

Chapter VI

At the summer's end, Caris remembered, it had taken him and the Archmage Salteris Solaris a week to walk from Angelshand to Kymil, ostensibly to seek the answer to the riddle of the mage Thirle's murder from Antryg Windrose, imprisoned in the Silent Tower. He had made the journey many times before, though that had been the first time he and Salteris had taken that road together. Always, as befitted the weapon of the Council of Wizards, it had been on foot.

Thus his memories of that journey had a slowness to them, in contrast to the hurried beat of the carriage team's hooves and the sting of wind on his face; then there had been the rhythm of a foot pace, the long flux of the amber and cobalt wings of summer days and nights, and the taste of dust and dew. The weather was well and truly winter now, the winds like flint and the roads either foul slime troughs or slicked with ice. Joanna and Pellicida were wrapped in rugs and mittens in the Princess' open traveling carriage, but Caris himself, high on the footman's perch behind them, barely felt the cold.

At times, the rage in him felt so hot that he thought he must smother; at others, his whole soul seemed to be nothing, down to its bottommost depths, but a pit filled with broken black ice. He hardly spoke, although, when Pella drew the team to a stop and jumped down to check their hooves for ice balled in their frogs, Caris sprang from his high perch to hold their heads.

Only that night, when Joanna had clustered all the lamps available on the table of the smoky, stinking, private parlor they had rented at the posting inn of the Plucky Duck to practice forging the Regent's signature, did he say, "Do you really think that's going to do us any good?"

He was weary, and the weariness came out as scorn; Joanna's head came up, her dark eyes hurt and a little puffy with sleepiness. But there was a spark in them, that spark of anger he had first seen in the alley behind the Standing Stallion in Angelshand, when she had cursed at him to act like a man. "If you've got a better plan for getting Antryg out of the Tower, I'd like to hear it."

Her fingers were chapped and red—it was very cold in the room, in spite of the grimy fire in the grate—and the imitation of Pharos' writing wouldn't have deceived a child.

He didn't, but Joanna's high-handed assumption of command chaffed him like a too-tight sleeve. "You haven't seen Antryg," he told her bitterly. "I have."

"It's the Sigil of Darkness . . ."

"Pox! It may have been the Sigil of Darkness that pushed him over the edge of madness, but taking it off him isn't going to restore what few wits he may once have possessed! *If* you can get it off him at all, which I'm waiting to see, in a Tower full of guards. And he's physically deteriorating as well . . ."

"Whose fault is that?" Joanna lashed at him.

"You're the one who put him there."

He could see her whole body tense, like the shutting of a fist. In the greasy orange glare of the two or three lamps before her, the thin face seemed to tighten in on itself, cold anger holding itself in. Stiltedly, as if counting out every word, she said, "I know I'm the one who put him there. But there's nothing that I or anyone can do to change things that have already happened. I can't know what to do about getting him out until I've seen him. For that, I need to get into the Tower . . ."

"And you think they're going to take the Sigil of Darkness off the outer doors to let *me* pass inside with you? Or that they're not going to ask about you having a mageborn sasennan with you?"

Her mouth stayed clamped shut, but he could see the tears of helpless anger gather in her eyes, and her small hands, that could not even wield a quill properly, shake.

"If that's how you feel about our chances of success, why did you come?"

"Because when you try to break Antryg out of the Tower," said Caris, quiet but suddenly harsh as broken stone, "Suraklin's going to hear about it. Suraklin will come . . ." He got to his feet, almost throwing the crude, heavy chair from him. "And then I will kill him for what he's done to me."

She answered him in a voice thinned with spite, "What makes you think you can?"

He took a step forward, wanting to slap her and hating that new spitfire glint in her eyes "If I can't," he said slowly, "then at least I can die as a sasennan should."

Joanna drew breath to speak, then stopped. Her brown eyes, in this uncertain light as black as the coffee cooling in its cup between the lamps, met his, narrow and gleaming; around her sharp face, her hair hung like a sulfury cloud. She said nothing. After a moment Caris turned on his heel and strode from the room.

If she had thrown it in his face that he was sasennan no longer, that he had broken his vows, and deserted the Way to which he had sworn his life, he thought he would have struck her. Sitting alone in the darkness of the inn stables, listening to the groan of the wind in the rafters and filling his nostrils with the clean, warm scents of horses and hay, he felt his rage rise at her, at Suraklin, at the mages who had disappeared from the Yard, at the stolid, silent, unimaginative Princess, and at the fool of an innkeeper who was little better than a robber for charging them a silver bit for a ladleful of stew and a hunk of bread the size of his fist. It was not the Way of the Sasenna to show rage, but he collected his rage, like steaming black liquid in a cup; a bitter drink that was all now that gave him strength.

It will sustain me, he thought, *until we reach Kymil*. After that it would not matter.

"Caris?"

The deep, husky voice made him realize with a start that he had no idea how long he'd been sitting out here. The sounds from the inn had fallen into muffled silence; the wind had risen, and when the door opened a crack, in the swimming well of shadows below the loft where he sat, he could smell the blowing snow. Mageborn, he could see in the dark when the tousled black head poked up through the ladder hole. He saw her looking around for him, peering in the blackness; he had automatically sought the deepest shadows, as it is the Way of the Sasenna to do, with the best field of fire to cover the entrance to the loft in case of attack.

He said, "Here," and the girl turned, tracking his voice without error. He heard the crunch and slither of her boots on the straw and the faint, light patter as she set Kyssha down beside her. He knew very little of this girl, save that she was a good driver, hopelessly disorganized, and that Joanna had somehow convinced her of her story. As the wife of the Regent she was, he realized, the first lady of the Empire, but it was difficult to remember that. For all her height, in her plain traveling dress she was curiously unobtrusive, speaking very little to the tense and preoccupied Joanna and not at all to him.

Not, he reflected dourly, that he would have made much of a reply if she had.

"Do you really think Antryg won't be able to help us?" She settled in the hay near him, drawing her thick tweed

cloak about her. A moment later, Kyssha's small, cold
nose came questing at his hand.

With a rueful smile, he gathered the little dog into his
lap, like a folded marionette. Softly, he said, "You know, I
think the hardest thing to give up when I went into training
was my dog? Her name was Ratbane." He sighed, not adding that the closest he had come to crying during the time
of his training had been when he'd received news of her
death. Of course he had not cried. He had been sixteen by
then, and it was in any case not the Way of the Sasenna to
mourn even the passing of one's parents, let alone a
shaggy-coated shepherd bitch with one blue eye.

After a moment he went on, "I don't know. Joanna isn't
sasennan, and she isn't mageborn. She doesn't understand . . ." His mind shied from the thought of the Seal of
the Dead God. It had taken every ounce of strength, every
knotted fragment of the hate within him, not to shrink
away when they'd fixed the iron collar around Antryg's
throat. The thought of touching the thing made him want to
vomit. "The Sigil's strength is in proportion to the strength
of the mage. It broke Antryg. He seemed to come through
the torture as well as anyone does."

Her voice was quiet in the gloom. "So you think it's
hopeless?"

Bitterly, he said, "Don't you?"

She made no reply, a curiously comforting silence, as if
she knew he had more to say and didn't want to divert the
course of it with words of her own. Outside, a gust of wind
struck the stable, like the flat-on blow of a monster hand,
and below them the horses stirred in their stalls. The air
was heavy with their smell, clean and curiously sweet, and
the sweetgrass scent of Pella's hair. Caris knew he should
rest, for they would be on the road as soon as it grew light
enough for the horses to see, but his whole body felt
charged with restless elation, as if he had drunk the *zam*
that professional boxers quaffed before their matches.

"I want one thing, Pella, and one thing only. I want to

kill Suraklin. I..." He hesitated, all the rage that had seethed in him since he had first stood in his grandfather's study with a handful of alien bullets in his hand taking shape, for the first time, into words. Slowly, stiffly, he said, "I loved my grandfather. A sasennan isn't supposed to love, but I loved him more than anyone else in the world, maybe—certainly more than my parents, though they were as good to me as they knew how to be. It's just that they were farmers, and he was ... he understood what it's like to be born with fire inside." He swallowed, struggling with the memory of those old hurts, wondering how after all the buried years they still seemed so fresh.

He went on, "I swore my vows to the Council because I loved him. He knew I loved him, maybe the only person I've ever told that I did. When Suraklin took over his mind, Suraklin knew that, too. And Suraklin used that, did all the things my grandfather did, things that I loved him for, played at being my grandfather, and used my love. He murdered him, killed him like a—a robber who wanted his cloak, only I was part of the cloak. He used me like a pimp."

It was the insult and the hurt, as well as the taking-away of the one person he had loved, Caris realized then, staring into the warm blackness, his blunt, powerful fingers toying with the soft fluff of Kyssha's ears. In his rage at the murder there was also rage at betrayal, as a man might feel who learns that the woman who came to his bed in darkness was not his wife, but a grinning succubus, counterfeiting the sound of her voice and the touch of her hands, in order to steal his seed. "There is no way back for me now," he finished softly. "I have betrayed my own vows. I'll have his life for what he has done and die."

They were under way again before dawn, the ice cracking sharply beneath the hooves of the newest relay of horses. Joanna dozed, exhausted from staying up half the night trying to master the techniques of forgery in an unfa-

miliar alphabet with writing implements she barely understood; when awake, she seemed anxious and preoccupied,
as if calculating how long a start the Witchfinder had on
them and whether he was able to make better progress than
they. At every postinghouse, she asked news of them, and
the news was depressingly the same. Peelbone was moving
south fast, not lingering more than was absolutely necessary to sleep or to eat.

"Can we pick up time by driving through the night?"
she asked worriedly as Caris helped her up into the phaeton
again after the barest stop for lunch while the horses were
changed. "Or part of it, anyway, since we're going to need
some time to work on those orders."

Pella and Joanna had both ended up practicing Pharos'
signature. In spite of Joanna's inexperience with the Ferr
style of writing, her efforts, though less than convincing,
were still far and away the best. Pella was simply too
clumsy-handed to be an artist. An attempt to transfer the
Imperial Seal from one document to another had already
resulted in cracking one of the three available; the other
two were secreted in one of the few corners of Joanna's
backpack not jammed tight with computer programs.

The backpack never left her these days, its straps wearing grooves in the thickly quilted crimson coat of one of
the Regent's pages which she wore over her gray traveling
dress. The scare she'd had when it had been in Magister
Magus' house at the time of his arrest had been enough.
Whatever the disk she carried would do to destroy Suraklin's plans—and Caris, in spite of her explanations, wasn't
certain he understood it—she was determined never again
to let it out of her sight.

Oddly, as he handed the backpack up to her, Caris found
in himself no trace of last night's impatience and scorn.
Though Pella had said very little in the stable loft, it was as
if her mere presence had allowed him to vent some of the
leading edge of his fury and, by speaking of it, to understand himself the hurt and the fear that underlay his wrath.

Standing by the horses' heads, Pella looked doubtful. "Even without the clouds we haven't had much of a moon lately..."

"If we get anything like a decent team, I can drive them in darkness," Caris said unexpectedly. "My sight in the dark isn't as sharp as a true wizard's, but I can see to drive." And, seeing the surprise in Joanna's glance, he added gruffly, "I'm not saying it will do us any good, but I'd be pleased to find out you're right about Antryg."

The words came harder than he'd thought—or would have liked to think—they would.

What they would do with the mad wizard or what was left of him if the deterioration brought on by the Sigil proved to be irreversible, Caris refrained from asking. Clinging hour after hour to the high footman's perch, or trading off the reins with Pella—Joanna not being a good enough whip to manage on the fouled roads—Caris watched the blond woman's sharp, worried face and wondered whether she was aware of the only possible option in that case. If Antryg could not be a help to them, with as powerful a mage as Suraklin alerted to his danger by the rescue, there was no way they could afford him as a hindrance. Caris knew Joanna to be not only learned in the ways of these mysterious computers, but intelligent as well. Her love of Antryg had not blinded her to the priorities of the situation. At least, he thought, it didn't seem to have blinded her mind.

And in any case, shooting the wizard like a lamed horse would be a far more merciful death than whatever was commanded by the Witchfinder Peelbone's warrant. Of that Caris was positive.

That night Caris got three or four hours' sleep in the hired parlor of the inn, while Pella and Joanna worked at what Joanna called their penmanship exercises and tried to figure out the tricky business of removing a seal from parchment without cracking it. They set out shortly before midnight in the teeth of a driving wind. Pella had to pay thrice the usual fee to take the horses out; but even driving with great care in the howling darkness, they managed to pick up six or seven hours on the Witchfinder's equipage. They had left the calmer weather of the Glidden Valley for the fringes of the Sykerst, and by dawn Caris could make out the barren gray hills rising beyond the ghostly clumps of birches beside the road.

"He's ten or twelve hours ahead of us," Pella reported, coming out of the stables of the next posting inn to where Caris and Joanna waited by the phaeton. Unlike those in the Glidden Valley, this inn was not attached to a village; it was a small affair and rather shabby, subsisting entirely on the traffic of the Kymil road. Indeed, there were no more villages between here and Kymil, only the bare gray hills of the Sykerst, stripped now even of their summer crop of wandering sheep.

It was also the inn at which, in Antryg's company, Caris and Joanna had once encountered the Regent and had been forced to leave the main road to flee his pursuit. Sitting at Joanna's side, the hood of his brown servant's cloak pulled well over his face, Caris felt just as glad they weren't staying. The events of that night had been far too spectacular for anyone not to recognize Joanna as the woman who had triggered them.

"Then if we drive all night, we can overtake him in the morning." Joanna looked exhausted. Unlike Caris, she had had no sleep last night, and she lacked Pella's ability to sleep in a moving carriage. Indeed, it took a special constitution to sleep in a small racing vehicle which could seat only two and was scarcely designed for even the small amount of luggage they carried.

"Did you come up with orders that will pass muster at the Tower?" Caris demanded.

She passed her hand over her eyes, pushing back the tangle of her fair hair. In the shadows of her dark green hood, her face looked white beneath the remains of its curious, unseasonable tan. "If we don't overtake him tonight, he's going to reach the Tower before we do anyway. I think what we have will do." Her jaw tightened. In a very small voice she added, "It will have to."

Pella swung up to the footman's stand, in spite of Caris' shocked admonition. Though no sasennan save those who had specifically sworn it owed allegiance to the Imperial Family, it still horrified his peasant heritage to see the wife of the Regent hanging on the footboard like a common groom. Caris steered the team out of the inn yard and once more onto the road.

It was a bitter day, the sky above the hills dark as a roil of ink. Periodic flurries of sleet soaked the road, the horses, and the passengers of the open phaeton, and made driving treacherous; the hard cold froze the road into a sheet of oiled glass. Caris and Pella traded places frequently, for driving under such conditions exhausted them both, and neither would even think of giving the reins to the inexperienced Joanna. Nor would either seek warmth from the bottle of plum brandy Joanna wordlessly produced from her bottomless backpack.

"I'm a cheap drunk," Pella admitted with a shy grin. "One glass of May wine and I start to sing."

Caris, holding the near horse's head while Pella picked the balled ice from its hoof, found himself thinking he would one day like to hear her sing. Her speaking voice was deep and husky, but had a sweetness to it, like an alto flute. At the moment there was nothing else sweet about her. Like him, she was splotched from head to foot with mud, her travel-dirty black braids twisted tight beneath her flat coachman's cap and her heavy mouth and chin pinched with exhaustion.

"I can't afford to take any of the edge off my concentration," Caris added. He and Pella scrambled back to their respective perches, and he took up the reins once more. "By the look of the sky, it's going to get worse tonight. But thank you."

It was four o'clock and graying toward sunset somewhere above the bruised darkness of the clouds, when the gray deadness, the numbness of body and soul, descended like a plague on the land. Joanna cursed, her small fists closing tight; she looked over at Caris, who had let the horses drop to a walk, feeling suddenly overwhelmed with a terrible sense of the futility of it all. "Do you feel it?" she asked, as if she hoped against hope that it was only her own weariness and not the draining of the world's life.

He nodded. Suddenly weary, furious with the exhaustion of the journey, he said, "It won't stop us. We can go on . . ." He picked up the whip, and Joanna reached out and caught his wrist.

"No. I *think* this is only a—a testing-out of one of the programs, rather than a major download. He only does that on weekends. It shouldn't last more than a few hours."

"And if it does?" Caris asked brutally, "Are you willing to risk that?"

"I think we have to." Pella leaned forward from her rear perch. "The roads are bad, Caris. It would be too easy to make a mistake and lurch us all."

"I've never lurched *anything* I drive . . . !" he yelled, suddenly furious. Another time it would have cut him to the heart to see her cringe. Now it gave him a kind of savage satisfaction.

Wearily, Joanna said, "We'll stop at the next inn and wait till it passes. We can't risk losing the time an accident might cost us."

Furious, frustrated, Caris made a move to lash the horses back into a canter. It was only when Joanna stopped him again that he realized the stupidity of the action in the dark and on such roads. Even so, he drove on, slowly, with blackness in his heart.

The spell lasted for just over four hours. It was less than half the long night, but sitting in the overpowering warmth of the posting inn's common room—for the place boasted no private parlors—it seemed to last forever. Pella came over to the inglenook where Caris sat, scruffy as a stagecoach driver in her travel-stained brown dress, with Kyssha huddled shivering in her arms. In spite of the poisoned weariness in his veins, Caris felt the stir of pity for them both, wordlessly facing a pain they could not understand; he moved to put his arm around those firm, square shoulders, then stopped himself, confused. It was not the Way of the Sasenna to give comfort—and certainly not to need it as he did. But even so, he found there was a certain amount to be derived simply from sitting in silence side by side and knowing he was not alone.

It had passed, and Pella had just paid the usual exorbitant fee to have the horses put to, when the Witchfinder Peelbone walked into the inn.

Caris heard his voice over the sound of the wind outside in the inn yard. For an instant, he did not recognize it. He was talking to Pella and Joanna by the fire in the nearly deserted common room, his mind on the drive ahead and on the nearly hopeless task of overtaking Peelbone before the Witchfinder could reach Kymil and deliver his warrant. He was aware of figures in the doorway and subliminally aware that he had heard no horses in the yard. Then the voice, thin and cold, said, "It was you who had the charge of such things, Tarolus. Such carelessness speaks ill for your devotion to our cause."

Caris' heart turned to ice in his body.

"My lord, I told you . . . I don't know what came over you . . ."

"Nothing came over me save the knowledge that each day Windrose lives, the chances increase of his rescue."

Joanna's head snapped around, her brown eyes wide with alarm. She made a move to leave, and Caris stayed her, knowing it was too late to do so without calling attention to them. Unobtrusively he turned his back to the room, and Joanna turned with him, holding her hands out to the fire. Caris found himself remembering that Peelbone knew them both.

"Rescue? My lord, surely no one . . ."

Behind him, the sasennan heard the Witchfinder's long tread. In the grimy mirror over the mantelpiece, Caris saw him, thin and middle-sized, a gray man—gray clothing, wispy gray hair. Even his eyes, though brown, seemed flat and colorless beneath the wide brim of his gray hat. He moved like a spider, slightly awkward, but with frightening speed; in his expression there was nothing, save a cold knowledge that whatever he chose to do was correct, and none would gainsay it.

"You are naive, Tarolus." The Witchfinder turned to his companion, older and shorter, like him clothed in the close-fitting, colorless suit of that self-righteous order. "There are many who would free him, either from desire to use his power or from mere perverse adherence to the heresy of witchcraft. Now that it is in our power to forestall such an attempt, we should lose no time."

"But driving at night . . . !"

"I see perfectly well in the dark!" The cold facade cracked; for the first time, Caris saw the vanity of the man behind it.

Beside him, Pella whispered, her voice barely able to contain her glee, "He lurched them! He put them in the ditch somewhere up ahead. They must have been walking for hours . . ."

The soaked clothing and muddied boots of Peelbone and Tarolus bore ample witness to this hypothesis. In the mirror Caris saw them making for the fire. His heart thumping heavily against his ribs, he moved away with what he thought was naturalness, still keeping his face averted. Peelbone had once gotten a good look at it, by the red glare of the burning books in the library at the House of the Mages. *Kill him*, he had said, as casually as if ordering the destruction of a stray dog. *We can't afford these waters muddied*. Even clothed as Caris now was in the rather grubby brown corduroy breeches and coat of a rich lady's groom, he knew the Witchfinder as a man who would not forget a face.

The innkeeper had come over to speak to the new-comers. Caris heard that chill, hated voice again. "... accident to our chaise ... ten miles up the road ... broken axle ..."

"He must have tried to drive on after dark, during the dead time," said Pella softly. Caris remembered his own violent impatience and felt an odd twinge of shame at himself. He would, he knew, have tried to do the same. "It will give us at least six hours ..." She turned toward Joanna, but Joanna was gone.

Caris muttered a curse. They still had several minutes until the phaeton was brought around, owing to the fact that the dead time had triggered in one of the ostlers a great desire to drink most of the contents of the inn's wine cellar. By remaining in the common room Joanna might have run the risk of being recognized by the preoccupied Peelbone, but disappearing and forcing himself or Pella to go search for her was not usual behavior in travelers, and would rouse more suspicion still.

Tarolus was arguing, "... a broken man. All he does is weep, and speak to the saints. He could help no one ..."

"He could help anyone who took the time to force from him the secrets of his former power," Peelbone retorted, holding out his thin hands to the fire, his shoulder close enough to Caris that the young man could feel the wet cold that radiated from it as it steamed with the heat. "Don't you understand? In the state he is in now, he is anyone's tool."

From the windy yard outside Caris heard the sharp rattle of harness and the crunch of hooves on the gravel. Peelbone looked up, his cold eyes narrowing. As Pella walked past him he said, "Is that your carriage, my lady? It may be necessary to commandeer it on the business of the Church ..."

"Not at all, not at all," the innkeeper said hastily, coming back to them, evidently mindful of the amount the Princess had paid. "There's a chaise your lordship can hire whenever you choose, though, as a wheelwright myself, I can tell you it won't take but a few hours to fix that axle . . ."

With great common sense, Caris thought, Pella did not reply or even remain to listen to this, but walked calmly out the inn door, slinging her massive tweed cloak about her shoulders as she went. Caris, buttoning his quilted coat and pulling up his hood, followed her out.

Joanna was waiting in the phaeton. The ostlers holding the horses' heads were shivering in their bulky coats and scarves; the wind had lessened, but still clawed the torch-flames into a jerky wildness of yellow light and darkness; spits of sleet still flew in the air. Caris knew the ice on the roads would be deadly. Still, driving at night here would be better than in the Glidden Valley. At least, there was no fog. He swung up to the seat and took the reins, Kyssha leaping up to snuggle near the heated brick, for which they had been charged extra, at his feet. His boot touched some unfamiliar piece of luggage as he did so. Looking down, he saw a bundle of bound-up cloth beside Joanna's back-pack; a corner had pulled aside to show bright metal within.

"What the . . . ?"

"The innkeeper's wheelwright tools," she said matter-of-factly. "Your software's only as good as your hardware. One of the linchpins from the wheels of the spare chaise is in there, too. I replaced it with a stick whittled down from the handle of a kitchen spoon; with luck, it should last a couple of miles and break at least a wheel, if not Peel-bone's neck. I suppose that's a case of replacing *hard*ware with *soft*ware. You'd better drive on. First and last, we've probably picked up at least a day."

"If a day will suffice," Caris said softly. "And if there's enough left of Antryg to save." He flicked the reins gently, picking out in the darkness the vague shape of the road. Beside him Joanna said nothing as they disappeared into the night.

CHAPTER VII

IN THE FEW HOURS OF SLEEP SHE HAD GOTTEN HUDDLED under the damp furs and rugs in the carriage, Joanna had dreamed. She had found herself again in a place she knew to be the Silent Tower, this time in a narrow and stinking room where the smoke of the chambers below collected in the darkness under the wheel-spoke rafters, a room chilly and damp as a pit, without fire, almost without light. She was trying to talk to a hunched, sobbing figure chained to the wall, whose crippled hands picked aimlessly at the vermin that crawled in his gray-shot beard and soiled rags. Vacant gray eyes squinted at her from behind a curtain of filthy gray hair. She had cried desperately, "Antryg, it's me!" and he had only mumbled, pointing off past her at some unseen vision of hypothetical saints. "Antryg, you have to help me! I can't defeat Suraklin alone!" For she sensed the Dark Mage to be somewhere near, listening in the gloom just beyond the turning of the stair.

But the figure had only whispered, "I tried to help—tried to help. I couldn't fight you all . . ." Awake, asleep, dead fifty years, she would have known his voice. It pierced her with grief for all the years they would never know, and she woke up sobbing, tears running down her face to mat in her tousled hair. Around her the hard gray hills loomed like granite under a sky milky with dawn.

Pella was at the reins, the look on her face one of exhaustion that bordered on physical pain; Kyssha, in Joanna's lap, was anxiously licking her hand.

Joanna's first waking thought had been, *We have eighteen hours.*

But the dream lingered with her, like the smell of vomit, as she rode out to the Silent Tower in the afternoon gloom.

The wind had sunk to an indistinct mutter among the hills; the sky was low and threatening, but still. They had reached the Imperial Manor of Larkmoor shortly before noon, and the servants there had been considerably startled when their mistress, as drawn and haggard as her two shabby-looking friends, had ordered three horses saddled at once. "We don't know what we're going to find at the Tower or what's going to be needed," Pellicida said, shaking out the cinder-hued robes of a clerk in her bedchamber, while Joanna sorted through her forged papers. "After that string of accidents on the road, you know Peelbone's going to suspect a rescue attempt."

She seemed calm and matter-of-fact, for which Joanna was profoundly grateful. After organizing the journey and keeping her head fairly well on the road, Joanna found herself increasingly frightened in the face of the physical danger of what they had come to do. And beyond that, she was hideously conscious that rescuing Antryg—and *we will* rescue him! she told herself fiercely. *We will* succeed! —was only the prelude to the true task, the true danger.

The Silent Tower stood only a few miles from the ruins of Suraklin's Citadel. Joanna had never seen that, but it loomed like a darkness at the back of her thoughts, shrouding the evil secrets of its past and, beyond a doubt, Suraklin's computer, the most evil secret of them all.

Her head emerged from the stuffy wool of the clerk's robe in time to see Pella putting on a pair of sharply tailored black trousers. The gold-braided tunic and coat of the Regent's sasennan lay on the bed, beside a neat array of weaponry. "Two sasenna will look more official than one,"

Pella had explained, seeing her look of surprise. "Besides, I can escort you while you leave Caris to look after the horses—that way we won't have any trouble when he can't pass the Sigil of Darkness on the Tower door."

She spoke calmly, braiding her black hair flat against her skull, as some sasenna did in preference to cutting it off. But as she turned away Joanna glimpsed something in her eyes that troubled her then and caused her now, as they rode together over the bleak monochrome landscape toward the Tower, to steal worried glances back at her, trying to read what might be in that stern young face.

Fear Joanna would have understood—she was scared almost witless herself.

But why, for one second, had she glimpsed the wretchedness of some buried knowledge, the suppressed tear-glint of a secret pain?

"There it is," Caris said softly.

Involuntarily, Joanna drew rein. Through a notch in the hills ahead she could see it rise against the slaty sky, a finger raised in warning—windowless, weathered, dead to magic, and old beyond speaking—the Silent Tower.

He's got to be alive, she thought. *He's got to recover when we get the Sigil off him. Those forged passes have got to get us in there. The guards can't look at them too closely. He's got to be able to help us . . .*

Deliberately, Joanna took several deep breaths.

I am a clerk bearing orders from the Regent, she told herself, fixing the attitude in her mind. *I have every right to be doing what I'm doing, and the words* UP TO SOMETHING *are not blazoned across my forehead . . .*

"What's that?!"

At the sharp wariness in Pella's voice, Joanna slewed around in her saddle. Silhouetted against the granite skyline, a small party of riders cantered away from the Tower.

"There!" Caris barked.

More men were visible, afoot this time, hurrying toward

the Tower from across the barren hills. "Something's
stirred them up."

Joanna swore.

"Do we turn back?" All Pella's grim coolness dissolved
into anxiety. "They're liable to look more closely at the
papers."

Caris, too, was looking at her uncertainly, and Joanna
felt a twinge of irritation. This whole mess, she thought,
came about because she was unable to make a correct decision.

She took another deep breath. "No. Those papers won't
look any more convincing tomorrow, and Peelbone's on his
way. We might be able to turn whatever's happening to our
advantage." Without waiting for Caris to reply, she kicked
her horse into a trot once more, hanging on grimly against
the jolting pace as she rode up to the gate. Pella fell in at
once behind her; Caris, rather unwillingly, brought up the
rear.

The portcullis was open. A little knot of men in the
quilted black coats of sasenna stood grouped there, gesturing as they argued; two of them wore the red robes of
Church wizards, like those Joanna had seen at the time of
Antryg's arrest. Past the darkness of the gatehouse passage, the courtyard was visible, alive with sasenna, running about, shouting, or fetching horses. A ferret-faced
man came striding through the gate to meet them as they
drew rein. With what she hoped was official hauteur,
Joanna reached for the leather satchel of papers, but the
man looked out past her at the two sasenna, and demanded,
"Any luck?"

"Luck?" Caris looked baffled. With a flash of insight,
Joanna remembered the Magus saying that the guards on
the Tower were changed frequently. With their black
quilted coats hiding the Regent's gold braid, the man
thought them part of the Tower guard. Then he took a second look at the cut of their breeches, and frowned sharply.

"You're the Regent's, aren't you?"

Pella looked momentarily startled, as if trying to figure out how he had known she was the Regent's wife. Caris said, "Yes. We're here to . . ."

"Are his men joining the hunt?"

"Hunt?" said Joanna blankly.

The man spat, and it froze to a diamond of ice on the granite doorsill of the Tower. "For that damned sorcerer. He's escaped."

"He'll be making for Kymil." Joanna drew rein on the brink of a stream which cut the roadbed, black rainwaters rushing with silken silence down the narrow channel between ice and frozen weeds. Behind them, the Silent Tower was a truncated spike against the darkening sky. Cold wind stirred their cloaks, tugging at her blond hair where it strayed free of her hood. Soon it would be night.

"Are you mad?" Caris demanded. "It's the first place they'll look—the Witchfinders will be searching house to house."

"Tomorrow, maybe. They've got a lot of men, but not unlimited numbers. It's my bet that tonight they'll be concentrating on the hills themselves and on the roads north."

Caris considered the matter for a moment in silence. Joanna guessed he was recalling, too, Antryg's foxlike skill in lying low and doubling on his own tracks. Tricky, devious, more than a little crazy . . . All the fears she had felt for his life and his sanity, all her plans for rescuing him, had vanished in a sort of thunderclap of delight, and it had only been with difficulty that she had restrained herself from laughing aloud by the gates of the Tower. Caris, for his part, looked brooding and angry, as if he felt that Antryg had made a fool of them as well as of his captors—as indeed he had.

Finally he said, "He'll have to wait until it gets fully dark, I think. There are people in Kymil who will recognize him, even with those absurd spectacles that were given back to him, if he's still wearing them. It's beyond

me how he plans to get into the city, but then I'm still
trying to figure out how he got past the Sigil of Darkness
on the doors of the Tower."

He touched his heels to his horse's flanks and reined
back toward the frozen Ponmarish and the city walls
beyond. Joanna followed him, grimly reflecting that tomorrow she'd have a whole new set of aches to go with
those acquired from four days of jouncing in the carriage.
The last horse she'd ridden had been a riding-stable plug at
the age of fifteen, and she was already sore.

As soon as they were well out of sight of the Tower,
Pella had ridden back cross-country to the manor of Larkmoor. No further purpose was to be served, she said, by
her staying with them to hunt for Antryg. The best thing
she could do was to brief the servants with a cover story
sufficient to divert the Witchfinders' inevitable questions
about the movements of strangers in the district. While
there was still enough left of the waning afternoon light,
Caris, like every other of the several dozen sasenna at the
Tower, had searched the grounds around the walls for
tracks and had found none. The frozen sleet of last night
had formed a brittle sheet over the dead grass, breaking
like glass at a touch. The only prints were those of the
sasenna of the Tower, searching like him without success.

"You don't think the story of his disappearance could be
just a cover, do you?" Joanna asked worriedly as they left
the road and swung north along the edge of the marshes.
"The guards said he just vanished—one minute he was
chained in his cell, the next minute he was gone. Even the
manacles were still locked shut. Could he have been murdered quietly, and all this search be for the benefit of
whichever member of the Council has been holding out
against his death?"

"The Council's in hiding," Caris said briefly. "You can
bet Bishop Herthe knew it the minute the last of them left
Angelshand—the Bishop of Angelshand's hasu would
have sent that news by scrying-crystal the same night.

They could have slit Antryg's throat with impunity any time in the last week."

"Maybe they did," Joanna said softly.

"Then why make a fuss now? No, the Captain of the Tower was genuinely furious." Through his teeth, Caris added, "And I can't say that I blame him." He urged his horse down a treacherous slope to the first iron-hard sheet of ice where the marshes began, scanning the rotted snow, frozen mud, and brittle, black weed stems for the print of Antryg's feet.

"He was barefoot, they said, in the Tower," he went on after a moment, with a kind of grudging compassion in his voice. "He'd sometimes wrap rags around his feet for warmth, or the guards would do it for him when he forgot, but they said he didn't walk much toward the end. He knows these hills the way a rat knows the sewers—he lived here for eight years with Suraklin—but in his physical condition, he won't be able to get far. He'll need food, he'll need shelter, and he'll need them before night. It's coming on to sleet again. He'll never survive it."

He has to, Joanna thought desperately, fear for him swamping again her lingering sense of delight at his escape. *Somehow, he has to survive. We have to find him before the Witchfinders do, before the sasenna of the Church and the Council.* It crossed her mind to wonder whether he would hate her for what she had done to him. It might not keep him from working with her to accomplish Suraklin's defeat; she was too familiar with his conscientiousness, his quixotic sense of duty, to think he would reject her help or even be openly hostile. But she had betrayed him, given him over to the savage usages of the Inquisition and the slow torture of the Sigil of Darkness. And, rather typically of Antryg, she reflected with a grin, he had robbed her of the opportunity to display her contrition by a spectacular rescue.

At least he's alive, she thought, as the darkness closed

round them and the wind began to moan among the hills. *Somewhere out there . . .*

The lingering daylight faded. Brutal cold settled in.

"My guess is he'll work his way around and come down from the north," Caris said softly, as they settled themselves in the lee side of a clump of naked alders on an islet in the marsh. Causeways led from the higher ground of the hills where they had hidden the horses to the tuft of ground where they sat, and thence to the city gates, a few hundred feet beyond. Around them stretched the marsh itself, the green fairyland of ponds and meres Joanna had crossed at the end of summer, now a solid lake of muddy gloom. Behind them, the wind throbbed shrilly over the hills. "They'll be watching the Angelshand road to the northeast, and the Stone Road that leads to the Tower itself, but this gate isn't much used. He'll have to come across the causeway—most of the marsh is frozen hard, but he'd be mad to risk a soaking in an ice bog."

"He is mad," Joanna said quietly. "And he's pretty desperate."

"He's mad but he's not stupid. If he got wet now, the cold would finish him long before daylight."

Joanna shuddered and tucked her gloved hands under her armpits in a vain attempt to warm them. The city gates were lit with torches and lamps, a promise of warmth and, she thought hungrily, food. The reflected orange glow showed up the cloud of her breath and brushed with fiery chiaroscuro the crumbling roof beams of the long line of trashy little shanties that crouched along the outside of the city wall on both sides of the causeway and its arched bridge.

"What are those?"

Caris followed her glance.

"Poor people live there in the summertime, fishing in the marshes for food. When the waters rise with the rains in winter, they're forced back into the town again. Most of those huts will be knee-deep."

"Could he be hiding in one of them?"

Caris leaned around the bare, coarse-barked trunk of the nearest alder to scan the dark line of pitiful dwellings. Then he settled back down at her side and whispered, "Someone thinks he might be."

Through the scaly trunks Joanna could see a line of black-clothed figures on the causeway. The glow from the gate beyond picked chips of light from the brass hardware of crossbows and pistols and caught the hard line of swords beneath dark, quilted coats. Church sasenna, she guessed, coming in from an unsuccessful search with the increasing cold of the night. One of them pointed down at the huts. "Have those been searched?"

And it seemed to her that her heart stopped.

The leader of the party cursed and gestured his men down the track toward the filthy, flooded little shelters. Her eyes on what were little more than black silhouettes, Joanna felt she was going to smother with anxiety, confusion, and overwhelming and impossible certainty.

"What is it?" Caris whispered, and she was aware that her hand had closed with convulsive strength on his wrist.

"Antryg," she whispered. "That was Antryg's voice."

"The *guard*?"

It sounded as impossible to her as it did to him, but she didn't take her eyes off the hut into which the tallest of the sasenna had vanished. It was close under the shadow of the bridge. She could see vague movements, men milling around, now and then caught in the gold lights from the gate. The tall man emerged briefly, wading through the half-frozen slime of marsh water and sewage to go on to another hut. Even at this distance, she could see that he walked with an odd, lithe arrogance, like a dancer.

"It can't be."

Her mind echoed it, over and over. *It can't be. It can't be*.

The sasenna reassembled. Somebody said, "Everybody here?" and there was a murmur of assent, though in the darkness, with that large a group, it would be impossible to tell. Scrambling in the slippery mud, they climbed the narrow track back to the causeway bridge.

Caris breathed, "They're one short."

"The hut there against the buttress. He never came out."

Caris was already checking the loads of the pistol he'd pulled from his sword sash. It was a local muzzle-loader rather than Suraklin's .45; in a stray glint of light from the gates, Joanna saw the runes of na'aar on the barrel. "He's got a crossbow," he said softly, and she remembered that, mageborn, Caris could see like a cat in the dark. "At this stage, he'll probably kill to protect himself." He rose to a crouch, glanced at the gate to make sure they were unobserved, then paused. "The fact that he's managed to escape from the Tower doesn't mean he isn't completely insane, you know."

The hut was low-roofed, half-fallen-in, a blot of darkness clinging like a dirty leech to one of the city wall's massive stone buttresses. It stood on higher ground than most, but getting there entailed wading through lakes of brown ooze which undoubtedly would have stunk, had it not been so bitterly cold. Joanna, her long clerk's robe hitched to her knees, was shivering, her toes numb in her boots and her thick woolen hose. Stalking ahead of her, Caris seemed not to notice. In the darkness, she could barely see him and certainly not see the ground; she slipped twice, nearly losing her hold on her ever-present backpack and the flashlight she had taken from it. The reflected glare from the torches at the gates overhead caught with a faint, citrous sheen on Caris' fair hair and the gold braiding of his coat as he paused before the darkness of the hut door. Then, before she could catch up with him, he stepped around the low doorpost, his pistol pointing into the blackness.

"Drop it," he said.

There was a long silence. Joanna paused, involuntarily frozen into stillness, waiting.

Then, slow and infinitely weary, Antryg's voice sounded within the hut. "Hello, Caris." There was the faint clatter and splat of something, presumably the crossbow, being tossed to the muddy ground. Joanna ran the last few slithery steps to Caris' side and shined the beam of her flashlight into the hut in time to see Antryg raise his hands in a gesture of surrender, his head bowed and a look on his face of utter exhaustion and the most total defeat she had ever seen.

He could have shot anyone, she realized, except Caris, who, in spite of everything, Antryg had never ceased to consider his friend.

The light flashed across the round lenses of his spectacles and he flinched; his hands, she saw now, in tattered, fingerless leather gloves, were shaking. He reached one of them out abruptly and leaned against the stone buttress for support; his face was cadaverously thin, bone-white against a frame of short, startlingly black curls; the hollows of his eyes were darkened still further with blue-brown smudges of exhaustion. After an instant, he raised his head again, squinting against the electric glare, and saw her.

Their eyes met. His expression did not change, but something in him seemed to settle into a kind of stillness, as if he were perfectly balanced between heartbeats on a razor's edge, awaiting the end of the world.

Caris shoved the pistol into his belt. "Suraklin's in Angelshand," he said quietly. "We're here to get you away."

Joanna said, "Antryg, I'm sorry."

She thought he was going to say something; but after the first sip of indrawn breath, he forcibly stopped himself. She saw the grief in his eyes, like a man pulling back his hand from that which he knows he must not grasp. In a conversational voice he began, "My dear Joanna . . ."

She took two strides forward and flung her arms around his waist.

In all her hesitant and approval-seeking life, she had never done such a thing, partly from fear of rejection and partly because it wasn't the sort of thing she did. Typically, she forgot to let go of either the backpack or the flashlight, so the ensuing embrace was lumpy and awkward, but of that she only became aware later. His arms crushed her against him, lifting her off her feet with his greater height; through layers of quilted coat and pilfered uniform, she could feel the desperate shudder of his breath. His ribs were like a washboard under her grip, and his pelvic bones like those of an old horse. For a time, she had the illogical sensation of wanting to lock their bones together, to meld his flesh into her body and never let him go, and the frantic strength of his embrace told her more than any words could have that her desire mirrored his own. Their mouths met. Had they been able to fuse then, truly lose their physical selves in one another's bodies, they would have done it. Joanna was aware that she was crying.

He set her down and pulled convulsively at the shabby muffler around his throat. Under it she saw by the dim glow of the flashlight the dark ring of the iron collar, harsh against the white flesh and edged with a mottled band of bruises and sores. "Get this thing off me," he said, breathless, and then, with a wry grin, "You don't happen to have a hacksaw about you, do you, my dear?"

Silently, Joanna dug into her backpack and produced one. He grinned like a pleased jack-o'-lantern, then seized her and kissed her again. "If this is all a hallucination," he said, his voice shaking slightly, "I'm going to be *very* disappointed in the morning."

He dropped to his knees, fumbling with the muffler; Joanna hitched the backpack up onto her shoulder and tucked the dirty green muffler between the iron and his neck. "Caris, can you hold the light for me . . . ?"

"No," said the sasennan briefly.

"Quite right," agreed Antryg, his voice blurred with the bending of his head. "Somebody has to keep watch. The noise may bring someone . . ."

"Maybe we could ride out first?" Caris suggested.

Antryg, who had taken the flashlight from Joanna and held it in one hand to light the collar, shook his head. "No. Just get rid of this thing."

It might not have prevented his escape, Joanna realized, but that didn't make the torment of wearing it any the less. It took surprisingly little time to cut through the soldered clasp—the iron had no kind of temper to it—and it made a hellish amount of noise. Joanna had broken two blades practicing before beginning her expedition and had brought several spares, but they weren't needed. The clasp broke apart as Caris whispered hoarsely, "Someone's coming!" Antryg stumbled to his feet, pulling the iron ring from his throat with hands that shook.

"Thank you," he gasped as Joanna shut off the flashlight. Amid the raw, scabbed flesh of his neck, a circular brown mark showed where the Sigil itself had touched, as if the skin had been burned with acid. Oddly enough, though he held the iron collar in his hands, Joanna had seen that he avoided contact with the Dead God's Seal.

"Hasu," Caris reported, ducking back in through the hut door. "Church dogs." He scooped up the crossbow from the mud and held it out to Antryg.

Antryg shook his head, pulled a board off the flimsy back wall and snaked his thin form through the gap.

Horrified, Caris gasped, "They can see us in the dark . . ."

"Of course they can." Antryg shoved the broken collar into his belt and made a dash toward the causeway.

Voices shouted behind him; they were evidently hasu who knew what Antryg looked like with his spectacles and without his beard. Joanna heard the *hrush* and whap of a crossbow bolt slamming into one of the nearby huts. Through gritted teeth, Caris snarled, "You're insane!" Antryg cut abruptly sideways between two crumbling board walls.

Through the gap in the back of the hut, Joanna watched him dash through the foot-deep standing water that flooded the ground hereabouts. She saw at once the reason that the water hadn't yet frozen—it trickled out of a sewer outfall just beneath the causeway bridge, a round stone pipe about four feet in diameter. It was, she realized, the way he had intended to enter the city.

On the other side of the hut, she heard the hasu splash by, running surely, unerringly in the dark. In the shadows of the causeway, it was difficult for her to see, but she caught the glimpse of Antryg's dark, spidery shape crouching for a moment before the outfall, and the moonlike flash of his spectacle lenses. Then he came sprinting back through the water, the black coat of the sasennan's uniform he wore billowing like a cloak behind him. He stumbled over some submerged irregularity of the ground, almost falling, but regained his balance and flung himself through the narrow opening in the wall through which Joanna had watched. She pulled the loose plank back over it as the two hasu came around the corner and dashed straight for the outfall pipe.

Beside her, Antryg was leaning against the wall, gasping for breath. His eyebrows stood out like india-ink against a face gone gray with fatigue; he was not, she realized, in any shape for this. In spite of the cold, his face was clammy with sweat, and the makeshift black dye in his hair ran in trickles down the high cheekbones and the dim shape of the scar left by the Regent's whip.

The two hasu jerked to a stop a few feet from the outfall. One of them reached forward hesitantly, then drew back his hand as if it had been burned. As one, they turned and pelted through the water for the little trail that led up to the causeway bridge, shouting for the guards . . .

"The Sigil of Darkness?" Joanna guessed, as the two small forms, their robes billowing suddenly red in the torchlight, ran with waving arms into the oven-mouth brightness of the city gates.

Antryg nodded, his old demented grin flickering through the lines of strain on his face. "Certainly superior to beavers, who are said to tear off certain of their bodily parts and throw them at pursuers to discourage the chase, though why it should do so has always escaped me. They're convinced I've gone through the outfall and are going to spend the rest of the night and all day tomorrow tearing apart the town. I hope whatever refuge you had planned for us *wasn't* in Kymil?" He was shivering violently with exhaustion, nerves, and cold. They were all soaked to the skin and the night was cruel.

She shook her head, "Larkmoor Manor." His brows dove together as he identified its name, then quirked upward, taking with them a whole ladder of forehead wrinkles. It was the first time she'd ever seen him put off-balance by anything she'd said. "We're guests of Pellicida of Senterwing."

"Good Heavens," he murmured, startled and bemused.

"The horses are at the end of the causeway...."

"Just a moment, my dear." And turning, he pushed aside the concealing boards. To Caris' utter horror, he dashed back across the open water to the outfall again.

As he came splashing back, Caris snapped, "You're not only mad, you're a fool! Every sasennan in town must be near the gates..."

"Nonsense." Antryg scraped the mud gingerly from the thing he held in his hand. "The Bishop had this made specially for me and it would be churlish to throw it away. Put this in your backpack, would you, my dear? We'll wrap it in lead when we get to safety..." He handed it to Joanna. It was the iron collar bearing the Sigil of Darkness.

They made their way back to the horses without further mishap, Antryg cheerfully directing the one group of sasenna they met on the causeway toward the town. Wet, cold, aching and exhausted almost to numbness, she scrambled up onto her horse behind Antryg, put her arms around his waist, and leaned her cheek against his bony back. She felt she could have gone to sleep that way and slept for days as the horses jogged into the windy darkness toward Larkmoor and what she knew would be only a relative and temporary safety.

One more subroutine successfully completed, she thought tiredly. They had rescued Antryg—or Antryg had rescued himself—alive, whole, and sane, or at least as sane as Antryg had ever been.

Now their troubles would really begin.

CHAPTER VIII

"SO WHAT WAS IT THAT FINALLY CONVINCED YOU THAT I was telling the truth?"

Extravagantly gowned in a robe of plum-colored velvet that had originally been made for the Emperor Hieraldus, Antryg sat at one side of a small table laid for high tea, in the course of which he had made his appearance, interrupting his fellow conspirators. Though it was early yet in the afternoon, the drawing room lamps at Larkmoor Manor had been lit on sideboards of carved maple, the glow of them pale against the uncertain grayness of the stormy daylight outside. Now and then wind would sigh along the northern wall of the house, and Joanna, if she stood too near that wall, found it cold to her touch.

With the blackish dye washed out of it, Antryg's hair was far grayer than Joanna remembered, and with the loss of flesh the tracework of lines around his eyes and running back into his hair had deepened to gullies. In the daylight, he looked thinner and badly the worse for wear. The fur collar of the robe framed a three-inch band of sores and raw flesh around his neck above the too-prominent points of his collarbone; the big bones of his wrists, similarly wealed, stood out from the wasted flesh. Even so, his hands, cradling the creamy smoothness of an eggshell teacup, had all their old lightness; and behind the cracked

125

spectacles, his gray eyes were daft as ever, but at peace.

"We've seen Suraklin," Joanna said quietly. "You were right. He needed an accomplice from my world, a programmer. No wonder you thought it was me. But he took over Gary, my—my boyfriend."

"Ah," Antryg said softly. "The one who got computers to do his stealing for him."

She nodded a little wearily, recalling the details of Gary's dealings with Suraklin, meticulously cataloged in the DARKMAGE files from the viewpoints of both seducer and seduced. Gary had never stood a chance.

For a moment she sat staring into her teacup, tracing the curves of its gilded handle with one fingertip. Then she took a deep breath, set it down, and plunged into a dispassionate account of her own belated conclusions and adventures, with Pella filling in, awkwardly but without omissions, her own experiences and suspicions of Cerdic's new Spiritual Advisor, the night at the gambling rooms, and the storm.

"The damn thing is that there's no proof," Joanna concluded. "It's only little things, nothing that can be pointed to. But these—these spells of deadness—are still taking place, though most people don't believe they're objective and not subjective. I'm starting to find that a little hard to believe."

"Are you?" Antryg said mildly. "Most people are firmly convinced there *is* a difference between objective and subjective reality and would find it extremely hard to believe otherwise. You're rather like someone looking down at a maze from the top, instead of wandering through it. There's really quite a nice maze at the Citadel of Wizards in the north, by the way. And since there's no proof of when any particular abomination appeared in this world, I suppose they're all credited to me whilst I was roving about loose at the end of the summer. I expect that, now I've escaped, the attempts on Pharos' life will start up again."

He set down his teacup and rubbed his fingers as if for warmth or to massage away some chronic ache. "I suppose there have been none since my capture? I didn't think so. Verisimilitude has always been Suraklin's strong point."

He glanced across the table at Caris, dressed in snuff-colored servant's livery and silently buttering and rebuttering a muffin which he clearly had no intention of eating. "I'm sorry, Caris," Antryg said softly.

The young man raised eyes like those of an injured wolf, ready to savage the hands extended to help him.

Antryg went on, "Suraklin destroyed a man we both loved very much—raped him of body and mind, used them for his own purposes, and threw him away when he was done. But the fact remains that I *was* the one who killed what was left."

Caris shook his head. Muffled and unwontedly low, he said, "If I'd found him the way the Emperor now is, I'd have done the same."

"I suppose Suraklin was counting on that—the fact that I couldn't stay long in that world and would never leave him there like that, helpless among strangers. But of course, whether I killed him or let him live, either way I'd have been blamed for it. Pella . . ." He looked across at the big girl, who sat quietly stroking Kyssha's head which lay on her velvet lap. "You were as much wronged by him as any of us, and it's worse, I suppose, since you just happened to be in the wrong place at the wrong time and married to the wrong person. Thank you for being good enough to help us. Caris, Joanna . . ." He turned simply to face them. "I do owe you my life. I wish I had a better way of thanking you than immediately hauling you both into greater danger with me, but I haven't. I'm sorry about Gary also," he added, turning to Joanna, who sat on the tapestried hassock at his side. "From the little I saw of him, he was never much of a man, but I suppose he was the best man he could be under the circumstances that made his life."

Joanna sighed, feeling as if she were seeing Gary clearly for the first time. "Not even that, I'm afraid." She reached out and laid her hand over his.

The night had been sleety and cold. In the late autumn dawnlight, Joanna had slipped out of the room Pella had given her, stealing down the silent corridor to the one where Antryg slept. A fire burned low in the grate there, its wickering the only sound but for the moan of the wind around the eaves and brief staccato of rain. Antryg had been in bed under a gray satin comforter, his hair close-curled still with the dampness of washing, profoundly asleep.

It was all Joanna had meant to do—to see him, to reaffirm to herself the fact that against all the odds in the world he was still alive. It had been her litany and her hope for two dreadful, endless months that she hadn't done the irrevocable and that somehow, somewhere, they would meet again.

Tomorrow or the day after, they would have to face Suraklin, break into whatever depths beneath his ancient Citadel housed his stolen computer, destroy him, or, as Caris said—as Joanna uneasily feared—die trying. Her thoughts flinched away from what would happen to her if she survived her own defeat as his prisoner.

But there in that still bedchamber of amber and gray, all of it seemed impossibly distant and very unreal. Yesterday she had been jolting miserably in Pella's phaeton, aching with fear and sleeplessness, feeling that the journey would never end. Tomorrow might see her, Caris, and Antryg dead, all hope and magic perished forever. Today, this morning, went no further than Antryg's preposterous profile against the bed linen, the whisper of his breathing and the spattering of wind and rain.

She had still been standing there, leaning one shoulder against the carved cherrywood bedpost, when his eyes had opened.

* * *

He had been sleeping again when she left. In fact, he had slept most of the day, and Joanna had the impression, looking now at the harsh lines around his eyes as he bent to refill his teacup from the ostentatiously garlanded pot, that he could have slept for the next twenty-four hours without trouble. He looked very tired.

Pella said gravely, "You know, they're going to put the blame for all of it on you now—the storm, the abominations, and the failure of the harvest." She held a fragment of buttered muffin out to Kyssha, and the little dog accepted it with as much condescension as if she hadn't been watching every bite with tears of bogus starvation in her eyes. "If you could work enough magic in the Tower to escape, they'll figure you could work enough to do all that."

Antryg sighed. "I know. But, of course, I didn't escape by magic. I couldn't use magic—not in the Tower, not with the Sigil welded against my flesh."

"Then how did you get out of the chains?"

He shrugged. "Picked the locks. Three or four years ago, the Bishop went through some kind of scare and threatened to have me chained; the rings had been in the wall there for hundreds of years. As a precaution, I took apart some of the toys I used to spend my time making and fashioned about a dozen picklocks from the wires in them. I hid them in the cracks of the floor and the walls all around the rings, and down in other areas of the Tower when I could get to them. And since I couldn't pass the Sigil on the door, I pretty much had the freedom of the Tower in those days.

"I picked the locks of my chains fairly regularly, to pilfer things from the guardroom downstairs—the uniform coat and breeches, a razor to cut off my hair and beard, and an outer coat to hide the fact that I wasn't wearing any weapons. I used a razor to whittle a stick to make the right sword-line under my coat—if I'd actually stolen a sword, it would have been missed, and they'd have searched the place. I'd stuff everything up under the rafters when I wasn't working on it. With no windows the place was pretty dark, but of course I can see in the dark and none of the guards, not being mageborn, could."

"I'd been doing this for over a month—as soon as I got my hands working again, in fact. For weeks all I did was crouch in a corner, mumbling to myself while I grew my beard and worked at my fingers. The Inquisitors had dislocated most of them, but only four were actually broken. I think they'll always be a bit crooked now. I had to wrap them up twisted again so the guards would think I was still crippled and not watch me too closely."

Caris glanced up cynically from some private contemplation. "And you played mad for the same reason?"

"For a number of reasons," Antryg admitted, his long fingers moving unconsciously over the dark fur of the velvet robe's cuffs. "The important thing was to keep any of the guards from knowing how I really look. For one thing, I'm nearly six foot three. No matter how I was disguised, I wouldn't have got ten yards if anyone in the Tower had ever seen me when I wasn't hunched over and sitting down. It's why I had the visions of obscure saints."

"*What?*" Pella demanded, half-laughing. Joanna had forgotten to mention to her that conversations with Antryg were apt to contain several wildly disparate topics per sentence.

He regarded her with his mild, mad eyes, as if surprised she didn't see the connection. "Most Church sasenna are halfway to being monks. After two years in a monastery, I could describe saints that only other novices would recognize. Did you know Saint Kalwiddoes was supposed to have a metal nose? He allegedly lost the original for his faith; one calls upon him to cure sinus problems. Eventually I won enough sympathy among some of the Church guards to prod the Bishop into changing the lot every few weeks."

Caris sniffed disgustedly. "It was all a blind, then."

Antryg was silent for a moment. Then he said, "Not really." Outside the window, the bare trees that surrounded Larkmoor thrashed uneasily in the wind, their black branches clawing like witch fingers at the mottled sky. "There were times when it all came home to me—where I was, and what was happening outside . . . Moments of sanity, I suppose, when I realized the truth of my position and my prospects. But one can't pound on the walls and scream all the time.

"And I was so tired. The Sigil of Darkness not only eats a wizard's magic, it devours him through it. The thing was literally killing me by inches. I could barely eat; I couldn't sleep, and when I did finally pass out from sheer exhaustion, the dreams made me wish I hadn't." He sat silent again, his head bowed, the white light from the windows glancing across the round lenses of his spectacles like circles of cracked and dirty ice. He had, Joanna noticed, acquired a pair of earrings as well as the Emperor's robe, solitaire diamonds of well over two carats apiece which flickered when he looked up again. "I had to get that thing off me," he said simply. "I had to break out. Even if no warrant of execution was ever issued, it was only a matter of time before I became too weak to do so."

"But the question is," Caris said suspiciously, "*how* did you break out? You say no wizard can pass the Seal of the Dead God. But it was on the door of the Tower as well. Even if you'd managed to disguise yourself as a guard, shave off your beard, cut your hair, and dye it, too—What did you use for dye, by the way?"

"Lampblack and dye soaked from the cover of a stolen book of scriptures. I'm told in Trembergil there's a root that will turn gray hair black permanently, if it's eaten, and Queen Darthirambis II once paid four elephants, ten lengths of second-quality silk, and two dancing boys for enough to cover the palm of her hand. The guards were forever stealing things from each other, the Church sasenna from the Council's and vice versa. No one noticed my thefts."

"But even if you managed to do all that," Caris said doggedly, "and went down among them with impunity, *how did you walk through the door of the Tower?*"

Antryg said nothing for a time, absentmindedly rubbing his fingers again. Joanna, glancing sideways at the round, brownish mark that seemed to have been burned into the galled skin of his throat, said softly, "Desensitization, wasn't it? They do that in my world as a cure for phobias."

A half smile flicked at the extravagant curve of his lips. "It was the one thing I was afraid of—that when it came down to the moment, I wouldn't be able to do it. And I almost couldn't. One never becomes desensitized—not to the Sigil of Darkness. Its hold never slacks. But I'd had it on me, welded against my flesh, for over two months. If I hadn't gone through that—if I didn't know that the alternative of walking past the Sigil on the door was enduring God knows how much longer of it before I finally died—I couldn't have done it. It took me about five minutes of standing there to work up my nerve as it was. But fortunately, I'd already roused the Tower with the news of my own disappearance, and the place was in such chaos that no one noticed."

He glanced over at Caris, half-apologetically, as if he sensed in the young man's folded arms and crossed knees his furious disapproval. The sasennan had come prepared to perform an heroic rescue and, like Joanna, still illogically felt slightly cheated. "Once I got through the door, I joined in the search while they ransacked the Tower and its grounds. I'd shoved my old robes and my cut-off hair and beard up into my hidey-hole under the rafters so the idea of disguise wouldn't occur to anyone. They thought they were looking for a barefoot and ragged cripple. Without my spectacles, I could see just well enough not to run into walls. Of course no sasennan wears spectacles. I'm told there have been those who've killed themselves as flawed when their eyes began to harden at fifty. Eventually I joined the parties going out to search the hills. Since they'd been changed so often, not only did no guard there remember what I'd looked like when I was brought in, before I grew my beard back, but they weren't able to identify each other by sight, either. After that..." He shrugged. "All that remained was to lose the other guards, put on my spectacles, slip into Kymil through the sewers, and pilfer a hacksaw. I had to wait until night, because in Kymil there are plenty of people who would recognize me —aside from the Church dogs, that is. But it's always easy to hide in a city."

He subsided back into his chair, the embroidered velvet settling around him like a royal mantle. Cradling his teacup once more in his big, deft hands, he stared into its henna depths as if he could read his own future there, as he had that of countless travelers on the Angelshand road to buy dinner for himself and his companions. And perhaps, thought Joanna worriedly, he could. At any rate, a small upright line twitched into existence between his brows, and he set the cup quickly aside.

She wondered what he'd seen there.

In time Caris broke the silence. "You know that was your last chance."

"Oh, yes." His deep voice was almost absentminded as his gray eyes flicked back to the young man's face. "By this time, there will be a mad-dog warrant out for me. If they find me now, they'll kill me out of hand. So this is quite literally our last chance to stop Suraklin—not merely to destroy his computer, which I'm positive is hidden beneath the ruins of his old Citadel at the node of the energy-lines, but to finish him." His lips pulled slightly in a smile again, but for one moment his eyes were quite sane—gazing, as he had said, when he spoke of his fits of screaming despair in the Tower, quite truthfully at his position and his prospects. Then he let it go, and the old, luminous mad-

ness of hope returned. "This time we'll just have to succeed."

"It came on very quickly, didn't it?"

Caris looked up, startled out of his own reflections,
from his absent gazing at the slatey shadows of the doorway through which Antryg and Joanna had passed. Pella
had been so silent that for a time he had felt he was alone
with the wind-mutter and the ruins of the tea, but now he
saw that the tall girl still sat on the pink silk settee where
she had been during tea and the subsequent conference, the
sleeping Kyssha cradled in her lap.

"'Like a storm from out of the east,'" he quoted scrip-
ture, knowing without asking what the girl meant.

She smiled, half-amused, "Like the second fence of an
in-and-out, really, that's hidden behind the first until your
horse is just about on top of it."

He recognized the cant term. "Do you hunt?"

Ruefulness flickered in the fine hazel eyes. "Not really.
I've always had too much sympathy for the fox, but the
riding was the closest thing to flying I could get. It was
another thing Mother and my aunt the Queen never ap-
proved of."

He returned her grin. "Along with being a sasennan."

"Well, Mother was terrified I'd get a cut on my face.
When I was ten I wanted a scar like my cousin Tybal's in
the worst way. I've been admiring yours all the way down
from Angelshand," she added sincerely, and Caris touched
the old slash on his cheekbone and laughed, picturing the
very well-brought-up daughter of the Royal House of Senterwing trying to convince her horrified parents that she
ought to have one.

She moved the stiff taffeta ruffles of her petticoat and
underskirt with her toe, and the shining fabric whispered to
itself against a lull in the wind outside. "I suppose putting
all our energies into reaching here before the Witchfinder

did and worrying how we were going to get Antryg out of the Tower . . . Is he always like that?"

"He was positively sedate, today," Caris said dourly, and Pella laughed again.

Then, soberly, she said, "I suppose it hid the real task."

"Not entirely." Caris' voice was very quiet. "But it made it possible not to think about it." It was the first time he had admitted, to himself or anyone else, that it was an event upon which he tried not to dwell.

"Do you think it's at the ruins of his Citadel?"

He sighed again and rose to his feet, Pella getting up too, Kyssha now tucked in her arms. "It has to be," he said. "I'm going to check the perimeter of the grounds before it gets dark. Would you like to come?"

It was something Caris had done at the posthouses where they had spent the nights or part of the nights, something, in fact, he did automatically when spending a night in an unfamiliar or potentially hostile place. It was a kind of patrol, an investigation of where things were and from what directions danger might or could come. At the posthouses, Pella had come with him on these rounds. He had welcomed this, partly because Pella, with her early training, would be the closest thing to a fighting ally he'd have if it came to trouble. In spite of her apparent clumsiness and absentmindedness in more domestic matters, the girl was silent, deft, and catlike on her feet.

But more than that, he had simply found himself glad of her company. In the gray times of deadness, it was good not to be alone; even outside of them, there had been times when he'd found his awareness of the upcoming battle with Suraklin, the knowledge that he would most likely die in it, more than he could hold at bay himself. He had broken his vows and had not even the strength of the Way of the Sasenna to comfort him. And in any case, he reminded himself, to seek comfort was not of the Way.

Pella slipped a smoke-colored cloak over her gold-beaded green gown; they moved like two shadows from the

side door of the house to the nearest of the line of bare elm
trees which surrounded Larkmoor on all sides, a windbreak
against the cutting Sykerst gales. In the summer, the grass
there was scythed close; now along the north and east
sides, last week's dirty snow lay in a filthy and broken
windrow, a frozen crust wide enough that it could not be
leaped by a man. From the shelter of the trees, Caris
squinted against the searing wind to study it for tracks,
mindful that the sasenna of the Council and now the
Witchfinder's men would be everywhere on the moor. But
there was no sign of tracks, either on the crusted snow or
on the iron-hard earth beyond.

They checked the outside of the stables, unobtrusively
avoiding the notice of the grooms and coachmen, and
moved on to the fodderbarn, out past the line of trees and
commanding the best views both of the nearby hills and of
the house. There were no tracks; Caris checked the small
chips of wood which he had imbedded in the half-frozen
mud of the threshold that morning and found them undisturbed. Pella stood out of the wind against the doorpost,
wrapped in the thick folds of her cloak, her breath a blowing cloud of white against the dimness of the barn and the
fading light from the moving sky.

"Would you do better to wait a day or two before going
out to the Citadel?" she asked, and Caris glanced up from
his study.

"We shouldn't have waited this long," he said bluntly.
"Yes, we needed a day's rest; Antryg was at the end of his
strength when we found him, and none of us in shape to do
what we have to do. But two days, or three days, won't
mend that. Suraklin's no fool. According to Joanna, Suraklin will be on the other side of the Void, in her world—
or should be. But we have no guarantee of that. And every
day that passes increases the chance that he'll come back
and hear of Antryg's escape. We might—just might—be
able to make it through whatever traps he's set up to guard
his Citadel, for Joanna to poison his computer and then lay

in wait there for him. But if he is there before us—if he knows that Antryg is coming—we'll stand no chance."

"That wasn't what I meant," Pella said apologetically and brushed a tendril of black hair from her face. "It's just that you might want to wait for better weather."

Caris stood up and grinned. "We'd be like three birds in a cellar, tucking our heads under our wings and waiting for sunrise. It's not going to be better until spring."

"Oh." Pella looked a little blankly out into that bitter landscape, her expression momentarily like that of a child who finds that coffee doesn't taste at all the way it smells.

Caris came over to stand beside her, shaking out the pleated linen ruffles of his shirt cuffs. After the relative shelter of the barn, the wind was stinging on his face, cutting like a knife through the coarse brownish wool of his livery. "I'm told people from the Sykerst miss it when they live in other lands," he remarked, shaking his head wonderingly. "They can keep it."

She glanced back at him. "Then you're not from here?"

He shook his head. "I was born in the Wheatlands, the black-earth country down on the Strebwell River. It's open country, but not like this—flat as your hand for miles, with deep black soil. Where there's water, the trees grow thick, in the marshes, and the bottomlands by the streams. It's a safe country—gentle. In the winter, Ratbane and I would wander for miles, with the full moon turning the snow luminous, as far as you can see to the edge of the sky, and the air so still you could hear a dog bark three villages away."

He stopped, his throat closing hard. It had been years since he'd thought of the country that was his home, years since he'd remembered the aching peace of those still nights.

"They wouldn't have let you ramble alone, would they?" he asked after a time.

Her smile warmed not only her great hazel eyes, but all the strong features of her face, the aquiline nose and the full-lipped mouth. "I wasn't supposed to," she said, "but I did. I used to sneak away and go bird shooting with my brothers and Cousin Tybal when we were staying in the country; sometimes I'd just go by myself. I enjoyed the clean skill of it—I like using things, tools, weapons—but more than that, I think I just liked to be alone and not have to worry about how I looked. And courts are so noisy." Her black brows pulled down over her nose, and a pain line like a pin scratch sprang into being between them. "It's as if people can't think of anything better to do with a summer evening and a garden than invite half the countryside to a garden party."

She was quiet for a moment, staring into the sunless distance, as if past the hills she could see the garden of which she spoke in the apple-green silence of a summer twilight. In her eyes, which were level with his own, Caris could see the silvery shine of tears. After a time she said, "If Suraklin succeeds in establishing this machine of his, that will all go away, won't it? No one will ever feel that —that magic—again."

"No," said Caris. Then, impulsively, "Will you come with us?"

She turned her head quickly; for one instant, he saw the leap of joy in her eyes, the warrior's eagerness for action. Then she looked away, so quickly her black hair made a sharp slithering over the collar of her cloak; he was close enough to her now that he could feel her tremble. "I can't."

"I'm sorry," Caris said instantly, realizing belatedly what he had asked. Only for a moment, it had seemed right, and the rightness had answered him from her eyes. "I shouldn't have . . ."

"It isn't that." Her eyes met his again. Now, clearly, he saw in them that haunted look he'd seen before in the last day or so of the journey and riding that afternoon in the hills—the despair of some unwanted certainty that could no longer be denied. "If it was just me, I would," she went on steadily. "It isn't that I want to fight to protect Pharos' life, though I know from what Gaire—Suraklin—was always hinting to me that he is in danger. He's a cruel man, vicious . . . I suppose I want to do this for—Rightness? Goodness? Do you believe in goodness?"

"I believe in evil," Caris said quietly. "And I believe that Suraklin has to be stopped." Here was another, he realized, who was more than a line fighter, more even than a campaign strategist like Joanna.

She looked away from him, her mouth flinching with an effort not to tremble. "It's just that I can't risk it." She went on, small and remote, as if trying to get quickly over pain or shame, "I think I'm carrying Pharos' child."

Anger hit Caris like a wave of night, disproportionate, illogical rage and revulsion, as if she had confessed to some filthy act. With an effort, he bit back words he knew would hurt her; she caught his arm as he whirled to storm through the door.

Her voice was desperate. "Caris . . ."

In the brittle light, tears shone on her face. He was breathing hard, the air cuttingly cold in his nostrils and lungs; everything in him was consumed with smothering heat. Confused, it flashed through his mind to wonder why this should be; the answer hit him like a thrown bucket of ice water, and in the next second, he saw that answer mirrored in her eyes.

It sobered him, the rage dissolving into horror and a grief he could not define. He felt as if he'd stumbled, accidently dropping and breaking something which he'd never known he had until it was gone, and which could never be replaced. In one instant the world was all changed from what it had been. Even then, he knew, there was no going back. Hoarsely, shakily, he stammered, "Pella, I can't do this."

She didn't need to ask what he meant. It was as if they had both fought the knowledge of it for days. "I know." Her greenish eyes met his, dark in the sweet-smelling gloom. "I know you need your hate to keep you strong—

to keep you alive, maybe, when you go to the Citadel to-morrow. But—" She shivered suddenly, and looked away from him, struggling against tears that it was not the Way of the Sasenna to shed. Tiny and choked, she whispered, "But please don't hate me."

They stood at arm's length, facing one another in the darkness of the barn while the ashy light bled away out-side. He felt a surge of hatred against Pharos for putting that fear into those fearless eyes. Then he stepped back to her and took her in his arms, willing himself desperately not to feel what he felt while she laid her head on his shoulder and cried.

"I had meant not to do this."

It was dark. Outside, the rain was falling, cold and steady now, with sudden splatterings where the wind flung it against the house wall in handfuls. A couple of candles burned at random out of the dozen or so on the desk and highboy. Antryg had lit them without getting up from the bed when the night began to close in.

"Does that mean you're going to press charges for rape?" Joanna looked up with feigned concern from the circle of his arms.

Antryg drew himself up, very much on his dignity, save for the wicked twinkle far back in his gray eyes. Then he sighed and let his head drop back to the pillow lace, his grip tightening around her shoulders. "It means that I don't want to make things more difficult for you than they al-ready are."

"Well," Joanna said consideringly, "we're going out to Suraklin's Citadel tomorrow; we're going to have to get through whatever defenses he's set up around his computer and keep them at bay long enough for me to program the worm into the system. After we take care of that, we settle down and wait for him to show up—if he isn't there de-fending the thing already. I've got Suraklin after me, and you've got the Church, the Regent, the Council, and the

Witchfinders after you, any of whom will be ready to nail me as your accomplice, plus any random abominations that happen to be around . . . It's hard to see how things *could* get more difficult, unless we get tangled up with invading aliens from another planet, or a crowd of peasants with torches. But I'll take your word for it."

He regarded her severely. "You know perfectly well what I mean."

"I know perfectly well that you're afraid I'll be hurt."

"Well, yes," he admitted, twining a tendril of her fair hair around one of his bony fingers and studying the resultant play of shadows thoughtfully. "But considering what we're up against, there's a good chance we're both going to be hurt and hurt badly. There isn't really anything either of us can do about that, except take the usual precautions and hope for the best. I have a general idea of what waits for us out at the Citadel, since I helped establish many of its original defenses, and it's not something I'd care to take any of my friends into. But I certainly can't deprogram the thing myself, and we need a warrior to watch both our backs. Neither you nor I has the option, as Caris and Pella do, of simply retreating."

"Caris won't retreat," she said softly. "Nor will Pella."

"No," he agreed. "They are souls who don't know the meaning of physical fear. But for them the danger isn't the same. Though I daresay Suraklin would use either of them as a tool, he wouldn't seek to establish the all-devouring grip on their minds that he did on Gary's—that he seeks to do on yours."

Joanna shivered, remembering the disjointed recollections of the Dark Mage's slow takeover, inscribed with clinical exactness by both perpetrator and victim in their separate files.

After a moment Antryg went on, "The whole time I was in the Tower, I was desperately frightened for you—frightened that Suraklin would get you under his influence somehow without your realizing what was happening until it was too late."

She was silent, drawing the soft, tatted pillow lace again and again through her small fingers. It was the screaming of his soul, Magister Magus had said, when the Sigil had touched his flesh, that she had heard in her dream . . . "You didn't hate me?"

The distant glow of the candles threw the long shadows of his lashes on his cheeks, as his gaze seemed to go out beyond those floating points of light. Then he looked down at her again. "I lived with Suraklin for eight years," he reminded her. "I grew to manhood in his household. I saw the kind of things he could manipulate people into doing." His jaw tightened momentarily, with shame and bitter anger. "Myself included. No, I didn't hate you. Mind you," he added suddenly, "when I was trying to talk you into letting me go, I was angry enough to knock your head against the wall."

Joanna laughed, and for a time they did not talk. The candles burned down in fluted columns of white wax over the shelled sea goddesses of their holders. Distantly they heard a harpsichord being played somewhere in the rooms below and muffled voices, Caris' and Pella's. A servant's footfalls creaked on a distant backstair. The rain eased to a trickle. In the glowing jewelbox silence of the room, even the wickering of the fire seemed loud.

For all intents and purposes, Joanna thought, the future ended with tonight. This warmth, this silence, might be all that they would ever have.

Tomorrow she would do what she had feared all along she must—walk into the heart of Suraklin's power and put herself in the one place where he could most easily get her.

But like Antryg, standing trapped between the abomination of the Sigil on the Tower door and the knowledge that, if he did not face it, its twin would remain welded to his flesh, she knew she truly had no option. If Suraklin were not destroyed, sooner or later he would seek her.

As if he read her thoughts, Antryg said quietly, "If we manage to demolish the computer without getting ourselves killed, and if it's possible to do so safely, I want you and Caris to come back here tomorrow. I don't think your presence will help me against him..." He hesitated, as if debating within himself how much of the truth to speak, then sighed. "And I don't think I'll be able to protect you from him."

"I see," Joanna said softly and did. She reached up and touched his chest, her sun-browned hand dark against the marble whiteness of his skin. "That's why you didn't want to—to tie me more closely to you, to make me feel committed to you—to let me love you. You don't expect to survive meeting Suraklin, do you?"

His gray eyes, enormous without their protective lenses, avoided hers; the candlelight caught a facet of his diamond earrings, held steady for a moment, a burning point of many-colored light. Then he sighed, and looked back at her with a half-rueful grin. "Frankly, my dear, I don't see any way that I can."

CHAPTER IX

THOUGH SHE HAD TRAVELED THREE TIMES THROUGH THE hills of the Sykerst, Joanna did not believe she had ever seen anything so desolate as the emptiness that surrounded what had once been the Citadel of Suraklin. Elsewhere the hills might be barren, the grass without life or color, combed like a dead dog's hair by the incessant winds, but at least the terrible silence had been broken by occasional signs of life. From Pella's carriage, she'd seen the start of rabbits in the thin clumps of naked birches which grew in the small pockets of soil in the bedrock; by the sluggish black streams near the Silent Tower, the prints of muskrat and weasel had latticed the half-frozen mud. At first sight a uniform pewter, the hills had a startling variation of color —mauves and sepias, the cobalt of shadow, and the occasional rich emerald of lichens clinging to the cold-cracked rocks.

Here there was nothing. In the wide dell with its scattered stringers of broken stone, its buckled pavements long veiled in a wind-flattened shroud of rotting weeds, and its crumbling pits and trenches like suppurating gray wounds, the only sound was the wind thrumming over stone and hissing in the dead grass. The jingle of the bridle-bits sounded very loud as the horses tossed their heads, made nervous by the silence, and the faint creak of Caris' sword belt as he turned suddenly at a noise that he hadn't really heard.

"That's very odd," Antryg murmured, frowning.

Caris looked quickly over his shoulder, then back in the direction of Antryg's gaze. "What is?" His quiet voice had an edge of fear to it. "I don't see anything amiss."

"Neither do I," the wizard said. "That's what's odd." He pushed his crazy schoolboy spectacles a little farther up on his long nose and dismounted with the light grace of a cavalryman. "Leave the horses here and follow me," he said softly. "It wouldn't do to get separated in this place." He turned to help Joanna down from her horse; the elderly blue roan, though the quietest Pella's stables had to offer, was sized for a woman of the Princess' height.

"We should split up," Caris said, his voice rough with nervousness. "You said yourself the spells you showed me this morning should keep Suraklin from scrying me out from afar. As long as Joanna keeps her backpack with the Sigil in it on her, he shouldn't be able to find her, either, protective wrapping or no protective wrapping. The Church knows whose pupil you were. They'll be expecting you to come back here. The hasu saw you beneath the walls of Kymil—they know you escaped dressed as a guard. If the Church sasenna see a search party sticking close together instead of spreading out . . ."

"Would you wander away from your friends to search Suraklin's Citadel?" Antryg inquired. "Particularly for an escaped renegade wizard who's known to be mad? Don't be obtuse." He turned away, a lanky figure in the crisp black-and-gold uniform of the Regent's sasenna, his sword —a real one now, not the whittled fake he'd worn in his earlier disguise—making the characteristic hard line under his long-skirted black greatcoat. "My only concern is that search parties came here yesterday and got caught in the place's defenses, whatever they are. You stay here," he added, suddenly turning back and catching his horse's bridle. He stroked the beast's forehead briefly. "And you," he added. His fingers brushed lightly the foreheads of the other two horses.

Ten yards away, Joanna looked back. The three animals stood grouped together, heads up, ears pricked, looking about them nervously, but they remained in place. She shook her head and followed Antryg along the broken, pitted ground.

From the hills above, riding down the track from the Silent Tower, the Citadel had been almost invisible—not as if a mist hid it, but as if Joanna's mind and eyes had simply skipped over that great, broken circle in the shallow dip in the hills. Caris had spoken of that effect, present even long after Suraklin's power had been rooted from the land. In the Dark Mage's heyday it was said men could ride straight through the gates and not notice where they were until the iron portals slammed shut behind them.

As they approached the remains of the outer walls, Joanna was conscious of the hammering the place had taken, the avalanche of power needed to destroy it so thoroughly. Huge sections of the ground had collapsed into the pits dug below, leaving vast, shallow subsidences half filled with rubble and knee-deep weeds. Chunks of stone the size of truck trailers scattered the landscape, half driven into the ground hundreds of yards from the nearest foundations. Weeds covered huge areas, a filthy carpet concealing treacherous breaks in the ground.

The rain had warmed the air, melting some of the stagnant brown ice where the land lay lowest. The surrounding hills sheltered the place from the wind. As they approached, cautious, ready for anything, Joanna was conscious of the nauseating foetor of decay that hung in the raw air.

Beside her, Antryg was tense, listening, it seemed, with senses beyond the human, sniffing the air with his long nose as if seeking some characteristic odor that would warn him when the first defenses closed in.

"Curious," she heard him mutter. "But logical, when

you come to think of it. Too many people come near this place to advertise that there's something here worth guarding."

"And then again," Caris added softly, "I've heard it was Suraklin's way to lure and lull at the same time by an appearance of harmlessness, until it was too late to retreat."

Antryg rubbed one side of his nose. "Well, there is that," he admitted. "Though with two of us mageborn, I think we'll have some warning."

"And you think that will do us any good?"

The mad wizard grinned. "Oh, probably not. But the object isn't to retreat anyway, so we needn't worry about it."

Sourly, Caris touched the .45 and the brace of na-aar pistols shoved in his belt—his sword was naked already in his right hand—and followed them without further comment among the hushed decay of the ruins.

They had spread out a little, Antryg picking his way unerringly through the maze of broken, knee-high courses of stone which had once been walls, Joanna keeping uneasily close to his side and fighting the urge to hang onto his coat skirts. In one place she saw crumbled slabs of rusted ironwork half buried in black weeds and fallen stone. . . .

"That was the kitchen," Antryg explained quietly. "Those pits behind it are where the storerooms stood. I used to hide there when I'd displeased him. Not, of course, that anyone could hide from him for very long, but being mageborn myself helped." He paused, a frown buckling his forehead as he scanned what was now little more than a reef of shattered rubble, seeing it, Joanna knew, momentarily as it had been—gray, massive, turretted, toothed, the stronghold of the terrible old man he had so desperately feared and loved.

She said, very softly, "Do you miss him?"

He looked down at her, startled. His brows, reddish as his hair had long since ceased to be, pulled together for a moment. Then he said, "I've always missed him. Missed him as I first knew him, missed what I thought I had. Even when I realized I didn't—that in fact, the care he showed for me was only because he knew I'd respond to care . . . I don't know. I still wanted it. But after that, it was difficult to believe in anyone else's caring." He rubbed his hands in their shabby, fingerless gloves, an absentminded gesture as the cold bit into the damaged tendon and bone.

"It was all right, I thought—I could put up with the beatings, and the bloodlettings, the spells and rites I performed in the dark of the moon, the blackest kind of magic, things I knew were evil beyond description . . . I could put up with that if he loved me as he said he did. I'd had a rather unhappy childhood. I suppose I felt honored to be given that love, trusted with the emotions so powerful a mage never dared to show anyone else . . ." The long, sensitive mouth quirked slightly. "Rather like a trout feeling honored to be trusted with an angler's worm. Because none of them were real. They were only facsimiles, copied from what he had seen others sacrifice themselves for." He sighed and added wryly, "They were just copied dazzlingly well. He used to take my blood, to bring some of his— creations—to life. There was a time when I'd have let him take it all."

Around them the Citadel waited, wreathed in its uneasy silence. Joanna remembered that it was built on a node where the energy-tracks crossed, lines that would feed the life-forces of two worlds into its magically electrified heart. Perhaps that was what Antryg and Caris listened for, feeling the pulse of intangible forces along the unseen veins of the earth.

At length Antryg went on, as if speaking half to himself, "Salteris told me they made a bonfire of all his possessions, everything they could find—books, implements of magic, jewels, paintings. Beautiful things, things he had deeply loved. He lived very intensely, you know. Everything about him had a burning quality that drew you and fascinated you. He would get almost literally drunk on the beauty of a cup or a gem or the angle of the sunset light. The high you get from working magic, the fascination of watching people play their intricate social games—he loved them with a passion I don't believe he ever felt for another human being. But of course, human beings are more difficult to control than possessions."

"He managed," she remarked.

"Yes." Antryg sighed regretfully, his eyes returning to hers. "Yes, he did. It never surprised me that he wanted to live forever—that he would do almost anything rather than let that beauty go."

Was that why, Joanna wondered suddenly, Suraklin had chosen Antryg as his student, his slave, his victim? Because he, too, had that passionate delight in the mere drawing of breath? But it was not the same. There were things for which Antryg would cheerfully give up that brightly colored life, among them the thwarting of Suraklin's plans. Awkwardly, because she had never learned the right things to say, she reached out and took his hand and was rewarded with the fleet warmth of his smile.

"Antryg!" Caris' voice rang out sharply behind them. "Over here!"

The wizard swung around in a swirl of gold-braided black coat skirts. Caris stood on the lip of a shallow subsidence, blond hair flattened in a surge of wind, a look of shock and revulsion on his face. Joanna wondered briefly if his appearance might be some kind of trap, a lure set up by the Dark Mage's defenses; but after an almost imperceptible pause, Antryg put his arm around her shoulders and drew her along with him as he strode through the crunching weeds to see.

The thing that lay in the wide depression had been dead for weeks. When the wind fell briefly, the stench was terrible; Joanna drew back, nauseated, at the sight of the bloated, blackened face, orifices agape and filled with maggots and worms.

Antryg and Joanna exchanged a quick glance. Caris said softly, "An abomination. It must have come through the Void and walked straight into one of Suraklin's defenses." The track it had left in the weeds was still plain to see, the dead stems broken in a jagged swathe which began at the creature's body and ended, abruptly, less than a dozen feet away.

Cautiously, the wizard took a step forward and sank to one knee. "Fascinating," he said. "The maggots are dead."

Steeling herself, Joanna moved to his side. Both Antryg and Caris had been adamant that she not adopt the uniform of a sasennan, on the grounds that she'd never be able to maintain the imposture at close range—she was dressed in the breeches, shirt, and short crimson coat of one of the Regent's pages, the backpack on her back and the .38 shoved in one pocket. Her boots crackled in the brittle undergrowth as she hunkered down to look.

"They're tiny," she said after a moment. "They must have died the minute they began to feed." Her revulsion evaporated in academic puzzlement. "Look, there are dead flies on it, too."

She frowned at Antryg for a moment, then back at the carcass. "Could—could Suraklin's defenses have done that? Killed even the maggots that fed on it after it was dead?"

Antryg raised his head and studied the gray skyline. Like a gunsite on the far hills, the last two stones of the line that stretched toward the Silent Tower notched the pale air. Directly opposite, to the east, a single menhir leaned like a weary drunk. Then he looked back at the unspeakable, rotting thing. "I wonder," he said softly.

"More likely this *is* one of Suraklin's defenses." With the tip of his sword Caris touched what was clearly a mouth at the end of a collapsed pinkish tube. Teeth like chisels stood out from the black gums.

"But in that case, what killed it?"

Caris shrugged. "Sasenna? Witchfinders? Peelbone was

keeping an eye on the place before you ever escaped the first time. There's a lot of breakage in the weeds around here, but it's hard to say how old it is."

"Odd that he never ran into any defenses." Antryg stood up again, scanning the ash-colored tussocks of stone and earth around them, his gray eyes narrowed and uneasy behind his specs. "Very odd. Come along, my dear." He took Joanna's hand. "Caris, guard our backs if you will. Twelve feet was the usual distance between the trigger and the rear edge of the trap."

With these comforting words he began to pick his way cautiously back toward the ruins of what had been the main keep.

The outer walls of the Citadel keep had been well over fifteen feet thick. Their foundations formed a broken platform in whose splintered and riven cracks grew straggling weeds, now black and brittle as burned wires. From its edge, Joanna looked down into a chasm like an enormous open pit mine, a hundred and fifty feet across and easily as deep. Collapsed spills of rubble tracked its sides and made little heaps on the bottom around the brim of a silent tarn of standing water, enigmatically reflecting the silver sky. In places, fragments of old floors and vaulting clung to the stone sides of the pit, showing how many levels down the Citadel vaults had extended. Joanna counted seven of them. Beside her, Antryg was very silent.

"Had you ever come here since—since its destruction?"

He nodded. "Salteris and I came here—oh, years ago, when we traveled together. I didn't want to, but he insisted. I think he wanted to prove to me that Suraklin was truly dead—to exorcise the fear of him from my dreams. Ironic," he added, forcing lightness over the sudden flaw in his deep voice, "when you think of it."

Salteris' own experiences with the Dark Mage's Citadel couldn't have been anything he particularly wanted to relive, Joanna reflected, remembering the old Archmage's digitalized memories of what he had found there when he led the triumphant armies in. Yet he had come back to the place to help a frightened and half-demented youth readjust to the world, gently trying to lead him back to sanity. What had it been for Antryg to come into a room in the Silent Tower to greet someone who had cared that much for him and to see Suraklin looking at him from his eyes?

"I wish I could have known him," she said softly.

He glanced down at her with that same half-wary expression, like a nervous horse, afraid to trust. Then he sighed and put his hand briefly on her shoulder.

"There used to be a stairway over here," he said after a moment. "It was hidden behind a false niche near the hall fireplace and enough spells to darken the noonday sun. The wizards' army destroyed the top part of it but never found the rooms below. That's where it will be."

"What about the way you got us out when I first came?" Joanna asked. "An underground passageway..."

He shook his head. "That was a subsidiary hideout, connected to the main pits by miles of passage. I think Suraklin went straight there through the Void from Gary's —his mark was all over the room."

He took a step away along the brink of the huge pit, then hesitated. "I should leave you here," he said after a moment. "But I don't know what defenses will be in operation, or if there's a delay-trigger and it's already too late to escape. It's hard to believe Suraklin would leave it this late—unless he's down there himself, waiting..." He paused, and Joanna thought that, against his black coat collar with its gilded braid, he seemed very pale. It occurred to her that Suraklin's aim of killing Antryg might only have been a contingency plan if he could not take him—his first, chosen, and well-prepared victim—alive.

"The trouble is," Antryg went on, "I can't feel a thing amiss here, and that's making me very uneasy."

"It's making *you* uneasy?" Joanna said, with a shaky grin in spite of the uncomfortable slamming of her heart against her ribs.

He grinned back. "Stay close, and be ready to . . ." He stopped, his head coming up like a dog's that scents sudden peril. "Oh, pox."

"What is it?" Joanna whispered.

"The Witchfinders," he said softly. "Peelbone."

"Antryg . . ." Caris sprang lightly up to the top of the broken platform. "Can you hear it? Along the energy-track . . ."

"Peelbone, yes."

"Can you use some kind of spell . . .?"

"They have hasu with them. Besides, apart from blowing a trumpet I can't think of a better way to let Suraklin know I'm here. Look, there they are . . ."

He pointed at the dark line of shapes on the colorless gray of the northern slopes. There was a red splash, like a drop of blood—a Church dog's robes. One thin gray form among them spurred his horse and began to canter down the slope.

"They must have been watching through a spyglass from a distance," Antryg said, catching Joanna's hand and hurrying along the top of the platform. "Peelbone knows me, of course. He was in charge of obtaining my—confession."

"Look!" Caris pointed to the western slopes above the Citadel; a dozen black forms could be seen riding down them. There was a thin glitter of drawn weapons in the heatless light.

"Where are Suraklin's defenses now when we need them?" Antryg wondered aloud.

"Should we split up?"

"Good heavens, no! Make for the pits . . ."

Caris skidded to a stop. "Are you mad? If the defenses are anywhere, they'll be . . ."

Clear and thin as the cracking of ice, Peelbone's voice rang across the broken Citadel. "Windrose!" He drew rein momentarily on the edge of the buckled pavement of what had been the court before the main keep, rising in his stirrups, his wispy gray hair streaming in the restless tweak of the wind. His hat had blown off; his eyes were hard and colorless as glass. "I should have known you would come here, back to the hold of your master!" The sasenna and the hasu behind him, galloping hard, had almost reached the edge of the pavement; the Witchfinder put spurs to his lathered horse and started across.

With a thin whine of steel Caris' sword was in his hand.

What happened then was almost totally without warning. In later nightmares Joanna saw it again in slow-motion and realized then that it was a thing she had dimly taken for a domed hummock of weed-covered stone which moved, bursting upward into the air as the horse trod on it in a flurrying scatter of dirt. But at the time it seemed as if it came from nowhere—as if suddenly it was hanging over the Witchfinder and his terrified mount, a huge, dust-colored thing like a monster jellyfish, slobbering tentacles dangling . . .

Adrenaline locked her lungs and circulatory system shut even before Peelbone began screaming. Sasenna were converging from all directions. Antryg grabbed Joanna's arm and made a run for the ragged spill of fallen stone and weeds that had been the head of the secret stair. From the tail of her eye Joanna saw Peelbone's horse running frenziedly in circles, the tentacles raking its flesh and almost wholly enveloping the shrieking, clawing man on its back as the floating body of the abomination lowered itself, like the canopy of a vast parachute, down over Peelbone's head.

She had no time to see more. Deep under the weeds were the broken rubble of old stairs. She clung to the brittle stems for balance as Antryg guided her down. Below the level of the pit edge, the weeds ended, leaving only a crumbling spiral of iced and treacherous gravel. Above her, she heard voices shouting, one scream riding over them. Dear God, she thought, how long will it take him to die?

Her feet slipped. She half fell, half rolled the last few yards, down what felt like a ladder of sharp and broken stone. Antryg pulled her to her feet and through a half-fallen archway like a skull's empty eyesocket, Caris panting and cursing at their heels. "What do you think you're . . . ?" the sasennan demanded hoarsely, as Antryg slipped his hand behind a shattered pilaster now barely distinguishable from its parent rock and cursed. He slid his sword scabbard clear of his sash, wedged it like a lever into the masonry and wrenched. Like the cries of some alien bird, the screams still drifted down to them, scarcely human anymore. A dark slot of ground opened in the grayer darkness.

Antryg thrust her unceremoniously through and was slipping after her when Caris grabbed his arm in a crushing hold. "You idiot . . . !"

"Oh, surely not!" the mad wizard protested. "Insane I may be, but not an idiot." With an easy movement of his elbow, he disengaged his arm from the baffled young man's grip. Dim daylight flicked along one spectacle rim, picked out the fracture in the glass and the facet of an earring. More soberly, he added, "They're never going to believe I didn't summon that thing. Most men would kill Peelbone for the things he did to me. And to Joanna," he added softly, touching her shoulder in the darkness. "And to you."

"And that's your reason for blundering straight into the heart of Suraklin's traps?" Caris' whisper was almost a scream of rage.

"Well, the odd thing is," Antryg murmured, "we don't seem to have sprung one." He slipped the scabbard casually back into his sash; Caris still held his, ready to draw and do battle. "We must needs have come here in any case, Caris. If it's a trap, it's a very good one. We might as well see the rest of it."

They moved forward, into a species of Hell in darkness. It was a darkness that chittered and whispered or, worse,

simply seemed to watch them in waiting silence beyond the
faint foxlight glow that Antryg called above his head.
Twice he killed the light, quickly, and thrust his companions back against the wall; in the darkness, Joanna heard
the slimy dragging noise that heaved itself slowly along the
passageway and felt the clammy cold that seeped in the
creature's wake. Against her arm, she felt Caris' muscles
tighten in utter revulsion and horror. He was mageborn,
she remembered. He could see in the dark.

Other things fled from the light, sometimes white,
squamous shapes like naked and legless pigs, other times
the more prosaic vermin of this world, swarming black
roaches and rats that had clustered around rotting carrion of
no shape known to her, whose putrefying stench poisoned
the air. In one place Antryg whispered to them not to touch
the bubbling orange mold that covered the whole side of
one rock-hewn chamber. Snared in it, Joanna saw two or
three other abominations of various sizes, all of them rotting, but none of them completely dead. There were rats
and roaches there, too, gummed likewise in the putrid
growth; by the faint, glittering radiance of Antryg's witchlight, she could see that several of the roaches were close
to the size of dinner plates, and the rats displayed unspeakable mutations.

But throughout that darkness, no magic, no malice, and
no trap touched its three invaders. It was a Hell unten-
anted, save by the abominations that crept, preying stu-
pidly upon one another, through its arched stone
passageways. Level by level Antryg led them deeper into
the surviving corner of Suraklin's mazes, and nowhere did
they find anything but the long-spent memories of his evil
and power. Even the ghosts, it seemed, had been calcined
away by the wizards' wrath.

"I don't understand," Joanna whispered.

They had come to the last, deepest chamber of all, a
vast black cavern where a broken stone cover showed the
inky waters of a stagnant well, and a round block of bluish

stone, like an altar, crouched amid darkness that even Antryg's faint witchfire could not pierce. Beside her, Antryg stood, his full, oddly curving lips now tight and rather gray, as if the aura of the place, like a remembered smell, nauseated him. The blurred remains of a chalked circle were almost eradicated from the floor. Dark stains blotched the top of the altar block and tracked its sides. And that was all.

"This is it, isn't it?" Joanna asked softly.

Antryg nodded. Under a sudden sheen of sweat, all the muscles of his jaw rippled, like rope under strain, then eased again.

She looked hesitantly up at him, not liking the haunted horror in his eyes. "Do you—do you see something that I don't?"

"Only the past, my dear," he murmured. "Only the past." His breath blew out in a sigh; he turned to her, his eyes returning to the present once more. "Yes, this is where it should be, the centerpoint of Suraklin's power, the place where he—or I—performed his great magics."

"You?" The echoes of Caris' suspicious voice murmured back at them from the hard stone of the walls.

Antryg's eyes moved to the altar, then away. As if speaking of someone else, he said carefully, "You understand, there is a type of magic which can be drawn from certain—acts—which by then he was too old to perform himself." He looked around him. "This was the place of his power, and I should say, my friends, that we have all been well and truly taken in." At his small gesture, an explosion of light filled the room, bright and clear as a sodium lamp, digging like the eyes of God into every bleached, clean cranny of its hewn stone walls and flashing like diamonds in the obsidian waters of the pool. In all the space of that room there was nothing.

"But the abominations . . ." Caris began.

"They weren't guards," the mad wizard said quietly. "Half of them were herbivores, by the look of their snouts

—even that thing at the top went for the man nearest it, God help his wretched soul, rather than for us, who were nearer the stair. We're on a node in the lines. Every time the Void is opened, gaps in it open for a short distance all around it—but when it is opened on a line, the whole line faults. Those poor things are mere blunderers-through, harmless . . ."

"*Harmless?*" echoed Caris indignantly.

"Comparatively harmless." The light around them faded again to the corpse-candle gleam above Antryg's head; he turned back to the stygian arch that led once more into the mazes and the hellish walk back to the outer air.

Caris strode after him. "Compared to *what*?"

Antryg shrugged. "Compared to what's going to happen when an intelligent one comes through."

They did not speak again until they had emerged from the pits, by which time darkness had fallen once more outside. From the protection of the passage, Antryg listened, stretching his senses out into the Citadel around them. The Church's sasenna had retreated, watching from the hills around. No one, no matter what his mission, was prepared to linger in the Dark Mage's fortress after the fall of night. They found Peelbone's horse lying half in a gravel pit, with the hacked and burned remains of the thing that had killed it. There was blood everywhere, soaking into the frozen weeds, and wide-strewn rags of clothing saturated with blood, acid, and slime. Elsewhere Caris found part of Peelbone's hand, most of the flesh eaten from the melted bone. Antryg looked somberly at it, rubbing his broken fingers in their shabby gloves, but said nothing.

It was only when they were on the hills again, having slipped through the scattered guards, that Joanna asked, "If Suraklin's headquarters isn't at his Citadel, where is it?"

"Elsewhere." Antryg sighed, and hunched his shoulders against the cold night. The horses had, of course, been confiscated by the Witchfinders when they had first surrounded the Citadel, and it was a long and tiring trek over the dark hills to Larkmoor once again. "And unfortunately, since now he'll be well and truly alerted to the fact that I'm at large and looking for it, I haven't the remotest idea where."

CHAPTER X

THEY LEFT LARKMOOR THE FOLLOWING NIGHT, TRAVELING north on foot.

It was a bad time of year to be taking to the roads, and Caris knew it, worriedly eyeing Joanna's small, spare form as she stumped along through the bitter darkness at Antryg's side; it would be worse still away from the main roads. The Sykerst was a land unkind to men.

Antryg's escape coupled with Peelbone's death had roused the countryside around Kymil and set patrols along the Angelshand road. But deeper in-country, Antryg argued, among the isolated villages that sprouted wherever there was soil enough to support thin crops of rye, they would stand a better chance of making their way northward in safety.

"There's another node, a crossing of the energy-lines, on Tilrattin Island about twenty-five miles upriver from Angelshand," he had explained, when the four of them had sat around a picnic breakfast in the darkness of the deserted fodder barn at Larkmoor, following their return from the Citadel ruins. "Suraklin has to have established his computer at some node in the lines. That one has a lot to recommend it; it's on Prince Cerdic's land, for one thing..."

"And what do we do if it isn't Suraklin's headquarters, either?" Caris demanded, sitting in the mildewed straw at

Pella's side, moodily stabbing his dagger into the floor. Reaction had set in on him. Having keyed himself for a death fight at the Citadel, he now felt empty, weary, and vaguely cheated. "Walk to the Citadel of Wizards in the taiga forests to check that one as well? And what if it isn't? What if it's somewhere on the other side of the world? Have you thought of that?"

"But we *do* know Suraklin's trying to take over control of the Empire," Joanna pointed out diffidently. "So it's a good guess that's where it is."

"I'm actually very taken with the notion of its being at the Citadel of Wizards," Antryg mused with a dreamy grin. "It is the next nearest node in the Empire. Lady Rosamund would have a seizure from sheer indignation. But going there wouldn't be necessary." He gestured with the muffin he was holding, his long legs folded tailor-wise under him and butter dripping on his gold-braided black cuffs. "By standing at a node in the lines when the computer comes up, I'll be able to feel the direction of the energy-flow and tell pretty well where it's going. I'd simply stay here eating your cook's excellent muffins, Pella, until I could do so from the Citadel node, only somehow I don't think that would be such a good idea."

Pella shook her head, missing the impish sparkle in his eyes. "They're going to be searching house to house," she said gravely. "I can keep my servants quiet about a chance visit, but not if you're still here."

So they had spent the day sleeping and quietly assembling provisions, and departed three or four hours after it grew dark. In that time Caris had seen seven or eight separate patrols on the hills, and two groups—one of Witchfinders, one of Church sasenna—came up to the manor itself, to ask questions. It would only be a matter of time, he thought, before the place was searched.

They traveled as physicians, Antryg wearing the old-fashioned, dull purple robes of a University doctor, torn and mended and stained with gin, Caris the cleaner, if

threadbare, gown of a medical student. To his outfit Antryg
had added his usual collection of the gimcrack beads of
which he was so fond and the long-skirted olive coat of
some nobleman's household cavalry, arguing that the
hooded cloak of an academic was wholly inadequate; the
worst of it was that he was right. Caris looked down his
nose at the scarecrow appearance of his purported instructor, but shivered in the cutting wind.

For her part, Joanna was relegated to the rough, baggy
trousers, sheepskin coat, and coarse woolen hood of the
lowest type of servant, since she could pass herself as neither sasennan nor student.

"That should teach you to learn to read the wrong lan-
guages," Antryg chided loftily, steadying her over the
gluey gray mud of the half-frozen potholes with effortless
strength.

"Eat hot death, dog wizard."

"I fear," sighed the wizard, "that we shall all do that
when—or if—we reach the inn at Plikey Wash this evening. The cooking there is notorious for miles around."

Joanna laughed, her breath a cloudly puff of silver in
the cold.

In the event, none of them was obliged to endure the
dubious hospitality of country inns. Raised in the populous
Wheatlands, Caris had previously had little idea of the
frightening isolation of the Sykerst and the knowledge that,
if something went wrong, there was almost literally nowhere to turn for medical aid. For all his decrepit appearance and jangling beads, Antryg was welcomed in every
village along their road, to tend illnesses, give advice, and
often to repair injuries that had been left to fester all summer—injuries brought about by carelessness and exacer-
bated by the uncaring apathy of the dead times. Again and
again, as Antryg examined mortifying flesh or bones set
crookedly because they had been carelessly splinted or not
splinted at all, Caris heard that tired refrain, ". . . don't
know what I was thinking of, that day. . ."

And rather to Caris' surprise, the lunatic mage proved to be an excellent doctor as well.

"Won't the Council and the Witchfinders be able to trace you by your use of magic?" Caris asked quietly as the wizard bent over the bed of a small boy, counting the pulse in one fragile wrist. The lantern hanging on the rafters not far over their heads threw little light, but both men were mageborn and able to see in the dark.

"They would if I used magic for a cure, yes," Antryg replied. "But a fever like this can be brought down with ginger and elder; I asked Pella to put some up in the medical satchel she gave me. If they can keep it down until the ailment has run its course, the boy should be all right." He half lifted the child to a sitting position, and the boy's thin, gasping breath at once seemed easier. Caris folded the limp pillow and frowned. A glance around the loft where the child's bed stood yielded no sign of spare bedding—the family was a poor one—but after a moment he collected several sacks of peas and seed-corn from their lumpish white ranks along the far wall and stacked them up behind the little boy's shoulders, wadding the pillow in over them. Antryg eased the boy gently back.

"It's pneumonia, isn't it?" Caris asked, listening to the thick wheeze of the boy's breath. "But his mother said it was cowpox..."

"It probably started out as cowpox... Thank you, my dear." Joanna's head appeared above the crude ladder from the room downstairs. She set a steaming tin kettle down by the entry hole and scrambled up the last few rungs. "Pneumonia is a common complication, particularly in children. Elfdock steam should help clear up some of the congestion..."

"His mother asked me if you were going to bleed him." Joanna hunkered down beside the bed and looked worriedly at the dozing child. Three days on the road had not been kind to her; she looked worn and tired in her coarse smock and heavy boots, and the greasy yellow light picked out hollows under the pointy cheekbones.

"I hope you told her that I was." Antryg removed from his medical satchel several bleeding cups and dipped a little of the hot water up in one of them. From his boot he pulled his razor, flipped open the blade, and drew off one of the fingerless gloves that he wore indoors and out to keep some of the cold from the damaged tendons of his hands. Carefully he slit across one of the smaller veins of his wrist, and squeezed the blood into the water. "Astonishing what a mess even a little blood will make in any amount of water. Rinse that round all the bleeding cups, would you, my dear?"

"*Aren't* you going to bleed him?" Caris asked, shocked.

"Of course not. The boy needs his strength, but there's no point in having his mother fret."

Caris frowned, watching Antryg as he crushed up the dried elfdock and kindled his portable spirit lamp to raise the water to steaming again. "Doesn't bleeding bring down a fever, then?"

"Not in my experience. In fact, the only time I ever bleed a patient is if they are intent on getting out of bed too soon and doing something silly." He thoughtfully ran the razor blade back and forth through the spirit lamp's flame a few times, closed it, and returned it to his boot. "Remind me to mark the boy's back a little before we leave. Otherwise his mother will never believe me when I tell her to keep him sitting up and let him breathe steam."

From his coat pocket he took a tin flask of gin with which he doused the wound in his wrist; below the pushed-up edge of his sleeve, Caris saw the ragged trail of ancient slits and punctures that followed the vein back up his arm, broken here and there by the distinct scars of small and vicious teeth.

"You speak as if you were a physician at one time," he commented later, when they were once again on the endless, nameless road from one minute village to the next.

That morning a farm cart had carried them a number of miles on their way before turning down a lane that was little more than a muddy slot in the broken and stony land. Around them, like the flanks of sleeping giants, the rolling land rose to rounded crests hundreds of feet high, barren, monotonous, and cold under a slate-hued sky. Whitish outcroppings among the dead whin showed how close the granite lay beneath the thin veneer of topsoil; only by the gradual strengthening of the light above the cloud cover could Caris tell that it was nearly noon. The wind blew from the north, smelling of snow.

"Well, wizards do learn something about healing, though we're not allowed to practice it on anyone but one another, and I've passed myself off as a doctor often enough to learn some conventional medicine. The borderlands of midwifery and granny-magic are fairly wide, if shockingly inaccurate in places." He frowned thoughtfully at the young warrior from behind his cracked spectacles. "You don't do badly at it yourself."

Caris blushed a little. "Grandfather..." His tongue stalled momentarily on the name, hate and vengeance and grief clutching in him like a fist. But just as suddenly, he remembered Salteris himself, the real Salteris of his childhood, and the anger in him gave way like melting ice breaking. Hesitantly, he went on, "Grandfather taught me enough to help him, when I was a boy. It was more of a game for me, picking out this herb from that and remembering what each of them was good for. Grandmother was a midwife, too." He grinned reminiscently. "Even before I became sasenna, I was always getting into scrapes, so I started early learning how to care for cuts and broken bones, mostly my own."

He fell silent after that, for the memories hurt him in an odd way—vivid not only to the way the old man had looked, but to the smell of warm hay and herbs in his robes and the summer's heat on his skin. Caris thrust them aside, knowing that he could not afford to warm himself too

much by those memories, as he could not afford to let too
near to him all the dozens of small scenes of the last week
that burned so clear now in his mind: the warm breath of
the horses on his hands while he held their heads so Pella
could gouge ice-balls out of their hooves; the lithe way she
moved, like a big, splendid panther, as she mounted the
footman's stand; the smoky-sweet timbre of her voice and
the strength of her arms around his waist that afternoon in
the barn. He had felt bitterly sorry for her, left behind to do
nothing but wait and feel the child of an unwanted husband
growing in her belly. During the last day between their
return from the Citadel and setting forth to the Tilrattin
node, he had avoided being alone with her, avoided any
but the most perfunctory good-bye.

She had not sought him out. She had understood.

She had trained as sasennan, he thought, and smiled as
he pictured what sparring with her would be like. She'd
probably be a little slow, he guessed, but she'd have a
forehand stroke like the blow of a timber beam. In the barn
at Larkmoor she had said, "I know you need your hate . . ."
When he had pursued Antryg through the darkness of the
Void, he had known that, if he took his eyes from that
flitting, tatterdemalion figure, he would be utterly lost. So
it was now. Pella knew what he knew—that facing what he
faced, to turn his gaze for one second on anything but the
pure, sharp strength of his revenge would be a weakness
that could be fatal to them all.

And in any case, any turning-aside from what he was
now would be hopeless. Not only could he not afford to
think of might-bes, but he knew that they could, in fact,
never be. She was Pharos' wife and the mother of Pharos'
child. As a recreant to his vows, Caris' life and soul were
already forfeit. There was nothing for him but to accomplish his revenge and to die, as was the Way of the Sasenna
to die, in the process.

Why then, in this gray journey, did he feel, not the

grimness of one who seeks only vengeance and death, but a medley of strange and hurtful joys?

The joy of friendship, unlike the hard-edged and competitive friendships of the training-floor, with this woman Joanna, blunt, uncertain of herself, awkward, and oddly logical with the logic of the computers who for so many years had been her only friends. The joy that he had put aside and almost forgotten in his years of training to be a perfect weapon, the painful, puzzling joy of seeing the lives of others, the people of the villages through which they passed as well as Joanna and Antryg. The joy of a reawakened awareness of life, even now, on the threshold of winter's annual death and perhaps of a greater death to come—his own, his love's, the world's. The joy of watching the last dark stringers of geese hastening south high in the pewter air, of the warm smell of stables, or of Kyssha nuzzling at his hands. The odd joy he had felt, standing in the window embrasure, listening to Pella play the harpsichord, with the candlelight dancing off her over-embroidered sleeves.

For years, it seemed, he had seen all things in terms of the Way of the Sasenna, of defense and attack. Only now he saw them in terms of her—a heifer-calf in a stable where they were forced to spend one night, the way the mist clung to the low ground in the morning, and the sound of hunting horns ringing across the hills the night it snowed. He wanted to crystalize those moments in molten glass, string them on a necklace, and carry them back to her. She, who so loved small beauties and simple things, would have wanted to know.

He knew what was happening and he fought it desperately. He could not, he told himself over and over again in the dark hours of the night, afford to let himself soften even a little, let alone fret himself with worrying over what would become of her, married to her spiteful and sadistic little lord.

By Antryg's very gentleness, he suspected that the wizard knew, and hated him for that knowledge, while silently thanking him for not speaking of it. And indeed, there was little anyone could have said.

Woven in and around these other joys and hurts there was the joy of finally, after so many years, touching and using magic, even the insignificant magics of healing that were all that lay within his scope. That was perhaps the greatest and certainly the most dangerous joy of all.

Caris pretended to himself sometimes that it was all in the interests, as Antryg said, of verisimilitude; he was supposed to be a medical student, after all. As a sasennan, he had learned the cleansing of wounds and the setting of bones, and there was, too, the vast, half-forgotten backlog picked up from his childhood fascination with the arts of his grandparents. From Antryg he learned a smattering of standard medical practice—to diagnose ailments from the different pulses of the body and from the colors of the whites of the eyes or of the tongue and the mucus. But threaded through this knowledge, like ribbon through bone, was the laying of spells upon the various herbs and salts to increase their efficacy and the sigils of healing to be written across the life-tracks of the body itself—matters not only outside the physician's knowledge, but outside the law, matters which interfered, however beneficently, with the ways of humankind.

To work magic at all, Caris found, required a softening of the soul, a listening to all things in a manner different from a warrior's instinctive caution—a dropping of one's guard.

What appalled Caris was that he found it so easy.

"I shouldn't be doing this," he said quietly to Joanna one evening in the ill-lit sitting room of some isolated manor deep in the Sykerst. Their host, the local squire, and Antryg had gone upstairs to see to the squire's wife, a girl of seventeen, far gone in what looked like a very bad pregnancy. Joanna glanced curiously at the little card of parchment that lay before Caris and raised her eyebrows inquiringly. He had been practicing drawing the Sigil of Air—one of the easier ones—from memory, a sign to summon all the qualities of lightness, openness of the veins and heart and mind, and freedom of the soul. He saw the direction of her look and shook his head, pushing the Sign from him.

"I don't mean this, particularly," he said. "I mean . . ." He hesitated, feeling tripped by what he *did* mean—so much more than he was prepared to say.

"You mean dealing in life?" Joanna asked softly, "instead of dealing in death?"

He ran his fingers through his short-cropped blond hair, and avoided her eyes. Behind him, the wood shutters of the window quivered under a sharp blast of the sleety wind, the candleflames on the table before him starting nervously in their holders of Kymil porcelain. Like most small manors, this one was built largely of wood from the stands along the Sykerst rivers, exquisitely carved and fretted, but apt to creak. Around them the whole house seemed to be muttering to itself.

"No," he said evasively. "That is, I've been trained as a killer . . ."

"I didn't mean other peoples'," Joanna said, toying with the small parchment rectangle that lay between them. "I mean yours."

Caris was silent.

The girl's small fingers traced the lines of the Sigil, simple as a magic circle on the stiff, cream-colored card. There was no magic in it, for Caris lacked the ability to imbue what little he had in any inanimate thing; he had watched the mages drawing Sigils for years, for various purposes, from small to great, but this was the first time he had ever set out to memorize them for himself.

She went on, slowly, because speaking was no easier for her than it was for him: "Ever since I first met you in Suraklin's hideout you've been—been ready to die. Ready to kill for your cause, yes, but most of all ready to die for it."

"It is the Way of Sasenna," Caris said, "to be ready to die at the will of the one to whom you have sworn your vows."

"I know." She looked up, the glow of the several candles layering traceries of shadow across her dark eyes. "Since we left Larkmoor, I've had the feeling you're ready to live, but—it's as if you don't know how.

"I know about that," she continued uncertainly, after a silence broken by the creak of the house beams, and the distracted sobbing of the wind. "I don't know how either, really. This is the first time I've—I've felt like—I don't know, coming out and saying what I feel. To you. To Antryg. Pella and I did a lot of talking on the way down to Kymil; I don't know why that was easier for me, but it was. It's as if in caring for Antryg I care for other people more, too, and don't want to see them hurt. For so many years I've kind of—of had a lot of reasons for not giving time to people or not saying things to them. Silly things mostly, really simple stuff like, 'I'd like to know you better,' or 'I care about what happens to you.' I don't know what I was afraid they'd say back to me."

Caris turned his pen over in his hands for some moments, studying the shadow of the quills on the red-gold grain of the table. Then, with half a grin at her, he asked softly, "What were you afraid I'd say back to you?"

Her eyes warmed; he was a little surprised that he'd managed to say the right thing, but evidently he had, for she returned his smile.

Stammeringly, he added, "Thank you." He set the pen down and looked over at her in the amber and sepia gloom. "It isn't that I don't know how to live—or not just that, anyway. At this point, it would not only be useless for me to learn, but dangerous."

He thought she would contradict him, but she didn't, only listened in silence, her small hands folded, cold-chapped and so fragile against the coarse linen of her smock sleeves.

"After you shot that Witchfinder on the island near Devilsgate, I told you that sometimes you can't afford to think too much—remember?"

She nodded. He remembered the oppressive heat of the hay barn that night, his own impatience with listening to her stifled sobbing in the darkness, and his sharp jealousy at the thought that she had done the one thing he had trained for but had never actually done—killed a man in a fight. Two men, for that matter. The memory of that childish jealousy still embarrassed him.

"Do you want to learn?"

He looked away from her. To put it into words, he thought, even to deny it aloud, would make it too real for him to stand. "It isn't an option."

"We don't need a hero that bad."

He turned back. Small and unprepossessing in her crudely embroidered brown shirt, her feathery blond curls tied haphazardly back with a leather strap, and her brown eyes worried in their sketched fans of crow's-feet, she looked like a mouse in a cheese compared with Pella's splendid handsomeness. Joanna and Pella and Antryg were the only people who had cared about what he thought or felt since he had parted from Salteris in his thirteenth summer. That they did so still surprised him.

The thought of Salteris made him remember Suraklin, and he raised again that cold shield of obsession deliberately before his heart. He might hate it, but he could not afford to put it down. "You do," he told her quietly. "Believe me, you do."

The candleflames curtseyed suddenly in the rush of a draft as the door was opened; he could hear Squire Alport's lumbering tread retreat down the stairs to the first-floor hall as Antryg strode in, all his grubby tatters fluttering, absently rubbing at his gloved hands.

"How is she?"

The wizard's long mouth hardened. "Frightened," he said softly. "With far better cause than she knows."

Caris had seen the girl when Squire Alport had first offered them hospitality, presenting them to his bride of less than a year. Half her husband's age, her delicate, flaxen beauty was far too thin for her swollen belly. Everything Caris had learned from his midwife grandmother had made his stomach curl with dread at the sight of those too-hollow cheeks and those sunken eyes. Looking up now into Antryg's face, he saw the struggle there; as if everything had been spoken of before, he understood what the wizard was going to ask of him.

He had watched the wizard work minor magics for days, little healings such as granny-wives used, to nudge a bit of extra strength into weary hearts or to hinder the growth of proud flesh on a cleansed wound. Those bits of piseog were undetectable to the Council of Wizards, listening along the pulses of the earth for the whisper of Antryg's name—small things, that lay within Caris' rudimentary powers as well. But such things would never save that frightened girl's life.

Their eyes met and held. Even before Antryg spoke, Caris understood what he was going to be asked, what he had to be asked, and illogical rage surged up in him, a hot flood of anger at the taste of all the things that he would never have.

"You have no right to ask that of me," he said softly, even before Antryg opened his mouth. "I'm a killer, not a healer."

The wizard drew in a sip of breath and let it out. Deranged he might be, but he did not pretend not to understand. His flamboyant voice was low in the half dark. "Well, you're only the one masquerading as the other for the time being, I'll admit . . . ."

"You need me for what I am." Caris' onyx eyes narrowed, blazing into the wizard's calm opal gaze. "Don't make it harder for me by showing me what I know I can never have."

The gray eyes did not waver. The fact that what Antryg wanted him to do was against the first law of the Council whose sworn weapon he was or the fact that it would make him an outlaw in the eyes of both Empire and Church was not spoken of. In a way, both sensed that it was not the issue, and neither pretended that it was. Gently, Antryg said, "I know it isn't fair to you . . ."

"Fair!" Caris' laugh was a harsh explosion, utterly without mirth. "Fair isn't even in it! If I don't learn whatever spell it is you want me to learn, to save her life—*if* I have the strength to use it . . ."

"You do," the mage said calmly.

The sureness in his voice stopped Caris for an instant with a split-second's leaping joy and then a rush of even more bitter rage.

"If I don't do this thing," he went on at last, "you will, won't you? You'll give yourself away to the Council by working magic to save her—give *us* away. Get yourself tracked and caught and killed, and never mind that Suraklin will go free—all to save the life of some half-educated petty noblewoman we don't even know?"

It was Antryg's turn to be silent. He stood for a moment, his big hands resting on the back of Joanna's chair, the flames of the two or three candles distorting even further the baroque shadows of his lips and nose. Around his neck and over the velvet collar of his patched green coat, his tawdry beads glittered sharply like a galaxy of trashy stars.

Then he said slowly, "I know that I should not—another of those great, awful laws that I can believe in at a distance. But I know myself well enough to—to doubt my own reliability at close range, with the life of another person in my hands."

"Reliability! That's rich!" Caris' voice shook with scorn as he turned away, the taste of the small magics he had learned warm in his mouth, and on his hands—things he knew he must not touch, for if he did, he would never want to return to being what he had been. He had been a good warrior, and a good warrior was what they needed. He knew he would never be even an adequate mage, useless against Suraklin's might. To work magic, to touch even the small power of which he was capable, would be like a drunkard's first taste of wine; it would be like lying naked in bed at Pella's side, knowing that he must not put a hand on her.

After a long moment, he turned back to where Antryg still stood silent in the candlelight. "You're such a damned sentimentalist you'd do it, wouldn't you?"

Antryg did not reply.

Disgusted with himself, furious with Antryg, Caris hooked one foot over the rungs of another of the carved chairs and thrust it in the wizard's direction. "I should have killed you in the Tower."

The spells were a deeper magic than Caris had ever before attempted, almost beyond his grasp; even shaping them in his mind, without putting his power into them, left him exhausted as after hard training. It was the discipline of his training that got him through, learning them as he would have learned a new sword form, and Antryg, trained as a sasennan himself, cast the lesson in those terms, the terms that Caris would unthinkingly understand.

Oddly, Caris trusted him. Antryg was clearly as mad as hatters got after years of breathing the mercury fumes of their trade, tricky, devious, and marked, far back in his soul, by all the dark abominations of Suraklin's magic.

Yet for reasons he did not fathom, Caris had felt drawn to the wizard from their first meeting and, though he knew he ought to guard himself, felt little hesitation in opening his soul to the scrutiny of those daft gray eyes.

Using the magic itself was like flying.

His power was slight, and nothing he or Antryg could

ever do would increase its strength. But when the hemor-
rhaging started somewhere in the endless hell of the girl's
childbirth, it took so little to reach in with his mind and
close the ruptured vessels. Even that took all his concentration, to focus and transmit the healing light from his
own palms to the small, sweaty, twisting ones so desperately clutching at him, summoning the vision of it by rote
until sweat ran down his face like rainwater, repeating to
himself everything Antryg had said, making himself see,
making himself believe . . . But the power came.

Antryg's voice drifted away somewhere, with the girl's
terrified sobs. The blood smell was everywhere, sweetish-
sharp in his nostrils as it had been the first time he had
killed a man—a thief, bound hand and foot to the big stake
in the rear court of the training-hall; Caris still remembered
the color of the man's eyes. Through the woman's hands he
felt her spirit, feeble and summery and rather stupid, hopeless in the grip of unimagined pain. When he felt that of
her living daughter, the shock of it nearly made him lose
his grip on the inner chain of light at which he clutched so
hard.

Then he heard the child crying.

After it was all over, on one of the terraced balconies on
the lee-side of the house, heedless of the raw cold that had
followed the sleety winds of the night, he put his forehead
down on the wooden rail and wept as if his heart had been
broken.

Joanna could hear the servants whispering in the hall
when the household's single footman came into the sitting
room with a tray of muffins. The lamps had been put out.
Through the opened storm shutters and the double-paned
windows, morning lay on a landscape, messy with patches
of snow and sheets of water frozen into plates of gray steel.
How Antryg could possibly have demanded breakfast was
totally beyond her; after the truly appalling mess of child-

birth, she thought queasily that she would never be able to eat again.

He was asleep on the divan now, only a tangle of gray curls and one crooked-knuckled hand in its shabby glove above the dull purple vastness of his patched cloak. Since she was supposed to be his servant, she took the tray from the footman and set it on the table near him, the table still littered with Caris' exercises in Sigil-making; she glimpsed one of the maids craning her neck to see in from the hall as the young servant closed the door.

So much, she thought wearily, *for traveling north unobtrusively.*

The events of the night seemed crowded and telescoped in her mind—the intentness in Caris' eyes as he drew the Sigils, and the bitterness in his voice, the stink of blood and her own nausea at the primal rawness of the birthing, the squire weeping as he knelt before Antryg, clutching his gloved hands. There should have been something faintly ludicrous about a fat, middle-aged man sobbing and jiggling awkwardly on his chubby knees, but there hadn't been. He had obviously never expected the girl he loved so desperately to survive.

She walked back to the divan, rested one hand on its scrollwork end, and looked down at the man sleeping there. The deep lines around his eyes aged him, as they had when he had worn the Sigil of Darkness; even in sleep he looked worried. Since his escape from the Tower, Joanna suspected that he was less resilient than he had been.

Voices rose in the hall downstairs. Tired as she was, it took Joanna a second to realize that there were far more of them than the small servant population of the house could account for and that their tread, clattering en masse up the wooden stairs, was far too numerous and heavy. Fear stabbed at her and she caught up her backpack from under the divan, fumbling the .38 from its pocket. Caris, where was Caris . . . ?

The door opened. Lithe and deadly in his dull purple robe, Caris stood framed against the brownish shadows of the hall. Beyond him, Joanna could see Squire Alport, like a fat brown bear in layers of heavy tweed. Massed around him were a dozen men and women in the coarse, bundly clothes of peasants, the damp sheepskin of their jackets steaming in the sudden warmth of the house after the cold outside. None of the them were armed. Feeling a little silly, Joanna made a move to pocket the gun, then saw the look on Caris' face.

"What is it?" Behind her Antryg sat up and fumbled his spectacles on, to blink at the mob.

"These people heard about you from that woman whose son you cured of pneumonia back in Bel Gulch," Caris said quietly. "They want to talk to you about the spells of deadness, and the draining of life."

"They want to *talk* about them?" The wizard's huge gray eyes widened still further with surprise.

"You mean someone else has *finally* noticed that they all happen at the same time?" Joanna demanded.

"In a way." Caris' voice was carefully neutral. "They say they know what's causing them. It's at their village."

Joanna said, "WHAT?" and thought, panicked, *We're not ready for this yet* . . . Her eyes met Antryg's and saw in his that he, too, had been taken completely off-guard.

He turned back to Caris, and asked cautiously, "What is?"

Expressionless, the sasennan said, "The Dead God."

CHAPTER XI

"THEY'RE NOT LYING, ANTRYG." CARIS PAUSED AT THE turn of the stairs, letting the squire lead the delegation down into the manor's big hall ahead of them. Through its open double doors, wan daylight filtered up to dispel some of the gloom on the landing, showing his face paler than usual against the dark of his eyebrows and his pleated robe. "I'm frightened myself."

"It has to be Suraklin." Joanna glanced worriedly up at the two men. "If he's established the computer *off* one of the nodes, off the energy-lines entirely..."

"Then it wouldn't work," Caris finished firmly.

"No, it wouldn't," Antryg agreed. "But for that reason it would be a splendid idea if it *could* be done—and, of course, all we're going on is guesses about what's happening, anyway. We haven't any more proof than anyone does."

There was an appalled silence, in which the muted scuffle of voices sounded below, and somewhere in the dim house rose the thready wail of the new baby. Hesitantly, Caris said, "Have we been wrong about *everything*? It can't *really* be the Dead God behind it all—can it?"

Antryg grinned. "Disconcerting, isn't it? Caris, for a man who doesn't even believe in the Old Faith, you're awfully worried about the return of something that supposedly never existed. I shall have to speak to the Archbishop of Angelshand about the general shakiness of religious training among the sasenna."

"Worried?" Caris retorted, his cheekbones staining red with annoyance. "I'm frightened, and if you had the brains God gave a chicken, you'd be frightened, too!"

The demented smile widened. "Oh, I am," he assured them cheerfully, "I am." In a swirl of patched coat skirts and robes he clattered down the stairs ahead of them and into the hall.

Caris' fine-cut nostrils flared and his upper lip seemed to lengthen. He started to follow, and Joanna caught his sleeve.

"It has to be Suraklin." She heard the uncertainty in her own voice.

"I agree." The young man threw a glance down at the brighter rectangle of the hall doorway, where Antryg could be seen, half a head taller than anyone else in the room, polishing on his shirt ruffle spectacles which had fogged slightly in the steam rising from their damp clothes. "They say the Dead God has been demanding his ancient sacrifices, ruling the town through terror. It's only superficially different from what Suraklin did for years in Kymil. A perfect setup."

Somewhere in the house, the baby's cries sounded again, sharp and demanding; there was the faint creak of floorboards, and the cries ceased in a contented gurgle. Looking up into Caris' face, Joanna saw for one moment in his eyes a look of such bitter yearning, such hopeless unhappiness, that she reached out with involuntary pity to touch his hand.

His dark eyes returned to her, briefly unmasked by the sound of the first life he had given instead of taken. Then his mouth twisted in a wry smile and he shook his head. With a warrior's deadly lightness, he strode down the remainder of the stairs to join Antryg in the hall.

Joanna followed, trying to collect and sort possibilities

in her mind—how Suraklin could have organized the energy transfer away from the lines and how his power might be met. But this exercise in logical explanations was hideously evanescent; the tale told by the mayor of Far Wilden and her frightened delegation was bizarre, disquieting, and bore no resemblance to what she knew of Suraklin's calm methodology.

It had started, they said, with noises, knockings, and scratchings in the Church. The old priest claimed that the place smelled of death and of the coldness of the Dead God and had refused to enter. The young priest, sent out two years before from Angelshand and still filled with the arrogance of the seminary, had insisted upon performing as usual the services of the Holy Sun, the Sole God.

"It was known from the beginning what it was, then?" Antryg drooped back in the carved chair by the hearth, his hands in their shabby gloves folded across his middle, his eyelids half-lowered behind the cracked and mended lenses of his specs.

"Oh, yes, my lord." Greer, the mayor of Far Wilden, a tough, sun-browned woman in her forties, nodded. Her white linen chemise under an embroidered peasant bodice hung baggy over wide shoulders and the slack breasts of one who has lost weight quickly. Men and women, they all had that look, Joanna thought, sitting curled in silence on the plank floor at Antryg's side—the slight bagginess of jowls and necks and clothes that no longer fitted as they had. She had grown used to it, traveling through the Sykerst—that, and that crushed-in grayness of stress and uncertainty, of knowing there was something desperately wrong and not quite knowing what it was.

What she had not seen before was the shadow that seemed to haunt the depths of their eyes, the way they tended to stay away from windows, and the way they always seemed to be listening for some noise in the corridor outside. She felt obscurely glad that outside the heat-steamed glass of the windows lay daylight, dreary though it might be.

"We're true Believers, my lord," Greer went on diffidently, folding her big, brown hands, "good children of the light. But the Dead God is different."

Thoroughly orthodox in spite of his long association with the mages, Caris looked on the verge of indignant speech, but Antryg motioned him silent with one crooked forefinger. "I know," he said, his deep voice scarcely louder than the croon of the wind round the eaves. "It's a belief that sleeps in the ground. And the Dead God was never like the other gods."

"No, my lord," the woman said simply. "Old Father Del, he knew. But in Angelshand the Bishops and the Witchfinders, they don't like anything that can't be written in their holy books of the Sun. It's why they sent out poor Father Sweelum to tell us it isn't true, to make sure the Green Mass isn't said in the fields, and to knock down the standing-stones and put fences round the churchyards to keep the conjures out."

Her dark eyes narrowed as she studied the tall man who sat by the hearth, his faded purple robe hanging slack over his bony frame like a blanket on a picket fence, the firelight and daylight sparkling on the magpie treasure of glass beads around his shackle-galled neck. "There's talk you're a conjure, my lord. Lord Alport said his lady's life was despaired of, and over to Bel Gulch that boy..."

Antryg shook his head. "I have worked no magic," he said softly. "And in any case it would be unlawful for me to do so, even if I could. What became of poor Father Sweelum, who went into the Church to sing the hymns of the Unconquered Sun?"

Greer's full lips tightened; she sighed and shook her head. "It was only a matter of time," she said. "He went there two, three times, evening and morning—cursed Father Del for refusing to set foot over the threshold. It was the Dead God's eve; Sweelum went in to say services at sundown, though for three days there'd been no one to go into the Church to hear them. I was one of those who stood outside the door. We heard him scream, the first time in fear, the second time... I can't say, but I've never heard a human being scream like that in all my life. When we looked in, he was dead, lying halfway between the door and the altar, blood round his nose and ears, and the look on his face as if he'd seen into Hell itself."

"Was this before or after sunset?" Joanna asked worriedly, remembering the hot glare of the slanting light on the San Serano parking lot and crouching in the dimness behind the door, waiting for Gary to pass.

"Before, surely," Antryg murmured, and Greer nodded.

"He'd just gone in to sing the services. He always had them timed fine, the sun touching the horizon on the first word of the Farewell Hymn, and no fadiddling about waiting for it. The light fell nearly straight through the doors on his body when we opened them."

Joanna shot a troubled glance at Caris, sitting on the black sheepskin of the hearthrug, his back to the fieldstone chimney; he seemed lost in his own thoughts. "And how long before this had the noises started?"

Greer frowned, thinking back. One of the younger men of the delegation said, "Three days? Four days?"

There had been a Tiger missile program review during the week before the Dead God's eve. Gary—Suraklin—had worked late at San Serano every night. And in any case, the computer had been up and running intermittently weeks before. Joanna subsided, feeling as if pieces of a jigsaw puzzle had fallen out of her hands. Beside her, she could sense the tension in the line of Antryg's shoulders and see it in the way his bony hand lay on the chair's carved arm and in the tilt of his head.

After a moment Greer went on, "We—we went and fetched Father Del. We didn't go into the Church. The smell of it was something dreadful, rot and corruption and worse besides. It was pretty near dark when we opened the doors again." Her voice sank to a whisper, and she glanced involuntarily at the window, as if even in daylight she feared what she might see looking in. "He was standing up, my lord—Father Sweelum, with blood running down from his mouth and his dead eyes staring at nothing with the lolling of his head. He said, 'I am the Dead God. I have returned, as I said I would.'"

"Ah," murmured Antryg. *"When the last of a thousand candles burns out, the darkness will always return; though a thousand voices sing all the hymns of life, silence always waits upon the inevitable failing of their breath.* Yes."

From the corner of her eye, Joanna saw Caris, white-faced, sketch the sign of holiness on his forehead and lips.

"Entropy always wins," she said softly, and Antryg's fleeting gray gaze touched her.

"Precisely." His eyes returned to the peasants, clustered close now, like sheep who hear the howling of the wolf, though Joanna guessed they were probably the dozen most fearless men and women in the village. "What did he ask of you?"

He spoke gently and as if he already knew. There was a terrible silence. Then Greer spoke without meeting his eyes. "Life," she said, her words barely to be heard in the hush of the room. "Lives."

"Ah," Antryg breathed, like a man who sees some piece to a riddle, but his eyes, on Greer's downcast face, were filled with compassion and pity.

She raised her gaze to the wizard's, as if asking that he understand that no horror or accusation of his could equal what she had already felt toward herself. "He would have destroyed us, else."

"I know." Something in the sureness of his voice, the absolute understanding, made Joanna shiver, but it melted some of the woman's wretched self-hate.

"And he can," she said. "He can draw the life out of a man like a fox sucking an egg, then stand there in its rotting corpse, speaking out of its mouth. He can call down spells of death, of ruin—at least so he told Father Del and the town merchant, Pettin, who spoke with him in the Church. It's they who tell us his bidding, now."

"Aye," interpolated a younger man, stocky and bearded, who sat near the door. "It's not Del I mind, for all I think his brain's been turned. But that Pettin! Him and his sons and a bunch of their hired men keep guard on the Church, and do the Dead God's bidding, as he does theirs. Three of my sheep he's had, for his own use and none of the Dead God's."

There was an angry mutter of assent, and Antryg murmured, "Fascinating. But the Dead God has no use for beasts?"

That silence returned. They had sinned and knew it; Joanna wondered how many people they had given to the terrible thing in the Church and how those had been selected. Then an older man with short white braids said, "None. Only men. Once he asked for a child..." There was an awkward pause, as if all of them heard the echo of some mother's frantic cries. "It used to be every day. Then none for three, four days at a time. Now he's had three in three days again..."

Greer took a deep breath. "You have to come, lord doctor. In the name of God, of whatever gods you worship. The nights he comes out of the church and walks abroad are those nights like we've had all the summer, when it's like all the life goes out of the air, the ground—out of all of us. It's he who's been causing them all along. It's got to be! We'll hear him, lurching and staggering, and in the morning there's a trail of slime like a rotting beast was dragged over the ground, out to the Witchpath Stone and back. He's destroying the village and all the countryside around; they say he's drinking the life out of all the world."

"Why the hell would Suraklin be doing something like *that*?" Joanna demanded, when they were once more gathered in the small sitting room and Antryg was placidly consuming the now-cold muffins. "And it can't be Suraklin himself anyway—I *know* where he was on the Dead God's eve at sunset . . ."

"If it isn't Suraklin," Caris said firmly, "we cannot afford to turn aside from our task, much less risk getting ourselves killed on a side issue." He was pacing like a caged thing, his dull robes billowing about him, the short quiff of his blond hair falling into his eyes.

Antryg glanced up. "I'm not sure we can afford not to. Would you care for a muffin? Curious to think the gentry hereabouts import white flour from Kymil at twelve crowns the barrel to make muffins, solely because it's the correct thing to do, when rye-flour muffins are just as good." He licked the butter from his fingers and looked up at Caris, who had stopped, staring at him in openmouthed indignation.

"You are the most frivolous . . ." the sasennan began.

"Going to Far Wilden may not be frivolous—that is, if by frivolous you mean apt to pursue side issues. I hope that it will turn out to be frivolous, yes, for all our sakes. But I can't know until I've been there." He wiped his fingers on a corner of his coat and reached over to pinch loose one of the long stalactites of white wax which had dripped down from the side of a sitting room candle. Even at this hour of the morning, the sky outside was darkening with coming rain; servants were lighting the candles once again throughout the house. Antryg rolled the wax deftly into a ball with his long fingers, his gray eyes growing dreamy and distant. Then he pulled free one of the several pins he kept stuck through the frayed velvet lapel of his coat, and began scratching signs into the ball.

"I'm leaving you behind here, Caris," he said. "Put this *lipa* where you can see it. If it turns red, beg a horse from Squire Alport *at once* and ride for all you're worth to Far Wilden, but enter the town carefully once you get there. If it turns black . . ." He hesitated, the pin suddenly stilled, and his odd mouth set. Then he sighed, and handed Caris the tiny spell-ball. "If it turns black, I'm afraid you're going to have to deal with Suraklin yourself."

"Is it that important?" Joanna hunched her shoulders under the damp sheepskin of her coat and the weight of the backpack. The day was ending; the thin wind cut her like a knife. The utter weariness that seemed to have settled into her bones during the past week of continual walking dragged on her less than it had, but she still felt tired to death, as if she would never be warm or rested again. Not, she grinned to herself, that she wouldn't have enthusiastically jogged the fifteen miles back to Squire Alport's had Antryg said, *No, not really, let's go back.*

The spire of the haunted church was visible through a dip in the iron monotony of the hills. When the wind shifted, she could smell the village's familiar stinks—cow-byres, woodsmoke, and privies. It was growing dark. Her worry over Suraklin ebbed and she began to be scared.

"I'm afraid so, my dear." In the shadows of his cloak hood, little was visible of Antryg's face save the lenses of his spectacles, which caught the final pallor of the evening sky like luminous, insectile eyes. "I have a bad feeling about what's in that church. For all our sakes, I hope it has nothing to do with Suraklin, but I can't risk the chance that it might."

For the last five miles, the group of villagers had been very hushed and had seemed to huddle tighter together as they walked. Even Greer, who for most of the journey had kept up a stolid appearance of courage while she told them details of the hideous visitation, had fallen silent. Now they stood gazing at that silent spire in the distance, like a spike against an iron sky.

Hesitantly, Joanna said, "What *is* the Dead God, Antryg?"

In the tail of her eye, she caught the movement around her, like the rustle of wind in a grove, as the villagers all blessed themselves with the air of people no longer sure of the efficacy of a charm. Though Antryg was still looking out across the hills at the skeletal black spire, he must have heard the stirrings of their clothes, for, in the shadows of his hood, she saw his lips twitch briefly in an ironic smile.

"Not, as many people believe, the God of Death, the Lord of Gates, who was worshipped in the Green Masses held in the fields. The legends have become conflated in the years. The Dead God is the God of Being Dead—not even the 'God of,' but just Deadness. He is entropy, if you will. The final flickering-out of the last candle in darkness, the ending of all songs of hope for want of breath, the dying of the last blade of grass when all life has been leached from the soil—that is the Dead God. As you yourself said, entropy always wins."

A surge of wind caught his vast purple cloak and tossed it like a huge wing around him. In the twilight, his tall, thin form, with his deep voice and round, alien-looking eyes made him seem almost like something from a Danse Macabre himself.

"That is why the Dead God elected to die, you see. So that he would have it all in the end, even though it meant being nothing himself. He is the god of stasis, of stagnation, of the utmost death without even regenerative decay. No matter how much life the other gods created, say the legends, the Dead God died so that he would get it all in the end."

"Like a black dwarf star," Joanna murmured, "that is so dense that even light can't escape."

Antryg nodded.

She went on doubtfully, "So it can't really be the Dead God—can it? The Dead God—the true Dead God— wouldn't need something as petty as the village; he wouldn't need to make all those strange and senseless commands they talked about, like keeping everyone indoors on certain nights or bringing vats of blood to the Church or all those other things Greer told us about. All the Dead God would need to do is . . . wait."

"Precisely." The wizard shoved his hands into his coat pockets, and began to walk down the crooked and ice-slippery path toward the first wretched sod shanties of the town.

Her half-frozen buckskin boots sliding on the stony ground, Joanna hastened to catch up with his longer strides, and he slowed to wait for her. "Then what *is* in the Church?"

A thin stream of white breath escaped from the shadows. "I believe it's something I've been rather fearing all along," he said. "An abomination that has intelligence."

Without enthusiasm, Joanna said, "Hot damn."

"And I sincerely hope," he added cryptically, "that's all it is."

Joanna sighed. "I'm not even going to *ask* how the situation could be worse."

"Don't," Antryg advised.

In the village itself, the silence was almost palpable and had a watching quality that raised the hair on Joanna's nape. Even the occasional muttered comment among Greer and her people had ceased; they walked close together, always glancing back over their shoulders at the heavy darkness that seemed to clot between the lumpish buildings of sod and logs. The village sounds to which Joanna had grown used, the lowing of cattle and the grunting of backyard pigs, were absent; through the door of a byre, she caught a glimpse of a couple of goats, huddled head-down as if ill, their green eyes gleaming in the darkness. Before them the square bulk of the church, with its cluster of turrets and single emaciated spire, loomed black against a cinder sky.

Joanna shivered and drew closer yet to Antryg. She thought it was colder here than on the hills, in spite of the windbreak of the buildings. The foetor of decay hung over the town, clogging her throat like putrid dust. Antryg had pushed back his hood; in the wan twilight, his face looked strained and old.

"So you have returned, Greer." From the shadows of a round, stumpy building a dozen feet or so from the church itself—a baptistry, Joanna knew, having seen them near several village churches already—other shadows separated themselves. A torch was brought forth, and its jerking orange glare played over the faces of half a dozen men and women armed for the most part with the makeshift weaponry of farmers, though at least two held heavy but businesslike swords. The man who swaggered in their lead was one of the few Joanna had seen who had not lost flesh in the harshness of a failed harvest; tallish, red-haired, the cut-steel buttons of his middle-class coat strained across an undiminished paunch. He was unarmed, but a couple of his bullies walked with axes at his back. "That was stupid of you." Joanna noticed idly that one of his front teeth was gold, with a tiny chip of ruby set like a stray speck of beef in its center.

Greer drew in her breath for an angry reply. At that moment, however, Antryg forestalled her by breezing forward, gloved hands outstretched. "My dear Pettin," he cried affably, "you really must forgive her concern. Of course the Unnamed One wouldn't communicate all his plans to a mere subcreature such as her—how could you expect him to? But they serve also who only act as the Dark God guides, and I'm here now, so there's no harm done."

And, as Pettin the merchant gaped in speechless surprise and Greer stared at the wizard aghast, Joanna thought, *Antryg, you'd better make this work.*

Antryg shook hands briskly with the stunned town boss and flung a friendly arm around his shoulder. "Surely you don't think He . . ." He nodded toward the silent church ". . . would have let her out of the village unless to fulfill his will."

"Uh—" Pettin managed.

"Where's Del?"

Greer's gasp of rage, of betrayed fury, caught Joanna's

attention like the rattle of a snake, and she turned in time to see the mayor twist an axe from the grip of the nearest of Pettin's guards. "Traitor!" Greer screamed. "You were its servant all along!" She strode forward, axe upraised, totally forgetting Joanna by her side until Joanna stuck out one booted foot and tripped her.

Joanna herself was a little surprised at the movielike patness of it. Even as a child, she had never dared to trip anyone deliberately and was astounded at how easy it was when the tripee had the momentum of rage. With a little more presence of mind, she supposed she could have dived in and got the axe away from her then and there, but didn't think that quickly; when she did, she decided to let Pettin's guards do that part—the axe looked damn sharp.

By the time Greer sprang to her feet again, covered in offal and mud, the guards were upon her.

"Stop it!" Antryg barked as one of them raised a fist to smash the infuriated woman across the face. Such was the authority of his deep voice that the man froze in midgesture. "Lock her up," he said coldly. "Don't hurt her." He glanced down at the totally discomposed Pettin by his side. "As you know, they must be untouched."

"Yes, my lord." Pettin clearly wasn't about to admit that nobody had communicated to him about *this*.

With a shrug that would have done credit to an Emperor, let alone the emissary of a god, Antryg shed the patched cloak from his shoulders. Joanna, with perfect timing, caught it and folded it over her arm. Casually, the wizard removed a club from the grasp of the guard nearest him and didn't even glance at it as its tip burst into flame. Pettin's bullies drew hastily back, murmuring and whispering; not a few made the signs against evil.

"Do as the god has bid you and keep everyone away from the doors," Antryg said. In the yellow glare of the new flames, Joanna could see the glitter of sweat on his face, but his voice was uncaringly arrogant. Magister Magus, Joanna recalled, had said he would have made the best charlatan in the business. "Obey my servant here as you would me until I come out." And he strode to the church steps as if he'd just closed escrow on the place.

"Liar!" As Antryg's foot hit the step, the doors slammed open; the rolling cloud of stench that swirled forth caught Joanna cold and she fought not to retch. With that stench, darkness seemed to pour out like smoke. The skinny old man framed in that vile and leaden darkness, Joanna saw at once, was completely mad.

Antryg ordered calmly, "Get out of my way, Father Del."

"Mountebank!" the old priest snarled. In the glare of Antryg's torch, drool gleamed on the old man's unshaven chin; by the black hollows of cheeks and eyes and the slack folds of filthy skin behind the ears, Joanna wondered, in the detached portion of her mind that wasn't sick with panic, if Father Del had eaten at all since the coming of the Dead God. *Not, living close to that smell, that anyone could . . .*

Antryg's voice was soothing, the deep notes played like an instrument against the shrillness of the lunatic's mind. "I am but a servant of the Unnamed One, as you are, who was once Del. He sent for me, and I came."

"Liar! Jackanapes!" Father Del advanced down the steps, leaning on a six-foot staff, heavy oak reinforced with plates of iron. Its iron tip grated on the stone. "Yes, he sent for you—it suited his purposes that you should come. He sees all, knows all. All things come at last to him! A mage, he says. Light shines through your flesh, he says, and the colors that halo you are not the colors of other men. You lie, he says." He stumbled a pace nearer, clutching at his staff with hands that shook as from palsy. At twenty feet, Joanna nearly gagged on the stench of his clothes.

Antryg did not move, but all around her Joanna sensed Pettin's men stir, hefting weapons in their hands. *If I run for it*, she thought, *it's an admission*. Adrenaline shot through her like gas to an engine racing in neutral.

"He smells your mind," Del's voice creaked. "Yours and this little girl's. You seek to destroy him. But he will have your flesh. Perhaps it will kill his long craving . . ."

Someone grabbed Joanna's wrist and she twisted the bone of it against the weak joint of her captor's thumb, at the same time slamming her full hundred and one pounds with her heel on the man's instep. The grip slacked. As hands snatched at her clothes, she plunged up the brick steps. At the same instant, the wizard thrust his torch at the priest's face and twisted the iron staff from his grip. Pettin's men surged up the steps at them, weapons flashing in the guttery light; Del's screaming, shrill as an angry hawk's, stabbed through Joanna's panic like the senseless sounds of nightmare.

With the hand that held the priest's iron-shod staff, Antryg thrust Joanna before him into the utter blackness beyond the great doors, and the doors thudded shut behind them.

CHAPTER XII

"HOLD THIS, PLEASE."

Antryg's calm voice was so quiet Joanna, stunned as much by terror as by the hideous stench and bone-freezing cold of the place, barely comprehended what he said. But she accepted the torch and the iron staff he shoved into her hands, even as the bolts outside the door were still scraping into place. The wizard was already down on his knees, a piece of chalk in his hand, sketching the wide arc of a circle on the stone floor around them. He must have practiced a lot, Joanna thought, as her panic drowned itself and left her feeling oddly cool; the circle was perfect to within a few degrees. Considering the bad light and the way her own hands were shaking, that in itself was astounding.

Around them, the pillared vestibule of the church was like a well filled up with evil, evil such as Joanna had never encountered—nauseating stink and gluey darkness pressing in on them, swamping the feeble torchlight. The cold here was intense, far more severe than outside, and she no longer questioned how the villagers had believed the assertion of the thing in the church that it was the singularity point of eternal death.

The chalk made soft crumbling sounds on the granite slabs of the floor. Straining her eyes into the aphotic depths beyond the carved and painted pillars—no two alike and

all gaily colored like psychedelic barber poles—she heard
the whispery hiss of the torch as it burned in her hands and
the faint, quick creaking of Antryg's belt as he moved here
and there, drawing out a five-point star within the double
circle around them. He hadn't made the original ring quite
big enough, and once the star was drawn there was only a
square yard or so in its center for them to stand. Joanna had
known Antryg long enough to know without being told not
to step over the chalked lines.

Somewhere among the pillars, something was moving.

She heard it blunder against the wood with a fumbling
hollow sound, heard a kind of wet slither that turned her
stomach with a dozen gruesome implications. The smell
was growing stronger, too, in spite of the killing cold—
meat long rotten, the fetid excrement of fear, and something else, something she had smelled in the Void. *Don't
panic*, she told herself, forcing herself to breathe slow and
deep in spite of the appalling stench. *If you panic, you'll
run, and there's nowhere to run to* . . . The cold was a living thing, malevolent, eating her bones. She wondered
briefly whether she could scream long enough and loud
enough to wake herself out of this nightmare and, if so, in
what place she would wake.

Antryg stood up, his face clammy with sweat in the
wavery yellow light. He took the iron-bound staff from her
left hand, the torch from her right. His voice was calm and
unstrained. "Joanna, get down and cover your head. It's
psychokinetic; I think it'll try throwing things first. Don't
try to move about to avoid me. I'll avoid you."

Joanna didn't even bother to try and guess how he knew
it would be psychokinetic. She merely dropped to her
knees, pulled off her backpack, tucked it beneath her—
mostly to protect the worm-program disk—and assumed
the position recommended by the California Public School
System as effective protection against atomic bombs. Antryg carefully laid the torch down beside him on the floor
and stood straddling her, the iron-bound staff in his hands.

He'd kilted up his robe almost to his knees, and the rough wool brushed her back, weirdly comforting, as was the sight between her slitted eyelids of the brass rings of his boot harnesses. She clenched her hands more tightly over the back of her neck and tried to make herself small.

Somewhere in the blackness of the church beyond the pillars, she heard a knocking.

It was impossible to say where it originated or on what kind of surface. There were a few experimental taps, soft and strangely hollow-sounding, then suddenly a huge crashing like thunder or the slamming of some massive door. Heavier and faster the sounds came, iron boulders falling from some unguessable height to an iron floor, a vast fist beating a ringing wall—*It's only noise*, Joanna told herself, shutting her throat on a scream. *The same as the darkness is only darkness, the cold is only cold, the smell is only a smell . . .*

It wasn't. It wasn't.

Something flashed through the air with vicious force— metal; copper, Joanna thought, glimpsing it from the corner of her eye. Antryg swiveled and smashed it with the end of his iron staff, sending it whirling, bouncing with a hideous clatter against the nearest pillar. Joanna saw it was an ewer, an altar vessel. Antryg whirled and batted again, catching a heavy piece of stone that had once been a sculpted cherub's head with a force that nearly snapped the staff in his hands. The next missile came in low and fast, aiming for his ankle. She gritted her teeth and turned her head away, but he caught that one, too. *Cricket as well as baseball*, she decided hysterically. At almost the same instant, she heard something connect against his other hip with vicious force and felt his knees give. The staff whined with an evil *swoosh* and she felt something strike him again and heard his grunt of pain.

Something glowing flashed between the pillars, swooping toward them with terrible speed. Fire, pale and flickering like ball lightning, streamers ribboning along the floor.

Joanna flinched as it hit the outer magic circle, heard the faint crackle, and saw the flames dash, scattering around the perimeter before they vanished. Looking up, she saw Antryg's face set and grim, blood tracking down from a cut over his right eye and spreading everywhere as it mixed with the sweat pouring down his cheekbones. His gray hair formed a matted halo in the weak torchlight, broken by the diamond glitter of his earrings.

Another flicker of light, wan and corpsish, appeared among the pillars, its reflections slipping wormlike up the lines of gold leaf. Joanna shut her teeth hard as something came rushing and weaving among the dark forest of columns, glowing with a horrible radiance. Antryg half swung toward it as it broke against the outer circle, then turned back as something else lunged, dark from the darkness.

A tsunami of stench struck them first, overwhelming. Even the brief glimpse Joanna got of the thing was heart-shaking, a slobbering, half-melted travesty of a face whose fangs, she realized, were broken-off ribs thrusting out from the corners of the rotting jaw. Bone showed where the flesh of two of the arms was falling off; the other two were reaching to grab. *It's material. It can cross the circle*, she thought. She half rose to run, then dropped to her knees again. In front of her, Antryg braced himself, the staff balanced before him. Tall as he was, the thing topped him by over a head. *He'll never thrust it off . . .*

The thing—monster, demon, god of rot—was almost to the edge of the circle when Antryg snapped the staff around and thrust its end like a spear into the creature's belly. His long legs locked and his weight dropped to take the shock, the thing's whole momentum slamming into the one-inch circle of the pole's end. The iron ferrule punched through the rotten meat like an arrow, and an unspeakable fountain spewed out behind. With a violence that seemed to shake the floor, the thing fell just beyond the chalked line of the protective ring. It raised its head, fluid trickling from the working mouth. Then it dropped squishily and lay still. Antryg had to twist and level the rod to pull its dripping end free.

The silence in the church was more terrible than before. Under the fallen flesh of the face she half believed she saw the silvery gleam of an eye move. She sat up, cold and shaking all over. "Can you cut it to pieces with your sword?"

"I could," Antryg whispered softly. "But if you'll look at the way the muscles are rotting, you'll realize that it's psychokinesis that moves the whole thing, and the limbs probably don't have to be attached to the torso for it to control them. So on the whole, I think I'd rather not."

Joanna worked out the implications of that one and swallowed queasily.

Rather white around the mouth, sweat and blood tracking stickily down his face, Antryg stepped to the very edge of the circle. Like an image losing itself down a corridor of mirrors, the echoes of his deep voice chased one another away into the endless darkness of the columns. "Can you understand me?" he asked softly. "I'm not here to destroy you."

It was waiting, Joanna thought.

Something wet fell on Joanna's hand. Looking down, she saw a drop of blood. Another drop struck her, falling from the darkness above; then a pattering, hideous rain. Trails of it threaded their way down the bright paint of the columns and curled like ribbon across the floor. The smell of it, coppery-sweet and harsh, stung her nostrils. The dying torch smoked and sputtered in it; the darkness edged closer, like a ring of wolves.

"Speak to me if you can," Antryg said. "I can help you if you'll let me."

Slowly the monster's head moved, white sinews breaking through the slimy flesh of its neck. Joanna saw the chest rise and fall as if pressed like a bellows to force air through vocal cords that were all but gone.

"I—am—the—Dead—God." The glottal stickiness of

timber made her flesh crawl, thinking of what caused it. "I drink the power that shines from men's flesh. All things are only lent to life, before they return to me. I am the Dead God."

Black fluid leaked from its mouth and from the hole in its gut as it swayed to a sitting position, head lolling gruesomely; fat droplets of slime hung from its wrists as it raised two of its arms; they elongated and finally dripped to the floor with a sticky splat. "The Dead God demands his due . . . transdimensional interface . . . I walk the boundless darkness in the pits of the world . . . universal field theory . . . xchi particles . . . structural shift at the ylem . . ."

"What?" whispered Antryg.

Joanna looked up at him, startled. "Don't you understand?" He shook his head, baffled. "Transdimensional interface?" She spoke the words in English, knowing that neither she nor Antryg had heard them in that language, though the Dead God had spoken, for the most part, in slurred and stammered Ferr.

He shook his head again. "You mean, you *do* get a translation through the spell of tongues? I mean, those words mean something to you?"

Joanna nodded quickly. The Dead God drew itself to its feet like a crumbling mountain, eyes gleaming slimily in the failing ruby light. "He's from another world, he's got to be."

Still holding the staff warily in hand, Antryg walked to the edge of the circle. "Look," he said, his deep voice echoing in the darkness, "I can help you. Send you back."

"A wizard," muttered the Dead God thickly. "Your power shines through your flesh. I will drink of your brain, your power will be mine. All power will be mine—psychokinesis at the molecular level—I am the Dead God . . ."

"I'm not getting through to him." His eyes never moved from the thing that had begun to lurch toward them, one staggering step at a time, huge arms outspread and broken claws bent to seize. Antryg's swollen knuckles shifted along the staff he held; his voice was low and rapid. "Do you have a weapon of any kind with you, my dear? I don't think the gun will do much good—my sword-scabbard, maybe, as a club. Remember it's only dead flesh . . ."

But Joanna frowned suddenly at the dark monster that loomed on the edge of the dying torchlight, her mind taken up with another question entirely. "You know, I bet it's a hardware problem," she said.

Any other companion in such adversity would have stared at her and said, *"What???"* in utter disbelief, but Antryg, who dealt completely in inconsequence himself, only said, "You mean with the physical bodies he's taken to make up what he is now?"

"Not the bodies—the brain." The stench was so terrible she could scarcely breathe, part of her mind screaming in panic, while another part, calm and calculating, worked out the logic of the situation. "Your software's only as good as your hardware."

"And he can't put his thoughts through the brains of the people he's taken," the wizard finished, his gray eyes lighting up like a truly mad scientist's on the verge of discovery.

"Yeah," Joanna breathed. "Only as far as brain chemistry is concerned, it isn't a simple binary—your hardware *is* your software. And his must be half-rotted anyway, even if he didn't get it from some not-very-bright priest and whatever town drunks or troublemakers the local sacrifice lottery decided the community could best spare. He's in there . . ."

"Poor bastard," Antryg whispered feelingly, and Joanna, looking at that filthy colossus of decay, felt a shudder of horror and pity. "But he can hear us."

"I'll bet he's only able to process information in terms of what was in those brains to begin with." She was on her feet now, her back to Antryg's; she slipped his scabbarded sword from his sash to hold like a baseball bat, knowing that her aim must be to strike, rather than to cut. The scabbard was lacquered wood and hard as iron, but it still felt like a hopelessly inadequate weapon in her small hands. "Look, we've got to get through to—to the original part of him, the part that still remembers what he used to be . . ."

"*If* he—or she—still remembers."

Joanna thought for a moment. Then, still keeping a wary eye on the creature that loomed in the darkness, she slid her makeshift weapon into her belt, dug quickly in a pocket of her backpack, and pulled out her Swiss Army knife. Kneeling beside Antryg's feet, she tapped the metal knuckle of the knife three times on the stone floor.

She paused, then tapped again, once, hard and small in the terrible stillness. "I saw this done in *Red Planet Mars*," she explained breathlessly, and tapped again four times.

"Don't get it wrong," Antryg whispered, still standing braced only feet from the swaying form of the Dead God, his dripping staff held at the ready. "And pray the thing's a mathematician."

"I'm just praying the value of pi is the same in its dimension as it is in mine."

Pause, one. Pause, five . . .

"Hmm. Sticky if it's not."

Pause . . .

Then, hollow and terrible, vast as the slamming of some great iron door, the knocking came as before—nine times. A silence, like the black weight of the air after thunder. Then two knocks, blows that shook the walls. Silence. Six.

The silence stretched into an elastic eternity.

"Five," prompted Antryg softly, as Joanna, suddenly panic-stricken, blocked on the next number.

Tapping it out, she realized that to be a wizard, the ability to maintain the concentration for working a spell in any kind of bizarre emergency had to be the most vital of survival traits.

Three hollow booms answered her; five; eight . . .

"Can you make a Sigil?" she whispered.

"For what purpose?"

"Hardware. They're only giant chips, after all—patterns of lines encoding symbolic logic, like the synapses of the brain. If you can draw one, or some, or as many as you need, on the floor, and give him an alternative communications hardware to what he has . . . Would that work?"

"I haven't the faintest idea," he said, an expression of dazzled, scholarly delight in his face wholly at odds with the bruises and blood that marked it, the hell-pit darkness around them. "I'll need metal . . ."

"There's about fifty feet of copper wire in my backpack."

He hesitated. "And I'll have to step out of the pentacle." He had not taken his eyes from the thing before him; her shoulder to his side, Joanna could feel the swiftness of his breath.

She said seriously, "Not if you drew them real small." For one second he glanced down at her, protesting, then realized she was joking and grinned. His hand was perfectly steady as he gave her the staff. Having seen him whip and twirl it like a cheerleader's baton, she was startled by its weight.

"Don't let it rush you head-on," he cautioned softly. "It weighs three or four times what you do."

"Do you want your sword back?"

He shook his head, dug a piece of chalk from the pocket of his coat, and gingerly stepped across the protective points of the magic circle. There was a flicker of blue light, like tiny discharges of electricity, among the pillars. Then silence again, that terrible waiting. Crouched like a lion gauging its moment to spring, the Dead God edged forward as Antryg knelt and began forming the complex shapes of the Sigils on the floor.

The torch was going; in the darkness Joanna thought she saw the lines on the floor begin to glow with a cold, frosty light, but it illuminated little save the mad wizard's long nose and cracked spectacles and the wet gleam of the Dead God's eyes. It was aware of her, she knew, watching with

the mind that seemed to fill the icy blackness around her—
as if it knew that it was she who held all the weapons, she
who was totally unsuited to use them. Her hands shaking,
she braced the staff under one arm and dug into her backpack, pulling out the copper wire and one of the several
candles stowed in a side pocket, which she lit from the end
of the dying torch. The light wasn't much, but she knew
Antryg could see in the dark. She felt the Dead God's
glance shift toward her and hastily set the candle down,
praying she wouldn't be panicked into stepping on it, then
gripped the staff once again.

There was no sound but the crumbling slur of chalk on
stone, and the swift lightness of Antryg's breath.

Watching the pattern of the Sigils take shape, Joanna
recognized some from Caris' practice drawings: the Sigil
of the Gate; the Sigil of the Single Eye; the Sigil of
Strength; and the horned Sigil of Shadows which governs
veiled and hidden things. Linking through them was the
Sigil of Roads, that curious, oddball Seal which, like the
Lost God who governed it, had no power in itself at all.
Across the protective points of the circle she tossed Antryg
the copper wire and duct tape, knowing from Caris' explanations that metal was necessary in their workings; and still
the Dead God edged forward, slime tracking down the broken ends of his bone fangs, his hands with their hooked
nails stirring hungrily, uneasily, at the ends of rotting arms.

When Antryg straightened up his face seemed very
white in the ghostly glow of the Sigils under the stitchwork
of tracked blood. Around him the Seals of those ancient
gods lay in a lace of light, wire, and duct tape, seeming to
float on the stone. He took a deep breath, walked forward,
and held out his hand to the Dead God.

With a gluey snarl, the Dead God raised two of its
hands; Antryg saw what was coming and ducked, but not
quickly enough. Claws raking, they caught him a stunning
blow, flinging him against the closest pillar, as if he'd been

in truth the scarecrow he so often resembled; then the Dead God was upon him.

Not knowing what else to do, knowing she could never cross the distance between them in time, Joanna swung the iron staff and caught the pillar behind her with a crack like a gunshot. The Dead God's head swiveled horribly on its neck, one eye glaring, the other drooping sickeningly as the muscles that held it began to come loose. Picking up one of Antryg's discarded pieces of chalk, she stooped and marked the floor:

//////
//////
//
/////
//////

The Dead God stood for a long moment, staring down at the pattern of chalked lines. Then it turned to where Antryg still slumped at the base of the pillar. Closing one huge hand around his arm and another around the nape of his neck it hauled him to his feet. Their eyes held, the Dead God's glinting like a half-mad animal's, Antryg's calm and completely without fear. At length he took the rotting wristbones in his hands, and drew the thing toward the pattern of Sigils; it let him guide its hands to the points where metal and magic entwined, and left them there when Antryg rose and walked to the other end of the symbolic Road.

The wizard glanced down at Joanna's binary code. "What is it?"

"Planck's Constant."

"I'm sure Mrs. Planck is pleased to hear it." There was a note of strain in his voice, and she guessed by the way he moved that he'd cracked a rib against the pillar.

"If he's a scientist he'll recognize it. It's the ratio of energy to frequency of light and it occurs over and over again in physics. Like pi, it was a way to tell him that we knew he isn't the Dead God. That we knew who he is really."

Antryg knelt down near the Sigil of Shadow and touched the glowing latticework of wire and light. "Perhaps he needed reminding himself," he said softly and wiped the trickle of blood from the corner of his mouth. Joanna set down the staff and, shivering slightly, stepped across the psionic barrier of the pentacle to kneel at Antryg's side.

"I think you're going to need a technical consultant."

Behind the blood-fleckred glass, she saw the quick flare of concern in his eyes, but he couldn't deny the truth of what she said. After a hesitation, he took her hands, his long fingers and the leather of his gloves sticky with the gross corruption of the monster's touch, and guided them to the wan stringers of criss-crossing light. "I don't know how much you'll be able to hear," he cautioned softly. "If you feel him trying to get a grip on your mind, pull out at once. Don't try to help me. All right?"

Joanna nodded uneasily.

"Good girl." He drew a deep breath and flinched at the stab of his injured ribs, then seemed to settle in on himself, half closing his eyes, not working magic, Joanna thought, but drinking of the magic of the Sigils themselves.

Not being mageborn, she felt very little, only a kind of warmth where the light lay under her fingers. For a time she heard nothing; but glancing up in the dim amber reflection of the distant candle, she saw Antryg's lips move and realized that her own nervous observation of the Dead God in the darkness that surrounded them was blocking her concentration.

Great, she thought bitterly. *What a time to have to pick up meditation techniques*. But she had read enough to have some idea of what she must do. Perhaps the hardest thing was simply to close her eyes, to release all thought, all fear, and all planning of what she'd do if . . . to think of nothing . . .

Like the distant murmur of a metallic wind, she heard the Dead God's voice.

". . . The more lives I take, the greater my power will grow. I can drink the magic of your brain, Windrose—magic to keep this flesh from corrupting, magic to take, to hold. Why should I return to my own world, when with the powers of a god I can spread my will across the earth here?"

"I suppose you can." Antryg's voice seemed distant in the darkness, but perfectly conversational, no more ill-at-ease than if they shared a tankard of beer at some alehouse hearth. "Provided, that is, you're more than semiconscious and still able to take care of yourself. But I don't think you will be. Human psychic energy is really a rather poor substitute for what you eat in your own world, isn't it? Not to mention the air."

"This flesh tolerates the air."

"You're poisoning yourself and you know it—or you did know it when you tried to cut back on human sacrifices and when you tried all those other things—beef blood or walking out to the Witchpath Stone on the nights the energy ran along it."

Joanna felt, through the whispering whiteness of the Sigils' light, the bloody stir of the Dead God's anger. "The hunger grows," it whispered.

Diffidently, she put in, "That's common with food allergies."

"In my own world I was nothing," the god whispered. "A technician, a tracker of xchi particles for other men's research. Here, I have power."

"Only as long as you retain your consciousness," Antryg pointed out. "My magic will give you more power, yes. But it won't stop the clouding of your mind. At best, you'll become a random force, a psychic whirlwind that grows with every human mind it devours until someone finally finds a way to destroy you as mad dogs are destroyed. At worst, you'll be controlled by others, as Pettin controls you now. I don't see another choice for you."

There was a rush, a surge, a blaze of light behind her eyes and half-drunken fury and hate slamming like a wave against her mind. Joanna jerked her hands free of Antryg's light touch and opened her eyes in time to see the wizard flinch aside with a cry. Though the Dead God had not moved, Joanna saw the fresh claw marks that scored Antryg's face and jaw, running with blood; as she watched, a second set gouged his neck; the air rumbled with a sound of rage that seemed to come from nowhere, the foggy rage of the Dead God's half-polluted brain. Antryg bent under the blows, blood streaming from his face and neck, but never took his hands from the curving horns of the Sigil of Shadow.

The angry rumbling died.

Her heart hammering, Joanna could not bring herself to touch the Sigils again, but in time she heard Antryg whisper, "Where is the body that you came here in from your own world?"

The Dead God must have made some reply, for after a time the wizard breathed, "Since it has not corrupted in this world, were I to guide you back into it and back through the Void to a place where you could get help, would they be able to save you?"

An even longer silence followed; then Antryg, still half in his trance, smiled. "Yes," he murmured, like a distant echo of his conversations with Caris. "Mad, too. You no more know that I won't destroy you when you open your mind to me than I know that when I open mine to you, you won't simply devour it. Do you believe that you need my help?"

If he was sane he might, Joanna thought desperately. *If he wasn't fogged-out, half-poisoned with the psychic and metabolic garbage he's been ingesting for weeks . . . Don't do it, Antryg. Don't give him what he seeks . . .*

But Antryg took his hands from the Sigils, and climbed slowly, wincingly to his feet. The Dead God loomed over him in the shadows and held out two rotting hands to help him up; together the gawky wizard and the monster vanished into the black hole of the haunted darkness. The glow of light in the Sigils themselves faded, seeming to sink into the floor, leaving only a smudgy tracing of chalk and the tangled snakes of copper wire, glinting faintly in the flicker of the single candle at Joanna's side.

How long she sat alone in the darkness, Joanna wasn't sure afterward, her every nerve strained, listening for sounds in the utter silence of the distant crypt. The candle burned itself slowly down. Reaction was setting in, after a day's exhausting walk and only hours of sleep snatched at intervals in the endless childbirth of the squire's lady the night before. Weirdly enough, the blood that had rained down during the combat with the Dead God had vanished without a trace, though Joanna was at a loss to say when. She wondered whether it had, in fact, ever existed.

Antryg was alone in the crypt with the Dead God. That he had said nothing to her at their departure didn't surprise her; she suspected that he was channeling all his strength into maintaining some kind of psychic link with the Dead God's mind, some lifeline to that lost abomination's sanity that he dared not loose. The cold deepened. Joanna huddled into her sheepskin coat, watching the mist of her breath, gilded by the dim candle-gleam, and wondering how long she should give it.

Before doing what?

The great doors were bolted from the outside. In her heart she knew she'd wait a long time before she dared make her way through the sightless forest of the pillared vestibule down to those ghastly vaults alone.

The noise, when it came, nearly made her jump out of her skin with shock—the slamming scrape of the door bolts at her back, and a man's angry curse. Then the night

air touched her face, close to freezing but almost warm
compared to the icy stillness around her.

"Joanna?"

Torchlight fell across the floor over her in a gold bar,
sparkling on Caris' blond hair and the blade of his drawn
sword. He fell back with a gasp from the threshold. "What
the . . ."

"Here!" She sprang to her feet and stumbled to him, her
knees almost giving way with the cramp of long sitting; she
was shaking all over as he caught her briefly in the circle of
his arm. He wore his sword sash and dagger belt strapped
over his scholar's robe; past his shoulder Joanna saw no
one in the trough of darkness between church and baptistry
save one man slumped unconscious at the bottom of the
steps and the arm of another projecting from the shadows
of the baptistry door. "Caris, we . . ."

"Where is he?" The young man held the torch aloft,
looking swiftly around the vestibule, concern overriding
for a moment both his nausea and his usual shield of aloof
and bitter calm. "Is he . . . ?"

"He went down to the crypt with the Dead God," she
said. "He was going to try to send the Dead God back, he
said . . . Caris. You do care for him, don't you?" For the
fear in his face was unmistakable and had little to do with
being left to deal with Suraklin alone.

"He's the most maddening mooncalf I've ever had the
misfortune to know," Caris retorted explosively, not answering the question. "If he's . . ."

He broke off and caught her arm. Around them the
freezing darkness seemed shaken suddenly, like a curtain in
a wind. Cold terror skated across Joanna's bones and she
clutched tight to the coarse wool of Caris' sleeve. For an
instant, the universe seemed to ripple into breathing near-
ness around them.

"The Void," Caris whispered.

Outside, thin and terrible as the death-cry of something
that has long since ceased to be human, Father Del's

wheezing voice could be heard, scaling up into a thin
scream that ended as if dispersed upon the wind.

Joanna said softly, "He's gone."

Caris raised his torch again and, sword in hand, led the
way into the black cave of the church.

After all that had gone before, what was in the sanctu-
ary did not do more than make Joanna gag, but she heard
Caris gasp and choke on the fumes that made the air there
almost past breathing. From inhabiting the body of the
luckless Father Sweelum, now an unrecognizable puddle in
a black habit in a corner, the Dead God had used the flesh
of his victims to fashion his own body. What was left over
lay strewn across the altar, the chancel, the steps leading
down to the crypt. Only the deathly cold which the Dead
God had gathered about him to preserve his borrowed flesh
intact saved the place from being more hideous than it already was. In the crypt, the swollen body of the Dead God
lay, a huge sprawl of carrion, beside a stone niche that had
once contained some local notable; dry bones lay heaped in
a corner, still bundled in the dessicated shreds of gold-
stitched winding sheet. In their place, stretched facedown
upon the stone, lay Antryg, one arm extended, his fingers
still twined with the Dead God's dissolving hand.

"Antryg . . ." She stepped forward; at the sound of her
voice, and the touch of the torchlight, he flinched. Then
his hand came up and groped for hers, seeking the touch of
a human mind or perhaps only of living flesh. She barely
even noticed what it was covered with as it closed convulsively around her arm.

He whispered, "Get me out of here."

On the outside steps of the church, Caris picked up Antryg's fallen cloak and put it carefully around his shoulders;
Joanna dug into the wizard's coat pocket for his tin flask of
gin, which he drank like a dying man receiving the elixir of
life. Then with a shaky smile he handed it to her, and she
decided after two swigs that there was a good deal to be
said in favor of the vile stuff after all. Torches had begun to

flicker around all sides of the square as dark forms emerged from the shadow—the merchant Pettin, looking white and scared and Greer the mayor, her face filled with concern and joy when she saw the three demon hunters gathered alive and more or less whole on the steps. Of Father Del Joanna never saw anything again.

"D'you suppose our welcome would extend to a cup of tea?" Antryg asked softly at last, when his hands had stopped shaking. He glanced up at Caris, the old impishness returning to his black-circled eyes. "You turned up with remarkable speed for a man we left back at Alport Hall."

"Don't be a fool," Caris said roughly. "I followed you here, of course." He sheathed his sword with a vicious click, but did not replace the scabbard in his sash. "The only delay was in putting Pettin's bullyboys out of the way."

Glancing around the square, Joanna identified only two of the merchant's hired men; of those two, one was nursing a closed eye and a lump the size of a pigeon's egg on his jaw, and the other was just pulling the remains of makeshift ropes off his wrists.

More gently, the sasennan added, "And you? Will the Council be able to track you through what you did here tonight?"

"I don't think so," Antryg replied and pushed the blood-tipped ends of his matted hair out of his face. "I did very little actual magic. Perhaps some, in the—the guiding of the Dead God's spirit back into his former body and back through the Void. Like the abominations we saw at Suraklin's Citadel, it was unable to breathe the air here, but for the same reason the organisms of decay here had taken no hold upon it. But the Sigils draw and transmit power of themselves. They are, as Joanna said, symbolic representations of the mind, in a way; they are fueled, like the teles relays, by the ambient magic all around us."

He frowned, as some other idea teased the back of his

mind; his reddish brows pulled together, twisting the crusted claw marks that scored the side of his face.

Caris stood looking down at him for a moment in the uncertain dance of the torchlight. There was some of the sasennan's old exasperation in his face, tempered by understanding and pity. In a low voice, as if for the mage's ears alone, he said, "You know you can't keep it up."

Antryg glanced up at him swiftly, but there was no question in his eyes.

"It's only a matter of time before you get yourself backed into a corner where you must use your power or die."

The wizard looked as if he would have shed this remark with his usual lightness, but hesitated on his indrawn breath and then let it go. "I know," he said, so low that Joanna almost could not hear. He sat for a time, looking at the battered metal flask still clasped in his stained fingers, tiredness settling on him as if some sustaining inner cord had been suddenly cut.

"My greatest fear was that Suraklin would have heard of the Dead God, and gotten here before us," he went on quietly. "Whether the Dead God joined him as a willing partner or was overcome and dominated as his tool when his consciousness deteriorated with the pollution of those it subsumed, they would have been a terrible combination. The thing is . . ."

He stopped, his gray eyes staring out beyond the torchlight, beyond the darkness, looking, Joanna sensed, at some additional horror, some piece of the puzzle that had fallen into place. So he had looked, Joanna realized, when in the Prince Regent's carriage Pharos had spoken of what had become of his father.

"What?" she asked quickly.

He glanced down at her and shook his head, his eyes avoiding hers. "Nothing," he murmured. Then, "Do you think we could talk these people out of a cup of tea, some food, and a bed for the night? I'm chilled to the marrow and like to die of weariness."

But though Joanna, once they were in the bed of sheepskins and quilts in Greer's house, fell almost at once into heavy slumber unbroken even by nightmares, the last thing she saw was Antryg's open gray eyes staring into the darkness of the ceiling. Whatever it was that his encounter with the Dead God had told him or caused him to guess, she was aware that it did not let him sleep that night.

CHAPTER XIII

IN THE ENSUING THREE DAYS JOANNA TRIED TO GET AN-
tryg to talk about his interview with the Dead God, but
found him silent and preoccupied. In Antryg's case silence,
like sanity, was always a relative matter; on the road he
chatted of the obscure customs of religious sects, the love
lives of past Emperors, and the odder methods of divina-
tion; or he listened in absorbed silence to her explanations
of computer hardware and the best methods of videotape
piracy. But she sensed that, behind this gentle barrage of
persiflage, he was worried and frightened.

They came out of the Sykerst and down into the lowland
countries east of Angelshand, working their way through
the brown valleys along the Glidden toward Tilrattin Island
and the node in the energy-lines. She had come to understand that Antryg was not a particularly brave man. Like
herself, he possessed far too vivid an imagination to contemplate the final confrontation with his ancient mentor
with anything like Caris' single-minded fatalism. He had
lived with fear for a long time. Then, too, Joanna realized
uneasily, he was the only one of the four conspirators who
truly knew what they were up against.

"As far as I can tell it looks like Suraklin knew what he
was doing," she said diffidently one evening, looking up
from the heap of photocopied programs on her lap in the

feeble illumination of a couple of flickering candles. An-tryg raised his head sharply from the makeshift pillow of his pack. She had seen the glint of the candlelight in his open eyes, staring up past the broken house beams that sheltered the abandoned cellar where they had made camp, studying the winter stars blazing above the naked trees.

As they had drawn nearer to their destination, they had avoided for the most part the farming villages; but, having left the brutal winds of the Sykerst behind them, this was less of a hardship. Here in the hedgerow country, too, it was far easier to find deserted barns or the ruins of old chapels or farms. Lord Alport and the villagers of Far Wilden had given them as much dried meat and the thick, heavily concentrated waybread as they could carry, so there was little need for them to seek out farmers who would spread word of strangers in the land.

Antryg rolled up onto one elbow and squinted myopically at her across the candles. "I'd certainly like to think so," he murmured, falling into the conversation, as was their habit now, in the middle, as if it were something they had discussed before. In the dim glow of the candles, his breath formed a little cloud; Joanna pulled her quilted blanket more tightly around her shoulders and brushed with her fingertips the papers that lay in her lap.

"As far as I can figure it without being a mage or a xeno-bio-psychochemist," she went on hesitantly, "the Dead God's problem stemmed from incompatible hardware-software interface—he'd put his consciousness into the physical brains of beings who were not of his species. I gather he was able to tap into human psychokinetic powers at will—which no humans but mages are able to do ordinarily—but he couldn't make the transfer until the human consciousness was absolutely gone—that is, till the poor yutz was dead. And I suspect he was doing it instinctively, rather than as a learned technique."

Antryg nodded. "More or less, yes."

"I don't think you need to worry that there will be a

similar problem with Suraklin. I don't have anywhere near all the subroutines of personality transfer—I was just pulling them off the disk as fast as I could, and a lot of this stuff is total gibberish to me—but from what I've been able to tell from the ones I *can* understand, he's got all the personalities digitalized down to the last detail. You're not going to get the kind of organic deterioration we did with the Dead God."

The wizard fished his spectacles out of their hiding place in his boot, which stood drying by the fire, and eased them carefully on over the narrow lines of bruises and Caris' stitching that marked the Dead God's final, furious attack. His coat, blanket, and cloak around his shoulders, he edged over to look down over Joanna's shoulder at the endless lines of the program.

"You haven't happened to come across any mention of *where* Suraklin's put his computer, have you?"

"Not yet." Joanna wriggled her way under the corner of the cloak he held out to her—though still, the night was icy. "I've been looking for it, but you've got to remember there's *tons* of this stuff. The copy isn't all that hot, either. Toward the end there, I was just photoreducing it, doing a fast cut-and-paste job and having it copied again, double-sided to save space, without looking to see what it was. For that reason, a lot of it's barely legible, but I had to bring as much as I could. And it isn't anywhere near the whole."

Antryg grinned ruefully and ran his thumb along the edge of the thick stack of unread papers. "That will teach me not to learn to read English."

She shrugged and smiled back. "Even if you could read English, you still couldn't read programming—the same way I can't understand the spells in here, even if they are in Fortran. At least, since Gary was doing most of the programming as Gary, the programs *are* in English—probably because Suraklin couldn't get a keyboard in those hearts-and-flowers you people use for an alphabet. I wonder what language he thinks in?"

She shivered suddenly and muttered, "Oh, damn," as the bitter, creeping grayness of depression whispered in like floodtide over her soul. Antryg's arm tightened around her, the warmth of it only a ghost, a memory that such things ought to bring her comfort rather than comfort itself. She bent her head wretchedly, steeling herself to endure what might be several hours, what might be the rest of a nightmare-laden night, or what might, she realized intellectually, be the beginning of forever. But she was too drained, too weary, to care.

She whispered, "I don't know how much more of this I can take."

Antryg sighed and rubbed her back with his big hand. "A great deal more, I'm afraid. Good parasites never kill their hosts." She gritted her teeth a little and rested her head on the bony hardness of his chest. She had never figured out how badly the energy drains affected him, though since they had become lovers, she suspected they did so more than he showed.

"Salteris—Suraklin—said something like that once," she commented dully. "That people grow accustomed— that in a few years no one will know what they're missing . . ."

Under her cheek, she felt him startle and raised her head to meet the hard, speculative glint in his eyes. "Did he?" Then his lips tightened and his long, narrow nostrils flared with the first real anger she had ever seen him display. He took a deep breath, almost forcibly releasing his hold on it, but there was still a kind of cold purposefulness in his face as he disengaged his arm from around her shoulders and began to dig through the capacious pockets of his greatcoat. "Will you excuse me, my dear?"

Joanna nodded miserably, thinking, as he rose to his feet, *I should have known he didn't really love me* . . . and then stopped herself irritably from that old and, she knew, quite untrue train of thought. His decrepit robe nearly black in the starlight, Antryg climbed halfway up the fallen rubble and beams at the other side of the cellar and dug from his pocket an astrolabe he'd gotten from Pella.

"Suraklin thought like that, you know," he said, making a minute adjustment to the rete and sighting along the alidade at the North Star, high in the frosty sky. "He operated on the assumption that he was more intelligent than anyone else. For the most part he was right, of course, but it led to certain habits of thought. He could never be got to admit that there were things he did not understand."

He turned the astrolabe in his hand, manipulating the rule on the back. Joanna watched him without much curiosity, having seen him take sightings before in the uncertain glimmer of starlight. Now and then he would turn his head, his long nose silhouetted black against the Prussian blue of the sky as he scanned the horizon. Once he turned quickly at the sound of a sharp rustle in the blackened woods that were all around the ruined house, but it was only Caris, returning cold and wet from his nightly patrol. The young man scrambled down the decayed steps, cursing. "Now I can't even move through the woods without making noise! This is all your fault..."

"Nonsense." Antryg repocketed the astrolabe and slid lightly down from the beam to pull on his boots. "If my calculations are correct, the energy-line should lie about three miles southwest of us; there's something I have to check, now, while the energy's moving."

"You mean you could have sighted along it any time, anywhere, not on the node?" demanded Caris furiously. "We've come all this way..."

"Because I enjoy hundred-mile hikes in the dead of winter, yes." The wizard straightened up, shaking back his straggly gray curls; behind the spectacles Joanna saw the gleam of annoyance in his eyes.

Caris, who had drawn breath to say something else, let

it out and looked away. "I'm sorry," he muttered. "It's just that . . ." He let the words trail off.

More gently, Antryg said, "I know." He held out his hand in its stained and ragged glove. "Joanna? Will you come with me? It isn't dangerous; but if what I fear is happening, it's better that I know."

They traversed the woods in silence. There was a village not far away—at one point Joanna could see the pinpricks of its lights across the stubble fields, like the dying glow in the heart of a burnt-out log—but on these cold and lifeless evenings there was little likelihood of anybody's being abroad so late. And it was not truly so late, Joanna thought, glancing at her watch in the starlight. Back in California, prime time television would barely have started. It was only here, in this bleak world, that the nights went on forever . . . here where she would be trapped . . .

She tried to shake off the depression, but knew it would do no good. Throughout the days of their journeying, the spells of deadness had become more frequent and longer, descending every few days as Suraklin completed, tested, and downloaded more and more of his programs. It was only a matter of time before he made his final transfer and, she suspected, not very much time at that. Her heart turned cold at the thought of it.

Our last chance, Antryg had said. At times like this, with her soul melting into a cold puddle of despair, she knew that she had no chance at all.

She felt nothing of the movement of the energy-line when they reached it, but Antryg evidently did. In the wet, brittle thickets of the woods he halted abruptly, looked this way and that in such thin starlight as filtered through the bare lattices of trees overhead, and turned west, holding Joanna's hand to help her over the rolling roughness of the ground. She'd forgotten to put on her mittens after repacking her backpack—laboriously rewrapping her Xeroxed files in plastic only because she'd made it a rule to do everything by the numbers when the depression was upon her—and her hands were almost numb save where his warmed them. She'd far rather have remained back in the cellar camp with Caris, but had come with Antryg, obscurely craving his company and now, in spite of herself, heartily resenting his preoccupied silence.

"Ah," he murmured at last. "Here we are."

Under a snarl of brown ferns and ivy stems a little standing-stone could be seen, like a child's coffin half embedded in the earth. The trees grew thick around the spot, sapling maple and elm; Antryg pulled off his gloves and waded through the dead underbrush, which rustled sharply as small animals darted away. He pulled loose handfuls of the stone's brittle shroud, baring the surface, then knelt before it, his spectacles gleaming in the cold starlight as he pressed his hands to the pitted rock. After a moment he leaned forward and touched his forehead to it, as if listening. Under his fingertips Joanna glimpsed the scratchwork shadows of traced Sigils and runes.

Shivering and weary, she folded her arms and bit back a number of smartass remarks. They stemmed, she was only too aware, from the gray exhaustion of her soul and her fear of that enormous woodland silence. What he could be seeking she could not imagine, but when he came back to her, she could see the anger in his movements, frustrated rage she had never seen in him before.

"Damn him," he whispered viciously, as they started back to camp. "*Damn* him. He may be the greatest mage in the world but he's a complete and utter fool . . ."

"What is it?" She had to hurry her steps to match his furious strides. Seeing this, he slowed immediately, offering her again a corner of his cloak for warmth. Beneath her encircling arm she could feel the jut of his ribs through several layers of coat and robe and the ripple of the muscle as they walked.

"It's difficult to explain . . ." He paused, looking down at her in the wan lace of star shadows. "No—it's difficult to *believe*. That is—you probably believe that objects are inanimate. So does Suraklin."

"Uh . . ." Joanna said, reminded once again that, in spite of his intelligence and charm and in spite of the fact that she loved him, Antryg was in fact several bricks shy of a load.

"Well," he said simply, "I don't. By the way, my dear —in your reading of the DARKMAGE files, did you ever find mention of where Suraklin hid the teles-balls that he collected over the years, the teles that he's now using to draw power—life-magic—down the energy-paths to convert to his computer's electricity?"

Joanna nodded, remembering one of those many cold little lists of facts that comprised all that was left of Suraklin's personality. "Something called the Bone Well?"

Antryg shuddered. "I was afraid of that. I can understand why no one wanted to look very closely there." She felt the shiver of his body against hers, and he started walking again, heading back to camp. In the starlight his face looked drawn and a little ill.

Glancing back, Joanna saw the little stone still standing like a stumpy dwarf. Pale against the black nets of ivy, the bald patch Antryg had torn seemed to glimmer in the darkness. Joanna could see no scratch on it, no mark of the faint web of signs that she had glimpsed beneath Antryg's hands.

It was, she realized, one of the first markers of the Devil's Road, the arrow-straight track that ran to Tilrattin Island and the crossing node of the lines.

Softly, she said, "Do you think he has them at Tilrattin Island? The teles-relay and the computer? Do you really think he'd put them that close to Angelshand?"

"He would, if he thought he could get the Archmage and the Council run out of that city—which of course he has done." He picked his way over the rocks that crossed a shallow stream, sluggish now with winter, the water like ink between beds of frozen mud lined with rims of ice. He held out a hand to Joanna; she noted, among the tracks on the bank, the small, deformed footmark of something unknown and hideous, a track that the marks of weasel and cony gave wide berth. "But from here, away from the node, I simply can't tell."

"In a way I hope they are there."

He glanced at her, his brows raised but no surprise in his eyes to hear her say it.

Stammering, she explained, "Time is on Suraklin's side. It isn't that I'm eager to face off with him, as Caris is. But if that computer's up and running when we get there—if Suraklin's already programmed himself into it—I don't know how much conscious control he'll have over his input."

"You mean he may simply spit it out."

Joanna grinned unwillingly at the anthropomorphic image. "Well, he can't, not physically. It's the trade-off he's made for virtual immortality and a limitless capacity for knowledge. He's at the mercy of his input. He can defend himself from a worm in the way computers fight human interference—with passwords and tricks and codes —but with enough time, and enough concentration, those *can* be worked through. The problem is that, with the teles relays in operation, such concentration is the first thing to go." She swallowed hard, frightened just to be saying it, thinking it and its implications. "If we get there while the computer's down, we're home free. But if that computer's on-line, I'm going to be making a *lot* of mistakes. And any delay's going to buy him time to bring up whatever second-line defenses he's got."

"I see." Antryg sighed and pushed up his spectacles to rub his eyes. "I *think* there's one last thing he needs to do before he goes 'on-line,' as you say—before he becomes his computer. But he may have done it already, whilst we were skulking about the Sykerst, pretending to be doctors. I wish I knew. I have a frightening feeling that time's getting very short."

He stopped, listening in the thin, starry darkness between the trees. Though one piece of woods still looked much like another, especially at night, Joanna thought she recognized the environs of the fallen cellar. She knew he was listening for any sound, any clue of danger. Still oppressed by the energy drain, physically weary and shivering with cold, she felt a flash of impatience and the urge to jerk on his sleeve and tell him not to bother. She forced herself silent until she felt, through his big hand in hers, his body relax, and they moved forward again.

She asked softly, "Is that what's been bothering you?"

He shook his head. "No. Since talking with the Dead God I've been uneasy about it, and feeling the energy-flow in the stone tonight I'm now sure; between his hardware and his software, with his input, once Suraklin enters his computer there is a very good chance that he'll be insane."

They reached Tilrattin Island two days later in the middle of a morning drowned in pearl-colored mist that limited visibility to a few feet. Moving cautiously through that clammy opal world, Joanna wondered if the fog itself were not some defense that Suraklin had thrown around his headquarters, but Caris shook his head. "It's always foggy in the river basin at this time of year."

"Convenient," Antryg murmured, pausing for the dozenth time since they'd entered the shaggy tangles of riverbank woods to listen. Though no countrywoman, Joanna remembered these woods at the end of summer with their myriad of bird calls, the hum of gnats above the boggy places, and the splash of fish in the streams. All was silence now, save for the muted clucking of the river itself, invisible in the fog. "Of course, tampering with the weather is very difficult to trace or even to detect, but if someone *is* watching from the island, all the fog rolling suddenly away so that we can see where we're headed is going to be a little hard to miss."

"Swell," Joanna muttered, tucking her mittened hands

into her armpits for warmth. Beside her, Caris said nothing, but his narrowed dark eyes moved here and there about them, trying to pierce the milky vapors. Since the spell of deadness the night before last, the cold armor seemed to have risen around his heart again, black and impenetrable. He had resumed the loose black fighting garb of the sasenna and seemed glad to have put the distractions and the temptations of passing for a healer behind him with his purplish student's robe. When one is getting ready to die, she supposed, one can not think too much about living.

"Tilrattin and, in fact, all the woods between here and the Devil's Road have been shunned for centuries," Antryg went on after a moment. "If it's been anything near what it was like at Suraklin's Citadel, the concentration of abominations won't have improved its reputation any..."

"This is getting better and better." Joanna threw a nervous glance over her shoulder. They had, in fact, come across the carcass of one abomination and what Antryg took to be evidence of another—a fairly extensive grove of oak trees which within the last few weeks had been burned to their stumps, pulled down and fired until nothing remained.

"Still," the wizard continued, "I doubt we're going to encounter any traps until we set foot on the island itself. Suraklin wouldn't want to call attention to the place—not this close to Angelshand, not this close to the manor at Devilsgate."

"He has Cerdic fetching his shoes for him," Caris put in bitterly.

"That's only been since the end of September," Joanna reminded him. "He was setting up the computer before then—pity you didn't check Devilsgate for Suraklin's marks when we were there."

"I did," Antryg replied. "It was in the study, and quite old—twenty or thirty years—but it hadn't been reactivated; at least it hadn't then." He looked around him again, scanning the matte dove-colored mist, the flattened cutouts of the trees that faded back into pencil tracings, streaked here and there with rust. "But I don't feel anything and I don't hear anything, except..." He frowned, his gray eyes narrowing behind his specs. But he only said softly, "Come on."

Caris slipped his sword sheathe from its sash, holding it loosely in his left hand, his right held ready at his side. Stained and blotched with weather and patched with coarse brown and butternut fustians, the dull purples and greens of Antryg's coat and cloak seemed to blend uncannily with the fog as he moved away. Joanna followed, picking her way carefully over the carpet of frost-stiffened leaves.

They shed their packs at the edge of the river, with the exception of Joanna's ever-present backpack; the water was low, and a long series of crescent-shaped riffles like brown glass marked the ford. The island itself was invisible beyond a wall of fog. Caris cursed, and Antryg shook his head.

"Use the shielding spells I taught you," he breathed, pulling off his boots and hose and shivering as he kilted up the skirts of his long robe. "I'll whistle if it's safe." He drew his sword and began to pick his way gingerly down the ice of the bank. Over his shoulder he added softly, "If you hear a great deal of splashing, but no whistle, I suggest you look for another way across."

"Thanks," Caris said bitterly as the wizard vanished into the grayish wall of water and mist.

After what seemed like twenty minutes but which was, by Joanna's digital watch, less than five, the sound of the wizard's low whistle drifted across the smoky water. Feeling horribly like a character in a science fiction TV show ("Gee, the Captain's vanished utterly so we'd better beam down the second-in-command to exactly the same coordinates to see what happened to him!"), Joanna pulled off her boots and rolled up the legs of her trousers, gritted her teeth, and waded into the icy river .38 in hand.

But when the dark wall of the wooded bank materialized in the mists before her, only the solitary shape of Antryg was visible there. He was balanced on a rock above the water, still barefoot, she saw; he helped her up and ordered curtly, "Put your boots on." Thankful for this display of male chauvinism, she obeyed, then stood guard while he did the same. At Antryg's whistle, Caris appeared out of the fog a few moments later, shivering a little and tense as stretched rope. The fog seemed thicker here, as it naturally would, Joanna reminded herself, surrounded on all sides by water; the silence of the crowding black trees was frighteningly oppressive.

"The island's less than half a mile across," Antryg remarked softly. "If Suraklin's here, I suspect he knows by this time he's got company, so I think we can dispense with the element of surprise." As he spoke, Joanna felt upon her face the chilly brush of wind that seemed to come from nowhere, and gradually, gently, the fog began to drift and part. Over the water it remained thick, a rolling wall of white cobwebs, but before them trees emerged, scabby greenish elms and oaks whose coarse bark was nearly black with dampness, a wiry carpet of knee-deep sepia underbrush beneath their feet. Through the trees, startlingly close, rose the pale heads of the stone circle.

"Do you feel anything?" she whispered to Antryg, and he shook his head.

"Not from the knees down, anyway," he added ruefully. "There's no sign of a roof among the stones—he can't have left the thing in the open air. Let's have a look, but I suspect all we're going to find is a vacant lot." On that irreverent remark he moved off through the trees toward the damp, bluish stone giants, but he did not, she noticed, sheathe his sword.

The stone ring on Tilrattin Island was centuries empty, silent and overgrown with ivy and wild grape, but even so, something about it made the hair prickle on Joanna's nape. She had seen the menhirs that made up the Devil's Road,

and the long tracks that crossed the Sykerst, some of them
twelve and fifteen feet high—the bluestone monoliths of
Tilrattin towered twenty feet high, dwarfing the humans
who trod so warily beneath them. Standing within the innermost circle of trilithons, Joanna had the queer feeling
that the ring was bigger than it was and that she stood in
some huge courtyard surrounded by watching entities on
the verge of speech. In its center, disturbingly reminiscent
of that central chamber of Suraklin's power, a circular pool
of water reflected the colorless sky.

"What was it?" she whispered, hardly daring to breathe.
"What was it used for?"

"Many things." The frayed hem of his robe swishing
wetly through the gray weeds, Antryg moved from stone to
stone of the five great inner gates, passing his hands along
their surfaces as he had that of the little menhir in the
woods. Joanna thought she saw, ephemeral as the silver
gleam of snail tracks in the daylight, the flicker of runes
beneath his fingers. "Healing. At a node in the lines, a
powerful mage could draw back life to the dying, back in
the days when you wouldn't be killed yourself for doing
so. Listening. Drawing on the strength of the stones themselves." His deep voice, always so flexible, had fallen to
scarcely a whisper, as if he feared the stones themselves
would hear. "They are ruinously old, Joanna. They pass
power back and forth among themselves, like cells in a
battery. They watch and they listen. They have seen so
much that some of them are close to developing voices of
their own."

"You mean they—they speak?" She followed him to
one of the fallen stones of the outer of the three rings,
crouched down as he knelt beside it in the dead bracken
while Caris remained, forgotten, on one knee gazing into
the mist-skimmed depths of the central pool.

"Not to us." The mad wizard pressed his palms to the
pitted stone as he had to the menhir in the woods, bending
his head down as if listening, until the long ends of his

tangled gray hair brushed the damp rock. Light seemed to rise up through the stone, a wan foxfire galaxy of crossing lines—Sigils, runes, the marks of mages long dead, glowing palely for a few moments under the coarse winding sheet of lichen, then sinking back again into the stone's secret heart. "To one another." Antryg rose, and moved on to the next stone. "We don't concern them much, though it's still interesting to listen to what they have to say. It's a mistake many wizards make to believe that their spells have no long-term cumulative effect upon their surroundings ... Caris!" He turned his head sharply. "Come away from there."

The young man looked up from the pool with a start. He got smoothly to his feet; his strides made barely a sound in the wet bracken.

More gently, the wizard asked, "What did you see there?"

Caris shook his head. "Nothing," he lied. He looked gray and sick.

Antryg tilted his head slightly to one side, studying him; the sasennan's brown eyes avoided his. After a moment Caris asked in a muffled voice, "They used that pool for divining the future, didn't they?"

Like the touch of black silk in the misty cold, Antryg said, "It took a great deal of power to get a true reading. It always does, with water. Most people just see lies, if they see anything at all."

The young man looked at him for a moment longer, an orthodox and unwilling pupil to this half-deranged mentor in his diamond earrings and scruffy cavalry coat. It seemed as if he would speak, but he only nodded and turned away. After a time he said, "Could Suraklin have his headquarters underground? Under the island?"

Antryg shook his head. "The digging would have been far too noticeable and too recent to have covered the signs. Suraklin's plan has been in preparation for some time, but the physical assembly of it—the computer, the teles-relay, and the conversion mechanism perfected by Narwahl Skip-frag—only took place in the last several months. No, we can only wait—there's a ruined chapel on the far bank of the river—until the next time the power relays come up. From here we can take a sighting along the lines . . . I can't believe it's at the Citadel of Wizards itself . . ."

Caris swung around, slamming the side of his fist into the nearest stone with a sudden explosion of pent violence. His dark eyes blazed, his voice shook with the strain of being released, once again, from the death-fight for which he must still hold himself ready. "And what then?" he almost shouted. "Take a month to journey through the taiga forest in the dead of winter and knock on the gates pretending to be wandering tinsmiths?"

Almost before the words were finished Antryg flung up one bent-fingered hand for silence. In the eerie hush Joanna could hear nothing but the distant mutter of the water beyond the trees, but Antryg and Caris both stood frozen, listening.

Caris breathed, "I don't . . ."

"Sasenna," Antryg murmured. "Mounted parties, big ones, on both sides of the river, by the sound of it—and coming this way."

The young man's face hardened, and his grip tightened over the sheath of his sword. "Then we've been betrayed."

CHAPTER XIV

Joanna whispered, "It couldn't have been Pella."

As Caris steadied her down the last few feet of rope, he could feel her shaking all over. Though he would rather have died than admit it, his own hands weren't too steady either. He wasn't sure whether the place Antryg had picked for concealment from the approaching troops wasn't worse than an open fight. It had certainly required far more nerve.

"Who else could it have been?" He wanted to shout the words, furious at her naïve trust and at his own. Though the energy-lines would have brought him warning long before they were anywhere in earshot, he strained his ears to catch any sound of the troop's return through the now-impenetrable blanket of fog that muffled the island. "They couldn't have seen us approaching—not in this fog—and we hid our tracks. Besides, they were on both banks of the stream. They knew we were here . . ."

"Did they?" The double line of rope that dangled against the clammy stone side of the nearest great trilithon shook, and Antryg shinnyed down neatly from the eiderdown masses of cloud-cover only a few feet above their heads.

The sasenna—several dozen of them, by the sound—had searched the circle and the entire island with unenthusiastic thoroughness, but it had never occurred to any of them to look above their heads, where the vast lintels of the trilithons loomed invisible on their twenty-foot supports. When Antryg had scrambled cautiously up a leaning stone and made that heart-stopping jump across to the nearest of the five monster gateways of the innermost circle, Caris had had to forcibly remind himself that the stones had been standing for thousands of years and were far too heavy and firmly set in the earth to be overbalanced by one man's weight. But climbing the rope and lying down at Joanna's side on the four-foot-wide stone lintel had turned his stomach, though in fact the lintel had been as firm as a floor. It was a four-foot jump to the next trilithon. He still didn't know how Antryg had gotten the nerve to do that.

Antryg drew on one end of the doubled rope, winding it neatly around his hands. "They searched the circle and the island, yes, but they're searching the woods as well—" His brisk movements paused, and he seemed to slide momentarily into something like a listening trance, "—out past the Devil's Road."

Caris half shut his eyes, trying to block from his mind his immediate surroundings—the dense, clinging fog and the iron-colored shapes of the looming stones—trying to hear out beyond the far banks of the river. He hadn't the power, but did not doubt for a moment that the mad sorcerer beside him did. "But they know we're somewhere in the land," he whispered. "They were expecting us, and they very nearly had us . . ."

"That doesn't mean it was Pella," Joanna responded coolly, falling into step with him as they began their cautious return to the ford. Her voice was very quiet in the deep hush of the fog-bound woods. "Don't think that because you want it so badly it has to be flawed, Caris."

He lengthened his stride, furious at this little mouse of a woman who had never done anything in her life, not caring that she couldn't keep up . . .

Her small hand seized the end of his sword sheathe,

checking him. When he swung around on her in blazing wrath she continued, "That's what I did."

It stopped him. For a moment they stood in the dripping underbrush, brown eyes looking into brown, and Caris felt his quick anger cool to bitter slag as he understood that she was right. Hate himself though he might, he realized also that some perverse part of him had wanted it to be true. Then at least he would have been able to justify to himself turning his back on his greatest joy to walk into death.

She went on, "We weren't exactly inconspicuous traveling through the Sykerst. After programming in binary for months, Suraklin's got to be able to put two and two together . . ."

Caris shook his head, his whole soul hurting. What she said was true, he thought, but she had not seen what he had seen in the gray waters of the divining pool within the circle. He turned, and Joanna followed him more slowly down to where Antryg waited by the ford.

"She could have been tricked," he said, pulling off his boots. "We both know Suraklin is good at that kind of thing."

To that Joanna could make no possible reply. The fog was thicker now, summoned back by Antryg as easily as he had sent it earlier away. But listening through it, Caris could hear no sound from the riverbank, invisible beyond its white wall. He waded across, whistled softly, and stood shivering with cold and impatience until the thin little woman appeared wading out of the brown silk waters and mist.

He put on his boots as soon as Joanna had waded across to stand guard and located the packs where they had left them concealed. The long, thickly quilted coat of the Prince Regent's sasenna, left behind in anticipation of action in the circle, would cover the lack of insignia on his uniform while he asked information. With as many troopers as it would take to search the area Antryg claimed was under scrutiny, they shouldn't all know one another.

"Where are you going?" Joanna asked, shivering violently as she pulled on her boots while he stood guard.

"The manor," he replied. "Whatever's happening, they'll use that as headquarters. I can listen there . . ."

"Try to steal some food if you can," Antryg put in cheerfully, scrambling up the icy bank, looking for all the world as if he'd just been on a holiday outing, except for the sword unsheathed in his hand. "I'm deathly sick of waybread and hardtack."

His soul one well of black pain—at the possibility of betrayal, at what he had glimpsed in the pool—Caris fought the momentary urge to strike him. But in spite of Antryg's clownish gangliness, Caris had seen the wizard fight and wasn't entirely certain he'd even be able to land a blow.

"There's a ruined chapel on the far bank of the river, down about a mile and a half and inland four hundred and twenty strides or so, in a grove of laurels," the wizard went on. "If the sasenna are still searching the woods on that side of the river, we'll fall back to the little range of hills about ten miles north and wait for you on the hill on the west bank of the Spelding Stream. Two stones fifty feet from the camp mean it's safe by day—two fires if you don't get there till after dark. Whistle like a nightingale before you come in. All right?"

Caris nodded ungraciously. Whatever else might be said of the mad wizard—and a great deal certainly could—at least he understood a sasennan's evasion procedure. "I'll be there."

The crooked hand in its half-fingered glove sketched a sign in the air. "Good luck."

It was an old kitchen-magic spell Caris' grandmother had used to keep cakes from collapsing in the oven; coming at this moment, from one who had been the Dark Mage's pupil and was universally acknowledged as one of the greatest mages in the world, it cracked the wall of

Caris' anger and grief and made him laugh in spite of himself. "Don't tell me you believe in that!"

The wizard grinned back. "Oh, I believe in everything."
He threw the corner of his cloak around Joanna's
shoulders; like ghosts the two of them faded into the fog.

During his earlier stay at Devilsgate Manor, Caris had
made mental notes of the layout and approaches to the
grounds. Naked with winter, the thin screens of trees and
the little ornamental groves that dotted the gardens between
the woods and the house walls of granite and rose-red brick
offered little concealment. The gardens themselves lay like
a peasant's patchwork of umbers and sepias within the
spiky enclosures of knee-high box hedges, offering an almost uninterrupted field of vision from the silvery glass of
the windows. Here on the higher ground, the river fog had
thinned to a mere vaporish white cast to the sky.

Against the fallow, liver-colored earth, the uniforms of
the men who moved through the garden beds stood out in
harsh splashes—the black of sasenna, flashing with the
glint of gold braid and the blood-crimson of the Prince
Regent's personal guard.

In the woods beyond the stables, Caris folded up his
spyglass and settled back against the warty bark of the elm
beneath which he sat.

So the Regent was coming to Devilsgate.

That would explain the troops searching the woods for
half a day's walk in any direction, whose sign Caris had
crossed again and again on his way to the manor. Pharos
was said to fear and suspect everyone and everything;
Joanna's first, disastrous, encounter with the de facto ruler
of the Empire of Ferryth had stemmed from the Regent's
insistence upon having any house he entered searched and
surrounded before he would set foot over the threshold.

But the old-fashioned manor was Cerdic's home, two
days' journey from Angelshand. The Regent was certainly
spiteful enough simply to take it away from his cousin on

general principles; nevertheless, Caris felt uneasy. What he had seen in the divining well on Tilrattin Island still echoed in his mind, like the harsh, ambiguous note of an iron gong. At the time he had the impression that what he had seen was at Larkmoor, but he realized it could just as easily have been here. The thought turned him cold with anger and hopeless dread.

Was that what I saw? he wondered bleakly. *That he lied to her, deceived her?*

In his heart he hoped that it was. That was, in a way, the lesser of his fears.

Along the pale streak of road between the gray cutouts of the trees an outrider came cantering, his coat gaudy as outseason poppies against the colorless afternoon. Caris knew what his coming heralded. He rose cautiously to his feet, making sure he was out of clear sight of the house, and began his slow drift through the rim of the woods, edging along the knotted knees of tree roots where he could keep above the frost-stiff mats of leaves between, covering his tracks carefully where he could not. In another hour, he calculated, it would begin to get dark. That should offer some concealment as he crossed the vast brown spaces of the empty gardens toward the house itself.

A marble gazebo of the sort popular forty years ago stood amid the open lawns to the west of the house; through his spyglass Caris had glimpsed the gold flash of sleeve-braid in its trellised shadows and the glint of a watcher's glass. He approached the house from the stables on the east; with his own glass, he watched the point at which the half-mile drive from the main road cleared the trees. When at long last the dark bulk of the Prince Regent's carriage appeared, its lamps primrose in the gathering darkness, Caris folded up his glass, straightened his quilted coat, strode boldly across the open space between the woods and the stable, and thence along the drive to the house. Sasenna and guards from all quarters of the grounds were converging on the front of the house to greet their master. Those that saw Caris as he entered the kitchen quarters questioned him no more than they questioned one another. Unerringly, he passed along the halls to his chosen destination and place of concealment.

A fire had been kindled in the room that had been Prince Cerdic's study. The long curtains of crimson velvet had been drawn over the north-facing windows, cutting out the sight of the dark teeth of the Devil's Road against the dun-colored hills. Pharos hated the thought of being spied upon. Caris settled himself into a window embrasure, one of his dirks unsheathed in his hand.

He was prepared to wait for hours, if need be. But a servant came almost at once, lighting a holocaust of candles in every holder and sconce in the room—Pharos abhored the darkness—and Caris felt a twinge of satisfaction that he had guessed aright. In a short while he heard the distant vibration of doors opening and closing and the rattle of the carriage teams being led around to the stables. Then, faint but approaching, high heels clicked on the parquet of the floor.

Caris had already arranged a small parting in the curtains, natural as a dark fold in the heavy velvet. Through it he saw a man enter from the shadows of the hall; from Joanna's description he must be the Regent's bodyguard Kanner, well over six and a half feet tall, scarred, ugly, and armed to the teeth. A former sasennan, Caris remembered, Kanner had been made deaf by a high fever and, instead of killing himself as sasenna did when they became physically flawed, he had recanted his vows to remain as Pharos' servant.

Immediately behind him walked a handsome, fresh-faced boy of seventeen or so in white velvet and far too many pearls, and behind him, like a dainty flame of black and gold in the refulgent light, minced the Regent himself, Pharos Giraldus of the House of Destramor, pervert, sadist, and Pella's rightful husband and lord.

It was the first time Caris had seen him up close. His

former glimpses had all been brief, and the last one—in the yard of the roadhouse on the way to Angelshand last summer—had been blurred by the changeable flicker of torchlight. This was the man who had legal power over Pellicida, Caris thought, feeling oddly cool—this doll-like, dainty, evil little creature with his painted eyes and bitten lips.

The boy in white was gazing around with wide eyes the color of ripe blueberries, his rouged mouth parted. He breathed, "Oh, my lord, it's beautiful. Thank you! Thank you."

Pharos smiled and reached up to pat the rosy cheek. "No more beautiful than you, my lovely Leynart. It was time my charming cousin Cerdic learned that, even though he's the biggest moneylender in Angelshand these days, the property of the Imperial House is mine to do with as I wish. If I wish to install you here for a year, ten years, or in perpetuity . . . you've certainly given me more pleasure than he ever did or is ever likely to."

The boy laughed and hugged him, the dark velvet curls mingling with the pomaded gold. Then he straightened up again—he topped the older man by a good five inches— and looked gravely down at the Regent, his hands resting on the bullion-stitched shoulders. "I wish I could travel with you."

"My pet," the Prince said, his rather shrill voice quiet, "you know that's not possible."

Leynart broke away from him, walked around the great desk of inlaid fruitwood to the pink marble mouth of the fireplace, close enough that, if Caris had reached out from his hiding place in the window, he could have touched a velvet sleeve. He extended his hands to the blaze, and the shape of them shone pinkly through the flawless lawn of his sleeve ruffle with the saffron glow. "Why not?" he demanded after a moment. "You know you can do anything you want. Who is she to object if you bring me with you?"

"She," said Pharos, folding his arms and regarding the boy inscrutably, "is my wife."

The scene he had glimpsed in the silver depths of the pool returned to Caris again, with cold and sinking dread, like the news of a cancer one has tried for months to tell oneself is indigestion. He felt no surprise, but only a grief that filled his body and hurt it to the marrow of his bones. As if it had been spoken aloud, he knew now where Pharos was bound, and why, and what it was that he had seen.

Leynart laughed, trying to be boyish and ingenuous and only sounding tinny. "I still think yours is the best description of her: one of those big black mares decked out to pull the processional cart on a peasant's saint's day. I still have nightmares thinking about that awful yellow riding habit . . ." The tone was of a familiar gambit, rallying for a response that he did not get.

"She's welcome to wear what she pleases," Pharos began impatiently.

"Not the lavender satin, surely!"

"I certainly don't have to look at her all the time. But I wasn't fooled by that tarradiddle about the cold. Her? Cold? Pah."

The young man shuddered with exaggerated delicacy. "What a bruiser! I'll bet she takes baths in rainwater straight out of the barrel! I can't think why you simply didn't take a crop to the slut when she slapped you."

"Can't you?" Pharos cocked his head a little, his pale eyes in their insomniac circles glinting oddly in the dancing light. "She would have taken it away from me and flogged the daylights out of me. A filthy little brute, that dog—but hers."

"As I am yours." Leynart turned from the fire and walked back to where the Prince still stood. Taking one lace-cuffed hand, he raised it to his lips. "You'd be welcome to torment any number of pets, for all of me. You know that."

"Yes," said the Prince softly. The boy's head was still

bent over his hand, so Leynart did not see the glint of contempt in those pale eyes. "Yes, I know that." Pharos turned abruptly away and walked out of the narrow field of Caris' vision. By the sound of his voice, he was near the other window, close to the pedimented niches where the statues of the Old Gods clustered between Cedric's beloved books of occultism and quackery. Leynart stood where he had been, anxiety and apprehension in his face.

"I won't be at odds with her, Leynart," Pharos' voice said at last. "I need a child."

The boy laughed crudely. "Is that all? Since when has a man needed to ask permission to mount his own mare? I'm astounded you can even rise to such an occasion. I certainly couldn't."

Caris was aware of the pain in his palm from the crush of the dagger's hilt in his grip and forced himself to relax it. There was the faint slither of satin against lace, the muted creak of the corner of the desk taking the Prince's slight weight perched upon it. "They're trying to murder me, Leynart," that soft, edgy voice said. "All of them are plotting against me—Cerdic, Magister Magus, the Council of Wizards who wouldn't let me skin and slice Windrose when I had the chance to do it. Who's to say they weren't behind his escape? Or that the Bishop Herthe wasn't, with her sanctimonious whining? The only reason I married that musclebound Amazon was that Cerdic is my heir, and I won't have the country given over to a pack of superstitious dog wizards when I'm dead. But having married her, the least I can do is give her the respect due to my wife."

Tears gleamed suddenly in Leynart's cornflower eyes. Impulsively he strode out of Caris' line of sight, leaving only Kanner in view, standing impassively, arms folded, near the door. There was the swirling flounce of laces and silk as the boy flung himself to his knees. "So what do you think she's going to do?" his voice demanded, suddenly trembling. "Drive you out of her bed with a stick? She has to want a child as badly as you do, to make her someone at

Court and not just the jumped-up provincial nobody she is! Your child for preference, to keep the family looks, but I'm sure anyone with blond hair will do! Pharos, I love you! I don't want anything from you except your love! If I don't have that, I swear I will die!"

Caris turned his face away, sickened, staring for a time out into the thin darkness beyond the windows' misted glass. Against a leaden sky, the Devil's Road was nearly invisible; the long stretch of open garden and lawn was lost in a lake of shadow, broken at the very edge of his sight by the gleaming white island of the gazebo's dome. He had no business here, he thought; no business hearing that spoiled child's hysterical sobs, or the dry swish of lace as, uncaring of his bodyguard's presence, Pharos stroked the dark, ruffled head.

Leynart wept, Caris knew, because he saw in Pharos' eyes the dawning of respect for his wife. And like Caris, he knew what that respect might become.

In the gray pool he had seen them together, Pharos and Pella, sitting side by side in talk while Kyssha slept on Pella's swollen lap. Pella's face had been grave, but in her eyes had been no fear, merely her matter-of-fact willingness to take people as she found them. Her husband's pale eyes, so shifty with everyone else, had been on her.

I will never have her, Caris thought, the desire for her consuming his flesh at the same time cold grief drowned his heart. When the sasenna had arrived to search the island, he had thought the scene was one of betrayal, but now he understood. In a way, for Pella to be tricked or forced into telling her husband of their whereabouts would have been preferable to what he now knew the scene had been. It was as it should be, he knew. He never could have had her anyway—neither her, nor magic, nor the brightly colored life that he sensed stirring like a perfumed carnival beyond the dark boundaries of his destiny. He wondered despairingly if it was a mark of love to wish that her husband would continue to hate her, so that she could be his, at least in his heart for the little that remained of his life. But having no experience of loving, he did not know.

"Antryg?" Joanna said softly and felt the movement of his pectoral muscles beneath her cheek as he turned his head. They had lain a long time in silence, twined together in a stone burial niche in the ruined chapel's wall. At some distance, in the center of the ruin, two small fires burned a few feet apart. The light of them filtered through the hanging curtain of brown vines, dappling Antryg's face in a moire of shadow and light. He'd put his spectacles back on, and fragments of red and orange skated across the cracked lens and glinted in the diamond of his earrings. "What *are* the long-range effects of magic upon inanimate objects?"

"I don't know." His mellow baritone was little more than a vibration in his chest against her ear. "In that, I'm like Suraklin, except that Suraklin always refused to believe that there were any at all. He has always discounted reasons for not doing what he seriously wanted to do."

"You said that the stones in the circle had voices, spoke to one another, because of all the magic that had been drawn through them over the years."

"Yes." His bony arm tightened around her shoulders under the pile of blankets, coats, and cloaks, as if to protect her against whatever lay beyond the black fog of the night. "Magic isn't a science, as the Council of Wizards claims it is, nor an art, as Suraklin always said. It's life itself. It imbues all things, and particularly those things it touches for long periods of time. I keep thinking about that poor scientist, playing the Dead God in Far Wilden, gradually poisoning himself by the very thing that kept him alive. You're right, Joanna—software is only as good as the hardware it travels through. Suraklin believes that, because the teles-balls that make up the power-relays, and the stones along the energy-lines that convey the life-force to him, don't speak to him, there will never come a time when they might. But they do absorb magic. The teles-balls are practically indestructible, and some of them are older than any memory. There were two or three in Surak-lin's collection that—frightened me. I don't like to think of them, lying hidden in the Bone Well beneath the Citadel with the black carrion strippings of half demons he called into existence and then imprisoned there because he couldn't quite kill them when he was done.

"Those teles, those stones, are now going to be in use constantly and have magic pouring through them twenty-four hours a day. It may all go as Suraklin believes it will for a year or two or ten—but how long will it be before those voices begin to bleed into Suraklin's mind, his self, locked in the computer and at the mercy of his input? All magic is balance, because all magic is individuated. When it all gets bound together into one giant interlocking web, *we have no idea what could happen*. Neither has Suraklin. But he's dangerous because he thinks that nothing will."

The travelers remained for three days in the ruined chapel on the north bank of the River Glidden, waiting for the next spell of deadness. The weather was cold, though not the brutal, piercing cold of the Sykerst; sheet ice broad-ened out from the banks, a film of it entirely covering the river between the shore and Tilrattin Island by night, only to crack away at midday. It was a still time, but desperately unrestful.

Antryg spent a good deal of his time in the stone circle and refused ever to get very far away from it. Though Caris knew he should have been concentrating his energies on honing his warrior's skills—on hunting the shy beasts of winter to sharpen his reflexes or on swordsmanship and shooting that he had perforce neglected during the days of steady walking—he found himself accompanying the wiz-ard there. Hungrily, guiltily, as he had learned healing, he learned from him a little of the lore of the stones and that of the energy-trails, listening down the lines for the voices alive in the air. The wizard tried to instruct him, too, in the arts of divining and of seeing things far away. For two nights Caris sat near that tall, gangly figure bent over the fire, gazing into the embers with his spectacles throwing back the fulvous glow, watching the roads for the approach of danger or, indeed, of anyone or anything that might come upon them and spread word of their presence. The Regent had departed the morning after his arrival, and Antryg kept an eye on Leynart at Devilsgate. But the boy remained listless and seldom left the house.

Tormented by the knowledge that he should not be doing so, Caris tried to fan his own slight talents into sufficient strength to do the same. If the wizard guessed why, he did not say so, and Caris never admitted that what he wanted, as well as a glimpse of Pella, alone at Larkmoor, was to know where the Regent slept that night and how soon he would reach his wife's side.

The circle at the node of the lines was silent. The brown earth dreamed undisturbed under the mantle of coming winter. Joanna, thin and grubby as a shabby little wood-elf, alternated between reading Suraklin's incomprehensible files and checking and rechecking the contents of her backpack and the hardcopy, as she called it, of her own "worm" that she planned to feed into Suraklin's computer to destroy everything on its disks. Caris reflected bitterly that, like her, he should have been readying himself for the coming battle, not spending his time in pursuit of what would not help them and in any case could never be his.

Once in the night he slipped away from the chapel to wade the ice-skinned river and knelt in the circle's darkness at the side of the divining well. But its unfrozen waters showed him nothing, save the chilly blaze of the watching stars visible above the rising river fog, and he found that being in the circle alone troubled him. He was hideously conscious of the stones standing behind him in the cold starlight and prey to the uneasy sensation that as soon as he took his eyes off them they might move.

By day he was seized with a violent restlessness. Once or twice Antryg stripped out of his cloak and voluminous green coat and fenced with him, using trimmed saplings for swords instead of the razor-sharp weapons. Caris invariably felt himself worsted and cursed his sloth still further. At other times he merely patrolled the woods, as if by constant movement he could outwalk his burning awareness of how far Pharos must be on his journey and how soon he would be at Pella's side.

It was on one of these patrols that Caris heard the approach of the troops.

It was a clear evening and sharply cold; sound carried a great distance in the colorless ranks of the bare woods. Caris heard the strike of hooves first on the hard-frozen roadbed, and slipped quickly down into the concealment of the overgrown ditch at its side. It was only as the sounds came nearer and he realized that the troop must number nearly a hundred riders and a number of carriages that it came to him that something was fearfully wrong.

Antryg had had no warning of their approach. Yesterday he'd noted the presence of a peddler on the way to the village on the other side of Devilsgate, the passage of a wedding party from the village church. How could he possibly have missed an entourage of that size?

Baffled, Caris raised his head. White facings stood out on the unfamiliar black uniforms of fifty mounted sasenna, like floating bars of moonlight in the gathering gloom; they were followed by nearly as many household cavalry in emerald green. For the most part, the sasenna looked very young, newly fledged, newly sworn, tough and cold and trained to a hair. They surrounded a four-horse traveling coach, while several smaller vehicles with baggage brought up the rear.

He couldn't have missed it, Caris thought, baffled. *Yet why would he lie?*

The only place they could possibly have been heading was Devilsgate itself. Moving cross-country through the woods, Caris was at the big rose-red manor before them. Without Pharos' sasenna in the gardens, the place was far easier to slip into. The marble gazebo with its thin screen of trellises offered ample concealment and a good view, through the spyglass, of the front of the house; with luck Caris calculated that he could be away from the place by the time sasenna or guards were posted around the house or, at worst, pass himself off as one of them in his black coat in the evening gloom.

Leynart was on the steps of the manor, his primrose silk costume glimmering like a ghost in the dusk. He looked weary and haggard, as if he had found the last two days no easier than Caris had; in the dark frame of his curly hair the lines and hollows of his face showed through a careful application of concealing paint. The carriage drew to a stop. Through the glass, Caris could see it was drawn by a team of the showiest matched sorrels he had ever seen, the carriage itself ablaze with claret-red lacquer and gilt. The boy Leynart's haunted eyes brightened. He strode down the steps, his hands held out in welcome as the footmen opened the carriage doors.

A man stepped down from the carriage, and Caris realized instantly why Antryg had not had warning of their approach. It was difficult, he knew, for mages to divine the movements of other mages; even the slight spells that he was able to hold around himself would thwart any but a very powerful scryer. And though Magister Magus was generally spoken of as a charlatan, according to Antryg the dapper little gentleman whom the footmen now assisted down did, in fact, have true power.

Presumably, thought Caris dourly, he had been persuaded to use it in trade for being saved from the Witchfinders.

The footmen and Magister Magus bowed low as the second man stepped down from the carriage, and Leynart came forward to catch the lace-gloved hands in his own. Prince Cerdic was a good bit fatter than when Caris had seen him last and wore a suit of plum-colored velvet which must have cost more than the carriage and team combined. Leynart bent over his hands—though the Regent had taken Devilsgate and given it to his eromenos, it was obvious that, from that moment, the youth considered himself Cerdic's guest.

It took Caris a moment to realize who the third man must be. There was something vaguely familiar about his face; it was young, not yet thirty-five, yet settled already into hard and arrogant lines. His clothes were simple, a court suit of dark green and apricot, yet the Prince and Leynart both bowed deeply, and Leynart knelt on the icy gravel of the drive to kiss the man's hand. Perhaps it was the hair that jogged Caris' memory. It was shorter than anyone but sasenna and laborers wore it, yet familiar. He had seen it . . .

The man moved, gesturing toward the house. With a chill that was not quite anger nor yet quite dread, Caris remembered.

The face was the face of the man he had glimpsed through a darkened window, whining excuses to Joanna while the chaos of music and drinking went on at the party around the courtyard pool, long ago and in another universe. The face was the face of the hapless Gary Fairchild, but Caris recognized the gesture as typical of his grandfather.

He realized he was looking at Suraklin.

CHAPTER XV

"IT'S JUST THAT IT ISN'T FAIR!" LEYNART TURNED, THE snowy embroidery that laced his coat skirts glittering like frost with the movement of his caged pacing. With a passionate gesture, he strode back to the fire where his guests sat, and his words became indistinct to Caris once again.

Caris had calculated that the boy's fulsome welcome of the Prince and the two wizards would have given him time to take up his old hiding place behind the study curtains, had he chosen to, but caution warned him against it. It was one thing to spy upon the Regent, paranoid though he might be. It was another to spy upon Suraklin. Instead, he had carefully jammed the sneck of the study door so it would sit slightly ajar and had stationed himself in the disused alcove down the hall, listening for the steps of the four men as they passed. It was his guess that they would not risk the posting of a guard, for fear of the guard doing precisely what he did—listening. But any passing servant in the dark corridor would not know it.

Through the crack he could see more of the room itself than he had before—dark-paneled in a fashion fifty years out of date, with a deeply coffered ceiling and heavy antique chairs. Its shelves were crowded with books whose titles Caris recognized from his days at the Mages' Yard—tomes of wisdom and charlatanry ranked side by side. The resinous glow of fire and candles mingled along the edges of the Five Mystical Forms carved from polished hematite, objects of mathematical meditation which had become semi-sacred to one of the more crackpot schools of dog wizardry and gave a queer life to the statues of the twenty-one Old Gods, lurking like watchers among the books of what had once been their faith. Most people these days did not even know their names.

Caris did. Aunt Min, possibly the oldest mage living and certainly the oldest at the Yard, was an Old Believer, though, like most of that discredited faith, she had only *chellim*, elaborately wrought slips of paper bearing the gods' names, pasted to the walls of her little room and now grubby with age and cooking grease. So he knew most of them, those silent watchers of diorite, hematite, malachite, and jade, who guarded shelf and mantle and whose eyes seemed to move with the shadow of Leynart's feverish stride.

Suraklin remained seated in one of the gilt chairs near the fire, arms propped before him, hands clasped on level with his chin, and forefingers extended to touch his lips. Caris had often seen his grandfather sit so, though not, when he thought of it, back in the days of his childhood. He wondered now how he could possibly have been so stupid as not to realize something was amiss even then. If nothing else, the mocking glint of irony in those brown eyes should have told him long ago that his grandfather had ceased to be grandfather.

But what, he wondered wearily, could he then have done?

Leynart's voice rose again, fighting for composure. "It isn't that I begrudge her position, please don't think that." His tone was that of a man trying to be just against his every inclination. "But she doesn't care for him. She can't. She only wants his affection for the status it will give her, to fulfill some petty, bourgeois moralities. She'll dull

him, stultify him, make him miserable if he tries to please
her..."

"I always thought," purred Suraklin, the very turn and
inflection of his voice recognizable as accents Caris had
heard in the Archmage's, "that a provincial moneygrub-
ber's niece was hardly the proper choice for a man of
Pharos' stature, even were she virtuous, which of course
she is not."

Only years of training let Caris suppress the smothering
heatwave of anger and stifle the harsh draw of his breath.
Wizards had sharp ears and a sixth sense of danger—spy-
ing on them could be unbelievably perilous. His only hope
was that Suraklin's mind was occupied with whatever
scheme had brought him here and that the man was con-
ceited enough to be at ease among these worshipful victims. The flame-flecked eyes did not even move Caris'
way.

Pella had told him of her seduction by the wizard,
though she was almost certain the child she carried was not
his. For that, too, Caris hated the man. It occurred to him
that he was within touching-distance of the end of his
quest, only yards from the man he had sworn to kill. The
butt of his pistol ground against his ribs; he had only to
open the door...

Except, of course, that the pistol was not na-aar. With
even an instant's warning, Suraklin could make it either
misfire or blow up in his hand. The house was full of the
Prince's sasenna and household guards; Caris doubted that
he would get away; and even if he did, where would he
run? The resulting dragnet would pull in Antryg and
Joanna. Then, truly, all hope would be at an end.

All this passed through his mind in an eyeblink, as Suraklin went on, "No, Leynart, it isn't wrong to begrudge
her the Prince's care. You aren't taking anything away
from her, you know. All you want, truly, is his recognition
of your love—which in fact your loyalty deserves." He
moved his hand. Like a whipped hound eager for forgive-

ness, Magister Magus got hastily up from his unobtrusive seat in the shadows.

It was the change in Magus that hurt Caris most, hurt and angered him, as if he had seen cruelty to an animal or a child. When he had been the man's guest in Angelshand, he had despised Magus as a dog wizard who made his fortune while the mages at the Yard ate oatbread and worried about the leaks in their roofs. But the Magus had always dealt with him well, had taken care of Joanna when her presence under his roof had been a clear danger to him, and had helped her as much as he could. Seeing how the dapper little charlatan cringed when he approached his new master, Caris could guess how that fear had been instilled. Once Magus had been arrested, there had been no hope for him. Cerdic and his Spiritual Advisor were the only ones who could have saved him from the Inquisition—and Suraklin needed a slave who was a mage.

"I have prepared this for you." Suraklin held out his hand. Magus gave the wizard the box he carried, carved rosewood varnished like satin, then bowed and stepped back out of Caris' line of sight. The Dark Mage opened it; Leynart and Cerdic looked within.

"Wonderful!" Cerdic murmured ecstatically and reached into the box. "It's fresh! Roses like this don't even grow in Mellidane at this season . . ."

"Whoa!" Suraklin drew the box back, laughing. "Don't touch it, my lord, unless you look to become a good deal fonder of our Ley than you are now!"

The Prince withdrew his hand hastily and put a few feet between him and the youth for good measure. Leynart bridled at the promptness of the gesture, and the wizard laughed again.

"Of such stuff are bedroom farces made, my lord. It's a simple enough spell, but effective." A mocking gleam of amber danced catlike at the back of the brown eyes. "So have a care, Ley, unless you want suitors all over Kymil pounding down your door and snubbing poor Pella for no earthly reason whenever they see her. And incidentally, don't touch it yourself, until the moment comes when you lay it upon his Grace's pillow, where he shall sleep that night. Else all shall be for naught. Do you think you can do it?"

The youth nodded. His dark ringlets, plum-black in the firelight, swung against his cheeks. "If you can get me to Kymil, my lord Gaire, as you say you can, before his Grace arrives, his Grace's men will let me into his house."

"Trust me, my boy." The warm brown eyes smiled into the blue. "As I trust you." The wizard put out a hand and affectionately tucked a stray curl back into the dark mass of Leynart's hair. His voice was gentle. "I've never had the taste for boys—but now I understand it. You'll be in a position to wield a good deal of power, there on the steps of the throne, little lover. But I trust you'll do so wisely."

"I want no power," Leynart whispered, his cornflower eyes grave in their gilt and paint. "Only his love."

"Well spoken. And that you shall have."

So this, Caris thought sourly, was a love-spell—this harmless-sounding manipulation of the heart and the mind. To make Pharos snub his wife again and turn to this perfumed little catamite—to condemn Pella to lifelong humiliation . . .

Part of Caris wondered why he should be angry. The thought of Pharos touching Pella, kissing her—the thought of her lying in those thin, flabby arms—had kept him sleepless for two nights. He ought to be thanking the boy. But he knew his meeting with the Dark Mage was very near now, and he knew he would not survive it. It was not fair to want to be the only love she would ever have.

The Council was right, he thought, his whole body hurting with indecision and grief. Great and small, the affairs of humankind should be safe from meddling by those who had the power to do so. But in his mind he heard the cries of a newborn infant and felt the flash and throb of a tiny soul like primal fire, coming to life beneath his hands, and he did not know what he thought.

Leynart knelt to kiss Suraklin's hands. Beside the hearth, Cerdic was beaming like the bride's mother at a wedding, no doubt thinking, Caris reflected cynically, that with this one coup he had guaranteed himself Heir in the place of those that Pharos would not beget. Or perhaps he was merely sentimentally pleased to be helping his young friend. *Blind, fatuous fool.*

"Come." Suraklin shut the box and handed it to Leynart with a glance at the ormolu clock. "It's time. It must be before midnight, and there is something yet I must do here. Magus . . ."

Caris slipped quickly away as Suraklin and the Magus turned toward the door. With all the silence of his long training, he glided back to the alcove, waited till he heard them pass, then drifted, silent as river mist, through the dim halls and out of the house. Without Pharos' horror of the dark, Devilsgate was far less well lit than it had been; it proved an easy matter to conceal himself near the stable-yard as grooms brought out three horses, their breath floating in clouds of steam in the yellow flare of the stable lamps.

Caris' mind felt shaken, torn as a hound's on a crossed scent. Everything else aside—Pella, the Regent, his doomed, frantic love—Suraklin was *here* at Devilsgate. Could Antryg have been wrong about the circle? *Was* the computer concealed somewhere underground, as Caris had guessed? For that matter, how close did it have to be to the actual node to drink the energy? As Antryg himself had said, all they had to go on was guesses and deduction. None of them, from start to finish, had one shred of actual proof. Antryg hadn't spoken or worked with Suraklin in twenty-seven years. How would he or Joanna know what was and was not possible?

Could the apparatus be concealed at Devilsgate itself?

Reflected lamplight splattered over the wet gravel of the

stableyard. He heard voices and Cerdic's jolly laugh, then Suraklin's voice, firm and deep: "My lord, forgive me for making you play groom, but in truth I dare not trust another."

They came around the corner of the stables, flanked by a servant with a torch. Cerdic, heedless of that servant or the watching grooms, fell to one knee and kissed the wizard's hand. "Groom? I'll put my hand under your foot to boost you to the saddle, did it please you, my lord." Suraklin laughed, raised him to his feet, and clapped an affectionate hand on his shoulders while a footman hastened to sponge the yard mud from the Prince's velvet knee.

They were only facsimiles, Antryg had said, *copied from what he had seen others sacrifice themselves for . . . But they were copied dazzlingly well.*

Heart pounding, Caris flattened himself back in the shadows of the coach-house door to watch, wondering desperately what to do. Suraklin, Cerdic, and Leynart mounted. The Prince took from one of the grooms a closed lantern—to maintain the fiction, Caris thought, that Suraklin, or Gaire as he was called, couldn't call whatever light he wished or see in the dark. The three horses passed through the yard gate, their hooves crunching softly on the ice underfoot. Slipping from shadow to shadow, Caris glided in their wake. If he lost sight of the Dark Mage now, in all probability he'd never be able to locate him again— wizards were notoriously difficult to find. Yet he knew he was completely incapable of dealing with the wizard himself.

I'm only a warrior! he thought. *And out of practice, neglectful, indecisive of heart at that. I'm no match for him . . .*

Joanna had repeatedly asked, *Why me?* But she'd always been willing to take on Suraklin, the Inquisition, anyone . . .

Whatever happens, at least I can witness it to tell Antryg.

Soundless as a moth, he followed the bobbing gold splotch of lantern light across the vast gardens, into the woods, and along the narrow paths that led toward the dark stubble fields of the hedgerow country, and beyond that, the mist-shrouded river. The three men rode single file, Suraklin in the lead, the warm reflection of the lantern tipping his short brown curls and the fur collar of his great-coat with gold. Cerdic, bringing up the rear and showing a surprisingly good seat on a horse, kept glancing behind him, though more, Caris thought, from nervousness about what people would say than from any real sense of being watched. Once they reached the woods, Caris kept easily out of sight, drifting from tree to stripped and rain-dark tree. Between Prince and wizard, Leynart said nothing, only clutched his precious spell-box to his chest and hud-dled deeper in this miniver cloak like a cold lapdog on a pillow. Overhead the clouds had grown thick; the scent of snow rode the wind.

The riders took a roundabout path, changing direction frequently, but at last Caris heard the muffled whisper of the river and dimly glimpsed the white heads of the stones above the dark branches.

The river was frozen nearly across; the horses' hooves broke through the thin ice, splashing loud in the black water of the ford. On the island, Suraklin and Leynart dis-mounted, handing the reins to Cerdic. Caris crouched in the shadows of a copse of birches, and the sable hem of the Prince's embroidered greatcoat all but brushed across his face as Cerdic rode back, lantern aloft now, still peering fearfully all around him. Suraklin, on the boulder where Antryg had stood, watched him for some moments, while Caris told himself firmly that he was sheltered in that direc-tion from those darkness-piercing eyes.

To cross the ford—to follow them to the circle and see what Suraklin did there—Caris would have to break cover. By the stars it was nearing midnight. Suraklin had spoken of something which must be accomplished by then, and the roundabout way they had taken here had nearly doubled their time. Did the computer come alive at midnight? Caris wondered. And in that case, would Antryg be drawn to the circle and walk into his trap?

At last the wizard turned away, vanishing in the darkness almost at once. Still hugging his precious box to him, Leynart followed. There was a momentary blur of white stockings and hat-plumes in the underbrush, then nothing.

Should he wait? Caris wondered. For how long? Whatever it was they had gone to the circle to do . . .

He took a deep breath and stepped from his shelter.

Cold and crisp, a voice from the woods at his back said, "Take him."

Caris swung around, sword leaping as of its own will to his hand. Dark forms he would have taken oath had not been there seemed to rise from the ground all around him, shadowy shapes, glittering steel. He slashed at one and it melted before his blade, cut at another, water splashing icy in his boots as he leaped to avoid the return slash. Steel grated on steel; at least some of his attackers were of human flesh and not illusion. In the woods he thought he glimpsed a slender form, the black splotch of a Van Dyke beard on a white face. He thought, *Magister Magus,* as movement from the corner of his eye made him spin to meet an attack. As an axe whizzed toward his head and he raised his sword to parry he thought, *No sound of that one's boots in the water . . .*

But by then it was too late. His turning to defend against the illusion cost him the moment to parry the real warriors on his other side. He cursed himself as a halberd hooked his feet from beneath him. Something struck his head as he fell. He had no recollection of hitting the stony bank.

Fighting upward as if from black water, Caris thought, *Magus hid his men by spells. If I'd been a true mage, I'd have seen them—if I'd been a true sasennan I'd have been more careful . . .* Then he sank again into clouded dreams.

* * *

He was in his grandfather's house in the Mages' Yard, in the narrow, low-raftered study; light from the diamond-paned window fell across Salteris' bald head where he sat before the dull black turrets of his tall desk. "Caris, please don't think ill of me, please don't run away," the old man was saying softly. "Why do you believe that I allowed Suraklin to share my body, share residence in my mind, without my consent? We are guest-friends, my son, not captor and captive. He has let me come with him into immortality. You have no idea of the capacity of the human mind— there is room here for us all. I am not dead, Caris . . . only my body that was finished anyway . . . Does the butterfly mourn the chrysalis? Come."

He held out his hands, thin and strong, the blue veins standing out in the white flesh. His brown eyes were dark and gentle, coffee-colored, like Caris' own, save for an amber gleam, like the spark of hidden coals, far back in their depths.

Caris backed away from him, confused. He missed the old man, missed him desperately, all the mourning he had held bottled inside for months welling to the surface in a surge of blinding pain. The magic pounded in his veins, the power to help and heal; a forbidden power, indulged in like unsanctioned killing.

As if he read his grandson's mind, the old man murmured, "Caris, I can help you. I, too, am a healer. I, too, cared for the sick in secret—we all did. It lies in the palms of your hands . . ."

Caris woke up sweating, smothered by a sense of panic. For an instant he thought he saw a silver scribble of light written on the wooden wall by the head of the bed where he lay, gleaming softly in the thin light of the foggy dawn. Then he blinked, and it was gone.

He lay back. His head ached, and his body felt chilled and shaken. A blanket covered him, thrown back by his restless tossings. His weapons were gone. By the slope of the ceiling, he guessed the room where he lay was in one of Devilsgate's attics; the single window was barred; when he rose and approached it, he found himself shrinking with loathing at the thought of touching the frame or the glass.

Fear-spells. Of course, he thought bitterly. Suraklin had known all the time he was being watched. He'd called Magus aside, given him time to set the trap at the ford by that drawn-out journey, set up this prison . . .

If they had taken him prisoner, he thought, it meant Suraklin had a use for him.

The thought turned his blood cold.

Or—*had* his dream been right? *Had* Suraklin found, instead of a selfish immortality that raped his victims of body and mind, a means of carrying them forward with him?

Caris shook his head, pushing the thought away as absurd. Why would Suraklin bother? He had already shown he would kill without compunction.

Yet within him, Caris was conscious of a nagging itch to talk to the Dark Mage, to ask him . . .

Ask him what? he demanded of himself in disgust. It was only Suraklin's influence, whispering to his mind. He wondered suddenly if this was how the wizard had lured Magus' mind to his, how he had lured Salteris'?

Antryg, Caris thought. *He'll know by now I'm missing. How long before he attempts to find me?*

Or has he already tried and been caught? His heart beat faster with dread.

A quick look around his prison served to tell him the room was utterly bare, barred, containing nothing but the bed on which he had lain, a covered latrine bucket, and a small table which bore a loaf of bread and a pitcher of water. Being at the top of the house, the room itself was fairly warm; outside he could see patches of new-fallen snow on the slaty roofs of the laundry and buttery wing. He touched the bread, found it fresh, that morning's. Hungrily, he broke a piece from it, then hesitated.

He set it down again and smelled the water in the pitcher. There was no scent of drug, but he remembered he was dealing with a wizard.

He had no experience with these sneakier tricks, the spells to deceive and sway the mind, for they were utterly illegal, unknown to the wizards he had served. Nevertheless he set both bread and water aside.

It was one of the longest days Caris had ever spent. The daylight was the livid yellow-brown of snow, which occasionally fell, thin as sifted flour, from a sky which seemed neither bright nor dark. His head ached. Not knowing how late in the morning it had been when he had come to, he found it even more difficult to estimate time. Sometimes he could hear movement in the house below him, the comings and goings of the Prince's sasenna, and now and then a servant's voice.

He wondered how long it would be, before Suraklin came up to see him.

When the draining deadness began, the leaden depression that told him that Suraklin's mechanical brain was in operation again, his captivity became a thousand times worse. Part of him thought bleakly, *So it is here. In the circle, or here in the house itself...* Most of him simply did not care. He was hungry and thirsty by that time; with the numbing of his mind he craved even the small activity of eating. The depression whispered to him that it didn't matter whether the food and drink were drugged or not— Suraklin would have him anyway. At last, unable to stand the temptation any more, he tore the bread in pieces, threw it in the latrine bucket, and poured the water from the pitcher out onto the floor.

They'd said that Antryg had spent a good deal of his time in the Tower pounding on the walls with his broken hands and screaming. Lying white-knuckled on the bed, Caris knew exactly how he had felt. *If this goes on . . .* he thought.

But it would go on. There was an increasing probability that it would go on, literally, forever. Antryg and Joanna would go to the circle to take their bearing and walk straight into Suraklin's trap.

Despair at their naïveté, at his own stupidity, and at the hopelessness of his fate drowned him like a velvet wave. They would be killed, he would be enslaved, Pella would be condemned to a living hell of mockery and derision, and what did it matter, anyway?

He slept, and Salteris sat on the foot of his cot and whispered to him in his dreams.

The sliding back of the door bolt was so soft that, had he been sleeping even normally—and he was, as all sa-senna come to be, a light sleeper—he would not have heard it. But after the passing away of the grayness, his dreams had changed. The despair faded again into images of his grandfather, kindly, gentle, speaking of how they had all misunderstood Suraklin's intent, while that amber glint of mockery flickered somewhere in the coffee-dark eyes. Troubled, Caris tried to pull clear of the dream. Once he managed to open his eyes, and thought he saw again the wizard's mark gleaming on the wall near the bed in the semi-dark. But the dreams were strong, dragging him down like the sodden weight of river weeds. Dimly he wondered how long he would last.

But the slight whisper of slipping iron pierced his consciousness like the first drip of rain from a leaking roof. He was fully awake and poised to spring, a straight leap from bed to door, even as it opened and Antryg drifted through.

Caris aborted the leap half-made, but he could see his lunatic mentor had been ready for it. Antryg touched his lips, signaling silence, and beckoned with his huge gray eyes; outside the window the sky was deepening toward final dark. Within, lamps would be kindling.

"Hold your breath as we go through the main attic," Antryg whispered, and Caris nodded, not asking why. In the attic outside, a lamp had been lit, illuminating the table where two sasenna slept over a spread of cards. Four more had rolled, unconscious, from various hiding places. *A double-baited trap*, Caris thought as they moved swiftly through the hazy scrim of lamp smoke, pausing only long enough for Caris to collect a sword. *They were expecting a rescue. Suraklin didn't need me at all, except as bait.*

"An opium compound in the lamp-oil," the wizard breathed, as they descended the attic stairs, holding close to the wall so the risers did not creak. "Part of my medical satchel. The woods are simply stiff with sasenna—not the Regent's, either..."

"Cerdic's." Caris kept his voice to a subvocal wind-murmur as they glided along the upstairs hall. "How did you get in?"

"Thank goodness for the sins of bygone Emperors; there's a stair from the master bedroom to a passage that runs out to that marble gazebo. From the way the guards are positioned I think they're expecting me to fire the stables by way of diversion. Did you know the Empress Chananda was credited with having forty-seven lovers during the time that her husband was keeping her prisoner here because of her debauchery? Here we are."

"Antryg, Suraklin's..."

Caris never afterward could decide what warned Antryg —whether it was natural caution or the magic that allows mages to see other mages in spite of cloaking spells. As his fingers touched the painted porcelain door handle the mad wizard suddenly turned, leaping aside as he thrust Caris back. The narrow corridor echoed with the whopping crash of a crossbow, and the iron bolt came slamming from the shadows at the far end of the passage, punching through the door panels where Antryg's back had been an instant before. On second look—and Caris *knew* he had seen no one there a split moment before—Caris saw the figure at the turn of the hall near the stair, dapper in its full-skirted dark coat, the pale green eyes wide and gleaming like a cat's in the dark.

Antryg cried, "Magus, no!" as the little dog wizard threw the crossbow aside with a clash on the parquet floor and pulled a double-barreled pistol from his coat.

The Magus hesitated for an instant, grief and shame contorting his white face. He whispered, "I'm sorry, Antryg," and leveled the pistol at his friend's chest.

At the same moment Caris glimpsed a shadow on the staircase behind the Magus, a blurred impression of emerald velvet and straggly blond curls, Joanna in the uniform of one of Cerdic's pages . . . Even as the pistol cocked she had her arm up, and flung something with all her strength at the Magus' back.

Caris heard the tap of it, no louder than if she'd thrown a clot of horse dung, but the result was astounding. The Magus screamed as if she'd thrust a knife in his spine, flung up his arms, and in that one bought second Caris had covered the distance between them. The brief, tangled fight with illusion at the ford was in his mind, and the long agony of the day, as he grabbed a handful of superfine coat front; the hollow crack of the Magus' head hitting the paneling seemed to shake the house.

Downstairs men were shooting.

Antryg flung open the bedroom door. "Come on!"

Caris bent to scoop up whatever it was that Joanna had thrown, even as the girl reached for it; before his hand could touch it he jerked back, realization slamming him like the butt-end of a barge pole in the stomach—he almost threw up with shock. It was the Sigil of Darkness.

Joanna caught it up, shoving it back into its protective lead wrappings and into her backpack as she sprang over Magus' limp body and ran for the bedchamber door. As he followed her, Caris saw the stains of lampblack on her velvet jacket sleeves—she must have disguised herself as a page to take up the poisoned lamp to the sasenna who lay in wait.

"He would have killed you . . ." She flung a last hurt look over her shoulder as Antryg yanked open the section of dark linenfold paneling near the head of the bed.

"Suraklin," Caris gasped. "He made the Magus a slave —they were all here together..."

"Suraklin was *here*?!" In the darkness of the little cubbyhole behind the panel, Antryg's gray eyes flared wide with shock. An instant later he was plunging down the narrow stair ahead of them into blackness, suffocatingly hot from the chimney against which it ran.

"But he couldn't be!" stammered Joanna. "The computer was up..."

"It has to be in the house." Caris' shoulder brushed the coarse plaster of the wall as they rounded a turn. "He was out at the circle last night; if you didn't trip over him taking a reading today, this is the only place it *could* be..."

Patched coat skirts swirling, Antryg stopped abruptly at the bottom of the stairs, caught Caris by the shoulder, and thrust him against the warm brick of the wall. In the frosty gleam of the witchlight that hung above his head his dilated eyes seemed almost silver. Soft as it was, his deep voice echoed against the close, earth-smelling arch of the low roof. "And did you speak to him?"

Caris shook his head. Even a few days ago he would have been furious at the implied mistrust; now he understood. "They—Suraklin and Leynart—had already gone to the circle on the island when Magus took me. I don't know what they were doing there, whether Suraklin wanted me for bait or to use me, whether he came back here or not..."

"Did you eat or drink anything," Antryg asked quietly, "whilst you were there?"

"No." Caris swallowed hard at the evil recollections. "There was bread and water. I threw them away. The room was marked—I had dreams..."

Antryg sighed. "So have we all." Turning, he led the way into the narrow, dirt-smelling tunnel that stretched away into darkness before them.

"But if Suraklin was here," Joanna protested, hitching

her backpack up onto her shoulders and hurrying at his heels, "the computer *has* to be somewhere near, and not . . ."

"Not necessarily," the wizard said, striding ahead of them, his sheathed sword gripped sasenna-fashion in his left hand. "Theoretically it could be at any node in the lines. The lines—the energy-tracks—used to be called witchpaths, though few remember anymore how to use them. As it happens, Suraklin was one of the few. He could have walked from Kymil to the circle in a night, and walked back in another . . ."

"Kymil!" Leynart's words came back to him, with the glow of the study hearth and the glint of the forgotten gods' watching eyes. "Leynart said Suraklin could get him to Kymil before Pharos reached there. Suraklin gave him a love-charm, a rose . . ."

"Specializing in it these days, isn't he?" inquired Joanna viciously.

Bitterly, he said, "Of course it's to Cerdic's advantage to make sure the Regent has a boy and not a woman in his bed."

"Don't be naïve." Antryg paused at the foot of a steep stair, almost a ladder, his tangled gray curls tugged by the draft from the outer air. "That was a smallpox rose. It's a favorite trick of his. It will trigger an epidemic so virulent it will take out Pharos, Pella, Leynart, most of their household, and a sizable portion of the population of Kymil in the most innocent possible fashion, coincidentally leaving our clean-handed and horrified Cerdic with Regency over his imbecile uncle. When we hit the open air, make for the woods—with luck they'll all be converging on the house." The witchlight that illuminated the tunnel faded; Joanna, who could not see in darkness as Caris could, took a handful of the mage's patched and ragged cloak as they mounted the narrow twist of the hidden stair.

The gardens above them were alive with sasenna. For a moment they paused in the gazebo, like a miniature marble temple with its fluted columns and domed roof, the dancing rush of light from the guards' torches splashing over their faces through the lattice of last year's trellised vines. The woods were over a hundred yards away with no more cover than was offered by the knee-high brown hedges that defined the fallow beds. Caris felt his stomach sink.

"Don't run," murmured Antryg's deep, confident voice. "Stride as if you knew where you were going and make for the woods. With luck they'll take us for other sasenna . . ."

"Are you . . .?" began Caris, and switched it to, "Not in those robes they won't."

"I'll have a cloaking spell over us—Joanna, you're going to have to keep up. Once someone notices there's something amiss, we can't get the illusion back."

"Sort of like being in love." She grinned wryly and gave her backpack an extra hitch.

"Less painful in the long run," he replied, with the swift flicker of a smile and, cloak swirling, strode down the pink marble steps and across the dark paths of the garden.

They made it less than thirty feet. "There!" shouted a voice. Turning his head, Caris saw Magister Magus come running from the house, twenty sasenna and guards at his heels. "Kill them!"

Antryg grabbed Joanna by the arm, leaped a knee-high hedge, and bolted across a brown sward, Caris running, naked sword in hand, at his heels. Around them in the darkness warriors were plunging out of the gloom, white markings dancing on their black uniforms, pale faces above the grass-green of Cerdic's household troops. Dim starlight flickered across drawn swords, pistol barrels dark with smoking and scratched with the signs of na-aar, the wicked barbed tips of crossbow bolts, closing around them like a tightening noose of razors. From the darkness of the woods far ahead Caris saw others emerging and knew they were trapped.

Seeing their way blocked, Antryg stumbled to a halt; as Caris took his stance beside him, sword in hands, he glanced back and saw the wizard's face in the darkness suddenly haggard and ill. The ring of sasenna was thirty yards away, closing, metal glittering in the moonlight. In Antryg's eyes was the despair of a man whom Fate has defeated against everything that he could do. Wretchedly, he whispered, "Oh, hell." Sheathing his sword, he thrust it into the sash at the waist of his threadbare green coat. "Hand me the flashlight, would you, Joanna?"

Caris, settling into fighting stance in the bitter knowledge of useless death, looked back at him and said, *"What?"*

As calmly as if he were back at the ruined chapel, Antryg was unscrewing the flashlight's bulb, tinkering with the cylinder's innards. In the advancing glare of the torches his eyes, behind their rounds of cracked glass, were invisible, but his mouth, usually flexible and silly as a rubber doll's, was suddenly hard and set.

There was a faint zap and hiss, the whiff of ozone as the batteries sparked . . .

And the spark leaped like tame lightning, tiny, vicious, living, between Antryg's forefinger and thumb.

He held it up before his eyes, the fey purplish light of it for a moment illuminating the lean, ridiculous nose, the tangled hair, the tawdry beads, and the claw-scarred cheekbones that seemed so delicate in that absurd face. Like a physical impact, realization hit Caris and understanding of what was going to happen.

Since he had first met Antryg, when he was a child of six, and later, when he had encountered the genial madman chatting of tortoise-shell rubbings and playing cat's cradle in the Silent Tower, he had known by reputation alone that he was a wizard. Though he had learned magic from him, he had never seen him display power of any kind, save in little things that he himself could do. Insensibly, he had come to think of him chiefly as a scatterbrained and devious lunatic, his maddening mentor, Joanna's lover, cheerfully pursuing a quixotic quest from which he could not hope to emerge alive.

He had almost forgotten that this man had been Suraklin's chosen student.

He remembered it now, as Antryg raised his hand, the spark still flickering, an inch and a half of baby lightning between thumb and finger.

Uncertain, the advancing sasenna slowed their rush. The wind caught Antryg's cloak and coat skirts in a bat-wing swirl, edged in that crackling glow. Caris, seeing that drawn face, the serene mouth, and the pain-filled, grief-haunted eyes, understood—it was a face of unhuman power, *the most powerful wizard in the world,* Salteris—Suraklin—had said, *including myself . . .*

A voice screamed, "Kill them!" and the ring closed.

Antryg's arm lashed down. As if he had a whip in his hand the lightning elongated, shattering out from his twisted fingers to smite the earth at his feet and show his face like a demented god's in the streaming mane of his gray hair. From the ground, the lightning sprang upward, vicious, living, swelling to a whirlwind in which Caris could see eyes, teeth, whips, claws, too bright to look upon in the exploding darkness. In a column of blinding fire it leaped from earth to sky, the sasenna still rushing toward them, as it was the Way of Sasenna to do, unflinching . . .

Whatever had taken shape within the lightning fell upon them, and the screaming began.

Blinded, shaken, shattered, Caris was aware of nothing else until a hand like an iron claw shut around his arm and he was nearly dragged off his feet by strength he never knew Antryg had. The wizard held Joanna by the other arm, dragging them both at a run within yards of the howling electric maelstrom, through the break in the lines of the sasenna it had caused, and across the huge darkness of the gardens, while the shrieks and cries behind them ripsawed the night. As he ran, Caris caught a glimpse of Antryg's face and saw it was like cut bone, a dead man's face; in his gray eyes was a terrible darkness over half a lifetime deep.

No one pursued them through the woods.

The ford was frozen, the river stilled. Snow lay thinly everywhere on the island, save upon the circle itself; their feet slipped in it as they climbed the graveled slope of the riverbank. Antryg stumbled as they reached the circle, as if all the strength had gone out of him, and leaned against the bluish granite of the outer ring, his face as gray as the stone. He whispered, "They never had a chance."

"Neither had we," Caris gritted through his teeth.

The wizard pressed his gloved hands together against his face, as if by doing so he could still their shaking; a spasm of shuddering wracked him, bowing his whole body. Behind the broken fingers Caris saw the hard glitter of tears.

More gently, he said, "It was them or us."

Antryg nodded, but his wretched sobbing did not cease. He had sinned, Caris knew, in the true sense of the word. Whether it had been necessary or not to protect them long enough to encompass Suraklin's defeat, the fact remained that he had turned his magic upon those unable to defend against it.

"An elemental?" Joanna asked softly, and Caris glanced back at her.

"How did you know?"

"They say Suraklin used to call them. I think he called one to destroy Narwahl Skipfrag, when Skipfrag caught him trying to remove his electrical experiments from his laboratory. From the look of it he used broken glass to clothe it, to make its substance."

Leaning against the stone, Antryg nodded and raised his head as if against the weight of some terrible yoke. "He could use anything," he murmured. "It was the only thing that would—would remain when we had left the area and that Magus couldn't brush aside." His breath blew from his lips in pale steam in the cold traces of glimmering moonlight that were able to pierce the clouds; he had taken off his spectacles. Tear tracks shone on his ravaged face. "They had no magic—most of them probably didn't even believe in it." He was shaking as if naked in a place of bitterest cold.

"You can't think about that," Caris said quietly.

Antryg shook his head, agreeing without the horror or the grief in his eyes abating one degree.

Joanna said softly, "They'll be coming after you now, won't they? The Council can find you . . ."

"Hence the circle." The wizard raised his head again and, with trembling fingers, pushed back the hair from his face. He looked spent, more weary than Caris had seen him except perhaps in the Tower after they'd put the Sigil of Darkness on him, all the colored fires of his absurd courage burned to ash by what he had done. "The other mages will guess I've used the wizard's path, but it will take them a while to guess where I've gone, and longer to follow. It's only a matter of time now, but then it has always been." He moved his shoulders against the cold slab, pushing himself to a standing position once again, his whole body moving slowly, achingly, like an old man's.

"Antryg, listen," Caris said quietly. "You and Joanna have to go to Suraklin's headquarters, wherever it is. I understand that—especially now, while he's in Kymil with Leynart. But Kymil is where I have to go. If what you say about the smallpox-rose is true, I have to stop Leynart before he delivers it. Does one have to be a mage to use the path? Would I have the power . . ."

"No," Antryg said simply. "But it doesn't matter. While the computer was up, Joanna and I came here to the circle and took a bearing along the line. The energy is flowing back to Kymil."

Caris stared at him, digesting this information, the implications sinking in . . . "But we went all through Suraklin's Citadel," he protested. "We looked—*You* looked. That's impossible."

"I know." Antryg replaced his spectacles on his nose, gingerly avoiding the healing wounds of the Dead God's claws. The ghost of his old lunatic grin brushed his lips. "But that's never prevented me from doing things before. Now come—it's growing late."

CHAPTER XVI

THE STRANGEST THING ABOUT TRAVELING THE WITCHPATH was that there seemed to be nothing strange about it. Though intensely cold, the night was clear. Only a layer of ground fog clung like white smoke about the feet of the menhirs as Antryg led his two companions across the circle and under one of the great trilithons, and Joanna, clinging apprehensively to Antryg's hand, shivered and looked around her, waiting for the magic to begin.

Only it did not begin. Antryg simply walked, holding her by the hand and Caris by the arm, along the aisle of broken menhirs. Beyond in the darkness Joanna could see the dark shapes of trees and the occasional patches of snow shining faintly through the gloom. A scrim of light clung like a thin frost about some of the stones nearest them; that was all. She wondered if Antryg would be able to overcome his revulsion at what he had done enough to work the magic that would carry them south. But looking up at him, she dared not speak. His face was set and very tired, his eyes seeming to look inward on some pit of haunted memory. The shimmer of the stones caught like starfire in his earrings, on the gimcrack tangle of his beads, and on the tears that still marked his face.

Give him time, she thought, wondering apprehensively how much time they had. *Give him time*.

It was only when they had been walking for twenty-five minutes by Joanna's digital watch and had still not reached the river—at best a hundred feet from the edge of the circle—that she understood. They were on the path already. The magic breathed so softly from the menhirs that neither she nor Caris could detect it. Only Antryg, walking silent between them, knew it was there.

"Can all wizards do this?" Caris asked quietly, and Antryg, at the request for specific information, seemed to rouse himself a little from the dreadful isolation in which he was trapped. "Or could they once?"

"Not all, no." The mage pushed up his spectacles to rub the smudgy circles weariness had painted beneath his eyes. "How to use them for travel was never knowledge held by more than a few, even in the old days before the Battle of Stellith. How they work, what they are, why journeys along them always take the length of the night, provided they are begun before midnight, why one doesn't sleep on the path, and can't do so, in fact, and why at certain seasons of the year they must not be traveled at all . . .

"There are legends, stories, conflicting accounts. I—I sense things about them, as I sense things about the Void, that I can't put into words. But I have no proof."

Joanna looked out beyond the line of light-edged monoliths and wondered where she would find herself if she stepped through one of those weedy gaps. She had, however, no intention of trying. Though the stones leaned tiredly, weatherworn and obviously ruinously old, nowhere did the lines gap, as she remembered them doing in the fields south of Devilsgate. She knew the lines did not run continuously clear to Kymil. Yet from the inside, the track was unbroken. Each stone along the way was individual, shaped and weathered to its own personality; each was cold and damp when she touched it, hard and real under her hand. Weeds grew thickly around them, stiff with frost. They bent and crackled under the brush of Antryg's heavy cape hem, and now and then Joanna could see in the frosted mud of the track other footprints, running on south ahead of them—the footprints of the Dark Mage.

They rested several times during the night, Joanna glad to be relieved of the weight of her backpack. By this time she had become inured to walking, though the cold troubled her; under her thick sheepskin coat, the velvet uniform of Cerdic's page was less warm than her coarse laborer's clothes had been. She felt shaken and depressed, the sight of Suraklin's footprints—Gary's footprints—disconcerting her unexpectedly, reminding her that soon they would meet. She tried not to think about that, about the possibility of defeat and enslavement, or about the possibility of her own death. Throughout the last few weeks, even trapped in the stinking Erebus of the Dead God's church, she had taken comfort in Antryg's presence. He had seldom used his power; but unlike Caris, she had always been conscious of its possibility and in her heart had never really believed in his defeat.

But though gradually the desperate tension of self-hate eased out of his body, she was conscious, through his gloved hand in hers, of his utter weariness. The power he had used to summon the elemental and to clothe it in lightning had left him spent and ill. Not knowing what to say, she only walked close to him, under the vast purple blanket of his cloak, her arm around his waist. After a moment, like a man seeking warmth, his arm tightened around her shoulders.

Freezing cold and nearly as black as the night they had just left, dawn found the three travelers at the nadir of the gaping pit that had been Suraklin's Citadel. Throughout the night Joanna had been prey to fears of what awaited them at the end of the witchpath, entertaining in her mind half a dozen hideous and mutually exclusive scenarios, from entrapment within the Citadel to cosmic rerouting to some distant point.

But when the mists faded around them as they stepped through the gap between the last two menhirs of the line,

Joanna saw only the barren sides of the pit funneling up around her, calcined, charred in places, dangling with stiff black stringers of cold-killed vines. Above the vast circle of the pit's lips, the sky was the blackish yellow of an old bruise. The air smelled of snow and of the sickening carrion whiff from the rotting doorways all about the pit's sides. On the ground high above, the wind screamed over the stones. Even down here in relative shelter, it riffled the lead-colored waters of a vast pool of seepage that lay before their feet.

Antryg looked around him, exhausted and baffled, his tangled gray curls shifted by that cutting wind. "It has to be here," he said softly. "Somewhere—hidden so deep Suraklin wouldn't even need to guard the place for fear of drawing attention to it. It *has* to."

"We've been through every pit, every vault, every passage of the few that are left," Caris said, his voice quiet but hard as chipped flint, "and we have proven to ourselves that it *isn't*. If he makes anything like the same time we did, Pharos should be at Larkmoor tonight. Whether you go there or not, Antryg, I'm going to be there to intercept Leynart before he uses that charm of his to trigger a plague."

"Do that." Behind his spectacles, Antryg's eyes seemed to have darkened to smoke color with tiredness, but they studied the young warrior evenly, as if he, like Joanna, realized that, given a choice, Caris placed saving Pella's life above what might be his only chance for revenge upon the man who had murdered his grandfather. But neither commented on the final breaking of his obsession. There was a brittle, desperate quality about the young man now, like a sword blade bent to the snapping point.

Deep and soft as silk velvet, Antryg continued, "Joanna and I will stay here, search once again—there has to be something I've overlooked. If we find nothing..." He hesitated, absently rubbing his crooked hands, then went on, his tone carefully neutral, "...if nothing finds *us*, we'll sleep the night at the Silent Tower. In the weeks past, I've scried the place by magic. Since my escape, it's been abandoned. If you don't come I'll scry for you..." He paused again, as if his mind stumbled over the promise of that casual use of little magic, the muscles in his lean jaw jumping, as if he had carelessly brushed a raw wound. Then he took a deep breath and forced himself to go on. "Good luck."

"Thank you," Caris said quietly. He stood for a time longer, studying his sometime teacher. Joanna could see the hardness of his dark soul armor, an almost visible aura about that muscular, black-clothed form, but his eyes were not the eyes of the young man who had begun the journey north. He had made his choice, whether he articulated it to himself yet or not, that the saving of lives was preferable to the taking of them. "Go carefully, Antryg." His glance moved to Joanna, and he said, "Take care of him," and was rewarded with the ghost of her grin.

Joanna and Antryg watched him as he ascended the long, steep ruin of the old stair to the weed-curtained pit rim above. After his black uniform had vanished against the mottled sky, Antryg stood for some time, head bowed, listening intently while the cold deepened and the wind moved his stained cloak and the gray tousle of his hair. Then he sighed and took Joanna's hand. Together they began again to search the blasted ruin of what had once been his home.

"He'll be here in a few hours," Pella whispered.

"I know." Caris started to rise. "His men were everywhere outside the house."

Her hand on his bare shoulder drew him down again. The muted reflection of lantern light through the ladder hole in the floor snaked along the gilt braid of his coat sleeves, where the garment lay in a heap with Pella's plain brown riding dress. Here in the stable loft the warmth from the horses below collected, though the winds groaned outside; now and then they heard the muffled clunk of a hoof or the distant voices of the grooms cleaning tack at the far end of the stone-flagged passageway. But that was all. Kyssha dozed, Caris knew, like a dropped muff at the foot of the ladder. His arms locked more tightly around Pella's shoulders; for a time he said nothing, only breathed the thick smell of the hay and the cardamom scent of her hair.

He would have been able to keep his distance from her, he thought, as he had resolved to do, had he only met her in the house. Their situation was impossible, and he knew it. No matter how much he hated the thought—and the hatred of it filled his flesh like slow-burning gunpowder in a flash wound—she was and always would be Pharos' wife. He had no right to come between them, particularly when he himself was very likely to die in the fight against Suraklin. His frantic love did not want to let this girl go, but fairness and caring told him that it would be monstrous to complicate whatever she and her husband would have with the torment of might-have-beens.

But he had found her, wrapped in her many-caped tweed coachman's cloak, silently patrolling the perimeter of the house as they had done together, and all his resolutions had come apart like soaked tissue paper at the first hesitant joining of their hands.

At last he whispered, "We'd better go back to the house. If Pharos is coming this afternoon, Leynart has to be ahead of him. You know none of the Prince's men will keep him out."

Pella nodded, but caught his hand as he moved to get up. She said softly, "I know. And I know we can't let Leynart succeed and unleash a plague, can't let Suraklin rule the country through Cerdic. It's all—the part of me that wants good rulership, the part of me that still wants to follow the Way of the Sasenna. But—there's a part of me that doesn't ever want anything but this."

He brought her hand up to his lips. "Joanna's right," he whispered. "These things have to be done one—one subroutine at a time." As he had hoped, her friend's logic made Pella laugh. "Then we'll see."

It was a lie, and he knew it. He knew now that there was no way he could go on living without her in his life.

But as they crossed the thin, hard snow toward the house, like a powdering of salt on the ground, he remembered the amber glint of Suraklin's eyes and knew also that there was very little likelihood that such a contingency would arise. And that, he thought, caught between his present bounding joy and the black emptiness of the future, was probably just as well.

The Regent's sasenna were in the house when Caris and Pella reached it, slipping quietly in through the kitchen quarters with Kyssha peering inquiringly from beneath the folds of Pella's capes. Caris said, "Is there a back stairs up to the state bedroom? Wearing this—" He touched his black-and-gold coat. "—was enough to get me close to the house, but if the captain gets a look at me, she'll know I'm not one of hers. It would only take one of the servants saying they saw me here with Antryg to destroy everything."

Pella nodded and set Kyssha down, then led the way to one of the several narrow back stairs which allowed servants access to the principal apartments to unobtrusively remove the chamber pots of their betters. As they climbed the enclosed flight, Caris was aware of the subdued turmoil in the house all around them; servants scurried to prepare a meal up to the Regent's exacting standards, and sasenna prowled quietly through the halls. In the great state bedroom, the curtains had been drawn and a forest fire of candles lit. Against the old-fashioned, gilt-edged paneling of the walls, the bed hangings of bronze and pink looked like columns of flowers, the embroidered coverlet like an autumn meadow. Standing before that symbol of dynastic duties, Pella's cheeks reddened as if scalded. Shakily, she began, "Caris..."

He put his fingers to her lips. "Don't." Then he took his

hand away and put it behind his back, for the touch kindled in him an overwhelming desire to crush her in his arms, drag her to that imperial bed...

He looked away from her, confused and hating himself. Hesitantly, stammeringly, not sure that he should even be speaking the words aloud, lest he give them power, he went on, "It isn't that I don't want to help you, Pella. But I can't. I am—sasenna—or at least I was, before I went north. But my determination to follow the Way is leaving me—daily, hourly now, I can feel it going, dripping out of me like wine from a cracked cup. It used to be I could—could take a woman... And take her was all I'd do, and a woman was all she was. That's not the same with you. It shouldn't be this way—I shouldn't let it be this way—but it is. I should be out at the Citadel with Antryg and Joanna now, not here, trying to save you—trying to save Pharos..."

He was, he realized, asking for her help, as he had not asked help of anyone since he had taken his vows. It was not the Way to do so, not even in small things, physical things, let alone in things that truly mattered, things that were not supposed to matter...

Like an echo of his troubled thoughts, he saw Pella's training and her understanding in her eyes. "I know," she said softly. "I'm sorry. If I'd been a true ruler or even a true sasennan, I'd have sent you away myself." She smiled wryly across into his eyes, for they were nearly of a height; her black hair lay thick over the collar of her cloak, like coarse skeins of silk tangled with flecks of hay. Then abruptly she turned away, and preceded him out through the main door of the bedchamber, and into the darkness of the hall.

From the great stairwell, voices could be heard, muffled and distant from the front of the house, and the scurry of feet. A shadow was flung on the dark paneling of the walls—the hall lamps below had been kindled—and there was the quick creak of weight on the stairs. A servant's voice called, "My lady? His Grace's carriage is coming. Shall I send your maid up?"

In the reflected glow, Caris saw the girl's jaw tighten and put his hand on her shoulder. In a voice of forced calm she said, "I—I'd better get myself ready..." Her fingers strayed to her tousled hair, the rough tweed cloak still over her shoulders...

"We should get a guard in that room," Caris said quietly, like her, hardening himself to speak of commonplaces. "Remember that it won't be enough to find the smallpox-rose. If Leynart touches it he'll be infected, and anyone he touches, according to Antryg. He has to be stopped the moment he enters the room, before he even opens the..."

At Pella's heels, Kyssha suddenly raised her pointed muzzle, her feathered ears snapping in the direction of the state bedchamber, and she let out a shrill bark. Pella's eyes and Caris' met for one instant. Then they were both striding back down the hall.

The first thing Caris saw when he flung open the chamber door was the great bed, its coverlet now turned welcomingly back, a red rose lying like a great gout of blood upon the pillows. The second was Leynart, standing beside the embroidered curtains, his speedwell-blue eyes enormous with startlement and alarm. Caris strode forward toward him, calling back to Pella, "Get the tongs and throw that thing on the fire!"

The boy gasped with horror. "No!" He snatched up the rose to his chest and dived across the bed a moment before Caris reached him, plunging into the dark rectangle of the back stairs door and slamming it shut behind him. Caris jerked on the hidden handle, but the door held fast.

At the same moment Pella said sharply, "Listen!" Caris heard the grinding crunch of carriage wheels on the drive outside. He swore, gave the handle one final yank, and nearly overset himself when the inner catch gave way; then he was racing down that dark inner stair, hearing the clatter of high, jeweled heels rattling around the narrow turns ahead of him.

He'd be making for the drive. Caris heard the slam of the door at the bottom of the stairs and swore again, called to mind in midrun that the door did in fact open out into the kitchen, tucked his head and his arm, and hurled himself straight off the steps at it with all the momentum he could summon.

The panels burst but the frame of the door held firm, entangling Caris in a splintery web of shards. Swearing, he managed to get his arm through and fumble free the latch that held it. Behind the heat of his anger at the fatuous Leynart, he felt cold dread, remembering the smallpox epidemic that had swept Innkitar during his first year of training there, the stench of smoke and corpses and the quicklime burial-pits at the streetcorners. Pella could be gotten out of here, but many others would die, either of the disease or of being forced to take to the roads in winter.

The clatter of Leynart's heels on the stone floors of the kitchen quarters led him on, and Caris ran lightly, dodging through the big house, knowing the boy was infected already and that he must touch him, must seize him . . .

He heard the boy cry out, "My lord!" like a sob, and burst through the green servants' door into the hall, where Pharos stood among his sasenna and his guards, tiny, glittering, an evil, jeweled doll. His head snapped around at the sound of Leynart's voice, and Caris saw Pellicida beside him, half a head taller, like a crumpled-looking hoyden in her tweed cloak and plain gown with her hair in black handfuls over her shoulders.

Leynart halted for an instant, the poisoned rose still in his hand, as sasenna closed in on Caris from both sides. As his arms were seized and his sword wrenched from his hand, Caris shouted, "My lord, don't let him near you!" and Pharos' pale eyes narrowed.

His mouth trembling, Leynart's eyes darted from Caris to Pella again. "You'd like that, wouldn't you?" He almost spat the words. "You'd like even to take my gifts away from him and most of all the gift of my heart, which he's always had . . ." High heels clicking on the polished floor, he walked forward, like a golden image in his buttercup coat, the rose in his hand. His childlike blue eyes were on Pharos. "Please, my lord, if you must send me away, at least take this, to remember me . . ."

"It's poisoned, Leynart," said Pella quietly.

The boy stopped, his eyes slitting. "You're lying, you frumpy bitch."

But she was sasennan now, not a girl uncertain of Court usages, and the insult slid off her without breaking her serene battle calm. "I wish it were a lie," she said in her deep, husky voice, "because I don't want to see you hurt. But you were tricked. Cerdic was tricked. The rose is imbued with a spell to cause smallpox."

There was a sharp stir, a murmur and a drawing back of Pharos' red-clothed retainers. Pharos himself blanched and backed hastily toward the door.

"You believe her!" Leynart's eyes flooded with tears of rage. "You'd cast me off on her say so!" He whirled on Pella. "If it is you'll never live to have him!" he cried, and flung himself at the girl.

In the split second of confusion, Caris kicked the ankle of the man on his right, jabbing back with his elbow to break his balance, and whirled to snap kick his other captor in the gut. He shouted "NO!" and sprang at Leynart, hands reaching, knowing there was no way he could stop the boy.

In a single fluid movement, Pella had her heavy tweed cloak free of her shoulders and tossed it over Leynart's head. The boy let out a shriek of rage and clawed at the thick fabric as Pella stepped aside, holding a corner of the cloak to further entangle him; the next second Caris caught the muffled figure and foot-swept him to the floor. Leynart ceased struggling almost at once. Under the stifling layers of capes, Caris could feel the slim body shaken with sobs, through which the boy gasped, "Liars! Liars!"

From the safety of the door, the Regent said, "Take him away. Let him be confined in one of the best bedrooms ..."

"I'd suggest the state bedroom, your Grace," Pella said quietly. "It was where he put the rose originally for you to find."

Other sasenna helped Leynart to his feet, taking care not to touch more than the entangling folds of Pella's cloak. The boy shook his head free, raven curls matted around his face, and tears of bitter frustration tracking the powder on his face with streaks of melting blue. As they led him to the door, he braced his feet and looked back at Pharos, who still hovered in the doorway behind his bodyguards. "My lord, if it's true, I knew nothing of it," he choked. "I—I only wanted your love. You have to believe that."

"If it is true," Pharos said with unwonted gentleness, "I fear that the reason will not much matter, my Ley. If it was false ..." His pale eyes slid sidelong to Pella close beside Caris. The calm of battle was wearing off her and embarrassment taking over; her brownish skin stained with a blotchy red blush. But she met the Regent's eyes squarely, a warrior, not a confused Princess trying to make herself something she was not.

After a long moment, Pharos asked, "Do you hate me, child?" He spoke as if there was no one else in the room.

"I don't know," Pella said frankly. "You're the ruler and my husband ... and generally, I *don't* hate people. Even if I did," she added honestly, "I wouldn't say so in public." Then she blushed even hotter, realizing the gaucherie of comparing her own manners with his.

But after a quick flicker of irritation, the Regent's sinful eyes smiled. "Then I shall take an opportunity to ask you the question in private, my little Princess." And as he stepped forward to kiss her hand, Caris faded silently out of the room.

* * *

"It has to be there," said Antryg quietly, raising his chin from his elbows, which were crossed over his knees. He had been sitting in much the same folded-up position in one of the crude wooden chairs in the watchroom of the Silent Tower when Joanna had fallen asleep beside the hearth—hours ago, by the grayish quality of the light. That he'd gotten up in that time she knew; the fire had been replenished, and his cloak lay over her like a dilapidated purple horse blanket. But she hadn't heard him. Weariness that she had carried all the way north crushed her, far more than a few hours' sleep would dispel. Like the bitter cold, it had eaten into her bones, and she wondered if she would ever recover from it.

They had found nothing in the Citadel ruins, nothing but the abominations, hiding deep in the dead ends of such of the underground labyrinth as had survived the wizards' wrath and the attenuated dreams of an evil long calcined to nothing. Not even the Church's sasenna watched the place now; they had long deserted the Silent Tower to the darkness of its memories. And so at last, as the day grew colder with the turning of noon and a thin, dry snow began to fall, they had come to the Silent Tower, the only shelter in all the bitter hills.

"All the signs point to it," Antryg went on. "It isn't just that the energy of the lines was flowing to the south to Kymil—dammit, Joanna, it's the only place it *could* have been flowing! I felt it, I knew it was going there! It's other things as well."

She sat up under his cloak, pulling the thick wool around her shoulders, though the watchroom, built into the thickness of the wall off the arched passage of the tower gate, was warm now. On the hearth she saw a tin teakettle and a big pewter tankard which had evidently been pressed into service as a teapot; an earthenware cup rested on the table near Antryg's chair, though no steam rose now from its long-cold contents. He had refused to enter the Tower itself. Though the Sigil of Darkness had weeks since been removed from its door and taken back to the Bishop's treasure house, the walls of the Tower were still thick with spells that prevented the working of magic—thick too, she thought, with evil memories.

Throughout the day, Antryg had been silent. In his eyes she still saw the darkness of the garden at Devilsgate and the blinding refulgence of the elemental springing to life, clothed in the lightning he'd given it to destroy those whose only defense was metal swords. The memory lay on him like the brown scar left by the Sigil of Darkness that marked his throat among his tattered shirt ruffles, but it was a pain that it would take more than a carbide hacksaw to remove.

He went on, "It's the logical place for it, you know. Yes, the Church has watched it from a distance, but seldom closely, I'll wager. Everyone else would have shunned it. And though there were abominations near the Tilrattin node in the north, they weren't anything near as plentiful as there."

"That's because the woods wouldn't concentrate them like the pits did," Joanna pointed out.

"Even given that," he insisted, "there are still more—many times more. I never felt—easy—going to look for it elsewhere. Everything points to the old Citadel. It *has* to be there. I know it. I feel it."

Joanna pushed aside her backpack, which she'd been using for a pillow, and poked at the rock-hard jerky and waybread Antryg had dug from what remained of the guardroom stores. "That's neither here nor there," she said reasonably. "We've looked twice, and it's *not*."

"Neither here nor there," the wizard repeated ironically, leaning back in his rickety chair and hugging his knees again. "From here to Tilrattin and back—from your world to mine—neither here nor there . . ." He paused, his gray eyes suddenly sharpening behind his spectacles; then he sat up straight, unfolding his long legs to the floor. "Neither here nor there!"

His eyes met Joanna's. For a time the silence in the guardroom was so intent that the silken *whump* of the log crumbling in the hearth sounded loud and individual beneath the chaotic drone of the wind in the passage of the gates outside. Doubtfully, Joanna said, "A—a vest-pocket dimension?"

His eyes widened. "You know of such things?"

"They're in all the comic books."

"Actually, a sort of enclave between universes, like a bubble in the fabric of the Void. They sometimes occur, but they're fairly short-lived because the movement of the Void pulls them apart. But now that I think of it, your universe and mine have been in phase for a long time, and certainly energy is being drained from both."

"Could he make something like that? Or find it?"

"Found, probably, and is shielding in some fashion to keep the dimensions together indefinitely and to keep me from being aware of it." He leaned forward, and the grief that had haunted him for the last twenty-four hours faded from his eyes in the daft glow of a theorist's enthusiasm. "You see, I'm the only person I know who can 'cast through' the Void—see things on the other side, touch its fabric with my mind. Suraklin never could; though he can cross it at will, he has no sense of how the Void operates. It is actually a rather specialized field of knowledge. Many wizards have them, some of them completely useless, like the ability to summon frogs or sculpt the wind. But all the same . . ."

"Could you find it?"

He shook his head. "That's the trouble. Before I can see through the spells of unseeing that guard it, I'd need to know what it looked like, know its shape and boundaries, even as I have to know what the Gate to it looks like before I can see it. And, of course, such things exist only in Suraklin's mind."

Joanna looked up at him, feeling inside her such a blaze of illumination that she wondered her flesh didn't glow. Her voice was not quite steady as she said, "No they don't." With shaking fingers, she reached out and touched her grubby backpack. "If he's programming it, he can't do it in patterns—only linearly. And I've found graphics programs in here, mathematical equations that translate into three-dimensional shapes—or four-dimensional ones. The human mind can't really picture a four-dimensional shape, but a computer doesn't give a damn whether a thing is supposed to be able to exist or not . . ."

"Rather like wizards," Antryg mused, "or madmen. Are all computers insane?"

Joanna hesitated, disturbed by the question for reasons she'd preferred not to examine, and the wizard went on, "Can you graph those equations? Give me a picture of it?"

She nodded, shivering all over with suppressed excitement. "It's really only reverse engineering. I'll need graph paper."

"There's paper in the Tower. Lines can be drawn on it."

"It'll take a hell of a long time. If I'd known I'd have brought my calculator . . ."

"I had a set of calculating bones—little slips of ivory about the size of your finger with numbers on them. They're probably still up there. A mathematician in Melli-iane showed me how to use them. They work very quickly."

He got to his feet, collected his cloak from around her shoulders, and started for the watchroom door. Then he stopped, came back to her, and seized her in a fierce hug of mingled joy and desperation, his face pressed against her hair. Her arms went around his waist, being careful of the rib he'd cracked during his encounter with the Dead God. For a long moment, they stood so, while she thought, *This is going to be it. We're really going to have to deal with Suraklin this time.* The thought left her weak with dread.

Then he was gone, striding across the courtyard in the

failing light with all his old gawky insouciance, the snowy wind whipping his cloak and coat skirts into lunatic billows about his thin form and fraying at his long gray hair. Watching him go, Joanna felt a stab of grief and the burn of tears behind her eyes; for all his height, his loose-limbed strength, and his scatterbrained cheerfulness, it came to her how fragile he seemed. She understood, suddenly, Suraklin's obsessive desire to preserve the things in his life as they were, to hold to those joys no matter who else suffered for them, and to keep the taste of them on the tongue, so they would not slide away into the fast-flowing darkness of time. She forced the feeling down, telling herself, *One thing at a time*. Caris was right. There were some times when it did not pay to think too much.

Shaken inside, she sat down by the hearth again and began digging through the DARKMAGE files for the four-dimensional equations whose significance she hadn't understood and whose importance, at the time, had seemed to her to be neither here nor there.

It was long past dark when Caris returned to the Silent Tower. Had he not been mageborn and able to see in the dark, he doubted he could have found it at all, for not even stars pierced the black sheet of clouds that covered the sky from horizon to horizon. To his mage's sight, the Tower loomed queerly against the ebon backdrop, black within black, utterly untouched by light. The wind had risen, driving the hard little pellets of snow like a sandstorm against his cheeks; the cold ate through his tunic, jacket, and cloak as if he had worn nothing but a thin shirt of cotton lawn. Nevertheless, he circled the Tower twice, observing the ground and the walls, seeking for a sign. It was only when he climbed the rear wall with the hook and line of the standard sasenna's equipment which he'd gotten from Pella that he saw the blue glow of witchlight from the watchroom's slit windows and the faint shiver of heat above the chimney, before the wind whirled the smoke away.

If they were here, he thought, they had not found Suraklin at the Citadel after all. His heart turned sick inside him. Another time of search, then; how many more weeks of forcing himself to be what he no longer was, of warming himself at a revenge that had grown cold, and of waiting to die?

But it would have been worse, he knew, to have returned and found them not there.

His feet made no more noise than did his shadow as he crossed the court. He stood in a lee angle of the gatehouse passage and listened until he heard Antryg's deep, beautiful voice before slipping up to the door. Before he could raise his hand to knock, he heard Antryg say within, "Ah, there's Caris." There was the scrape of a chair, and the door opened to the cool brilliance of witchlight and the warmth of the fire. Caris reflected that there were times when he wanted to hit the wizard up alongside the head with the hilt of his sword.

He said dully, "It's done. I got there in time—Leynart's under guard, and they know about the rose."

Joanna looked up from the vast graph spread across the table—a bedsheet, in fact, ruled with penciled lines, on which she was marking dots in the midst of half a dozen wax scribbling tablets that were covered with mathematical formulae in the spiky little numbers her people used. "And Pella?"

"She's gone back to Pharos." Caris stripped off his cloak and jacket and folded himself up beside the hearth, his arms crossed before his chest. There was hard bread and dried beef there. He realized he hadn't eaten all day, save for a few mouthfuls of bread and ham Pella had stolen for him from the kitchen, but didn't care.

Joanna set down her pencil, startled and aghast. "Pharos . . ."

Roughly, Caris said, "It doesn't matter. It's better. There was nothing for us."

Except joy, he thought, leaning his forehead against the stones of the hearth and closing his eyes, feeling the warmth of the fire like the brush of Pella's fingers on the lids. *Except joy.*

Behind him, Antryg said quietly, "We've found Suraklin."

"Good," Caris mumbled. He lay down and drew his cloak over him. *At least,* he thought, *it will then be over.*

And on that thought he slept.

He was wakened by grief, dull and uncaring, beyond even the effort of tears. Pella was gone, and it seemed to him that even his pursuit of Suraklin was futile, a waste of his time, a fool's errand. Opening his eyes he saw wet grayish light seeping through the watchroom windows that let into the courtyard, making the small chamber seem dim and frowsty, with its stink of old smoke and wet clothes. The vast graph spread over the table was now covered with arcane lines and symbols, with scribbled marginal calculations half-hidden by tablets, by the disgorged contents of Joanna's precious backpack, and by Antryg's little ivory calculating bones. Under the grubby curtain of her straggling blond hair, Joanna's face looked thin and old, as it had by the candle light of the postinghouses on their journey south, ravaged by lack of sleep and weariness, the sharpness of her cheekbones and chin emphasizing the awkward nose and the shrew lines around her eyes. She was looking at the strange magic watch that was strapped to her wrist. Antryg, sitting on the bench beside her, seemed strangely subdued.

She said quietly, "It's nine in the morning."

The wizard glanced across at her, his fingers, as if idling away from his conscious thought, beginning to make a corral of his mathematical ivory bones. "There have been daylight spells before."

"Not on weekdays. This is Tuesday, Antryg; if Suraklin

was still being Gary, he'd have to be at work. He needed to stay working so he could program on the San Serano computer. The fact that he isn't means he's done with that."

The sleep cleared from Caris' mind, but left it still muzzy, as if he were half-drunk. He realized that his depression and grief were not solely his own. "You mean he's gone into his computer." He sat up, scrubbing his fingers through his cropped blond hair, wondering why it didn't matter to him that they had lost their race with the Dark Mage.

Joanna nodded. "I think so." She began folding up her papers, mechanically, as she always did, like a task she was forcing herself to perform. Her eyes were dull; she looked beaten, wretched, and badly scared. "I hate to say it, guys—but I think the system just went on-line for keeps."

CHAPTER XVII

UNDER A CUT-STEEL MORNING SKY, WHAT WAS LEFT OF THE Citadel of Suraklin lay cold and bleak, the puddles of slush frozen, and skiffs of hard, powdery snow blowing restlessly over ground barren now of any living thing. Save for those ghostly flurries, even the snow did not lie here, though it blotched the hills all around with white. Joanna, hugging Antryg's patched purple cloak around her, wondered if Hell would look like this after Judgment Day—inhabitants gone, Devil destroyed, even the glamour of evil burned out of it, leaving nothing but a few lines of stones that stank of forgotten corruptions.

Beside her, Antryg looked ghastly in the dun-colored light. "Can you feel it?" he whispered.

Joanna nodded, though she was not certain what it was that she did feel. Her mind felt clouded, dulled with the now-familiar uncaring depression of the energy drain; but added to that was a hideous sense of wrongness, as if she might extend her hand and push it inadvertently through the structure of the universe itself.

"He's weakened the whole fabric," Antryg said softly. "The enclave is being maintained from moment to moment now by the computer's power, by the energy relays. It's unstable; where it touches, this universe is unstable as well." He spoke barely above a whisper, as if he feared that too loud a sound would shatter the very semblance of reality around them. Wind stirred his hair and swirled the long skirts of his coat; a foot from him, Joanna felt none.

Something caught her eye, and she whirled, her heart in her throat. She thought she had seen something near one of the old pits, scraggly with wet stones and frozen slush, but there was nothing . . . or . . .

Try as she would, she could not focus her eyes on the place. It was like a puzzle with pieces missing, though she could not describe what was preventing her from seeing the spaces in between.

"Yes," Antryg murmured. "There are abominations here."

"Let's get this over." In spite of the day's freezing wind, a rime of sweat glittered on Caris' face. His long sword flashed naked in his hand, cold in the daylight like a living thing; it was his eyes that seemed dead.

"It will be in the pits." There was no doubt now in Antryg's deep voice. "In the bottommost room, at the center of his ancient power. It's fairly easy to see something invisible, if you know what you're looking for, have a picture of it, as the graphic program delineated it. My dear . . ."

For an instant Joanna seriously considered giving Antryg a quick rundown on how to input programs from floppies to mainframe, then stopped herself. Experience had taught her that whatever could go wrong with a computer would, even ones that didn't house the corroding souls of dead wizards. Though her own soul felt dead within her, she knew intellectually that she still loved this man and that he'd need her help. After several nights of little or no sleep, he looked like ten miles of bad road; if he felt anywhere near as bad as she did, he would, she told herself, need all the help he could get.

Trying to keep the whimper of fear out of her voice, she said, "Once I program the worm in, we'll have five or ten minutes. That's how long it would take that program to wipe the whole Cray at San Serano—ops, systems, everything."

"All right." He was glancing all around him as he spoke, his long nose pointing like a nervous dog's, the diamonds in his earlobes flashing like nuggets of dirty ice. "That will give us time to get out before the enclave itself collapses. Presumably, you can't tell which programs will be the first to be devoured, so there is the chance that we—won't make it out."

Joanna swallowed. During the spells of deadness, she always felt anxious—the anxiety now had intensified to a wretched sense of almost-panic in which she wanted only to do whatever she had to do *quickly* and then run away, run to safety . . . She said in a tiny voice, "You mean—die?"

His gray eyes were somber, looking down into hers. "I don't know—but probably not. There's a good chance," he added carefully, "that, though the enclave will seal up once the power goes down, Suraklin won't die. He will only exist in the enclave, unable to touch either of our worlds again, but . . . his consciousness may remain."

Joanna whispered, "Oh, swell." *No Exit*, she thought: the Sartre play about the damned sealed into a room with those who understood them all too well, for all eternity.

"So when you get your program input, I suggest you run like hell. It's certainly what I'll be doing."

She thought, *I'll never make it.* Antryg, with his longer legs, might. The door would close between them, and she would be Gary's—Suraklin's—forever . . .

With the hideous sensation of plunging down a limitless elevator to nowhere, she stumbled after Antryg and Caris toward the brink of the monster pit.

"Antryg . . ." Caris whispered, his voice fading to nothing.

Antryg turned his head, to follow the young man's eyes. A ragged stringer of ground mist whirled aside, and Suraklin stood before them at the head of the broken stair.

Joanna's throat felt as if it had been shut with a valve.

Whatever else Suraklin was now, he was not Gary anymore.

It was Gary's body, Gary's jeans and jacket and Nikes
under the black cloak of a Council wizard. Even the face,
she supposed, was still Gary's, though the expression had
changed it so completely that she was no longer certain she
would recognize the man she had once made love to, years
ago on a hot Los Angeles night. There was nothing left of
that slightly vapid, good-natured selfishness, amoral and
greedy without being actively offensive to anyone. Nothing
left at all. The lines of the cheeks and around the brown
eyes with their queer golden luster were the lines of age,
age infused by driving will and a single overmastering purpose.

Suraklin smiled, like something wound with a key.
"Antreges." His voice, nothing like Gary's now, softened
the hard *g* of Antryg's name into a diminutive, the name of
the boy he had known. "Like the windrose on a map, you
point in all the directions of the wind—but I did suspect
you'd finally point your way back here, to your home, to
me. Babe . . ." His eyes touched Joanna, the nickname
turning her stomach. "Do you think, if I can make a roulette wheel stop on red or summon lightning, I can't degauss a disk? You're just not thinking, babe . . ." As Joanna
gasped, sickened with shock, the brown eyes moved to
Caris, the inflection of the voice shifting again. "My son."

The sasennan began, "You dare . . ."

At the same instant, Antryg whirled utterly without
warning, caught Joanna by the shoulders, and flung her to
the ground. Lightning seared up like a blue-white snake
striking from the earth as he dived on top of her. Caris, his
breath and attention momentarily diverted in anger, wasn't
so quick. The lightning flung him a dozen feet, its earsplit-
ting crack drowning his final cry. It was over before Antryg
had time to react. Her face in the dust, her nostrils filled

with ozone and the stink of burned flesh, Joanna was still nearly blinded by an explosion of light that seemed to ignite the very air. She felt Antryg spring to his feet and wisely stayed where she was; his coat skirt brushed her face briefly and that soft, flexible voice whispered, "Get under cover and keep hold of the backpack." Then he was gone, his footsteps thudding through the ground in her ear.

Even faced with death, the effect of the energy drain made her want to stop and argue—the backpack was too heavy, the disk it contained was now useless, Suraklin had said so...

Do it by the numbers, she told herself fiercely. They'd been standing near a shallow subsidence. She rolled over and over, nearly blinded through her shut eyelids. The ground dropped away beneath her and broken masonry dug into her ribs through her heavy coat as she skidded down. The searing white glare seemed to sicken and purple; raising her head a little, she could see Suraklin with his head down, squinting against the light. Antryg, sword in hand, was within thirty feet of him by the time the Dark Mage could see enough to use the implement he had whipped out from beneath his cloak.

Quite sensibly, somewhere along the line, Suraklin had acquired a submachine gun.

Joanna had to clamp her hands over her mouth to keep from screaming. Antryg flung himself down, sliding and rolling, his sword screaming in a steel arc toward Suraklin's ankles. Bullets stitched the dust in front of him. He jerked and twisted like a cat flung in water, diving for the minimal cover of a broken wall; the glaring, unnatural light faded as he let the spell slip from his mind. It had served its purpose, but he had been just too late.

"Really, my dear," Suraklin said, amused. "You used to be quicker than that."

"Old age comes to us all." Antryg was moving already, flattened to the single broken course of stones, though Joanna thought his voice still seemed to come from where he had first gone to ground. He'd done voice-throwing, she remembered, as one of his dog-wizard tricks to earn supper when they'd first traveled the post road from Kymil to Angelshand during the summer. Behind the truncated wall, there wasn't much of anyplace to go, but already she could see the dead weeds around the place begin to smoke and wither as if under blasting heat.

"Not to me, my love. Never to me."

Antryg had reached the limit of the wall. He lay crushed to the ground, to keep from Suraklin's line of sight; Joanna could see blood black on the dull green of his coat sleeve, the sweat of concentration beading his face. "No," he said. "Nor youth, either, nor warmth, nor cold. Don't you understand yet what you've done to yourself?"

The snout of the gun never wavered from the wall. The bare ground was blackening there, the dead weeds starting to smoke inches from Antryg's feet. A counterspell, Joanna guessed, held the burning at bay, but for how long?

"Indeed I do. What you see is only what our little Joanna would call a waldo, operated by my mind at a distance. Now that I've taken steps to put Pharos out of the way for good, I'll have plenty of them. Cerdic will see to that. But the mind is not in any of them. I have made myself immortal."

"You have made yourself like the Dead God."

Suraklin's brows came together, his voice sharp. "Nonsense!"

"The Dead God isn't immortal," Antryg pressed. "The Dead God is dead. Without feeling, without caring, even for himself—without changing. More stagnant than the very stones, which transmute from rock to air and sand. What do you have, Suraklin, that makes you want to continue? As a computer, as a metal thing of electricity and knowledge, what do you want? *Are* you Suraklin anymore? Or have you become like Joanna's Xerographs, a fourth-generation copy of what you once were, with each copy a little less legible than the last, a little more mixed in with other peoples' minds? What is deathlessness on those terms?"

Around her, Joanna was conscious of the smell of dust, rising from the ground as if blown by imperceptible wind. She fought to stifle a choke, but found the air increasingly thick with it, grayish, stifling, clogging her breathing and burning her eyes. A gust of wind cleared it a little. Through it, she saw Antryg's face taut with concentration, fighting the spell of the dust's suffocation. The heat around the wall was still intense; she could feel it, even at this distance, on the unsteady wind. A computer is capable of millions of operations per second; she wondered how many subroutines constituted a spell, and how many spells could be maintained by a computer as opposed to a man.

"I was in the Silent Tower for years, Suraklin," Antryg went on. "I risked death to win my freedom. But you have walled yourself into a tower from which there is no escaping."

Suraklin laughed. "Are you tired, my love? You're older than I am, now . . . Trying to talk me into surrender, when you know you cannot defeat me by magic? I suggest you save your breath—I can outlast you, you know. Entropy always wins. I will still be here, waiting for you, when your concentration begins to crack from starvation or weariness—just how many spells *can* you hold off? Shall we see?"

Antryg's hand moved, flinched as if with sudden cramp; Joanna saw his face contort with pain. The wind faltered, the dust almost suffocating her. A moment later something stirred in the thick grayness, like a whirlwind rising from a slush pool between the buckled pavement of the old court, droplets of slime shivering into the air, half-forming into the shape she recalled from the electric darkness of the Devilsgate garden. The countering wind died. Through a curtain of silt, she saw Antryg gather himself together for a rush that would take him under the muzzle of the waiting gun.

Then she saw Caris move. His face was white where it wasn't smeared with mud, twisted with pain, but the hand that held his .45 was completely steady. Suraklin turned his head in the same instant that Antryg yelled, "NO!" With a shattering crack of flame the gun blew up in Caris' hand.

Caris screamed, doubling his body over the ruined bone and bleeding flesh; Antryg was already moving. One sword stroke severed Suraklin's right hand where it held the Beretta's trigger before the Dark Mage could bring the gun back to bear on him. At the same moment, Antryg backfisted the Dark Mage across the face with his other hand, sending him staggering back. Suraklin swung around, as if blood weren't pouring from the stump of his right arm and his shattered nose, and with the heavy lock of the gun, still clutched by the left handgrip, cracked Antryg across the temple.

Antryg fell to his knees, a yard from the edge of the chasm that had been the Citadel vaults. Before he could raise his sword again, Suraklin swept the spouting stump of his arm through the air, and the blood itself whirled—red, hideous, multiplying—into the form of an elemental that plunged down on Antryg in a reeking wave.

White light stabbed like a laser beam from Antryg's bony fingers as he sprang back. The elemental dissolved before it in a torrent of flying gore, even as the pit edge gave and crumbled under Antryg's boots. He tried to catch himself, but Suraklin was upon him, wreathed now in fire, his single hand weighted with the gun flashing through the air to crack like an iron club on the side of Antryg's skull.

Antryg clutched at the brittle weeds on the edge as he went over; then even his shabby half-gloved hand slithered from sight.

Blood streaming from his severed arm, Suraklin stood looking down into the pit. "That was very foolish, my darling," he said. Joanna's heart lurched into beating again— Antryg had to be holding onto some projection, some ledge, not too far down the abyss. He was alive—and just for the moment she wasn't going to have to cope with the Dark Mage alone.

Suraklin's back was to her. She could hear Caris still moaning faintly where he lay among the broken, weed-grown pavements, remembered his scream as the gun exploded in his hand and thought detachedly, *Thank God I decided against explosives.* Had that been a general spell, she wondered as she dug the .38 and the Sigil of Darkness from her backpack, or only against Caris, because Suraklin had seen him? She was shaking so badly she could barely tear the Sigil's lead wrappings free or hold the gun straight. One shot, she knew, was all she'd get, if she got that much. After that, she reflected in weirdly wry terror, he could not help but notice her.

The Dark Mage hitched the submachine gun under his arm, switching his left hand from the grip to the trigger. "Killing this body won't do you any good, you see."

Joanna braced the .38 in both hands, straightened her elbows and took time to align the sights as carefully as she had done during her few practice sessions; she pressed the round lead plaque of the Sigil tight against the lock as well as she could while keeping her fingers clear of the cylinder flash. It seemed to take forever; blood and terror pounded in her head, an almost palpable roaring noise that she was certain Suraklin had to hear. The first night Gary had kissed her flitted briefly through her mind, and her elation that for the first time in her life someone found her desirable.

Suraklin—Gary—braced his weapon under his arm, to aim down. "There's plenty of time left before it bleeds to death to . . ."

Here goes nothing, Joanna thought, and squeezed the trigger.

She saw the explosion of bone and hair and brain shatter outward as the automaton that had been first Gary, and then Suraklin, bowed forward and fell into the pit.

Dust still hung heavy in the air as she stumbled to the

edge, still clutching her backpack and the gun. She sensed
a shifting somewhere in it, not far off, and remembered
that there were abominations about, drawn to the smell of
blood. *Caris*, she thought desperately, but did not swerve
aside to where the dying sasennan lay.

Blood was puddled everywhere on the lip of the pit,
steaming faintly in the cold air. Her head ached with the
weight of the drained weariness that clutched her soul. Her
hands, as she fumbled at the pocket of her backpack for the
nylon rope, seemed to belong to someone else. And what,
after all, she wondered bleakly, would it matter? Suraklin
had been right. Killing him—killing Gary, or what was left
of Gary—had done no good. The disk was wiped, and she
knew that, while the computer was running, she'd never be
able to maneuver through the long and complicated process
of putting together another worm.

And the computer would run forever.

Tears of despair nearly blinded her as she peered down.
There was no dust below the level of the ground. She could
see Antryg clearly, pressed flat to what had once been the
wall of some vaulted room. One hand gripped about three
inches of what had been ceiling molding; the other spread
out over a sharply sloping piece of stone that offered little
if any purchase. One boot toe was wedged into the remains
of a broken capital. Below his heels gaped a hundred and
fifty feet of straight nothing, with Gary's body lying
smashed like a road-kill at the bottom.

Her hands shaking, she made a loop in one end of the
rope and stumbled back four or five feet to wrap the other
end around the nearest broken rocks. Things were moving
in the dust, converging on them—abominations, she
thought, for they lacked the deadly speed of elementals.
But that, she knew, would come soon. Antryg's over-
stretched concentration couldn't keep them at bay forever.
She had killed the Dark Mage's last body, but he was far
from dead.

Antryg came scrambling, gasping, up the rope, crushed

her in one fast hug, and planted a kiss on her sweat-soaked hair, even as he was dragging her toward the matted weeds which hid the broken stair. "Caris . . ." she began, and he shook his head.

"There's nothing to be done," he said hoarsely. "We have a few moments now when Suraklin can't see us, when he must marshal his influence on the minds of whatever he can—the abominations, for a guess—to stop us. Before he does . . ."

"But it's no good!" She balked, her feet sliding on the ice that had turned the broken rubble of the hidden stair to treacherous glass. "Antryg, Suraklin was right! It wouldn't take anything to demagnetize the disk; you can do it by leaving one too near the telephone! There's nothing we can do in there!"

He stopped on the slippery track below her, looking up; in spite of its coating of dust and grime, his face seemed suddenly very white in the frame of his unruly hair. "Are you positive it's blanked?"

She shook her head, the stringers of her wet hair trailing against her numbed cheeks. "But it's Suraklin's logical move."

He took a deep breath, as if bracing himself, then nodded. Sweat tracked down through the dust on his face, and Joanna realized that, dead though Suraklin's latest body might be, his magic still lived, pressing against Antryg's hard-held counterspells with the relentless patience of a computer. It was only a matter of time, she thought, until the human wizard tired, and then . . .

He said, "All right. Give me your backpack and get as far away from here as you can. If this deadness doesn't end, it will mean I've failed. Find the other wizards of the Council, tell them everything, make them believe you. If it does, find them anyway . . ."

"What about you?"

His gray eyes shifted away from hers, behind their cracked rounds of glass, then returned, after a moment.

"Whatever happens, my life is forfeit," he said quietly, his long fingers closing around the dirty webbing straps of the backpack. "If it wasn't when I broke out of the Tower, it has been from the moment I summoned the elemental to hold Cerdic's warriors at bay. I don't know whether I'll succeed or fail, but once I go into that enclave, I won't be coming out."

She heard it as if from some great distance, her soul numbed by exhaustion, terror, and the leaden ache of the energy drain. He started to move off down the ruined stair again, and she tightened her grip on the packstraps, holding him back. "What are you going to do?"

"Put the Sigil of Darkness where the teles-relay feeds into the electrical converter. It will break the flow of the magic and seal off the enclave."

"With you in it," Joanna said. "Imprisoned alone with Suraklin, forever." It had, she realized, been his backup plan from the first.

He looked away again, his face contorting with momentary pain. "I can't think about that now, Joanna," he said softly. Desperation shivered in his deep voice. "Now let me go. We've wasted too much time already—every second he'll be rallying new defenses, and I don't know how long I'll be able to hold them at bay. Can't you feel the spells around us now? It'll be worse within the dimensional enclave. If my concentration breaks, we'll both go up like touchwood."

"And the minute your fingers touch the Sigil," she returned, "all your defenses will vanish anyway, won't they?" Cold panic and the scorch of adrenaline stifling her, she drew the backpack from his hands and slung its familiar weight once more onto her shoulder. "Let's get this over with."

The entrance to Suraklin's enclave opened directly above the black pool in the stone chamber of his ancient power. Joanna couldn't see it at all until Antryg reached out over the water and touched it; then it flared into smoky life in the darkness, more like an optical illusion, a trick of mirrors and light, than a real gateway. The burning, unnatural glare of the witchlight that he'd called added to the sense of surreality. Through the clotted darkness of the labyrinths they had heard the lumbering, slurping tread of abominations, closing on the place, tracking them by the scent of their blood, and only the searing radiance of all the light that Antryg could summon had held them at bay. His sword was gone, lost somewhere in the frozen, weedy rubble of the pit where it had fallen when he'd gone over the cliff edge; with the abominations gathering and Antryg's face growing grayer and grayer from the strain of the tireless spells bearing down upon him, there had been no time to search. Even maintaining the light, Joanna sensed, was taxing him, draining his strength like a cut artery. His hand was shaking as he sketched a glowing sign on the wall of the underground chamber.

"When I tell you to run," he said, "run for this. Don't distract me, don't interrupt me—do exactly as I command. All right?"

She nodded, the fear in her growing, swelling—fear, and the sense that there was something she was forgetting, some detail knocking at the back of her mind . . .

He sprang lightly to the threshold of the gate, his boots resting on the glowing surface that seemed to be no more than a projection in the air. Her heart beating heavily, positive she was going to end up falling through into the accursed pool, Joanna reached across, twined her small fingers in the bone and grubby leather of his hand, and jumped.

It was deathly cold within Suraklin's enclave. This didn't surprise Joanna, in view of the physical preferences of computers, but it depressed her further and weighted her down with a physical exhaustion, as if her very body were unable to produce enough heat, enough life, to keep her going. There was a noise there, too, a kind of whispering hum that tugged oddly at her attention. She sensed the presence all around them of unseen forces, the shift of the stone walls—or were they stone?—in the darkness that stopped the moment she turned her head, and the tingle on her skin that made her wonder in terror what would happen if Antryg's concentration on his protective spells broke. Once she smelled a burning, a spot of itching on her thigh that swelled suddenly to searing heat. In numb panic, she pressed her hand over it as hard as she could, not daring to speak for fear of distracting Antryg's mind and making things worse; in a moment the heat passed. *We'll both go up like touchwood*, he had said, and panic sweat rolled down her sides under the dirty sheepskin of her coat and the green velvet jacket underneath.

Then the darkness opened out before them. It swallowed the beam of Joanna's repowered flashlight, which she'd turned on to save Antryg's strength; a vast chasm stretched in all directions, colder than the bitterest of the Sykerst nights. Faint and bluish, a glow rose from the double ring of globes on the floor, some of them no larger than a good-sized grapefruit, others the size of soccer balls; around and between them, like a monster web of brass, glass, and scribbled Sigils of Light, lay the apparatus Dr. Narwahl Skipfrag had invented for converting the ambient energy of life into electricity. The wires spread like weed runners along the floor, interspersed with Sigils and marks written in light, so that the web seemed to sink into the physical fiber of the place itself. Joanna had a sense of those veins of power fanning out over the walls and ceiling of the place, if there were any, hidden in the darkness. And eerily like the trilithons on Tilrattin Island, in the center rose the tripart bulk of what Joanna recognized from articles as an experimental fiber-optic superconductor Cray Three, undoubtedly the one which was rumored to have dropped out of sight early in the year from the Alta Clara Research labs—harder to steal than the 250-odd microcomputers necessary to make up a parallel-process Cube, but far easier to program. Like a vast monolith behind it rose the biggest power conditioner Joanna had ever seen.

Joanna whispered, "Damn!"

"What is it, my dear?"

The whispering in her mind was growing stronger, and with it was the sense of a half-guessed pattern, like an optical illusion of negative space—do you see a lamp, or do you see two faces?

And whose faces?

"It's a UPS—an Uninterrupted Power Source—a backup battery. It means that, even when we pull the plug, the computer itself will be up for at least a day, maybe more. We'll be able to get out . . ."

"But his spells will continue. And he'll be able to summon reinforcements."

Joanna walked forward, her heart slamming against her ribs, loathe to step across the teles-ring. Wan and blue, their sickly light was worse than darkness; as she passed between them, she felt a cold sense of evil, as if she heard the tittering whisper of laughter in the darkness beyond the reach of any light. Her mouth dry, she whispered, "I'm going to check the disk. You start pulling the leads out that connect the power conditioner with the spare battery packs —those small boxes stacked beyond it. They're to give it still more running-time if the power goes down. Just unfasten the clips and pull the plugs out . . ."

Antryg moved to obey, his flowing robe and long-skirted coat incongruous against the hard-edged metal and plastic, his face set now and lined with intolerable strain. Near the chair before the computer's central monitor, a single teles sat in its copper housing, the focal point of the vast spiderweb of wires and leads. It was by no means the largest; Joanna could have closed her two hands over it, had she dared. But nothing in the world could have induced her to touch the thing. She didn't know why she felt that it was aware of her, watching her; old, far older than Suraklin, it was far more evil—and alive.

Her hands were shaking as she pulled the flat disk box

from her backpack. She dropped it twice before she got it open, sweat streaming down her face in spite of the intense cold. And all the while in the back of her mind, that whispering suspicion nagged at her, the feeling of being faced with a quadratic equation, with two solutions . . .

She managed to get the disk in the drive, trying not to think about the process of bringing it up, and let her hands go through the motions automatically.

The disk was blank.

Resolutely, aware that the computer was Suraklin and might be lying about it, she tapped through the entry sequence, but the machine made no sound.

Then, before her eyes in the darkness of the screen, the green words formed up:

WELCOME, JOANNA.
I HAVE WAITED A LONG TIME FOR HIM TO BRING YOU TO ME.

Rage hit her like a falling wall. Betrayal, grief, horror, realization, and fury at herself for not seeing that she had been led all along, tricked into coming to this single place that she had most feared, deceived into walking into Suraklin's hands at last. Hate exploded in her as she swung around in her chair, her hand diving blindly for her backpack, coming up with the .38.

He had been Suraklin's servant from the first.

The crash of the gun was like thunder in the vast darkness. The bullet took Antryg in the side, knocking him back against the power conditioner—Joanna had not paused to take aim, and the kick jerked her aim awry. He raised his head, the sulfurous glow of the teles turning his spectacles to opaque rounds of gold and glinting in the star-fracture of the left lens. She braced herself carefully for a second shot, aiming for his forehead in the spiral strings of his blood-tipped hair. He had used her, used her . . .

She never knew what he shouted at her. Her name, she

thought, and some other word, a spell-word that sliced through the calm fog in her mind like thrown ice water. At the same moment, she felt the burning scorch of fire on her hair, her back, and her arms. He stumbled to his feet, caught her, and held her, smothering the heat between her skin and her coat, pressing her to him, heedless of the gun wedged between their bodies.

After a moment the heat faded again. She brought up her hand from his side and saw her fingers covered in blood.

She began to shake uncontrollably. "Antryg, I'm sorry," she sobbed. "I'm sorry—it was a spell—Suraklin's spell—"

"Don't!" he whispered desperately. His breath came as if he fought for every lungful, his face chalk-white with shock and strain. "Don't say anything. I understand. Put the Sigil in place and let's get out of here. Someone's coming; he's summoned help, and we have to stop them before they get here..."

"Who..." she began dazedly.

"Never mind that!" Behind his specs, his eyes were frantic.

Her hands shaking, Joanna tore open the velcro pocket of her backpack, fumbled with the lead shielding in which the Sigil was wrapped. She felt an increasing reluctance to touch the central teles under which she knew she must place it, a distaste for the whole project—she would be killing the last vestiges of Suraklin, Salteris, the Regent's father, Gary... It was murder...

So was your trying to shoot Antryg, she reminded herself disgustedly. *And Caris, dying up at the top of the cliff* ...Antryg made a swift gesture toward her, swiftly repressed; looking up she saw the strain on his face and the sweat tracking down through the grime and blood, and realized that in his mind, too, Suraklin was whispering.

Her fingers shrinking from the task, she swiftly pushed

the teles aside in its copper bed and slid the Sigil of Darkness into place.

The breaking of the energy drain was like the snapping of a metal band encircling her brain. She felt almost shocked, once more aware of the bone-numbing cold, of the danger in which they stood, and the smell of gunpowder and of Antryg's blood. The bluish gleam of the teles-balls died, and the scribbled light of the runes on the floor faded. Only the red and green lights of the Cray gleamed, baleful stars in the darkness, picking out Antryg's nose and lips and spectacles and winking in the haphazard collection of tuppenny beads and Imperial jewels around his neck. The drone of the UPS kicking in filled the black emptiness around them, broken by the shrill hooting of the alarm. At the same time, she felt the power all around her grow; the crackle of inchoate hatred in the darkness was held at bay only by Antryg's failing spells. Heat seemed to whisper, inches from her flesh.

"How long?" he breathed as they stumbled through the darkness, back toward the beckoning glimmer of his mark.

She shook her head. "A battery that size can keep a computer going for about a day." She felt him shiver and knew he'd never hold out that long. "But he'll be drawing energy from it for his spells to keep the enclave open for his repair crew, whoever they are, to get in—and to destroy you."

Antryg managed a crooked grin. "Added incentive for my death, I see." He was leaning on her, the sleeve of his coat warm and scratchy on her frozen face, permeated with the smells of sulfur and blood. Joanna realized Suraklin would never have needed an added incentive—Antryg was the only wizard who would have been able to hold out this long against the defense-spells. No wonder Suraklin had tried at every opportunity to have him killed.

"I don't know how much that takes, but I'd guess an awful lot." She cocked an ear back, listening to the alarm hooters. Was it her imagination, she wondered, or were they more frequent than before? "With all the spare battery packs disconnected—maybe an hour?"

He shuddered again at the endless length of time. "Unless he can break me first."

The inner chamber of the Citadel, beyond the Gate of the enclave, was crawling with abominations. Pausing on the insubstantial threshold above the pool, Joanna heard them and smelled them in the foul darkness, and all her innards seemed to contract with dread. She whispered queasily, "Can you summon light?"

Antryg shook his head. "Not now," he breathed. "Joanna, I can't. He's in my mind, tearing at it with his spells . . ."

"Okay. Don't worry about it." She unslung the backpack from her shoulder and found her flashlight. Its feeble beam glanced off the obsidian waters beneath their feet and caught the glitter of slime, the flash of mismated eyes. The beam shook as it traveled over them: fat things like monster slugs with foul, dripping snouts; something like a daddy longlegs skittering nervously near the wall; bloated, mutant rats; and things that must once have been cockroaches before some effect of the Void had changed them. She clenched her teeth hard, trying not to make a noise. Beyond them, the door into the sightless mazes of the vaults stood open, and she could sense movement in the darkness beyond.

"We've got to close it," Antryg whispered desperately. "Block it, barricade it . . ."

Behind them, the grating rumble of the backup battery echoed like a bass thunder; the alarms were hooting faster. If nothing else, thought Joanna, they had to get out of the gateway before it collapsed . . .

"Here goes nothing." She pulled open her backpack, removed the first of the DARKMAGE files, and wadded the photocopied pages into a ball. *Thank God*, she thought obliquely, *I brought lots of matches* . . . The abominations shrank back from the fire when she tossed it among them.

She lit five more crumpled balls and flung them, some to one side, some to the other.

"Screw the sheets into torches." Antryg was already doing so as he spoke. "If we can make it to the door . . ."

"We really have to bar it with us on *this* side of it?"

"Believe me, Joanna," he said softly, "I guarantee you it's preferable."

She didn't believe him until they reached the door—ancient, dusty, thick wood strapped and reinforced with iron on the inside and sheeted with copper on the outside. It was hung perfectly on steel hinges and it would swing with a touch. For a moment Joanna stood in the black arch, listening, and heard the footsteps in the passage beyond. They were slow and dragging; once she heard the thud of a body falling against a wall, and the clash of a dropped weapon, then a scrabbling noise as it picked itself up again.

She looked up at the tall wizard beside her, her revulsion stark upon her face.

"Bolt it," said Antryg softly. "Suraklin's magic will still be in his flesh."

Behind them, the abominations closed in. Joanna formed a barrier of wadded paper, crumpling and lighting all the DARKMAGE files, the pounds of paper she'd lugged on her back for hundreds of miles, the last details of the lives of two wizards, an Imperial Prince, and a computer programmer—the final records of their existence. From the enclave gate, still hanging, glimmering, above the pool, the tempo of the alarms had increased, shrieking, desperate, calling help, blocked on the very edge of immortality. All through the horrible shadows of the room the abominations stirred, prowling back and forth, the rats' eyes gleaming, outsize chisel teeth bared. Listening behind her, Joanna imagined she could hear the approaching footfalls in the hall, stumbling, slurring. Leaning against the door beside her, Antryg looked gray and drawn, his eyes shut,

reaming the last strength, the last magic, from the marrow
of his bones.

The blow on the door, when it came, seemed to shake
the very stone from which the vaults were cut. Antryg
flinched, but turned a little, to press his face and hands to
the iron-bound wood, his eyes shut and his face twisted
with pain. Joanna heard a sharp hissing behind her, smelled
damp smoke, and swung around to see a trickle of water
from the pool snaking toward the flickering line of her
barrier blazes. That was impossible, she thought, terrified,
as the abominations moved forward with the lessening of
the fire—the floor sloped up . . .

She pulled more paper from her backpack, twisted it
into another torch and lit it. Gritting her teeth, she strode
toward the slobbering, pulsing things on the other side of
the light, lashing at them with the torch.

The water was indeed seeping up from the pool. Wider,
thicker streams of it, like black slime, flowed up the slope
of the floor toward their feet, dousing another one of her
little fires. Another blow fell on the door, and she saw,
close to Antryg's head, the solid oak timbers heave and
crack. Antryg himself seemed hardly to notice; he appeared to be almost in a trance, except for the gasping of
his breath and the desperate contortion of his face. Grimly,
Joanna stuck the torch into a crack in the wall and twisted
another one, then caught at the first as it fell—she could
have sworn it had been firmly wedged. With quick-blazing
fire in each hand, she swung at the abominations. One of
the rats, the size of a dog and grossly fat, hissed at her; for
a hideous second, she thought it would leap, but it backed
away, its twisted face a nightmare.

Another blow drove a shard of the copper sheathing
through the door and made the strapping jerk and pull in
the wood. It was Gary out there, Joanna thought as she
swung again at a tentacled thing like a groping black wart
that edged toward them. Gary with the top of his head

blown off, Gary with his nose a bloody mash, Gary with nothing in his eyes but Suraklin's will . . .

Antryg made a small sound of pain. At the same instant, Joanna herself felt a stab of sickness, deep in her guts, the burning wrench like poisoned heat. From the enclave, the alarms were screaming, thick and fast now, louder and louder, like a heartbeat skipping out of its rhythm, spiraling up into the danger zone. Blackness swam in front of her eyes, and pain and nausea twisted at her guts as she pulled another handful of paper out, lit it with shaking hands from the last, and swung it at the things that waited greedily in the ankle-deep waters of the flooded floor.

The pounding on the door seemed eerily to pick up the tempo of the alarms, faster, more urgent, more desperate. Antryg cried out again, blood tracking down from the corner of his mouth as his counterspells began to crack under the inexorable pressure of the computer's strength. The alarms scaled up, blending into a single, screaming note. Beneath the screaming, Joanna could hear voices, like the wicker of colorless flame. Some of them were thin, unformed whispers of minds that had never been human; others were terrifyingly familiar . . .

Babe, you're coming out to my place this weekend, aren't you? I've got four new games for the computer, some good beer . . . new jet system for the Jacuzzi . . .

You must do as you think best, my son, but I think you would be a better healer than a fighter . . .

My father won't hear of it, but if you say Suraklin really is a danger, my lord Archmage, then I am behind you with all the support I can raise . . .

And far back of them all, half obliterated by those random snatches of memory, an old man's voice, high and harsh and terrible, whispered, *You were my only love . . . my only love. Of course I can still love . . . I can still feel . . . I can still taste the wine of life . . . It's all in the programs and will be forever. I still live . . .*

The silence falling was like a blow over the head with a

club. For an instant Joanna wondered, *What now*? and turned to look back toward the shimmering gate of the enclave and the distant glitter of the red computer lights that were like evil stars in some impossible darkness. But the lights were gone. With a tired gurgle, the water around her feet had already begun to slither away toward the well again; the abominations, sniffing and hissing, backed further from the crude bundles of burning paper still in her hands. A moment later, like smoke dispersing, the dark gate faded away.

Antryg's voice was no more than a thread. "Entropy always wins," he murmured. With hands that would barely close, he shoved back the door bolts. Neither of them looked at what lay across the threshold as they began their stumbling ascent once more to the light.

CHAPTER XVIII

THEY FOUND CARIS LYING WHERE HE HAD FALLEN, TWENTY feet or so from the lip of the chasm, a broken black shape in a pool of blood. Joanna knelt beside him and felt his face and his remaining hand, searching against hope for some sign of life. She had thought all emotion wrung out of her by the ordeal in the vaults, but now realized that that had only been the result of the energy drain. Now tears collected in her eyes—for Caris and for the fact that she had left him to die without a backward glance.

It had, of course, been what he would have done—what it was the Way of the Sasenna to do.

The short winter day had passed noon. The sky was a low sheet of steel-colored billows, like the undersurface of murky water; the air smelled of snow.

She heard the crunch of Antryg's boots on the hard frost behind her. Glancing up, she saw he'd retrieved his cloak from the subsidence where she'd rolled wearing it. In the daylight he looked ghastly, his haggard face tracked with runnels of blood through the sweat-matted dust, and spreading stains of it dark on his left sleeve and side. He moved stiffly, slowly, like an old man. His crooked hands shook as he covered Caris with the cloak.

"We'll have to get word to Pella," Joanna said dully.

"I'm sure the wizards will do that." Antryg knelt beside

312

her and pushed back the short-cropped fair hair from the young man's still face. "They'll be here very soon now."

The thought of the effort flight would entail turned her stomach, but she said, "We'd better go." She started to get to her feet, then gasped with startled pain. Under her coat and jacket, half her back was burned and beginning to throb. She gritted her teeth, fighting the tears and the wave of faintness that came over her at the pain. It was nothing, she knew, to what Antryg was going through or to what Caris must have gone through, raising himself for that final shot. "We've got a lead on them—with any luck they'll think you and Suraklin destroyed each other..."

Something changed in the air, some shock—blast—impact—as if the reverse side of the universe had been kicked by a giant foot. The air as well as the ground seemed to shudder with a noise that Joanna was not entirely certain was not solely in her own skull, the crying of voices in a dream. She caught Antryg's shoulder in fear. Dust rose in a white column from the abyss that had been the Citadel vaults, slowly mushrooming into the freezing air, then slowly dispersing.

"The enclave," Antryg said softly. In the ashy daylight, his face looked as deathly as that of the boy at whose side he still knelt. "He's used the last of whatever power was left to him to implode it completely—to destroy himself. So he did remember, after all."

Through the pain in her back and her grief over Caris, it was hard to think, but Joanna said, "Remember what?"

"Why he wanted to live forever." Tears made a shining track through the grime on either side of his beaky nose. "The operative word in that phrase is not 'forever,' but 'live.' And living is not only listening to songs, but singing them; not only possessing the wine in bottles, but tasting it in the company of those you love. Part of the beauty of a sunset is the way its colors change and intensify as it fades to night. Maybe he did realize at last that he was only the copy of a copy, a series of subroutines condemned to an

eternity of Read Only. . ." He sighed and pushed up his
specs to wipe his eyes with the back of his glove. "Or
maybe, like me, he simply couldn't abide the thought of
being locked up once again."

She looked down at his face, half hidden by his hair,
and the grief that haunted his gray eyes. "You still loved
him, didn't you?"

A smile flicked at the corners of his mouth. "Oh, not
actively anymore. But I, too, remember." He sighed and
stopped himself sharply, pressing his hand to his side
where her bullet had grazed.

Gently he raised Caris' right arm, the burnt chunk of the
gun-butt dropping from the two remaining fingers. Blood
oozed stickily from the wound.

Through a blur of exhausted tears, Joanna scanned the
barren hills. The iron-colored earth was streaked with snow
beneath a leaden sky. Cold wind stirred the singed ends of
her hair. Though the landscape was utterly desolate, she
had the uneasy feeling of being watched. She said, "We'd
better go. The wizards will be here soon."

"I know." He folded Caris' hands on the young man's
breast, and laid his own on top of them, the long, crooked
fingers stained with blood. "I can feel them seeking me
with their minds, seeking my magic. But here at the node
of the lines, there is one more magic that it's possible for
me to perform." He sat for a moment, gathering the remains of his concentration and his exhausted powers
through the staggering weight of pain and weariness.
Joanna did not understand what he meant, until his eyes
slipped shut and his head bowed, and she realized he had
gone into a healing trance.

She stood for a long time at his side, her throat hurting,
half-sick with her own pain and exhaustion. Then slowly,
painfully, she sat down again on the gray earth. Despite the
thick sheepskin of her coat, the quilted velvet page's
jacket, and the lace-trimmed shirt beneath, she felt cold to
the marrow of her bones. Tears burning at her eyes, she

leaned her head against Antryg's shoulder and tucked her chilled fingers for warmth around his arm. The wind spat snow at them from the surrounding hills and groaned among the charred bones of the Citadel all around.

After nearly an hour of silence, Joanna saw Caris' eyelids move, his ribcage rise, sink, and, after a long moment, rise again.

After two hours, with the darkness beginning to thicken in the louring sky, she was wakened from a half doze of sheer weariness by the strike of hooves on stone. She raised her head to see the ring of mounted sasenna who surrounded them, halberds and spears glittering like metal teeth in the failing light. Half a dozen horses stood apart in a group, the black robes of their riders whirling like storm-clouds in the sleety wind. At their head sat Lady Rosamund, her face like stone and her green eyes pitiless as jade.

"It's odd, you know," Antryg said quietly, steam blurring his spectacles as he poured bubbling water from the kettle into a cracked earthenware teapot. "The two places I've lived longest in my life—really the only two places where I've stayed long enough to qualify as 'home'—have been Suraklin's Citadel and here in the Silent Tower. Would you care for some tea?" he inquired of the pair of red-robed Church wizards who sat stiffly watching him by the door. Both of them glared and the older of the two, a woman, made the sign against evil.

Antryg sighed, wincing a little at the pinch in his cracked rib, and replaced the kettle on the narrow hearth. He handed Joanna a cup of tea with a rueful smile. "In any case, they can't put the Sigil of Darkness back on me." He rubbed absently at the brown mark on his throat. "Have you heard how Caris is?"

Joanna shook her head. The sheer mass and darkness of the Silent Tower oppressed her. Curiously, though the wizards, both Church and Council, who kept guard over her solitary cell on the lower level of the Tower, treated her far better than the Witchfinders had when she had been their prisoner, she found herself far more frightened. Perhaps this was because, when she had been a prisoner of the Witchfinders, she had known Antryg, and Caris, and Magister Magus, were still free and capable of helping her escape, as indeed they had done. She was now without options.

Then, too, she thought, watching Antryg's tall shadow move across the smoke-stained granite of the ceiling vaults, her sense of utter hopelessness might simply stem from exhaustion, the physical reaction to pain and overexertion, and to the repeated emotional shocks of the previous day. Upon being locked into her cell in the Tower, she had fallen almost immediately asleep, in spite of her wretched conviction that Antryg might very well be dead by the time she woke up. Looking at the weariness that seemed to have ground its way indelibly into the deep lines of his face, she wondered if he had done the same.

"I know he's at Larkmoor," she said in a small voice. "And that they say he'll live."

He took the battered and mended chair at her side, and his long, swollen-jointed fingers automatically sought hers. The room in which the Council had imprisoned him was his old study, crammed with his books, his astronomical instruments, and his mechanical toys. In shadow at the far end, Joanna glimpsed a narrow cot, heaped with a haphazard collection of furs and faded quilts. It did not look as if it had been slept on.

"He'll live," Antryg repeated softly and sighed again. "Now I wonder why they said that?"

"Because there are certain members of the Council who insisted upon it."

Both of them looked up quickly at the sound of that cold, sweet voice from the doorway. Lady Rosamund stood there, framed in darkness, immaculate as ever, the red-purple stole that marked her position in the Council sparkling faintly in the fire's reflected light. The Church wizards bowed to her and stepped past her through the door, though Joanna sensed they were in the narrow stairway still, listening for the slightest rise in her voice to summon them back.

"And because in your latest confession, you swear that he was injured in trying to apprehend you for your attempt upon the Regent's life. Or didn't you read it this time?"

"No," Antryg admitted, with a ghost of his old airiness, at which her Ladyship's pink mouth tightened disapprovingly. "I didn't think there would be much point." He looked down and met Joanna's frightened glance. "They didn't hurt me," he added, seeing the way her eyes darted to his hands, as if to see what new injuries those threadbare half-gloves might conceal. "But I told them I'd sign anything, as long as it contained a clause saying that I had forced you to help me by means of my spells, and that you were not responsible for what you did. At least they didn't have to tie the pen in my fingers this time."

Joanna opened her mouth protestingly, his image in the firelight and shadows suddenly blurring with her tears. He put out a hand and brushed her tangled blond hair.

"Joanna, there was never a shred of proof that things were as we said they were. Even the DARKMAGE files are gone now."

Crushed and miserable, she looked away. After a moment, he gathered her in his long, bony arms, holding her against him, the fabric of his shabby purple doctor's robe and the ruffled shirt he wore beneath it soft and scratchy as an animal's pelt against her cheek. She wondered what had happened to her, whether it was the pain and shock of her burns in spite of the wizards' treatment of them or whether she was simply too weary to go on fighting. She seemed to have come to the end of her subroutines. For the first time, she understood that she, too, stood in danger of imprisonment or execution in this world—that she, too, faced punishment as Antryg's accomplice. But she felt only

exhaustion, her mind too tired to grope for the next possible course of action. It was very odd, she thought detachedly, only to sit here in the strong ring of his arms,
comfortable in the single present moment, and let events
take their course into a black and hopeless future.

Past her shoulder, she heard Lady Rosamund say, "Minhyrdin has gone to Larkmoor, with Issay Bel-Caire, to deliver your confession to the Regent and to ask for clemency
for the girl. Whether that perverted mad dog will grant it or
not, I cannot say; but beyond a doubt, before they return,
the Regent's messenger will arrive with the orders concerning the manner of your death."

Joanna felt Antryg shiver, but he only murmured,
"Thank you." A moment later she heard the two Church
wizards reenter and the whisper of the Lady's black robes
as she passed down the stairs.

"Why did you let me live?"

Caris was a little surprised at the weakness of his own
voice. Once the words were spoken, he doubted they had
carried as far as the carved armchair between his bed and
the window, through which the bare trees of the windbreak
could be seen clawing the dun-colored sky. But the old
lady who slumped there like a bag of black wool raised her
head, the thin light catching silvery on the cap of her hair.
The steady click of her ever-present knitting did not stop.

"Tush, boy," was all she said.

"Whatever you told the Regent, you know I broke my
vows," Caris went on, finding every word an effort against
the lassitude of weakness and drugs. "I may have turned
my back on the Way of the Sasenna, but I know what it
means. They say a sasennan who breaks his vows, for
whatever reason seems good, proves nothing about that
reason, but only that he is a man who will break his vows.
And then," he added, moving his bandaged hand on the
coverlet, and wincing against the stab of the dulled pain, "I

don't imagine the Council had much use for broken sword blades. No one does."

"Nonsense." The old lady gave her knitting a tweak to clear its tangled strands and glanced sidelong at him with those faded blue eyes. "All things have their uses—even broken sword blades. Was your reason so good?"

"I thought so."

Partly from weakness and partly from his bitter self-recrimination, he spoke half to himself, barely audible, and perhaps the old lady did not hear, for she lapsed back into fussing with her knitting like any old granny by her hearth, muttering to herself as she did. "I knew him," Caris heard that thin, wavery old voice mumble. "Not well, but I knew him—no one really knew him well but that poor boy of his. And I knew your grandfather and the Emperor, that was the Prince then, and so handsome. I talked to Antryg when he signed all those papers they wanted him to sign last night—meddler, oathbreaker, and mad, yes, completely mad. But I knew them all." Her weak blue glance flicked to him, suddenly disconcertingly bright. "You do as I say, little son. You get well . . ."

"For what?" he burst out desperately. "To live as a cripple? I was no good as a wizard, and now as a weapon, too, I am flawed . . ."

"Then be just a man." She seemed to forget that her yarn had become tangled in her too-long black sleeves and resumed the steady clacking of her needles, her little white head bent over them, her face in the crossed lights of the window and the fireplace nearby like a very wrinkled apple at the bottom of the winter barrel. "Is it so hard?"

Caris said softly, "Yes."

"*Are* you sasennan of the Council?"

There were times when Aunt Min reminded Caris of the old weapons riddle among the sasenna—that hatpins could also draw blood. After long silence he stammered, "I vowed to be so, to the end of my life. But I don't know."

She made no reply to that. Caris realized the clicking of

the needles had stilled and, turning his head on the pillow, saw that she had fallen asleep.

For a long time he lay still, staring at the play of honey-colored firelight on the red cedar of the rafters overhead. He felt as if his life had been laid down on the coverlet beside his remaining hand, and that it was now his choice as to whether he would pick it up again.

The numbness of his soul, cracking these long weeks, had broken like spring ice, and pain welled through like a dark fluid—the pain of a child whose soul will not bow to the responsible rhythms of seedtime and harvest, no matter how he loves them and those who try to teach them to him, the pain of a youth whose inner magic is simply not strong enough to make him a mage. At the age of sixteen he had vowed away that pain, the pain of choosing and of want-ing. As a result, he was aware now that he had little experi-ence of either.

Tears leaked from his eyes, hot on his temples—not the stifled, hurtful tears of anguish shed at his grandfather's murder, but tears of weariness and of deeper grief that leached from his soul poisons of which he had long been unaware. As a sasennan, it was expected of him that he refuse to continue as a cripple in his life—he who, like a fighting-dog, had been trained for nothing else.

And yet . . .

As if a door had been opened, he seemed to smell again the fragile sweetness of the dried herbs in Antryg's medical pouch that had been left behind, with so many other things, in the chapel on the north bank of the Glidden. The kines-thetic memory of sifting salts and powders together came back to him and Antryg's deep voice, speaking of the qual-ities of certain plants—ground holly for rheumatism, slip-pery elm for disorders of the bowels, the white berries of mistletoe for bleeding. He recalled the way his hands had warmed when the healing light passed from them into the body of another and the shattering touch of a newborn child's mind on his . . .

He was not aware that he had slept until he began to wake again, floating, it seemed, a few inches beneath the surface of dreams, aware that the firelight had deepened to amber with the turning of the afternoon light. He was aware of the small warmth of Kyssha lying curled against his side, her nose under what was left of his bandaged hand, and of the strength of Pella's fingers over his own. From somewhere in the room, he heard the rustle of silk taffeta and Pharos' voice saying softly, "I thought I should find you here."

The hand over his flinched, but did not release its hold.

"I just thought you ought to know, my little Princess, that Leynart has indeed fallen ill with smallpox. The mage Bel-Caire is with him. So it seems you did save my life."

He heard her take in breath to answer, then hesitate for a moment, as if not sure what to say to those inscrutable blue eyes. Then she spoke, her deep voice like an alto flute in the gloom. "I'm sorry Ley is ill."

Pharos sniffed. There was the muted click of high heels on the parquet of the floor—Caris remembered, half-dreaming, that the Regent walked very quietly—and the overwhelming waft of orris-root perfume. "Tedious little bitch. I expect if he survives, his looks will be gone, though I'll see he gets some reward for his devotion."

Pella's voice was angry. "He only did it for love of you."

"Let himself be made a dupe? Tried to work magic on me that he didn't understand, on the bare word of someone he didn't know that it was for his own good and mine, and not my heir's? That silken rat you call a dog has more brains—more courage, too."

"That's still no cause to be cruel."

"As far as I've ever been able to ascertain, my little— Pellicida . . ." Caris heard him change his form of address to her and knew that, again, he had met her eyes. ". . . the world has never had any cause to be cruel to me or to you. But I think we've both suffered a certain amount of pain anyway. I'm sorry," he added, his voice halting on the words. "You did not have to save my life. I pay Kanner to do things like that. Hurting the weak is a habit with me—a bad one, like biting my fingernails. I'll try not to do it to you again. You had at least one good reason to wish me dead—was this young man another?"

"No." Pella's hand closed more tightly around Caris' fingers, and he heard the slide of her hair over her satin shoulders as she bowed her head. "Neither of us wished you dead."

"Ah." The way she had spoken the word "us" was, even to Caris' ears, unmistakable. "I thought I did not recognize him as one of my men, in spite of the uniform." There was a slight, undefinable shift in the harsh voice. "They say you're with child. Is this true?"

Again he heard the dry slither of her hair.

"Mine?"

"Yes."

Caris opened his eyes, to see those two forms silhouetted in the amber light, Pharos standing like some pretty doll in black and gold, two white fingers emerging from an explosion of sable lace to rest lightly beneath Pella's chin. The girl was gazing up into his face, her green eyes unwavering, looking very young and yet very calm, as she had in the clash with Leynart—the face of a sasennan who is also a queen.

Pharos' mouth twitched in a wry expression. "A pity, in a way," he said at last. "A madman, a credulous fool, and an idiot are no advertisement for a dynasty, whatever our respective families might say. I am not good myself, any more than I am a man for women, but I do know goodness when I see it—and I know that the good are often happy as well."

There was a long pause as he studied her, this girl whose spirit he had never been able to break, and the scorn in his eyes with which he looked upon a hostile world seemed to abate, as it had abated a little in the study at Devilsgate.

"Well," he said at last, "God knows I have little use for a woman, except to bear me an heir, and you seem to be fulfilling that part of what strikes me as a rather agricultural custom. So I will ask of you only that you raise my child and whatever other children you may happen to bear, with a sense of responsibility for the Empire and whatever happiness you can manage to give them as well." Picking up her other hand, he kissed it, turned in a great rustling of black silk ribbons, and walked toward the door.

Pella rose, holding out her hand. "Pharos . . ."

He paused, looking back. "Yes, Pellicida?"

"What about Antryg and Joanna?"

The Regent hesitated for a long moment, the old vindictive paranoia gleaming once more in his pale blue eyes. "They betrayed me," he said at last, with soft and vicious finality in his voice. "Both of them."

"They were trying . . ."

"We have Windrose's confession," Pharos cut her off, his shrill voice suddenly harsh. "That same document exonerates your friend here . . ." The diamonds of his rings glittered sharply around the great, cut hematite in the middle, live stars circling a dead one, as he gestured to Caris. Then, he went on quietly, as a ruler explaining a decision to a counsellor he trusts, "You must have known there was never hope for his reprieve. The messenger has already left for the Silent Tower. Sentence on them both will be carried out tomorrow."

"Both?" protested Pella. "Joanna . . ."

The small hand waved aside her fear. "Oh, never fret. It isn't your affair . . ." Pella started to rise, and Pharos went on hastily, "Of course, nothing fatal will be done to her— banishment—imprisonment . . ." But Caris saw his pale eyes shift from hers as he turned toward the door and heard the careless evasiveness of the voice. Caris knew that Pharos lied.

* * *

Even through the thick walls of the Silent Tower, Joanna heard the stormwinds rise, groaning in the wheel-spoke rafters overhead. As Antryg had said, even in the summertime, the Tower was icy cold; now in the dead of winter, the wind slipped like black snakes through the barred and hidden ventilation slits to drain the warmth of the room. She and Antryg had sat for a long time before the fire, sharing his scruffy cloak and one of the quilts from the bed, while the two hasu watching them shivered slightly, having indignantly refused Antryg's offers of other blankets.

They had talked, of California, of Mellidane, of Antryg's village of Velskonoe on the edge of the taiga forest deep in the Sykerst, whence Suraklin had taken him as a child, of Star Wars and the different types of magic, and of the possibility of Joanna's imprisonment for a greater or lesser time in this world.

"I tried to do what was best," Antryg said softly, his breath stirring the ends of her hair on top of her head. "Unfortunately, it's something I've never been terribly good at. I couldn't leave Caris; and if I'd simply sent you away, you wouldn't have gotten far before the wizards caught you anyway. There were still abominations about, too."

"And I wouldn't have gone." She raised her cheek from his chest long enough to push clear one of his trashy glass necklaces, then settled it back again.

"Oh, Joanna." He sighed, and tightened his arms around her shoulders. "I did want to keep you out of it, as much as I could. It isn't the first time my friends have been hurt through my meddling. It's just that I needed you too much . . ."

"Hey, they always said computer consultant was a high-demand field."

He laughed softly and looked down into her face. "That wasn't what I meant."

She knew it hadn't been and felt her throat tighten again with tears. But all she said was, "I knew the job was dirty when I took it." She wondered, feeling the hardness of muscle and rib through the baggy folds of the robe beneath her cheek, how long they would keep her prisoner here, and if she would ever make it back to California. Her old life seemed very strange and distant to her. The thought of being here alone made her feel weak and frightened, but it was totally peripheral to that blacker grief she resolutely refused to contemplate, the knowledge that Antryg was going to die.

She had fought it as a rearguard action for so many months that at times it seemed completely unreal, and his perfectly genuine cheerfulness tricked her mind away from it still further. But she'd seen it in the eyes of the Church dogs and heard it in the whispers of the mages who guarded her cell. Antryg was going to die and, in all probability, die tomorrow.

After tomorrow, she would never see him again.

Except, perhaps, in dreams.

In the darkness of the twisted stairwell, Joanna heard the moan of the wind and then the Lady Rosamund's voice, raised in indignation, "Don't be absurd! The Regent has no intention of letting her go and you know it!"

Then she heard old Minhyrdin the Fair's creaky little wheeze, coming closer with the scuffle of her laborious feet. "Nonsense. What know you of the Regent's plans—or care?" The two women, lady and crone, appeared in the darkness of the doorway. With an impatient sign, the Lady Rosamund dismissed the two guards. Aunt Min peered up at the elegant Lady with a shrewd old eye and added, "Or *do* you care what Pharos thinks?"

"Of course not!" her Ladyship retorted hotly. "But simply to go against his orders . . ."

"His orders have not yet arrived," the old lady pointed out blandly, turning her head a little, because of the stooping of her bent back, to look up at Lady Rosamund. "How are we to know his intention? His messenger has been delayed by the storm." Aunt Min's black robe was wet through and her cloak, patched, shabbier even than Antryg's, was covered with flakes of melting snow and ice. She was drawing off her knitted red and green mittens and getting the ends of her muffler tangled in her eternal knitting, which, clotted with ice, was still in its basket under her arm.

Lady Rosamund's eyes narrowed suspiciously. "When I scried the skies this morning, I saw no trace of a coming storm.".

Antryg smiled graciously from his seat beside the hearth and chipped in, "Well, these things come with practice." Joanna almost stifled, trying not to laugh at the way the Lady's green eyes flared with rage.

Unperturbed, Aunt Min continued, "But since we have received no orders, run along now and fetch what I asked you."

"We have no right . . ."

The withered little ancient drew herself with some effort to her full height—an inch or so less than Joanna's five-foot-barely. And Joanna, looking at that old, seamed face in its thin tatter of white hair, suddenly understood why she had once been called Minhyrdin the Fair by all. In a voice totally unlike her usual vague mumbling, she said, "*I* am the Archmage. *I* have the right." Then she dropped her knitting and bent laboriously to pick it up, dropping the needles as she did so. She fumbled for them. The Lady Rosamund bent to help her, and Aunt Min waved her fussily away. "Oh, let it be, Rosie! Now run along and do as I asked."

Stiffly, her Ladyship straightened up and strode with an indignant billow of black robes into the darkness of the stair. Joanna and Antryg both got to their feet and went to help Aunt Min, Archmage of the Council of Wizards, collect her scattered belongings.

"Thank you," the old lady said, shoving the sodden tan-

gle of wool haphazardly back into her basket and sticking
the needles into it at random. "Thank you, my dears." She
had to twist her spine to look up at Antryg's great height.
She reached out to pat his big, crooked-fingered hand.
"You always were a good boy."

He smiled down at her and held out his hand to help her
to a chair. "No," he said, with genuine regret. "But I
always did want to be. I never thanked you for speaking
out for me at the end of summer when they brought me
back here . . ."

"Only to escape again." She shook her head, clicking
her tongue pettishly, as if at a child's scrapes. "I knew him,
you see—knew Suraklin. I knew them all."

"I remember." Antryg smiled. "In fact I remember you
taking a broom-handle to him, the one time you were at the
Citadel . . . at the time I was shocked to death, of course."

The old lady chuckled, her pale eyes warming briefly
with a trace of their old color. Then she sobered and said,
"It cannot be so again."

"I know," Antryg said quietly. The brown mark left by
the Sigil of Darkness showed up more darkly against the
whiteness of his face. "Just please get Joanna out of here."

"Since we have received no orders from the Regent
concerning the girl Joanna," the old lady said, "though we
have no jurisdiction over her, as Archmage I think it best
that she be taken back to the place where we came through
the Void, the shed marked with Suraklin's marks."

Joanna felt Antryg's long fingers close tightly around
hers; then he said, "Thank you."

She was looking up into his face as he glanced past
Aunt Min to the shadow of the door and saw what was left
of the color there drain away. Her glance flicked after his.
Lady Rosamund stood there, silent and disapproving, in
her hands a cup made of gold and horn.

Aunt Min looked, too, and nodded her little head. "Set
it down, dear, set it down," she instructed, making vague
little gestures toward the table and dropping her knitting

again. Automatically Antryg stooped to retrieve it, then straightened up again as the old lady continued, "And be careful of it, Rosie—it's poison, you know."

Her Ladyship's beautiful mouth flexed with disapproval as she turned and stalked from the room once again. Aunt Min plucked her knitting needles from Antryg's yielding hand and said, "You know there is nothing we can do for you. The original sentence of death is still in effect."

Joanna remembered Antryg's airy recital—*hanged, broken, skinned, and sliced*... At the time, that day-long public torture had seemed so far away.

Antryg whispered, "I know."

The old lady added, "I am sorry."

Antryg nodded and patted her tiny hand where it curled around his own.

Joanna caught his sleeve, her mind refusing to take it in. It seemed to her that the warmth and the color of the afternoon was still on her and the taste of the deep and nebulous joy of mingled friendship and love. She had the helpless, protesting sense of being suddenly forced to leave a party long before it was over, of losing something which had been, and should have been, part of her for years.

Aunt Min touched her arm. "You had better come along, my dear. The storm won't be a long one." She said it with a serene knowledge that was almost comical, but for the circumstances. "There is no knowing when the messenger will come and then, of course, whatever orders he bears must take effect."

Joanna shook her head, her mind a blank of darkness and grief. Antryg folded her gently into his arms and bent his tall height to press his mouth to hers. Her hands tightened over the patched robe and tangled in the long gray hair. For a moment, it was as if she were trying to memorize, once for all, the sinewy movement of the loose-jointed frame, the magpie sparkle of beads and diamonds, cracked spectacles, and those wide, intent gray eyes, and the brocaded flamboyance of his deep voice.

Then he murmured, "Good-bye, my love." The word he used in the language of Ferr was the equivalent of *Adieu,* —to God—the long good-bye from which there is no returning.

Aunt Min took her hand and led her into the narrow darkness of the stair, where she saw that Lady Rosamund waited. As they escorted her down, to lead her far enough away from the Tower so that no chance weakening of the veil between worlds within the Tower itself would permit Antryg again to escape, she looked back at the gold rectangle of the door.

Through it she saw Antryg standing beside the table, the cup between his hands, his face like chalk in the firelight. As she watched, pulling against the Archmage's coaxing, she saw him raise the cup to his lips, drain it, and set it down, his fingers shaking uncontrollably. Then he walked back to his bed, lay down in the shadows, and turned his face to the wall.

CHAPTER XIX

IT WAS JANUARY, AND LATE-BLOWING SANTA ANA WINDS flowed over Los Angeles like a river of silk. After weeks of winter in the Sykerst, the balmy desert warmth was even more disorienting to Joanna, the crystal magic of the air adding to her sense of separation from this world to which she had returned, as well as from that which she had left. That was another thing, she reflected detachedly as she stepped through the double-glass doors of the Building Six lobby and looked out across the tepid twilight of the nearly empty parking lot, that they never mentioned in tales of adventure—the sheer amount of cleaning-up the participants had to do afterward and the gut-wrenching period of letdown.

Antryg was dead.

She was young enough never to have lost anyone close to her in her life—certainly not someone as close as he had been. She felt stunned and empty, not only of him but of everything. She had not imagined it possible to miss someone that much.

As she descended the shallow concrete steps, she thought to herself that she had not realized in the fall how lucky she'd had it. There was a good deal to be said, after all, for fear of Suraklin, terror of crossing the Void again alone, obsessive paranoia, and her frantic mantra that Antryg was not—could not be—dead. At least it had kept her

330

busy. There had been almost no time to think or to feel.

Now there was.

During the Santa Anas it was as if Los Angeles had never heard the word "smog." All around the low concrete bunkers of San Serano, the hills seemed to have crept nearer during the day, vast, rounded cutouts of matte cobalt cardboard against a periwinkle sky. The wind lifted strands of her hair like a sensual ghost; the air was milky against her bare arms. Weeks of freezing, she reflected, did have the one advantage of making her temporarily proof against all but the chilliest evenings. She hitched her massive purse with its dangling tassels and rabbit skins more firmly onto her shoulder, still kinesthetically missing the familiar weight of the backpack. When it brushed the bandages over the worst of the burns she flinched, though after four days the pain had dulled to no worse than a really bad sunburn.

It was after six o'clock, and most of San Serano's employees had braved their way onto the freeway an hour ago. Joanna had stayed, as she had stayed late the last two nights. Part of it was catching up on the horrible volume of work left undone at her departure, but a great deal of it stemmed from her unwillingness to face the emptiness that waited for her at home.

The snow would be deep around Larkmoor now. Aunt Min had assured her that it was possible now for Caris and Pella to be together. She wondered how Pella was, whether they were happy and how Caris was adjusting to the new life that had been Antryg's final gift to him. She wondered, too, whether Magister Magus had recovered from his slavery to Suraklin, whether Cerdic had helped him regain his ostentatious house, and whether Marquises and Countesses again clustered to his pink-and-black drawing room, waiting to pay him lavish sums to tell them what they wanted to hear.

She would never know, of course. It was as if they, too,

were dead. Sometimes in these last three days her loneli-
ness had seemed to fill the earth.

Most of the time it seemed as if Ruth believed her.
From the gas station near San Serano, she had phoned Ruth
to come and pick her up. All the way back to Van Nuys,
her friend had not said much, but had looked at her sidelong, where she had sat slumped in the corner of the front
seat in her grubby green velvet knee breeches, squalid
peasant boots and tattered, lace-ruffled shirt. She must, she
knew, have looked very different, besides being much
thinner and having three inches of her hair singed off. That
first evening Ruth had treated her with a care very much at
odds with her usual breeziness and did not dismiss what
she said.

Wherever she had been, thought Joanna wearily, she at
least must look as if she'd been *someplace*. As ever, she
had no proof.

She'd gotten something of the same reaction from her
colleagues at work who saw her and a great deal of sympathy regarding her fictitious sister-in-law's three-month bout
with terminal cancer. Most, though not all, respected her
flat request not to talk about it.

Slowly she began reacclimating herself to driving a car,
gauging traffic speed, taking showers, and having noise
around her virtually all the time. It was odd to have possessions again, odd not to be always on the move, and odd not
to be terrified of capture half the time.

But it all felt hollow and strange, as if it, and not the
past three months, had happened to someone else.

Antryg was dead.

Gary was dead, too, of course, she thought, feeling the
residual heat of the pavement radiating softly against her
sandaled feet as she crossed the parking lot. But it wasn't
Gary's voice she remembered, lying awake at night.

I'll get over this, she told herself, fighting the wave of
grief that threatened to swamp her. *It won't always be this
bad.*

She didn't believe it. She felt a flash of sympathy for Suraklin. It wouldn't be too bad, she thought, simply to program herself into a computer and forget what it was like to feel.

She raised her head, scanning the parking lot for her blue Mustang. It sat in solitary splendor beneath one of the tall lamps which, like a network of artificial moons, cast primrose light against a luminous blue dusk.

Someone was sitting cross-legged on the hood of her car.

She stopped, regretting the absence of her hammer and reflecting that miscellaneous weirdos were things she hadn't had to put up with on the other side of the Void. But after Suraklin and the Inquisition, she found the thought of minor hassles of this kind far less frightening than she once had. Then he turned his head.

She saw the flash of round spectacle lenses, the gleam of a silver-foil rock concert logo on his baggy t-shirt. As every drop of blood in her veins transubstantiated painfully into straight adrenaline, she thought, *Supposition A cannot be true*. And then: *Whoever it is, I'll kill him for doing this to me*.

She crossed what seemed like twenty acres of black pavement, first quickly, her heart squeezed like a fist inside her, then slower and slower as she came near the spot.

He unfolded long, jeans-clad legs and scrambled to his feet. The lamp overhead sparkled on the cracked spectacle lens, the diamond earrings snagged in the curly tangle of gray hair, and the strands of gimcrack beads. Even at this distance, she saw there was a bandage on the bare arm where Suraklin's bullet had grazed.

"Joanna?"

Her arms crushed him in a hug before she remembered he had a cracked rib—she could feel the stiffness of the dressing under his t-shirt. If it was a dream, she thought obliquely as his arms closed painfully around her burned back, it was an awfully accurate one . . . His embrace lifted her off her feet.

When they'd finished the first hundred-year kiss, he managed to say, "Look, I swear I won't be a burden to you—unemployed wizards can *always* find work . . ."

She dragged his mouth down to hers again, the familiar awkwardness of their mismatched heights convincing her finally that it couldn't be a dream. She must have caught him on his cracked rib again because his convulsive grip suddenly relaxed. "I'm sorry," he gasped. "I forgot about your back . . ." He looked around at the empty parking lot. "Did they make you stay on after everyone else left as punishment for desertion?"

He must, she realized, have been sitting on the hood of the Mustang for an hour at least, watching the sun go down. He was wearing only the jeans, boots, and t-shirt he'd had on when she'd first met him, but didn't seem chilled—like her, he had come from a place of bitterest cold.

"No. I had some things to finish . . ." She paused in the midst of her usual excuse, then said, "That's not really true. I just didn't want to go home to be alone."

"Ah," he said softly. For a few minutes they didn't speak, only stood wrapped in one another, as they had done under his grubby cloak in the Sykerst, silent and content.

After she quit crying Joanna said, "I guess I shouldn't be surprised."

"It's flattering of you to say so, my dear. I'm speechless with astonishment that I'm not dead."

Her arm tightened briefly around his waist. "You've never been speechless in your life," she said, with unkind accuracy. "Don't tell me the Council miscalculated the distance they had to be away from the Tower when they opened the Void to send me through?"

He shook his head. "No. It was—rather unlikely. A *deus ex machina*, so to speak." He sounded a little shaken, as if it still puzzled him, not only the manner of his escape, but that he had escaped at all.

"Don't tell me Cerdic came through at the last minute? Or Aunt Min?"

He grinned, and shook his head again. "Though I wouldn't swear Aunt Min was as asleep as she seemed to be when she was allegedly keeping the deathwatch over me. She seldom is, you know." He rubbed his hands absently, as if trying to massage some old ache from the swollen joints. "No, it was quite literally a *deus ex machina.*" For a moment he was silent, as if still trying to puzzle it out. At last he said, "It was the Dead God who saved me."

A technician, thought Joanna. A scientist. She remembered the rotting tower of borrowed flesh and bones, the gluey, freezing darkness of the haunted church, and the poltergeist knocking, hammering out the numbers of pi. She wondered whether the thing he had built out of the bodies of others had been meant to resemble his true physical form.

Lamplight snaked along Antryg's spectacles as he turned his head. "Universal structural theory was his specialty, you know. In fact that was why he got trapped on our side of the Void to begin with, because he was investigating the Gate that was opened, rather than running away from it like a sensible person. After having crossed the Void twice—through and back—he knew of its existence and was doing experiments with it. He picked up the heavy disturbances on his instruments when Suraklin destroyed the enclave and was focused on that area when the Council sent you through. Since he had telepathically touched your mind as well as mine through the Sigil net he recognized you; and he realized you were being sent through under guard and against your will. Having located you, he was able to backtrack the mages to their starting point and locate me."

He fell quiet again, staring out into the Prussian-blue

darkness, as if through it he could look into some other, deeper night. The lamplight overhead glinted on his earrings, and among the trashy finery around his neck Joanna recognized the necklaces given to him by Pella and earlier by Pharos, delicate as Fabergé work among dimestore beads.

"I had already taken the poison," he said softly, as if to himself. "Considering what was in Pharos' warrant, the Council was doing me the greatest favor they could. The Dead God—he told me his name, which is really only an identification sequence—was working on a machine to open Gates in the Void, but it was only in the experimental stages. He ran a considerable risk coming to get me at all. If Aunt Min had been awake, she could have stopped him easily, trapped him on that side of the Void, and destroyed him. But she wasn't, or didn't seem to be."

I knew them both, the old Archmage had said. Aside from Antryg, Aunt Min was probably the only person living who had known both Suraklin and Salteris well.

Joanna reached across and put her hand over his. "Are you all right?'" Her voice sounded smaller than she had meant, her thoughts on that silent stone room and Antryg lying there alone.

He brought his other hand around to cover hers, the big, crooked bones of it reassuring. "A little surprised at the Dead God. I hardly suspected him of that kind of sentimentality, or honor, or whatever it was that motivated him. I was nearly unconscious when he fetched me through to his own world and then I was ill for days, living on artificial air while he got the poison out of my system. And then I came here."

He put an arm around her shoulders and drew her mouth once more to his. In the midst of the kiss he added absently, "You know, you really *are* going to have to do something about your height . . .

"I promise I won't be a burden on you any longer than it takes me to find something to do for money and my own

place to live," he went on after a few moments. "I can tend
bar—read tea-leaves—heave coal . . ."

"There hasn't been a coal heater in Los Angeles since
before World War II."

"Another promising career blighted. You have to give
them numbers to tell them apart?" He dubiously regarded
the car as Joanna unlocked the passenger-side door, then
clambered in and pulled the door shut behind him. Joanna
got in, gave him a brief lecture on the operation of the
windows, started the engine, and, blithely disregarding the
white lines, roared off across the parking lot, out the gate,
and down Lost Canyon Road.

She braked where the road crested the hill above the
Ventura Freeway. Full dark had come, warm and magic;
the electric wind had fallen; and in the dry, brilliant air, the
San Fernando Valley lay before them in a glittering carpet,
with the outlying blaze of the greater city of lights in the
distance. Beside her, Antryg was silent, gazing out across
the jewel-box glory of the world in which he would now
live as an exile.

Quietly, she said, "Your magic is gone, isn't it? You
have no power in this world."

"Probably not." Against the reflection of the light, his
face was only a dark profile of extravagant nose, shining
steel spectacle rim, and a point of light caught in the beads
at his throat. "Considering the uses to which I put my
magic in the past, that may be for the best, at least for a
time. Later . . ." He shrugged. "Is later. Right now I'm only
glad that there is a later—or even that there is a now. And
in fact, that's really all there ever is."

" 'Had I world enough, and time,' " Joanna quoted
softly, wanting nothing more than that moment, the velvet
voice in the darkness, the liquid warmth of the night, and
the miles of flame-sprinkled blackness stretching out to the
encircling hills that hemmed a flame-sprinkled sky.

His lenses flashed as he turned his head; his deep voice
was rueful in the dark. "All those weeks you were in my

world, under my protection, I never fully appreciated how uncomfortable it must have been for you to be that dependent on someone."

Joanna nodded, her small hands resting on the worn plastic of the steering wheel as she gazed out into the night. "Well, let me warn you, dog wizard, now that you're in *my* world under *my* protection, I intend to take advantage of you to the fullest."

She couldn't see in the dark, but she sensed his grin. "Oh, good... What do people here eat? And will you teach me how to drive one of these things?"

She shuddered as she put the car in gear and headed down the hill toward the freeway. "That will be all I need ... We'll talk about it later. In the meantime, let me explain to you about tacos..."

ABOUT THE AUTHOR

At various times in her life, Barbara Hambly has been a high-school teacher, a model, a waitress, a technical editor, a professional graduate student, an all-night clerk at a liquor store, a karate instructor. Born in San Diego, she grew up in Southern California, with the exception of one high-school semester spent in New South Wales, Australia. Her interest in fantasy began with reading *The Wizard of Oz* at an early age and has continued ever since.

She attended the University of California, Riverside, specializing in medieval history. In connection with this, she spent a year at the University of Bordeaux in the south of France and worked as a teaching and research assistant at UC Riverside, eventually earning a Master's Degree in the subject. At the university, she also became involved in karate, making Black Belt in 1978 and competing in several national-level tournaments.

Barbara Hambly now lives in Los Angeles, California.